Romeo & Juliet

THE GRAPHIC NOVEL
William Shakespeare

PLAIN TEXT VERSION

Script Adaptation: John McDonald
American English Adaptation: Joe Sutliff Sanders
Character Designs & Original Artwork: Will Volley
Coloring: Jim Devlin
Lettering: Jim Campbell
Design & Layout: Jo Wheeler & Jenny Placentino

Editor in Chief: Clive Bryant

Prospect Heights Public Library
12 N Elm Street
Prospect Heights, IL 60070
www.phpl.info

Romeo & Juliet: The Graphic Novel
Plain Text Version

William Shakespeare

First US Edition

Published by: Classical Comics Ltd

Acknowledgments: Every effort has been made to trace copyright holders of
material reproduced in this book. Any rights not acknowledged here will be
acknowledged in subsequent editions if notice is given to Classical Comics Ltd.

Images on page 161 reproduced with the kind permission of The Shakespeare Birthplace Trust.

All enquiries should be addressed to:
Classical Comics Ltd.
PO Box 7280
Litchborough
Towcester
NN12 9AR
United Kingdom
Tel: +44 (0)845 812 3000

info@classicalcomics.com
www.classicalcomics.com

ISBN: 978-1-906332-62-4

Printed in the USA

This book is printed by CG Book Printers using environmentally safe inks, on environmentally
friendly paper which is FSC (Forest Stewardship Council) certified (SW-COC-003110). This material
can be disposed of by recycling, incineration for energy recovery, composting and biodegradation.

Mixed Sources
Product group from well-managed
forests and other controlled sources
www.fsc.org Cert no. SW-COC-003110
© 1996 Forest Stewardship Council
FSC

Contents

≫⮜ ⮞⮜

Romeo & Juliet

≫⮜ ⮞⮜

Dramatis Personæ

Romeo
Son to Montague

Chorus
Introduces the first two acts of the play

Lord Montague
Head of the Montague house (a Veronese family), at feud with the Capulet family

Lady Montague
Wife to Montague

Benvolio
Nephew to Montague and friend to Romeo and Mercutio

Balthasar
Servant to Romeo

Abraham
Servant to Montague

Escalus
Prince of Verona

Mercutio
Kinsman to Escalus, Prince of Verona, and friend to Romeo and Benvolio

Paris
A young nobleman, kinsman to Escalus, Prince of Verona

4

Juliet
Daughter to Capulet

Lord Capulet
*Head of the Capulet house
(a Veronese family), at feud
with the Montague family*

Lady Capulet
Wife to Capulet

Tybalt
Nephew to Lady Capulet

Nurse
*A Capulet servant and Juliet's
foster–mother*

Peter
A Capulet servant to Juliet's nurse

Sampson
Servant to Capulet

Gregory
Servant to Capulet

Friar Laurence
A monk of the Franciscan Order

Friar John
A monk of the Franciscan Order

5

Romeo & Juliet

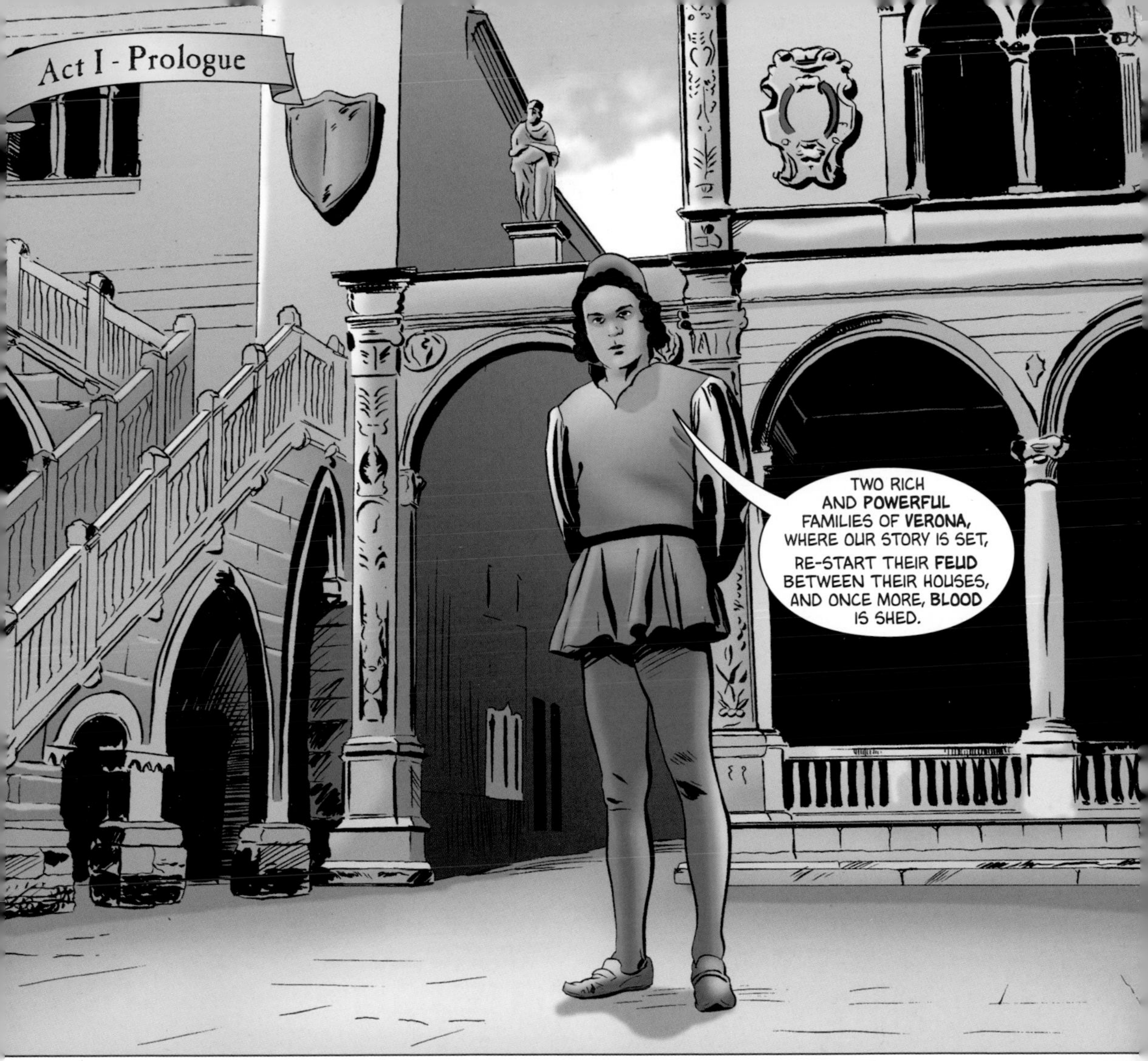
Act I - Prologue
TWO RICH AND POWERFUL FAMILIES OF VERONA, WHERE OUR STORY IS SET, RE-START THEIR FEUD BETWEEN THEIR HOUSES, AND ONCE MORE, BLOOD IS SHED.

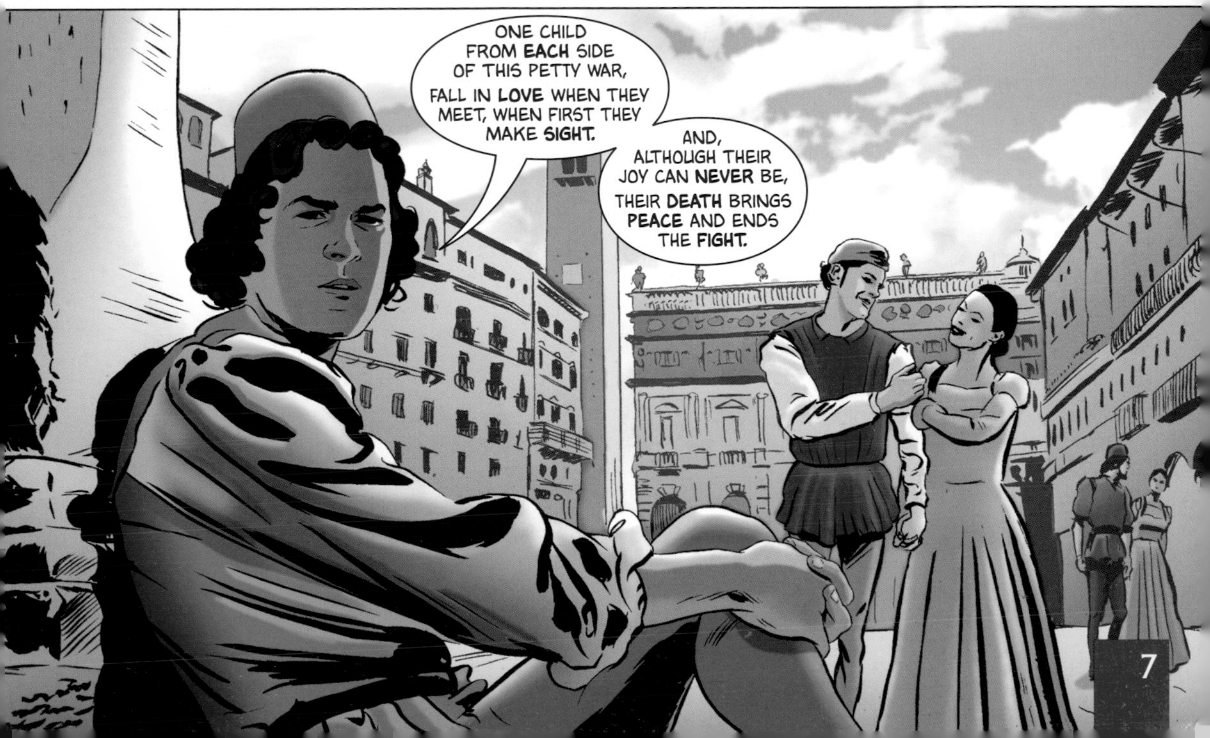
ONE CHILD FROM EACH SIDE OF THIS PETTY WAR, FALL IN LOVE WHEN THEY MEET, WHEN FIRST THEY MAKE SIGHT.
AND, ALTHOUGH THEIR JOY CAN NEVER BE, THEIR DEATH BRINGS PEACE AND ENDS THE FIGHT.

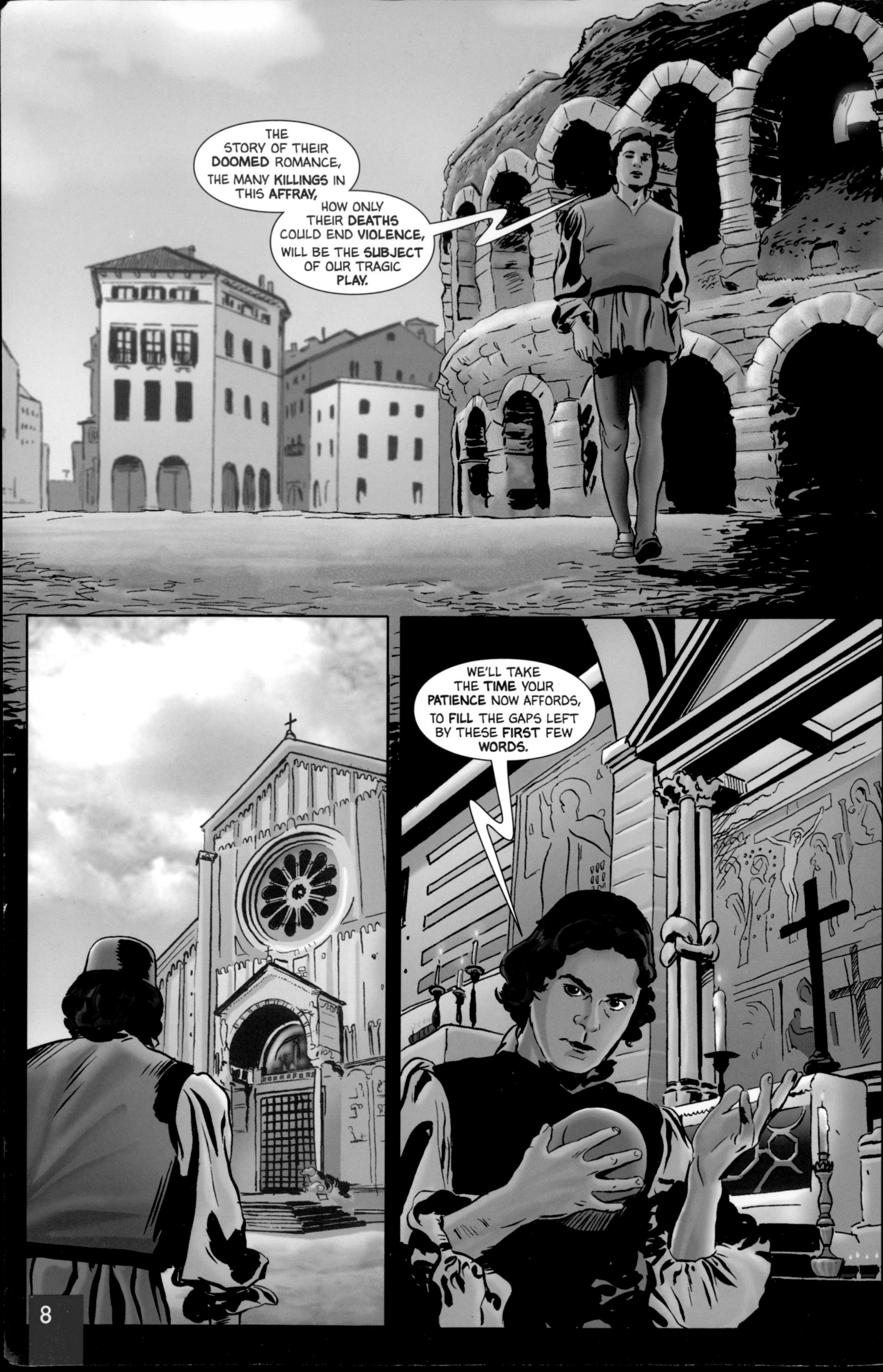
THE STORY OF THEIR DOOMED ROMANCE, THE MANY KILLINGS IN THIS AFFRAY, HOW ONLY THEIR DEATHS COULD END VIOLENCE, WILL BE THE SUBJECT OF OUR TRAGIC PLAY.
WE'LL TAKE THE TIME YOUR PATIENCE NOW AFFORDS, TO FILL THE GAPS LEFT BY THESE FIRST FEW WORDS.

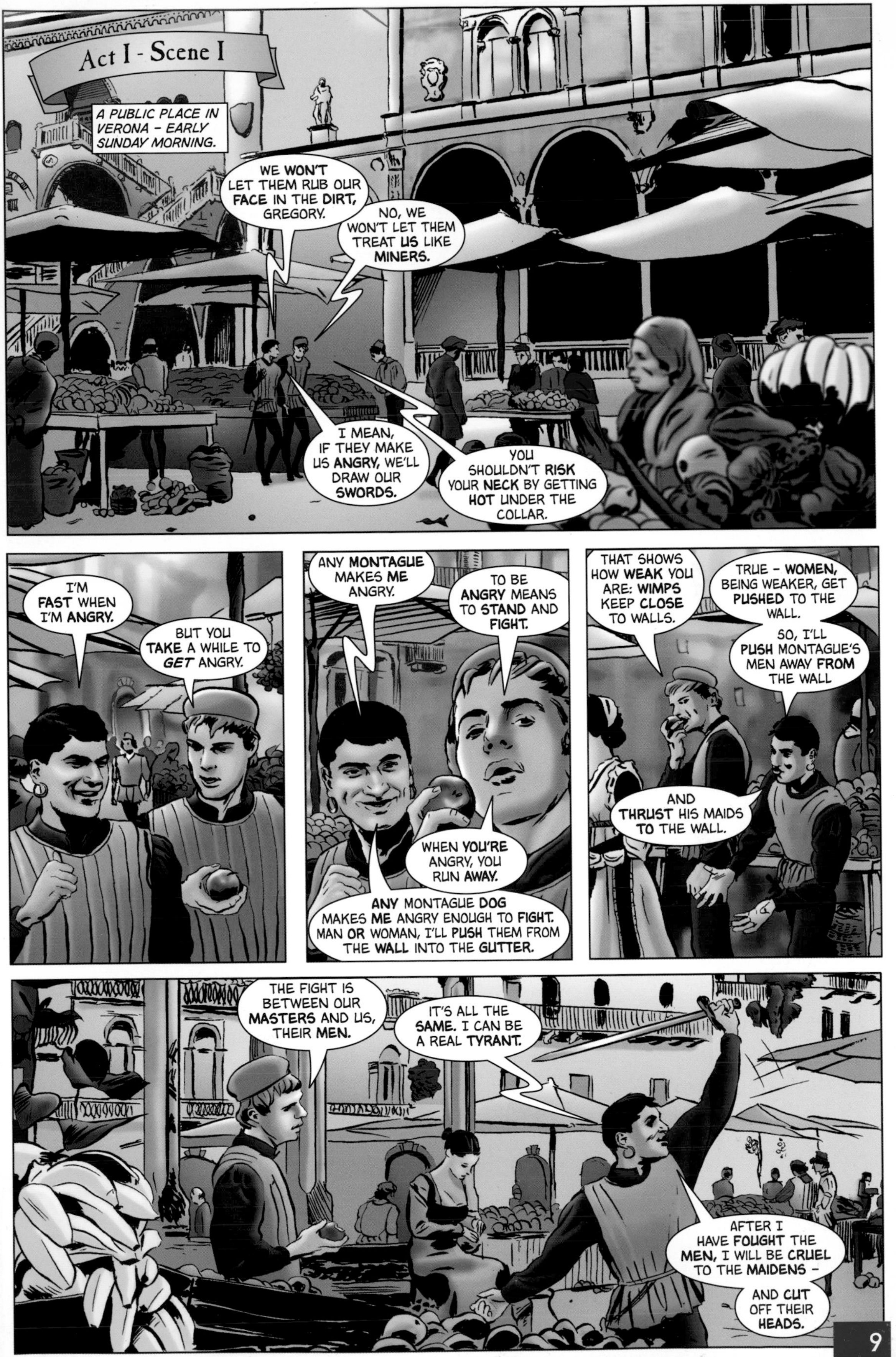
Act I - Scene I
A PUBLIC PLACE IN VERONA – EARLY SUNDAY MORNING.
WE WON'T LET THEM RUB OUR FACE IN THE DIRT, GREGORY.
NO, WE WON'T LET THEM TREAT US LIKE MINERS.
I MEAN, IF THEY MAKE US ANGRY, WE'LL DRAW OUR SWORDS.
YOU SHOULDN'T RISK YOUR NECK BY GETTING HOT UNDER THE COLLAR.
I'M FAST WHEN I'M ANGRY.
BUT YOU TAKE A WHILE TO GET ANGRY.
ANY MONTAGUE MAKES ME ANGRY.
TO BE ANGRY MEANS TO STAND AND FIGHT.
WHEN YOU'RE ANGRY, YOU RUN AWAY.
ANY MONTAGUE DOG MAKES ME ANGRY ENOUGH TO FIGHT. MAN OR WOMAN, I'LL PUSH THEM FROM THE WALL INTO THE GUTTER.
THAT SHOWS HOW WEAK YOU ARE: WIMPS KEEP CLOSE TO WALLS.
TRUE – WOMEN, BEING WEAKER, GET PUSHED TO THE WALL.
SO, I'LL PUSH MONTAGUE'S MEN AWAY FROM THE WALL
AND THRUST HIS MAIDS TO THE WALL.
THE FIGHT IS BETWEEN OUR MASTERS AND US, THEIR MEN.
IT'S ALL THE SAME. I CAN BE A REAL TYRANT.
AFTER I HAVE FOUGHT THE MEN, I WILL BE CRUEL TO THE MAIDENS –
AND CUT OFF THEIR HEADS.

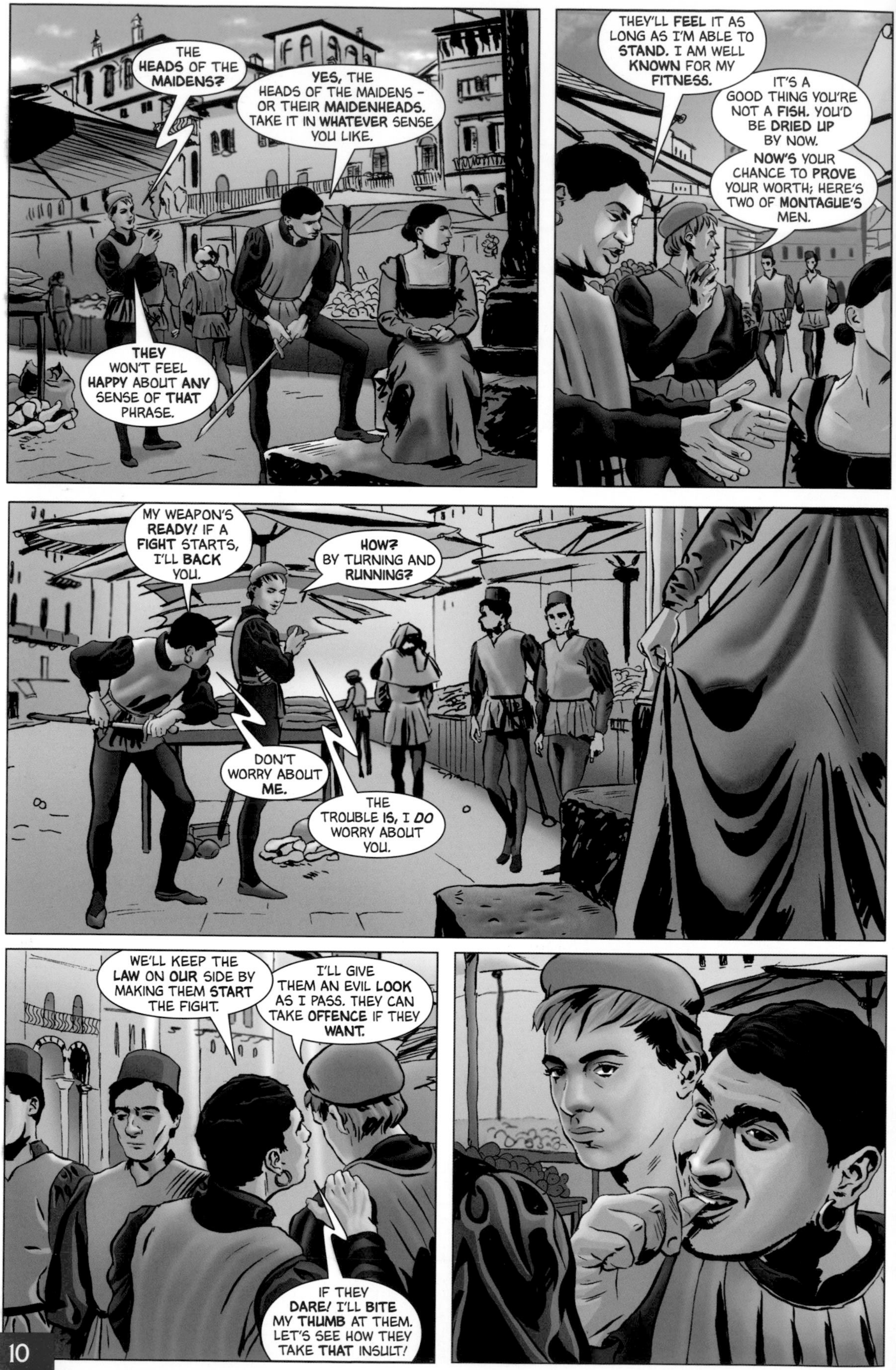
THE HEADS OF THE MAIDENS?
YES, THE HEADS OF THE MAIDENS – OR THEIR MAIDENHEADS. TAKE IT IN WHATEVER SENSE YOU LIKE.
THEY WON'T FEEL HAPPY ABOUT ANY SENSE OF THAT PHRASE.
THEY'LL FEEL IT AS LONG AS I'M ABLE TO STAND. I AM WELL KNOWN FOR MY FITNESS.
IT'S A GOOD THING YOU'RE NOT A FISH. YOU'D BE DRIED UP BY NOW.
NOW'S YOUR CHANCE TO PROVE YOUR WORTH; HERE'S TWO OF MONTAGUE'S MEN.
MY WEAPON'S READY! IF A FIGHT STARTS, I'LL BACK YOU.
HOW? BY TURNING AND RUNNING?
DON'T WORRY ABOUT ME.
THE TROUBLE IS, I DO WORRY ABOUT YOU.
WE'LL KEEP THE LAW ON OUR SIDE BY MAKING THEM START THE FIGHT.
I'LL GIVE THEM AN EVIL LOOK AS I PASS. THEY CAN TAKE OFFENCE IF THEY WANT.
IF THEY DARE! I'LL BITE MY THUMB AT THEM. LET'S SEE HOW THEY TAKE THAT INSULT!

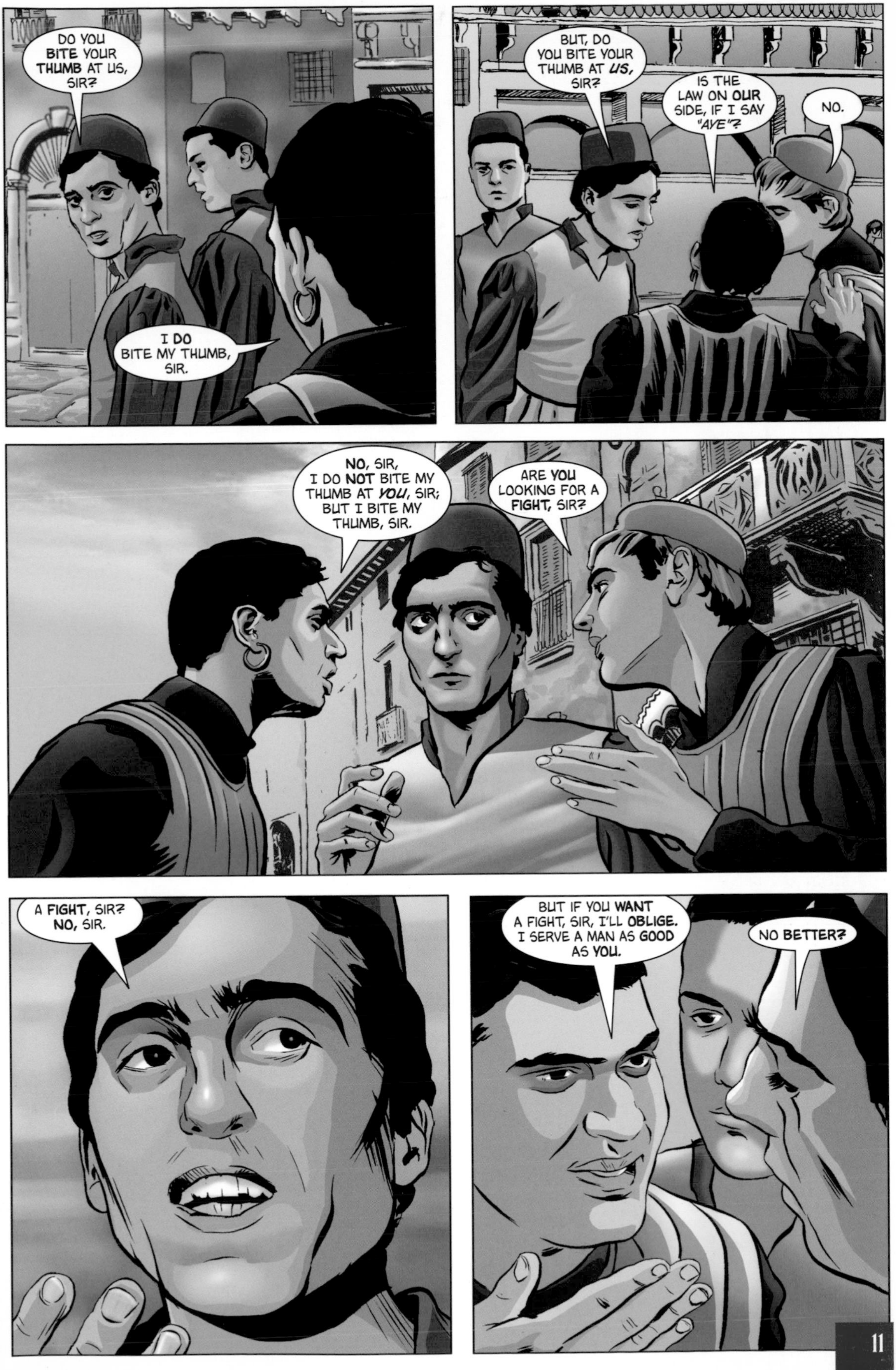
DO YOU BITE YOUR THUMB AT US, SIR?
I DO BITE MY THUMB, SIR.
BUT, DO YOU BITE YOUR THUMB AT US, SIR?
IS THE LAW ON OUR SIDE, IF I SAY "AYE"?
NO.
NO, SIR, I DO NOT BITE MY THUMB AT YOU, SIR; BUT I BITE MY THUMB, SIR.
ARE YOU LOOKING FOR A FIGHT, SIR?
A FIGHT, SIR? NO, SIR.
BUT IF YOU WANT A FIGHT, SIR, I'LL OBLIGE. I SERVE A MAN AS GOOD AS YOU.
NO BETTER?

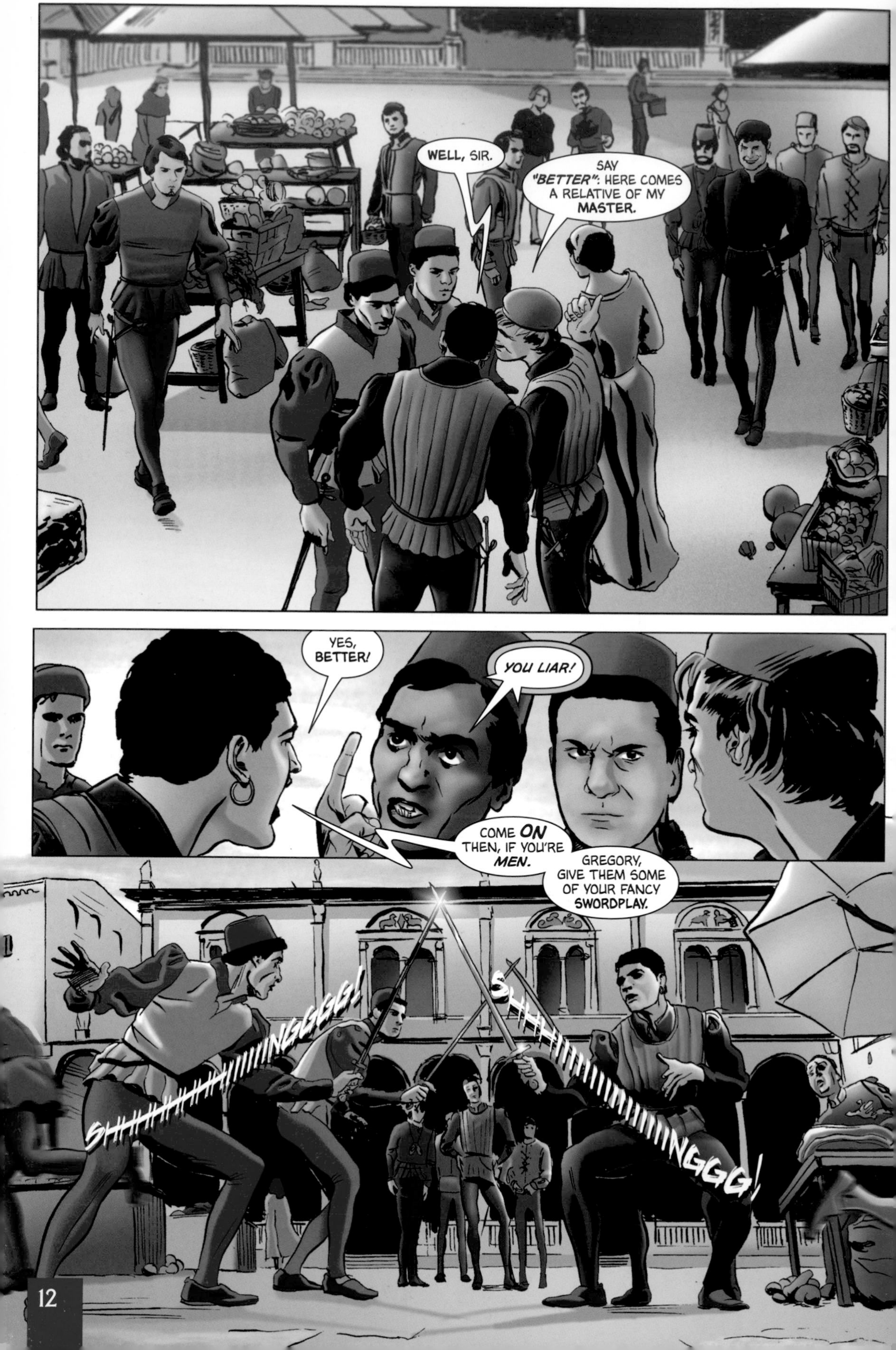
WELL, SIR.
SAY "BETTER": HERE COMES A RELATIVE OF MY MASTER.
YES, BETTER!
YOU LIAR!
COME ON THEN, IF YOU'RE MEN.
GREGORY, GIVE THEM SOME OF YOUR FANCY SWORDPLAY.
SHHHHHHHHHHIIIIIINGGG!
SHHHIIIIIIIIIIIINGGG!

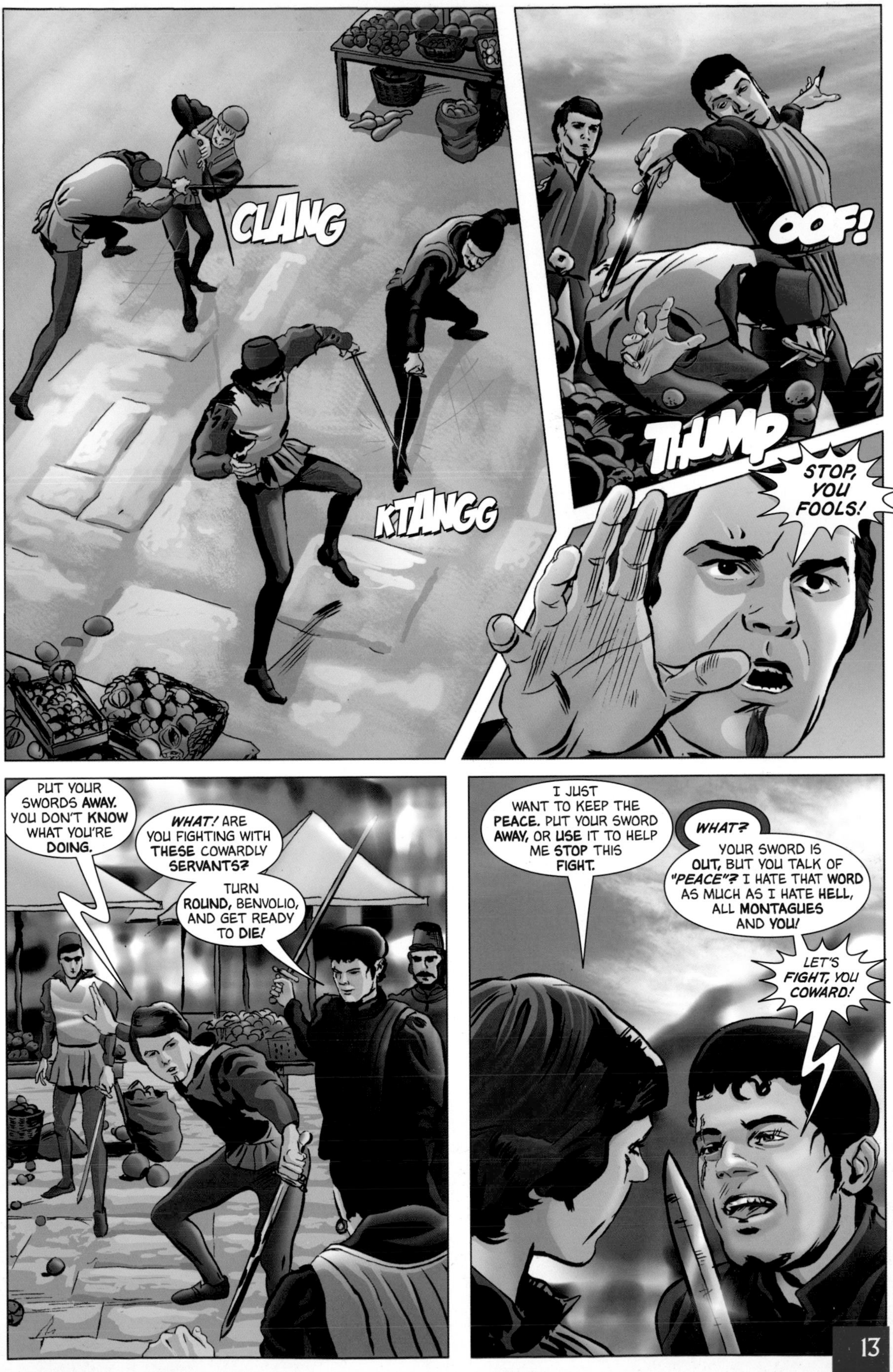
CLANG
KTANGG
OOF!
THUMP
STOP, YOU FOOLS!
PUT YOUR SWORDS AWAY. YOU DON'T KNOW WHAT YOU'RE DOING.
WHAT! ARE YOU FIGHTING WITH THESE COWARDLY SERVANTS?
TURN ROUND, BENVOLIO, AND GET READY TO DIE!
I JUST WANT TO KEEP THE PEACE. PUT YOUR SWORD AWAY, OR USE IT TO HELP ME STOP THIS FIGHT.
WHAT?
YOUR SWORD IS OUT, BUT YOU TALK OF "PEACE"? I HATE THAT WORD AS MUCH AS I HATE HELL, ALL MONTAGUES AND YOU!
LET'S FIGHT, YOU COWARD!

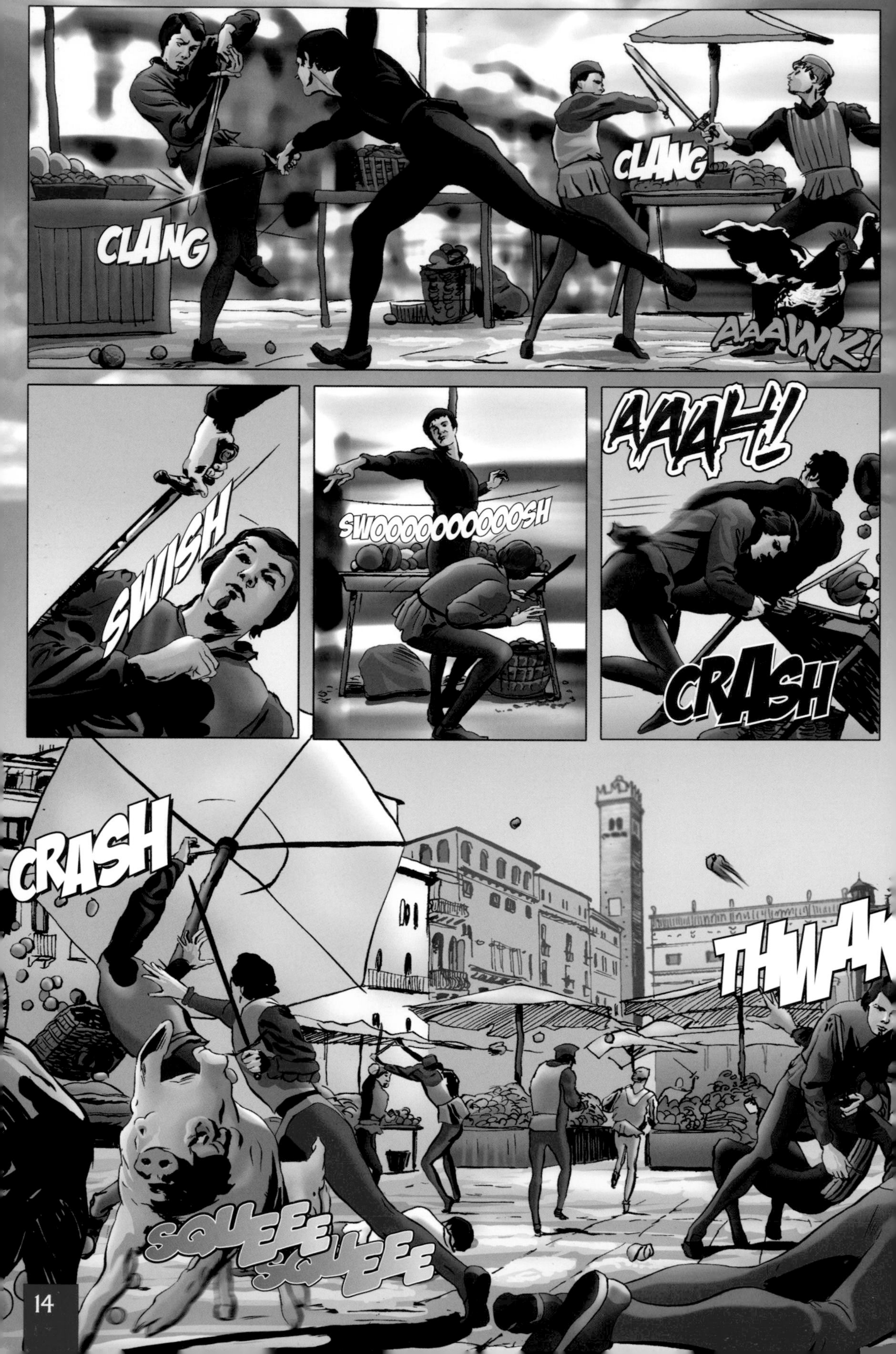
CLANG
CLANG
AAAWK!
SWISH
SWOOOOOOOOOOOSH
AAAH!
CRASH
CRASH
THWAK
SQUEEE
SQUEEE

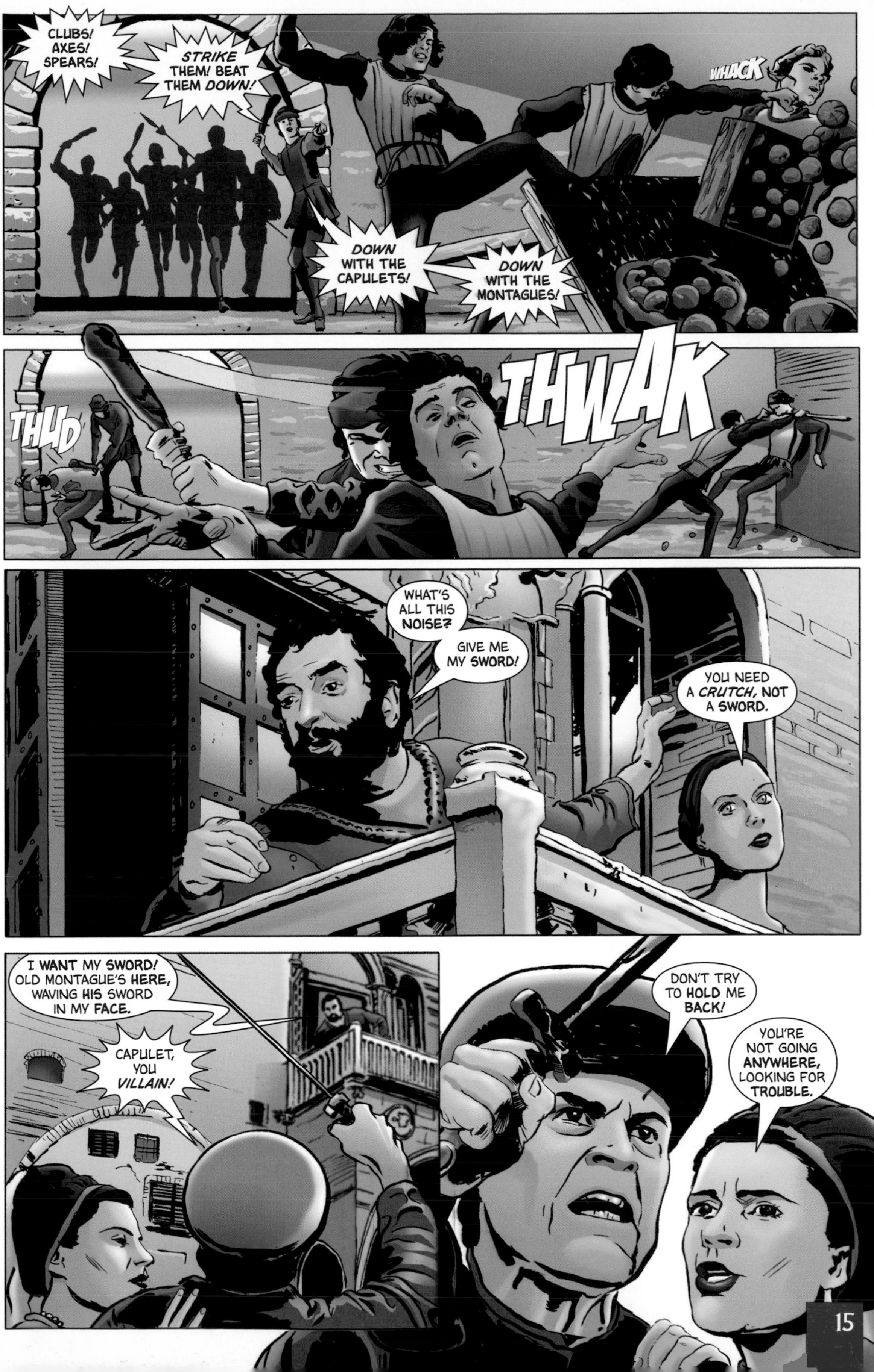
CLUBS! AXES! SPEARS!
STRIKE THEM! BEAT THEM DOWN!
WHACK
DOWN WITH THE CAPULETS!
DOWN WITH THE MONTAGUES!
THUD
THWAK
WHAT'S ALL THIS NOISE?
GIVE ME MY SWORD!
YOU NEED A CRUTCH, NOT A SWORD.
I WANT MY SWORD! OLD MONTAGUE'S HERE, WAVING HIS SWORD IN MY FACE.
CAPULET, YOU VILLAIN!
DON'T TRY TO HOLD ME BACK!
YOU'RE NOT GOING ANYWHERE, LOOKING FOR TROUBLE.

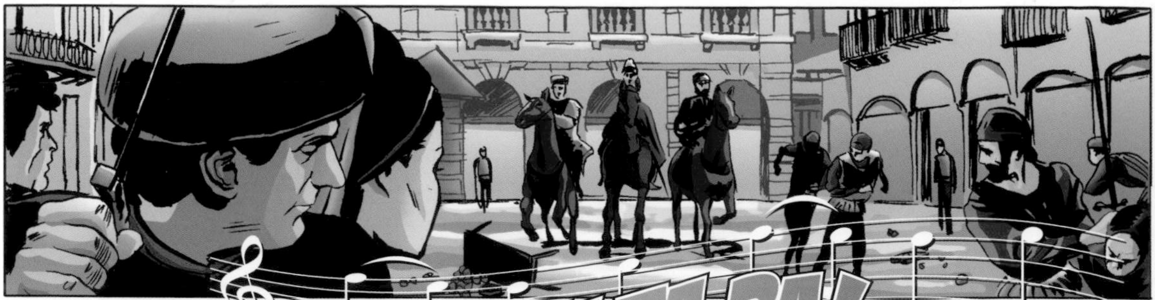

TA-TAN TA RA!

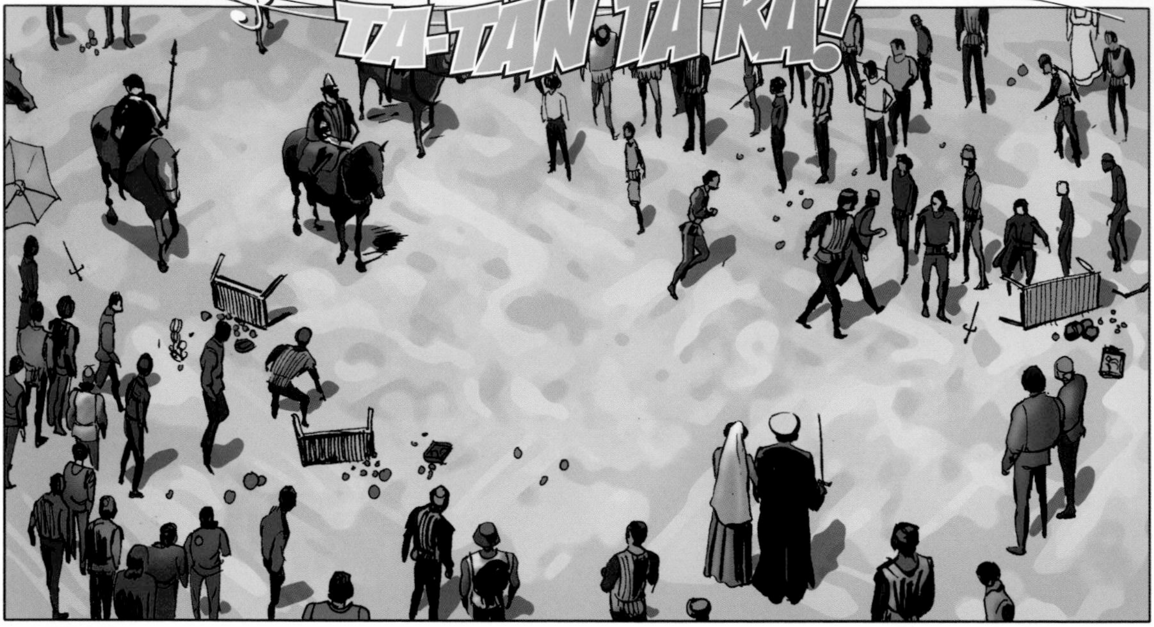

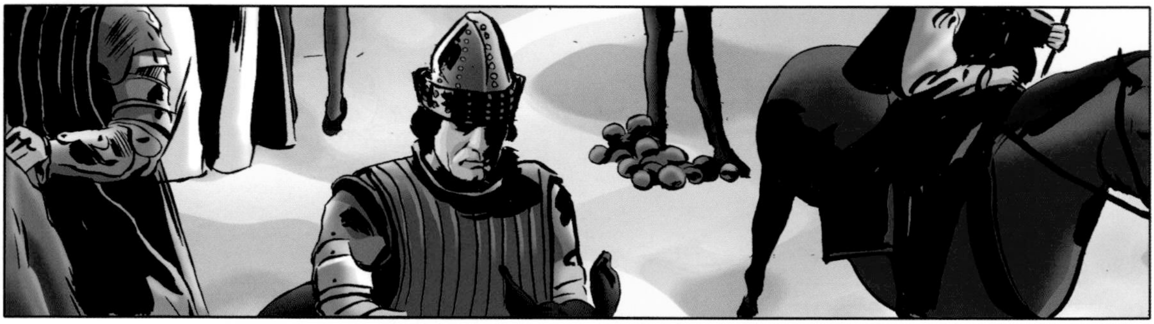

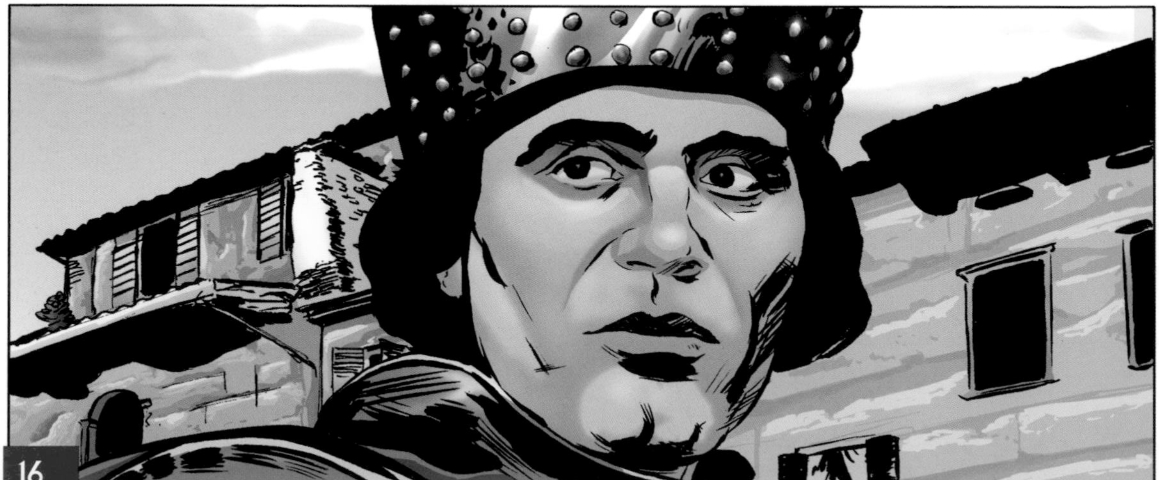

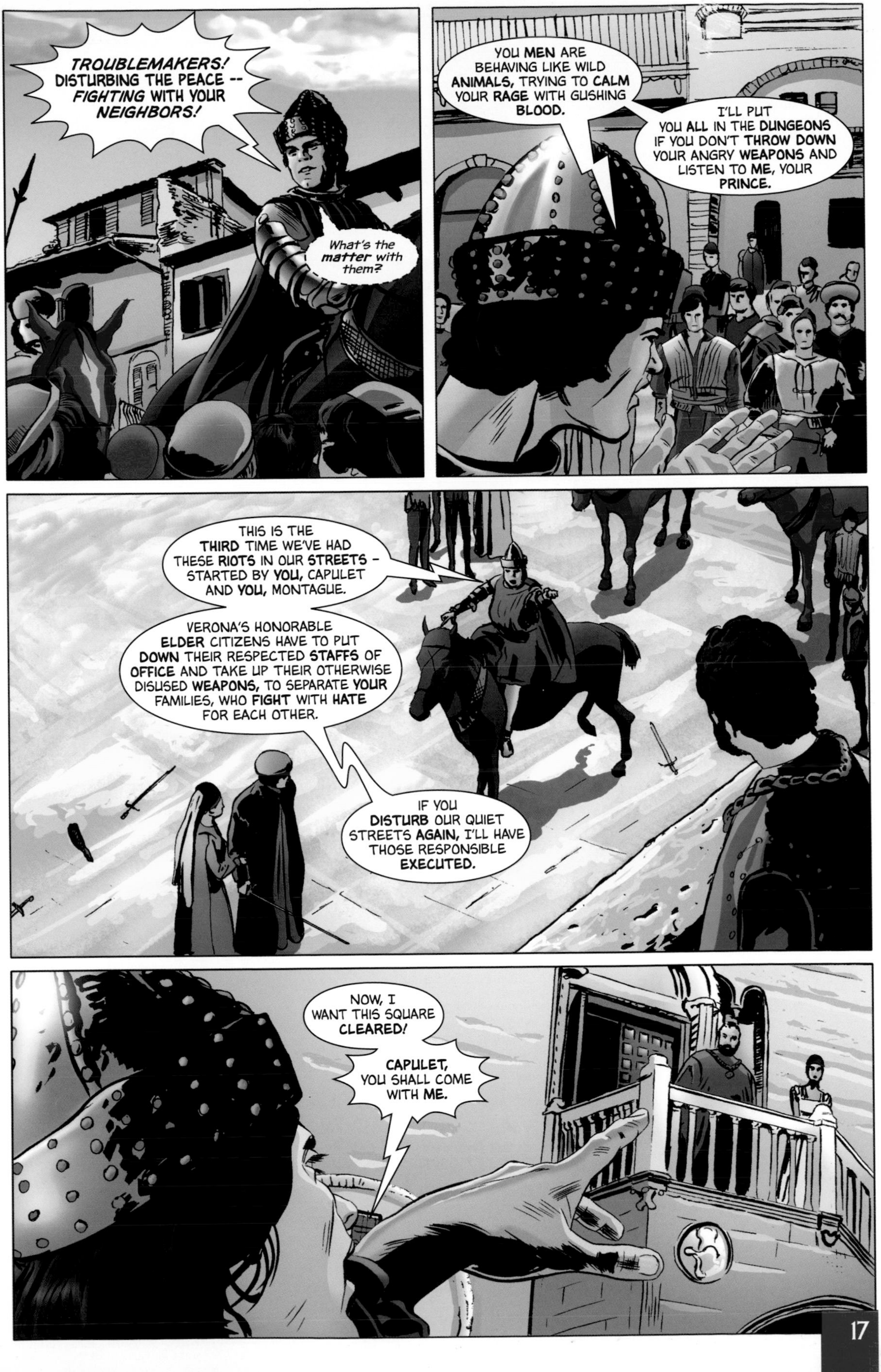
TROUBLEMAKERS! DISTURBING THE PEACE -- FIGHTING WITH YOUR NEIGHBORS!
What's the matter with them?
YOU MEN ARE BEHAVING LIKE WILD ANIMALS, TRYING TO CALM YOUR RAGE WITH GUSHING BLOOD.
I'LL PUT YOU ALL IN THE DUNGEONS IF YOU DON'T THROW DOWN YOUR ANGRY WEAPONS AND LISTEN TO ME, YOUR PRINCE.
THIS IS THE THIRD TIME WE'VE HAD THESE RIOTS IN OUR STREETS - STARTED BY YOU, CAPULET AND YOU, MONTAGUE.
VERONA'S HONORABLE ELDER CITIZENS HAVE TO PUT DOWN THEIR RESPECTED STAFFS OF OFFICE AND TAKE UP THEIR OTHERWISE DISUSED WEAPONS, TO SEPARATE YOUR FAMILIES, WHO FIGHT WITH HATE FOR EACH OTHER.
IF YOU DISTURB OUR QUIET STREETS AGAIN, I'LL HAVE THOSE RESPONSIBLE EXECUTED.
NOW, I WANT THIS SQUARE CLEARED!
CAPULET, YOU SHALL COME WITH ME.

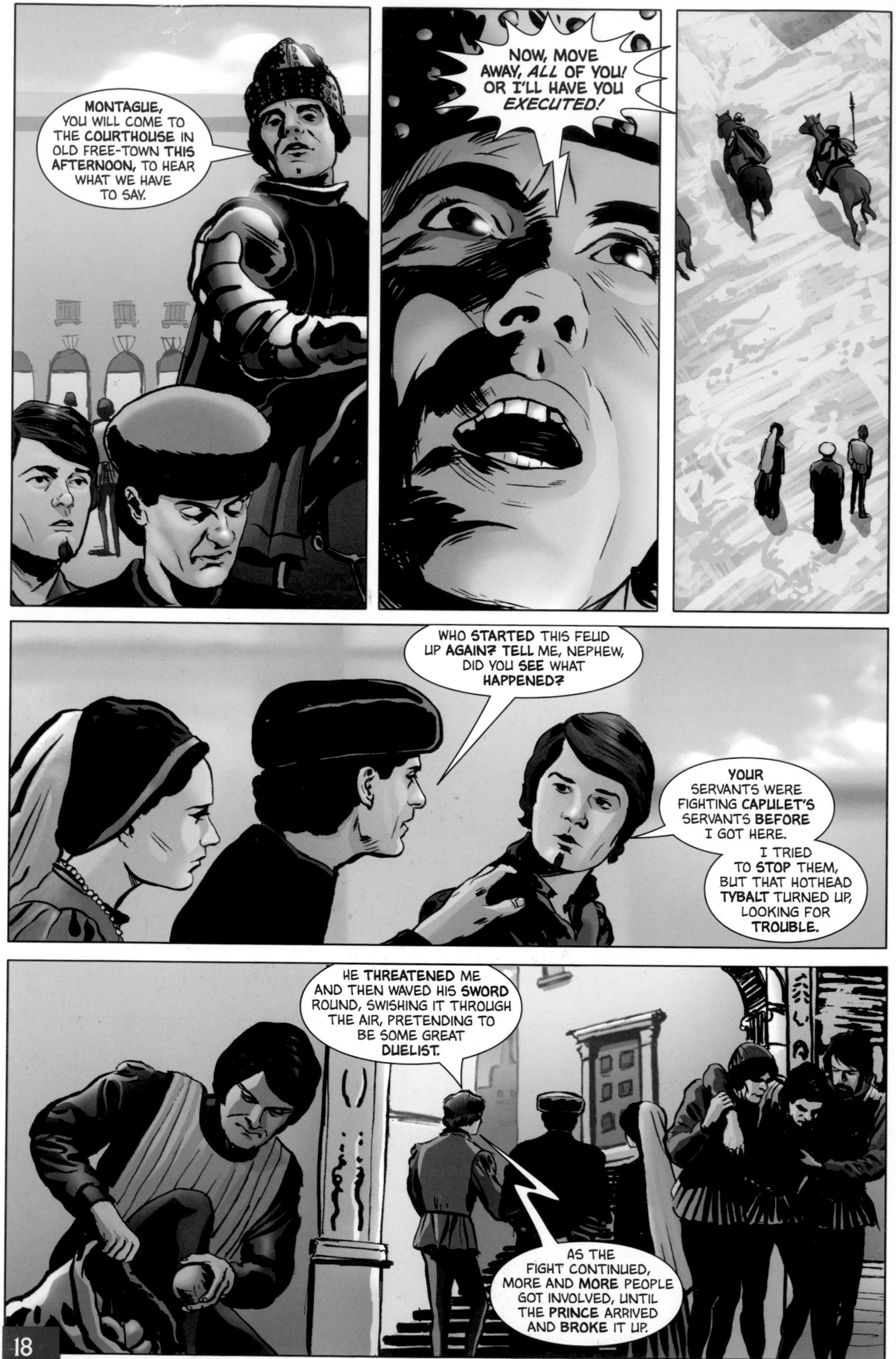

MONTAGUE, YOU WILL COME TO THE COURTHOUSE IN OLD FREE-TOWN THIS AFTERNOON, TO HEAR WHAT WE HAVE TO SAY.
NOW, MOVE AWAY, ALL OF YOU! OR I'LL HAVE YOU EXECUTED!
WHO STARTED THIS FEUD UP AGAIN? TELL ME, NEPHEW, DID YOU SEE WHAT HAPPENED?
YOUR SERVANTS WERE FIGHTING CAPULET'S SERVANTS BEFORE I GOT HERE.
I TRIED TO STOP THEM, BUT THAT HOTHEAD TYBALT TURNED UP, LOOKING FOR TROUBLE.
HE THREATENED ME AND THEN WAVED HIS SWORD ROUND, SWISHING IT THROUGH THE AIR, PRETENDING TO BE SOME GREAT DUELIST.
AS THE FIGHT CONTINUED, MORE AND MORE PEOPLE GOT INVOLVED, UNTIL THE PRINCE ARRIVED AND BROKE IT UP.

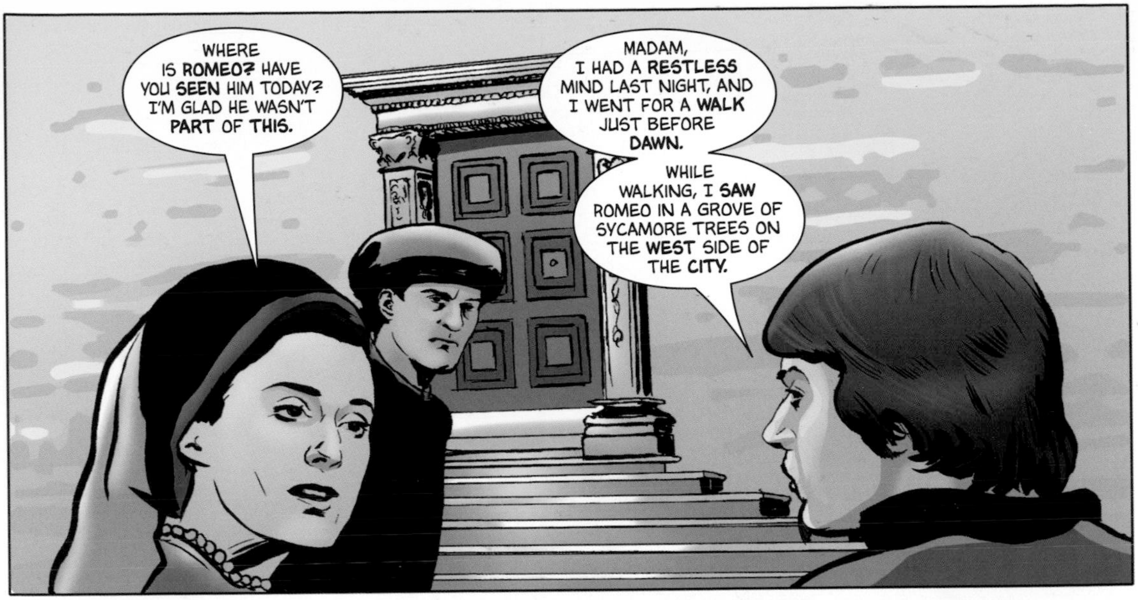
WHERE IS ROMEO? HAVE YOU SEEN HIM TODAY? I'M GLAD HE WASN'T PART OF THIS.
MADAM, I HAD A RESTLESS MIND LAST NIGHT, AND I WENT FOR A WALK JUST BEFORE DAWN.
WHILE WALKING, I SAW ROMEO IN A GROVE OF SYCAMORE TREES ON THE WEST SIDE OF THE CITY.

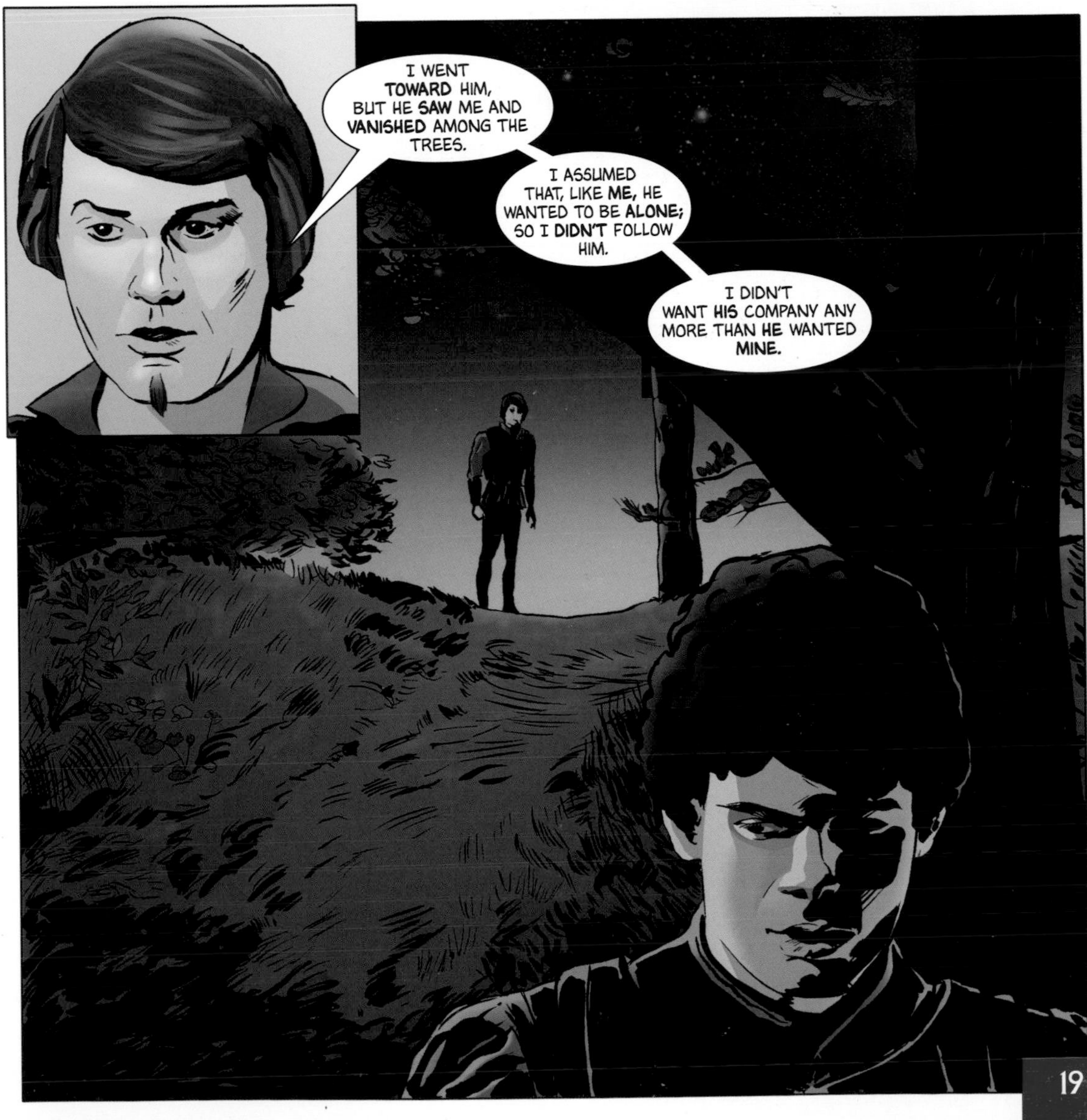
I WENT TOWARD HIM, BUT HE SAW ME AND VANISHED AMONG THE TREES.
I ASSUMED THAT, LIKE ME, HE WANTED TO BE ALONE; SO I DIDN'T FOLLOW HIM.
I DIDN'T WANT HIS COMPANY ANY MORE THAN HE WANTED MINE.

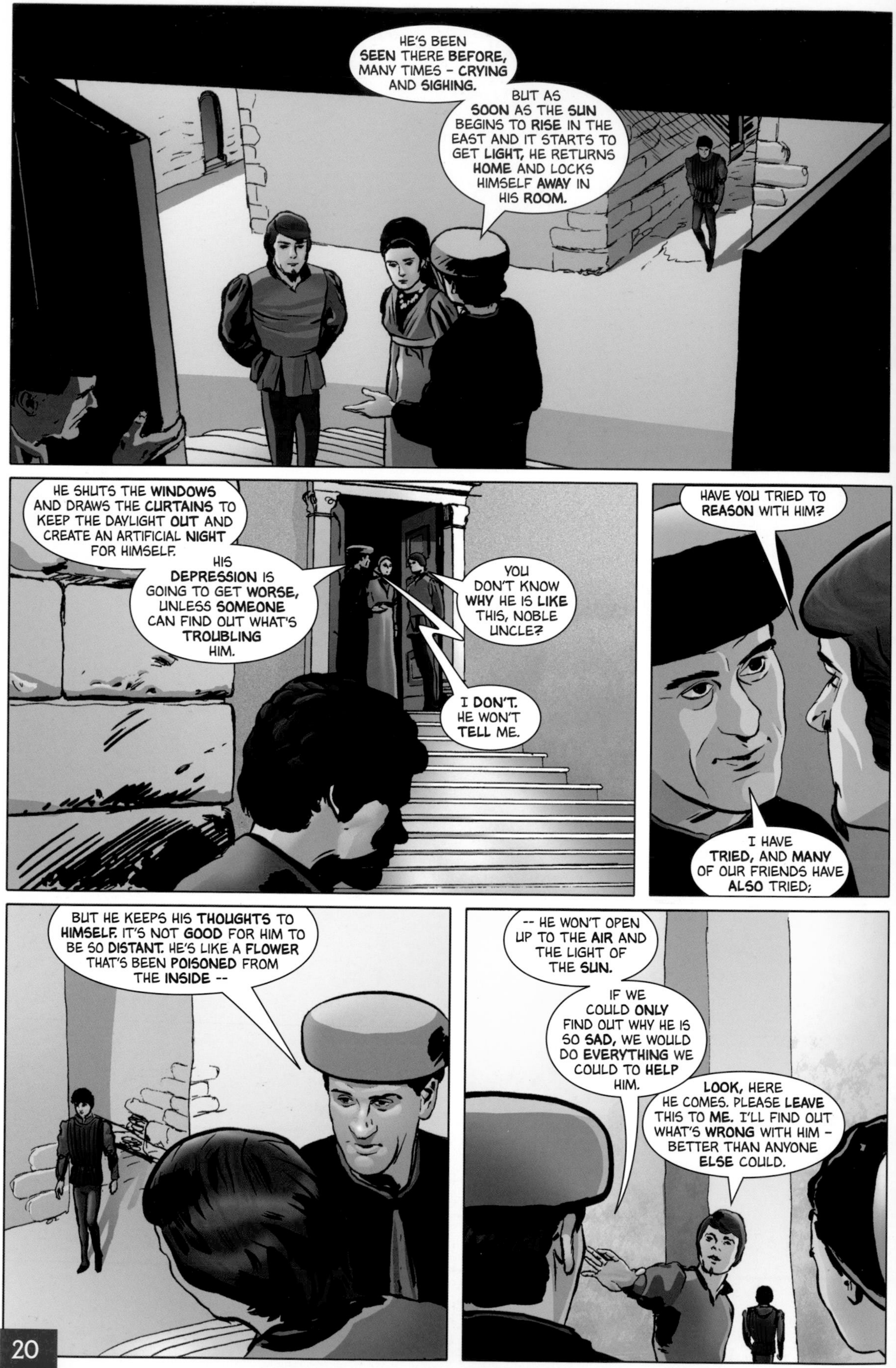
HE'S BEEN SEEN THERE BEFORE, MANY TIMES – CRYING AND SIGHING.
BUT AS SOON AS THE SUN BEGINS TO RISE IN THE EAST AND IT STARTS TO GET LIGHT, HE RETURNS HOME AND LOCKS HIMSELF AWAY IN HIS ROOM.
HE SHUTS THE WINDOWS AND DRAWS THE CURTAINS TO KEEP THE DAYLIGHT OUT AND CREATE AN ARTIFICIAL NIGHT FOR HIMSELF.
HIS DEPRESSION IS GOING TO GET WORSE, UNLESS SOMEONE CAN FIND OUT WHAT'S TROUBLING HIM.
YOU DON'T KNOW WHY HE IS LIKE THIS, NOBLE UNCLE?
I DON'T. HE WON'T TELL ME.
HAVE YOU TRIED TO REASON WITH HIM?
I HAVE TRIED, AND MANY OF OUR FRIENDS HAVE ALSO TRIED;
BUT HE KEEPS HIS THOUGHTS TO HIMSELF. IT'S NOT GOOD FOR HIM TO BE SO DISTANT. HE'S LIKE A FLOWER THAT'S BEEN POISONED FROM THE INSIDE --
-- HE WON'T OPEN UP TO THE AIR AND THE LIGHT OF THE SUN.
IF WE COULD ONLY FIND OUT WHY HE IS SO SAD, WE WOULD DO EVERYTHING WE COULD TO HELP HIM.
LOOK, HERE HE COMES. PLEASE LEAVE THIS TO ME. I'LL FIND OUT WHAT'S WRONG WITH HIM – BETTER THAN ANYONE ELSE COULD.

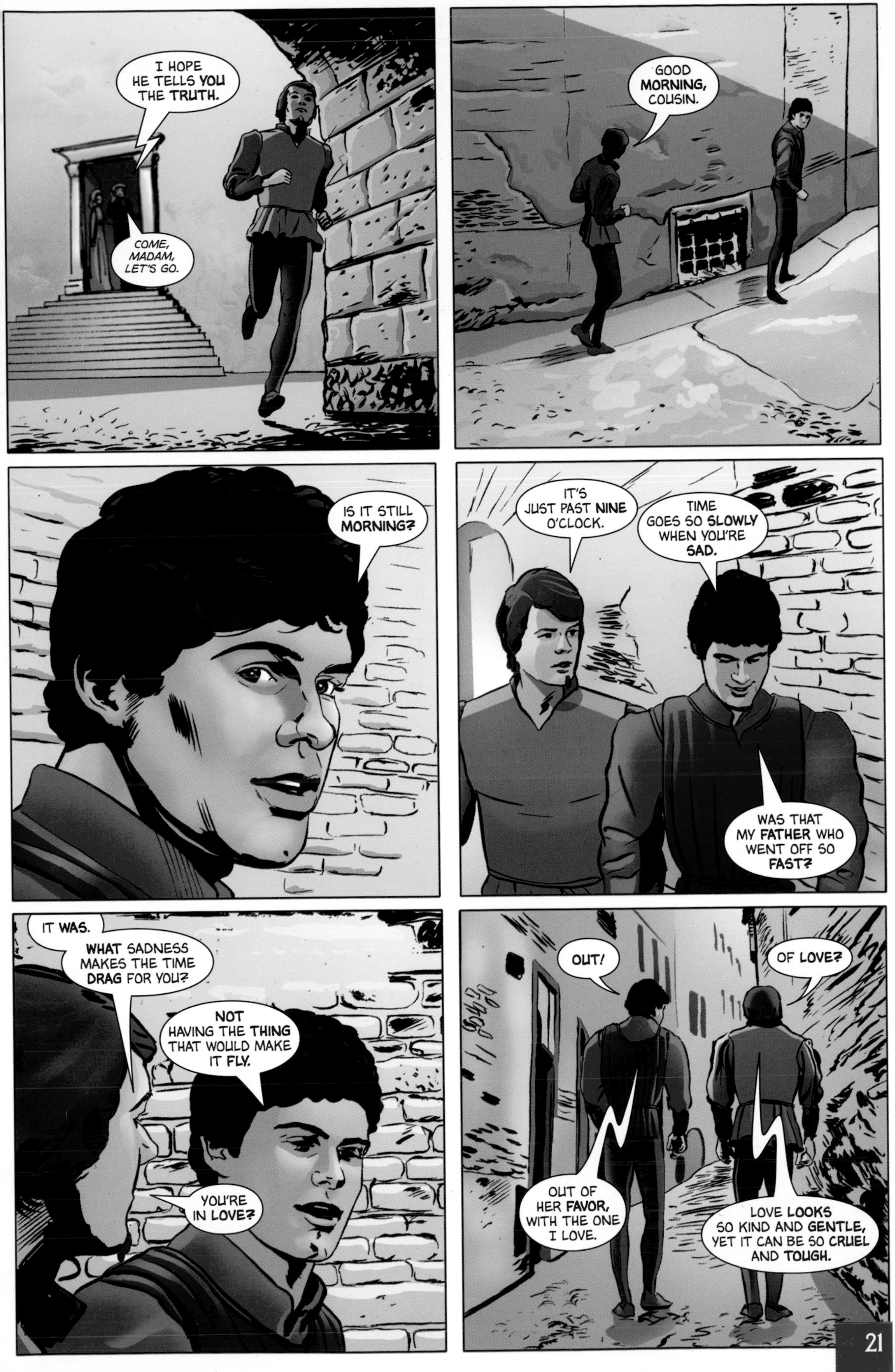
I HOPE HE TELLS YOU THE TRUTH.
COME, MADAM, LET'S GO.
GOOD MORNING, COUSIN.
IS IT STILL MORNING?
IT'S JUST PAST NINE O'CLOCK.
TIME GOES SO SLOWLY WHEN YOU'RE SAD.
WAS THAT MY FATHER WHO WENT OFF SO FAST?
IT WAS.
WHAT SADNESS MAKES THE TIME DRAG FOR YOU?
NOT HAVING THE THING THAT WOULD MAKE IT FLY.
YOU'RE IN LOVE?
OUT!
OF LOVE?
OUT OF HER FAVOR, WITH THE ONE I LOVE.
LOVE LOOKS SO KIND AND GENTLE, YET IT CAN BE SO CRUEL AND TOUGH.

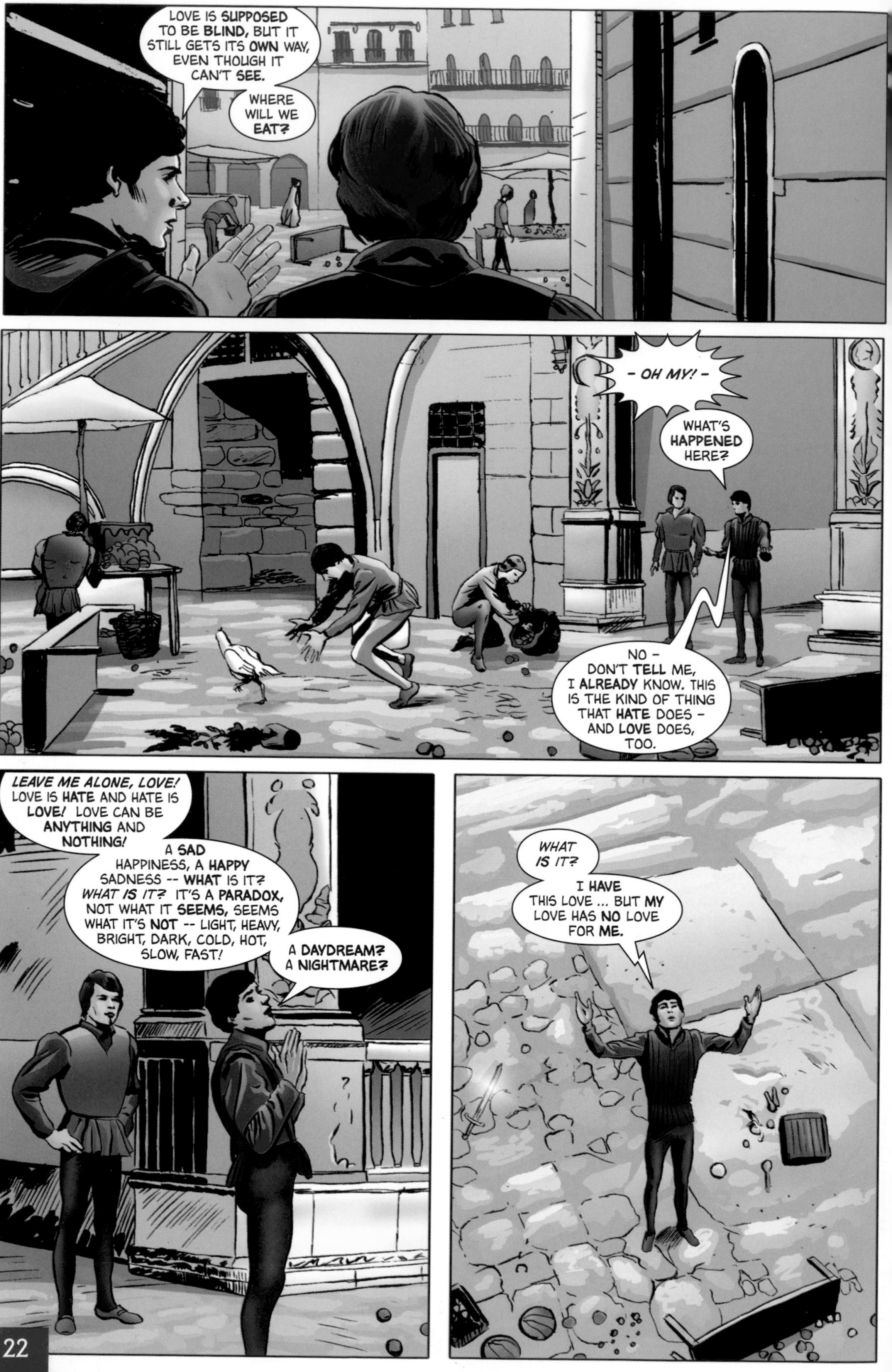
LOVE IS SUPPOSED TO BE BLIND, BUT IT STILL GETS ITS OWN WAY, EVEN THOUGH IT CAN'T SEE.
WHERE WILL WE EAT?
- OH MY! -
WHAT'S HAPPENED HERE?
NO - DON'T TELL ME, I ALREADY KNOW. THIS IS THE KIND OF THING THAT HATE DOES - AND LOVE DOES, TOO.
LEAVE ME ALONE, LOVE! LOVE IS HATE AND HATE IS LOVE! LOVE CAN BE ANYTHING AND NOTHING!
A SAD HAPPINESS, A HAPPY SADNESS -- WHAT IS IT? WHAT IS IT? IT'S A PARADOX, NOT WHAT IT SEEMS, SEEMS WHAT IT'S NOT -- LIGHT, HEAVY, BRIGHT, DARK, COLD, HOT, SLOW, FAST!
A DAYDREAM? A NIGHTMARE?
WHAT IS IT?
I HAVE THIS LOVE ... BUT MY LOVE HAS NO LOVE FOR ME.

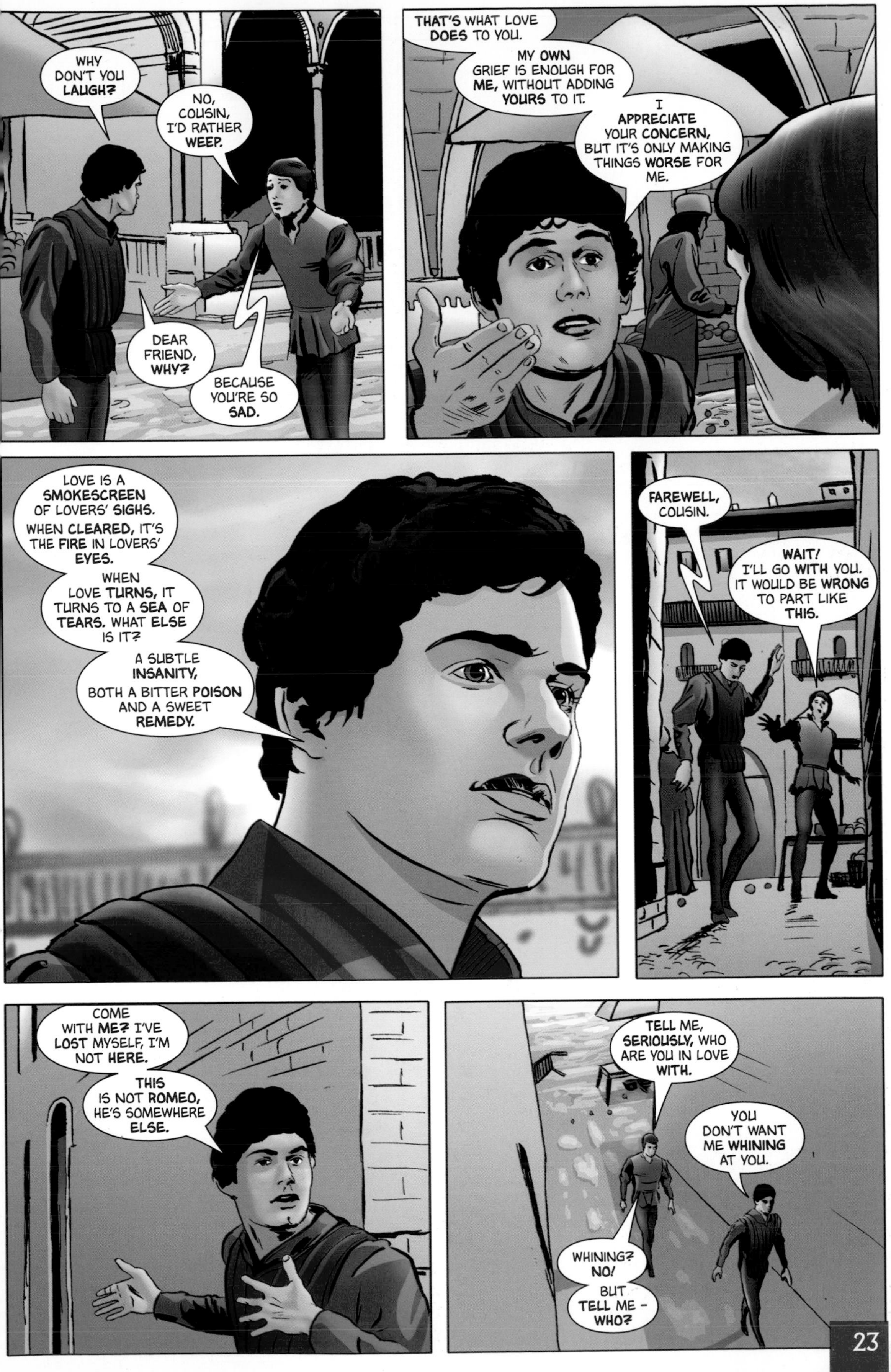
WHY DON'T YOU LAUGH?
NO, COUSIN, I'D RATHER WEEP.
DEAR FRIEND, WHY?
BECAUSE YOU'RE SO SAD.
THAT'S WHAT LOVE DOES TO YOU.
MY OWN GRIEF IS ENOUGH FOR ME, WITHOUT ADDING YOURS TO IT.
I APPRECIATE YOUR CONCERN, BUT IT'S ONLY MAKING THINGS WORSE FOR ME.
LOVE IS A SMOKESCREEN OF LOVERS' SIGHS.
WHEN CLEARED, IT'S THE FIRE IN LOVERS' EYES.
WHEN LOVE TURNS, IT TURNS TO A SEA OF TEARS. WHAT ELSE IS IT?
A SUBTLE INSANITY, BOTH A BITTER POISON AND A SWEET REMEDY.
FAREWELL, COUSIN.
WAIT! I'LL GO WITH YOU. IT WOULD BE WRONG TO PART LIKE THIS.
COME WITH ME? I'VE LOST MYSELF, I'M NOT HERE.
THIS IS NOT ROMEO, HE'S SOMEWHERE ELSE.
TELL ME, SERIOUSLY, WHO ARE YOU IN LOVE WITH.
YOU DON'T WANT ME WHINING AT YOU.
WHINING? NO!
BUT TELL ME - WHO?

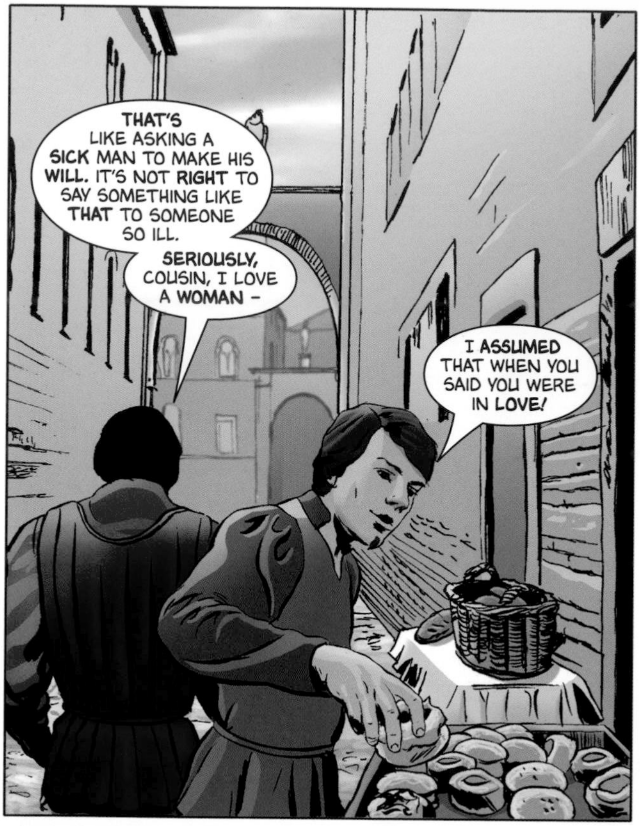
THAT'S LIKE ASKING A SICK MAN TO MAKE HIS WILL. IT'S NOT RIGHT TO SAY SOMETHING LIKE THAT TO SOMEONE SO ILL.
SERIOUSLY, COUSIN, I LOVE A WOMAN –
I ASSUMED THAT WHEN YOU SAID YOU WERE IN LOVE!

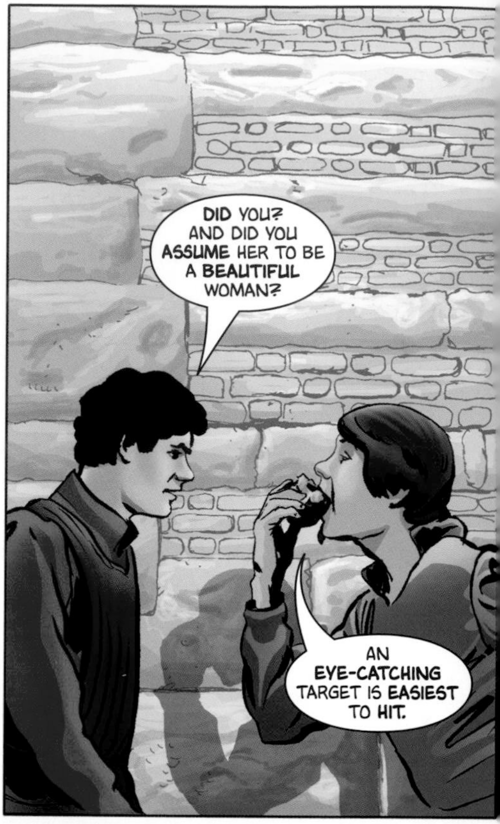
DID YOU? AND DID YOU ASSUME HER TO BE A BEAUTIFUL WOMAN?
AN EYE-CATCHING TARGET IS EASIEST TO HIT.

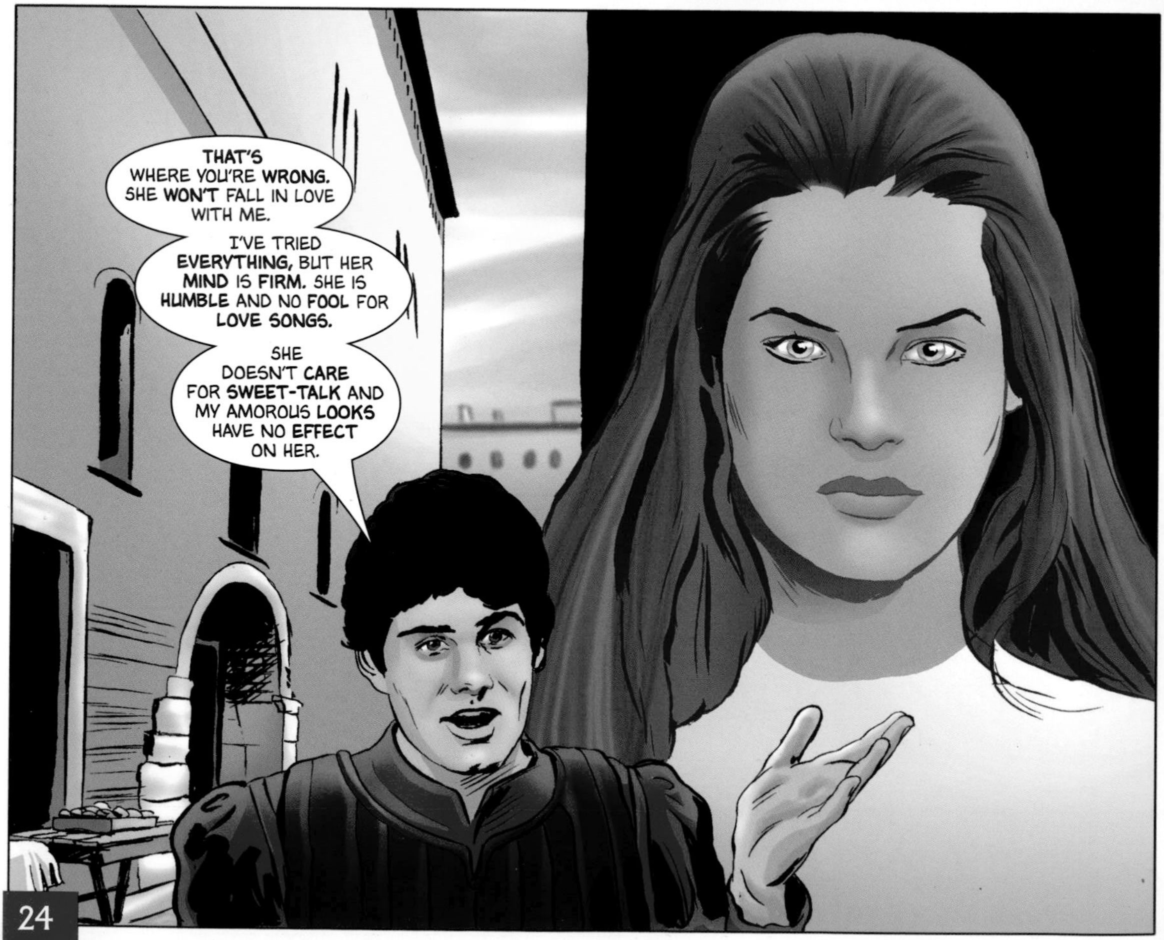
THAT'S WHERE YOU'RE WRONG. SHE WON'T FALL IN LOVE WITH ME.
I'VE TRIED EVERYTHING, BUT HER MIND IS FIRM. SHE IS HUMBLE AND NO FOOL FOR LOVE SONGS.
SHE DOESN'T CARE FOR SWEET-TALK AND MY AMOROUS LOOKS HAVE NO EFFECT ON HER.

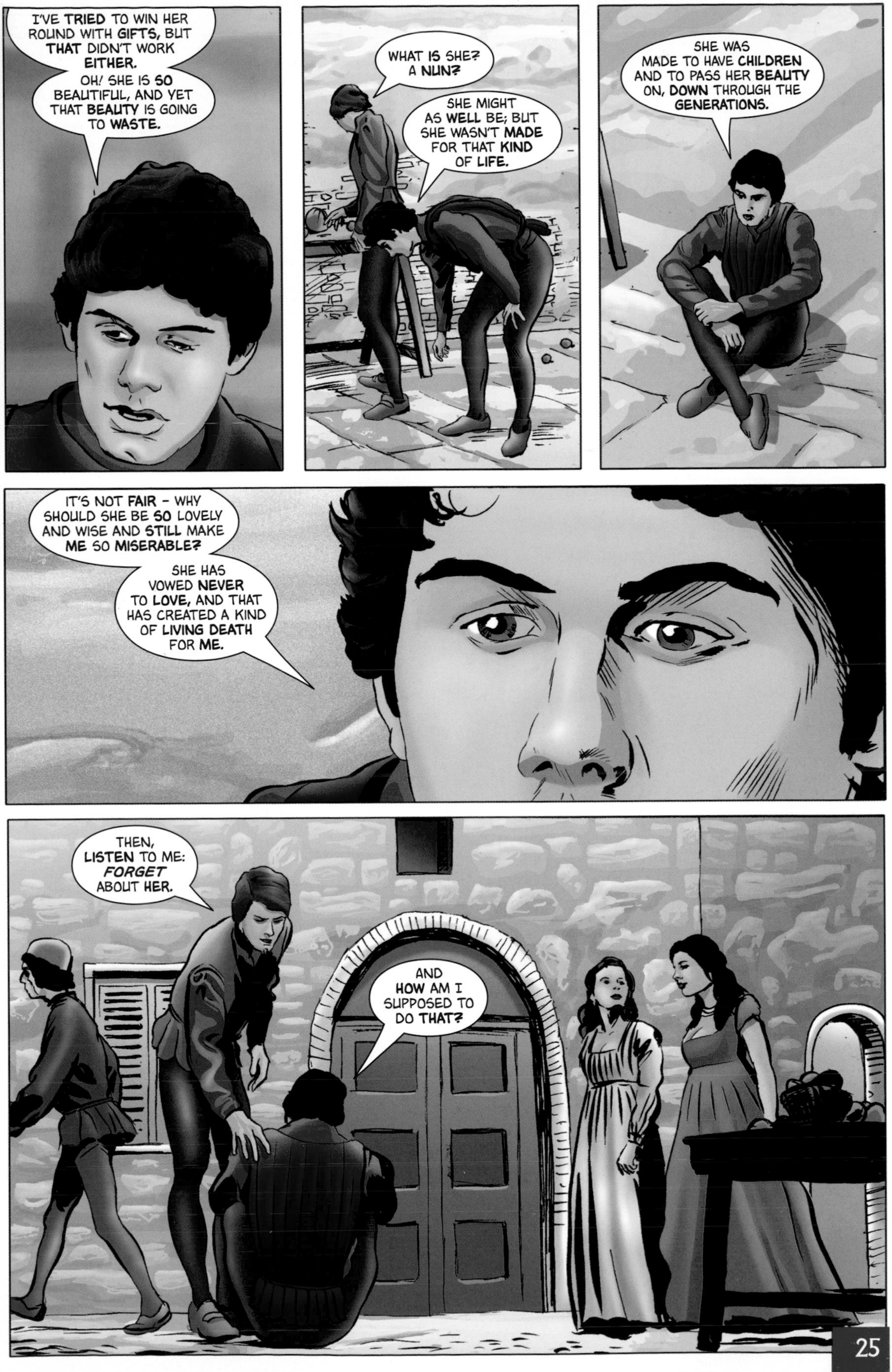
I'VE TRIED TO WIN HER ROUND WITH GIFTS, BUT THAT DIDN'T WORK EITHER.
OH! SHE IS SO BEAUTIFUL, AND YET THAT BEAUTY IS GOING TO WASTE.
WHAT IS SHE? A NUN?
SHE MIGHT AS WELL BE; BUT SHE WASN'T MADE FOR THAT KIND OF LIFE.
SHE WAS MADE TO HAVE CHILDREN AND TO PASS HER BEAUTY ON, DOWN THROUGH THE GENERATIONS.
IT'S NOT FAIR – WHY SHOULD SHE BE SO LOVELY AND WISE AND STILL MAKE ME SO MISERABLE?
SHE HAS VOWED NEVER TO LOVE, AND THAT HAS CREATED A KIND OF LIVING DEATH FOR ME.
THEN, LISTEN TO ME: FORGET ABOUT HER.
AND HOW AM I SUPPOSED TO DO THAT?

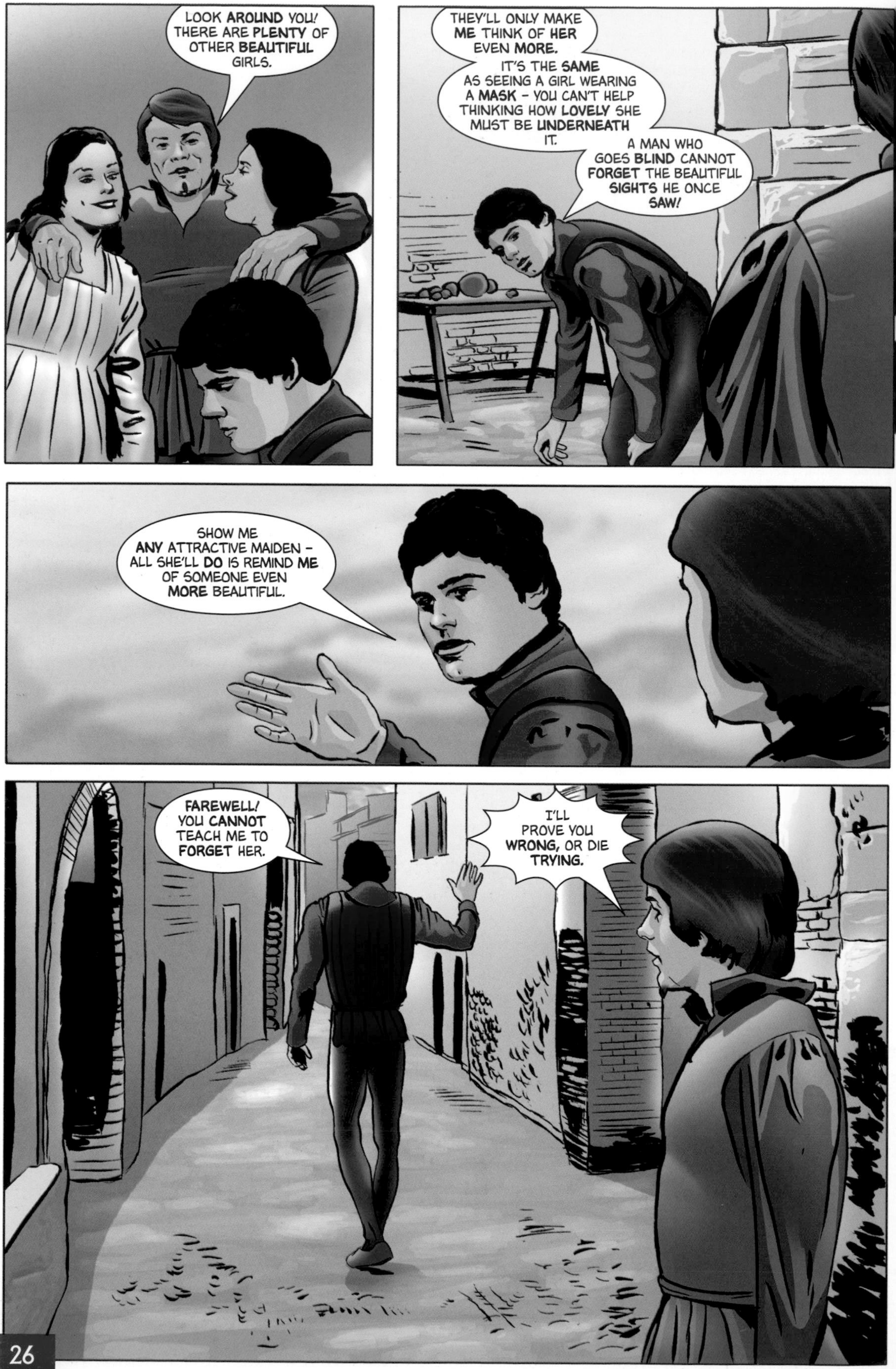
LOOK AROUND YOU! THERE ARE PLENTY OF OTHER BEAUTIFUL GIRLS.
THEY'LL ONLY MAKE ME THINK OF HER EVEN MORE.
IT'S THE SAME AS SEEING A GIRL WEARING A MASK – YOU CAN'T HELP THINKING HOW LOVELY SHE MUST BE UNDERNEATH IT.
A MAN WHO GOES BLIND CANNOT FORGET THE BEAUTIFUL SIGHTS HE ONCE SAW!
SHOW ME ANY ATTRACTIVE MAIDEN – ALL SHE'LL DO IS REMIND ME OF SOMEONE EVEN MORE BEAUTIFUL.
FAREWELL! YOU CANNOT TEACH ME TO FORGET HER.
I'LL PROVE YOU WRONG, OR DIE TRYING.

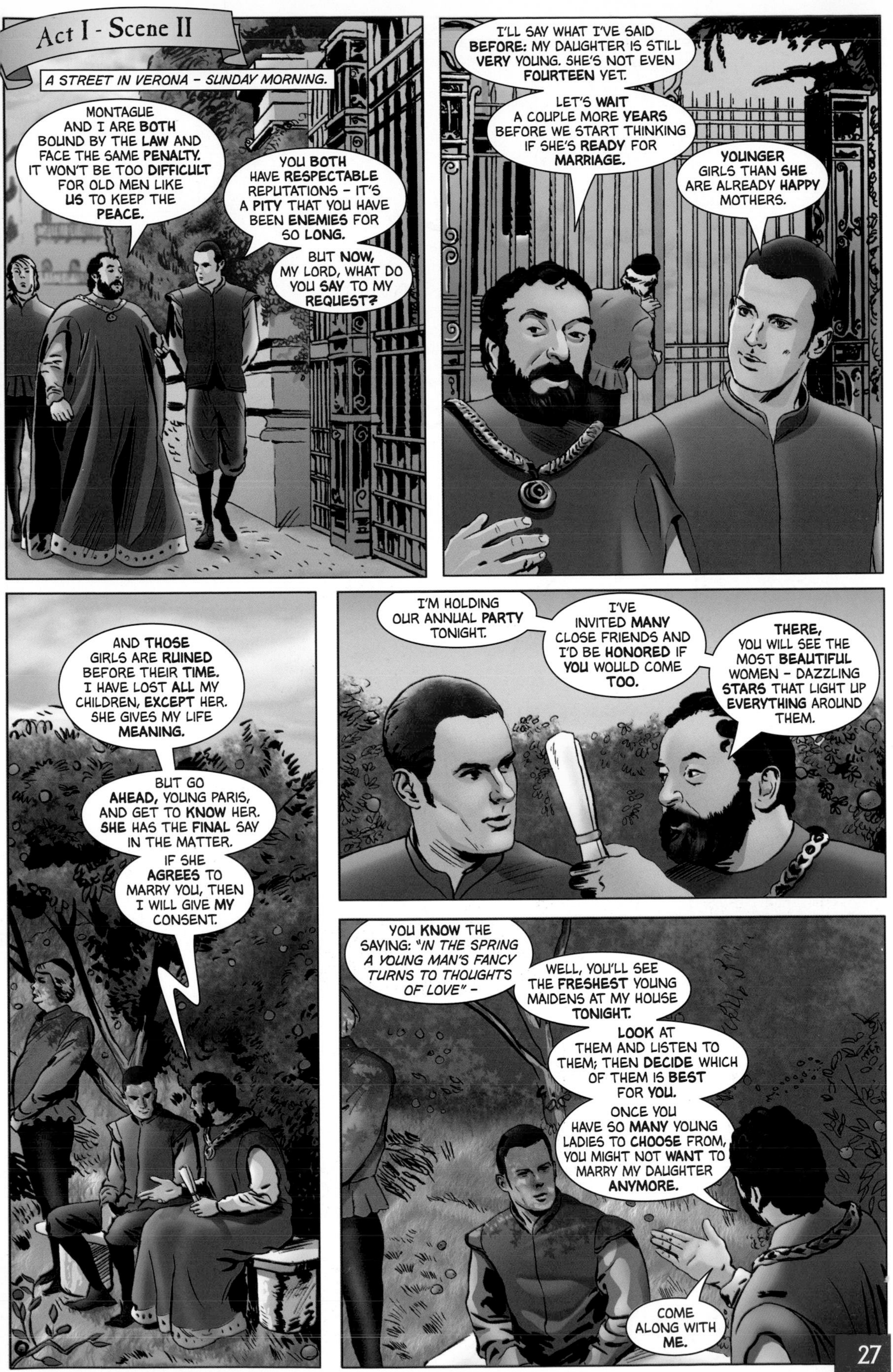

Act I - Scene II
A STREET IN VERONA – SUNDAY MORNING.
MONTAGUE AND I ARE BOTH BOUND BY THE LAW AND FACE THE SAME PENALTY. IT WON'T BE TOO DIFFICULT FOR OLD MEN LIKE US TO KEEP THE PEACE.
YOU BOTH HAVE RESPECTABLE REPUTATIONS – IT'S A PITY THAT YOU HAVE BEEN ENEMIES FOR SO LONG.
BUT NOW, MY LORD, WHAT DO YOU SAY TO MY REQUEST?
I'LL SAY WHAT I'VE SAID BEFORE: MY DAUGHTER IS STILL VERY YOUNG. SHE'S NOT EVEN FOURTEEN YET.
LET'S WAIT A COUPLE MORE YEARS BEFORE WE START THINKING IF SHE'S READY FOR MARRIAGE.
YOUNGER GIRLS THAN SHE ARE ALREADY HAPPY MOTHERS.
AND THOSE GIRLS ARE RUINED BEFORE THEIR TIME. I HAVE LOST ALL MY CHILDREN, EXCEPT HER. SHE GIVES MY LIFE MEANING.
BUT GO AHEAD, YOUNG PARIS, AND GET TO KNOW HER. SHE HAS THE FINAL SAY IN THE MATTER.
IF SHE AGREES TO MARRY YOU, THEN I WILL GIVE MY CONSENT.
I'M HOLDING OUR ANNUAL PARTY TONIGHT.
I'VE INVITED MANY CLOSE FRIENDS AND I'D BE HONORED IF YOU WOULD COME TOO.
THERE, YOU WILL SEE THE MOST BEAUTIFUL WOMEN – DAZZLING STARS THAT LIGHT UP EVERYTHING AROUND THEM.
YOU KNOW THE SAYING: "IN THE SPRING A YOUNG MAN'S FANCY TURNS TO THOUGHTS OF LOVE" –
WELL, YOU'LL SEE THE FRESHEST YOUNG MAIDENS AT MY HOUSE TONIGHT.
LOOK AT THEM AND LISTEN TO THEM; THEN DECIDE WHICH OF THEM IS BEST FOR YOU.
ONCE YOU HAVE SO MANY YOUNG LADIES TO CHOOSE FROM, YOU MIGHT NOT WANT TO MARRY MY DAUGHTER ANYMORE.
COME ALONG WITH ME.

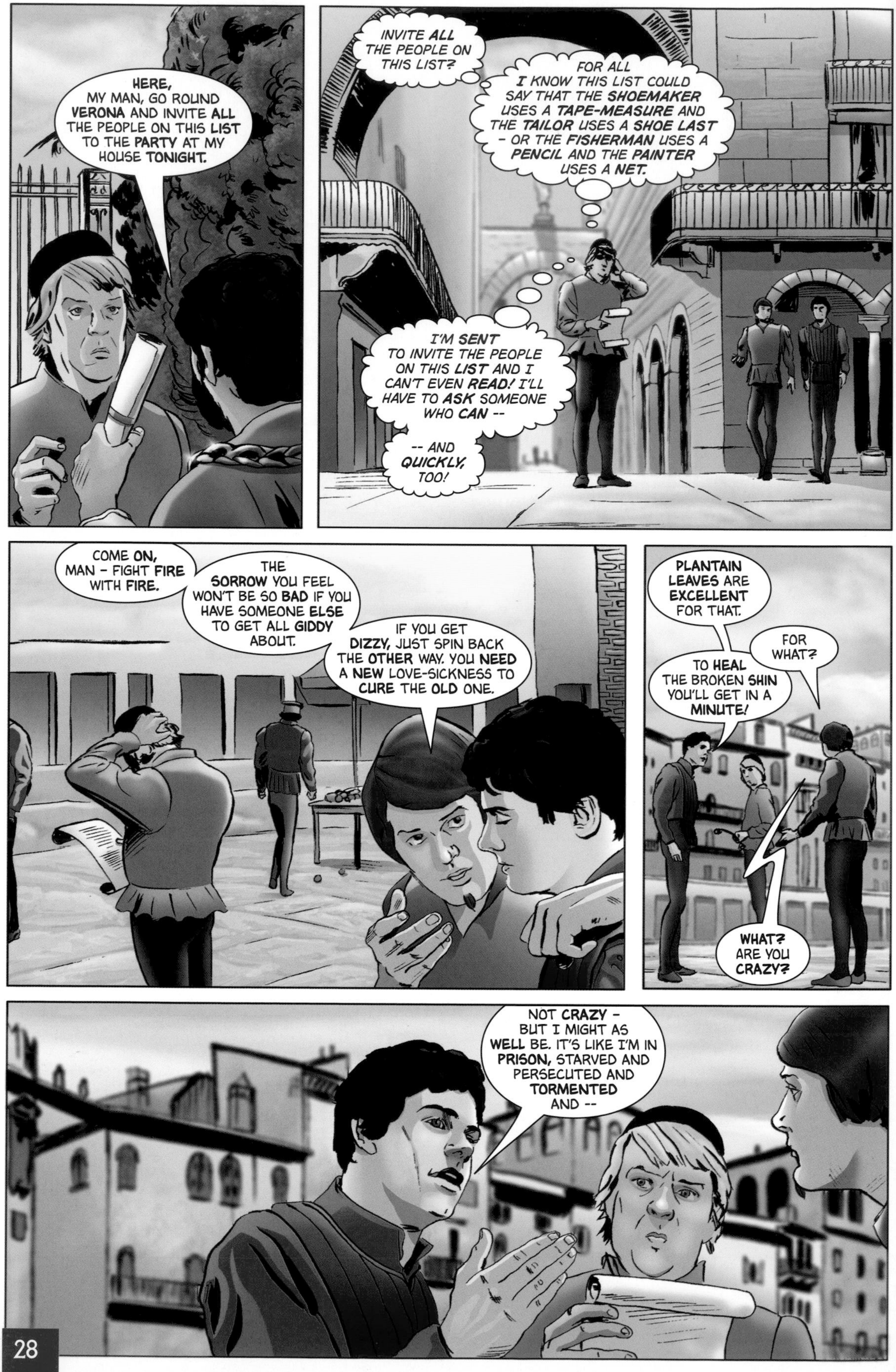
HERE, MY MAN, GO ROUND VERONA AND INVITE ALL THE PEOPLE ON THIS LIST TO THE PARTY AT MY HOUSE TONIGHT.
INVITE ALL THE PEOPLE ON THIS LIST?
FOR ALL I KNOW THIS LIST COULD SAY THAT THE SHOEMAKER USES A TAPE-MEASURE AND THE TAILOR USES A SHOE LAST - OR THE FISHERMAN USES A PENCIL AND THE PAINTER USES A NET.
I'M SENT TO INVITE THE PEOPLE ON THIS LIST AND I CAN'T EVEN READ! I'LL HAVE TO ASK SOMEONE WHO CAN --
-- AND QUICKLY, TOO!
COME ON, MAN - FIGHT FIRE WITH FIRE.
THE SORROW YOU FEEL WON'T BE SO BAD IF YOU HAVE SOMEONE ELSE TO GET ALL GIDDY ABOUT.
IF YOU GET DIZZY, JUST SPIN BACK THE OTHER WAY. YOU NEED A NEW LOVE-SICKNESS TO CURE THE OLD ONE.
PLANTAIN LEAVES ARE EXCELLENT FOR THAT.
FOR WHAT?
TO HEAL THE BROKEN SHIN YOU'LL GET IN A MINUTE!
WHAT? ARE YOU CRAZY?
NOT CRAZY - BUT I MIGHT AS WELL BE. IT'S LIKE I'M IN PRISON, STARVED AND PERSECUTED AND TORMENTED AND --

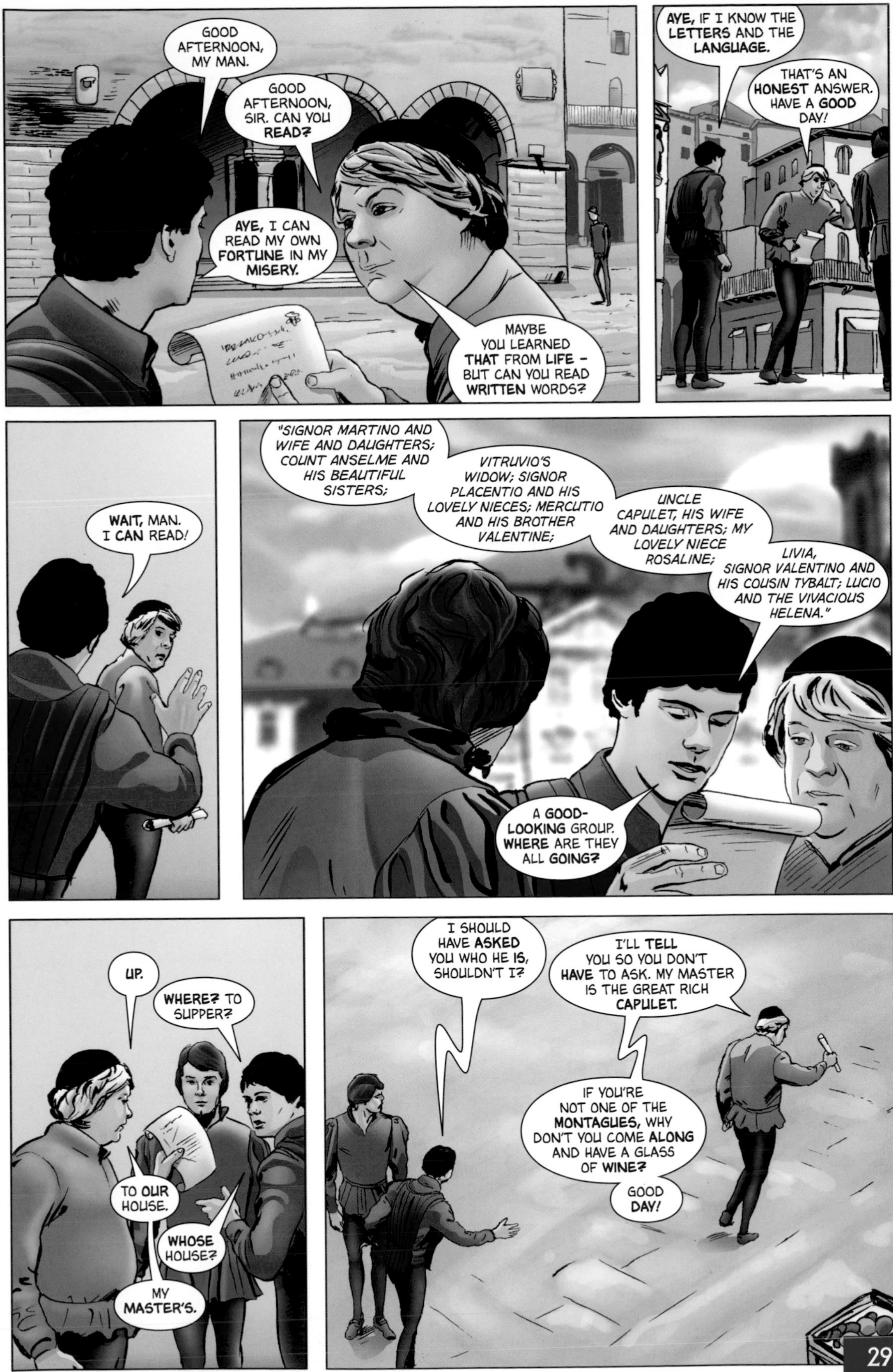

GOOD AFTERNOON, MY MAN.
GOOD AFTERNOON, SIR. CAN YOU READ?
AYE, I CAN READ MY OWN FORTUNE IN MY MISERY.
MAYBE YOU LEARNED THAT FROM LIFE – BUT CAN YOU READ WRITTEN WORDS?
AYE, IF I KNOW THE LETTERS AND THE LANGUAGE.
THAT'S AN HONEST ANSWER. HAVE A GOOD DAY!
WAIT, MAN. I CAN READ!
"SIGNOR MARTINO AND WIFE AND DAUGHTERS; COUNT ANSELME AND HIS BEAUTIFUL SISTERS;
VITRUVIO'S WIDOW; SIGNOR PLACENTIO AND HIS LOVELY NIECES; MERCUTIO AND HIS BROTHER VALENTINE;
UNCLE CAPULET, HIS WIFE AND DAUGHTERS; MY LOVELY NIECE ROSALINE;
LIVIA, SIGNOR VALENTINO AND HIS COUSIN TYBALT; LUCIO AND THE VIVACIOUS HELENA."
A GOOD-LOOKING GROUP. WHERE ARE THEY ALL GOING?
UP.
WHERE? TO SUPPER?
TO OUR HOUSE.
WHOSE HOUSE?
MY MASTER'S.
I SHOULD HAVE ASKED YOU WHO HE IS, SHOULDN'T I?
I'LL TELL YOU SO YOU DON'T HAVE TO ASK. MY MASTER IS THE GREAT RICH CAPULET.
IF YOU'RE NOT ONE OF THE MONTAGUES, WHY DON'T YOU COME ALONG AND HAVE A GLASS OF WINE?
GOOD DAY!

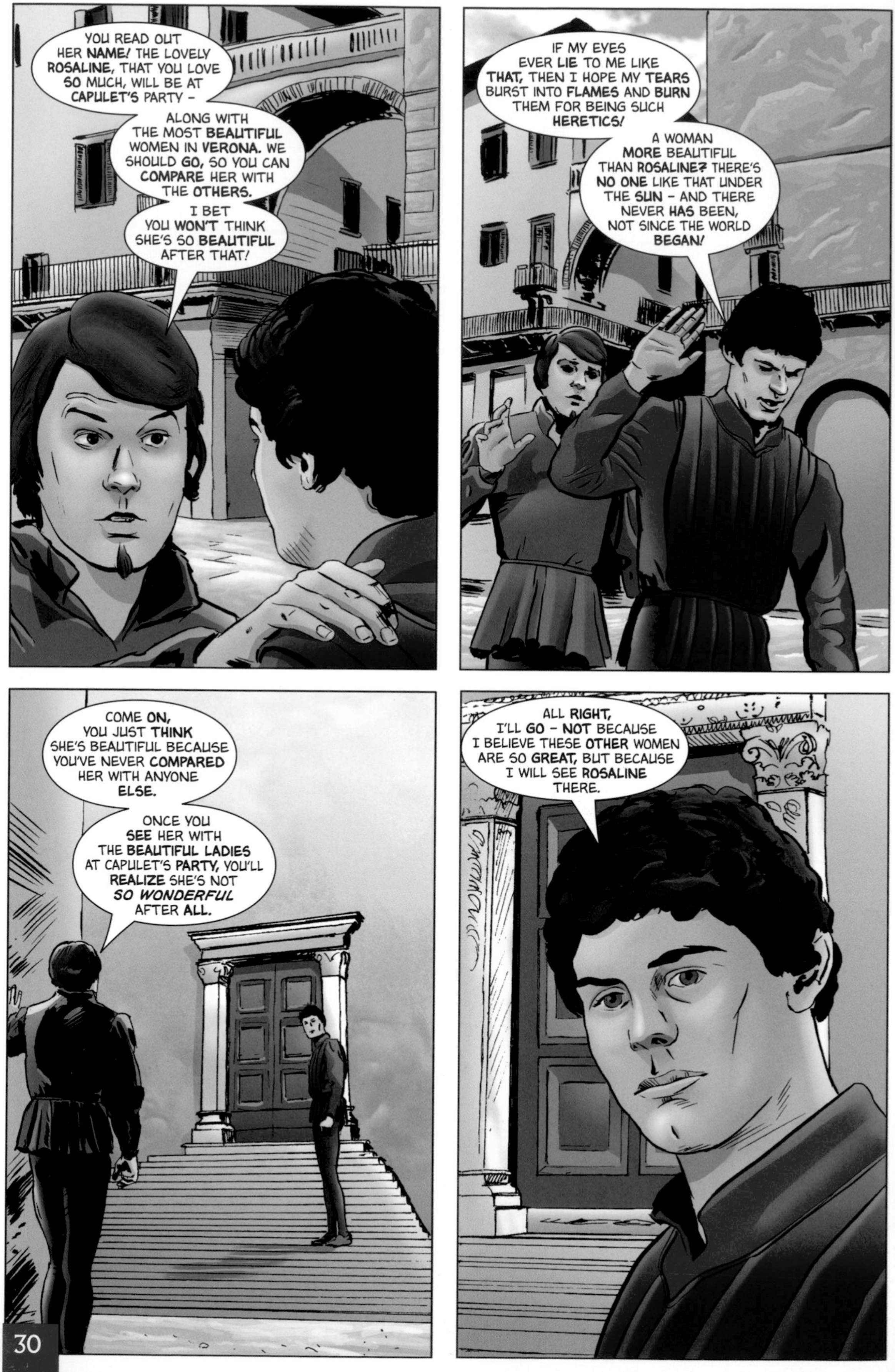
YOU READ OUT HER NAME! THE LOVELY ROSALINE, THAT YOU LOVE SO MUCH, WILL BE AT CAPULET'S PARTY –
ALONG WITH THE MOST BEAUTIFUL WOMEN IN VERONA. WE SHOULD GO, SO YOU CAN COMPARE HER WITH THE OTHERS.
I BET YOU WON'T THINK SHE'S SO BEAUTIFUL AFTER THAT!
IF MY EYES EVER LIE TO ME LIKE THAT, THEN I HOPE MY TEARS BURST INTO FLAMES AND BURN THEM FOR BEING SUCH HERETICS!
A WOMAN MORE BEAUTIFUL THAN ROSALINE? THERE'S NO ONE LIKE THAT UNDER THE SUN – AND THERE NEVER HAS BEEN, NOT SINCE THE WORLD BEGAN!
COME ON, YOU JUST THINK SHE'S BEAUTIFUL BECAUSE YOU'VE NEVER COMPARED HER WITH ANYONE ELSE.
ONCE YOU SEE HER WITH THE BEAUTIFUL LADIES AT CAPULET'S PARTY, YOU'LL REALIZE SHE'S NOT SO WONDERFUL AFTER ALL.
ALL RIGHT, I'LL GO – NOT BECAUSE I BELIEVE THESE OTHER WOMEN ARE SO GREAT, BUT BECAUSE I WILL SEE ROSALINE THERE.

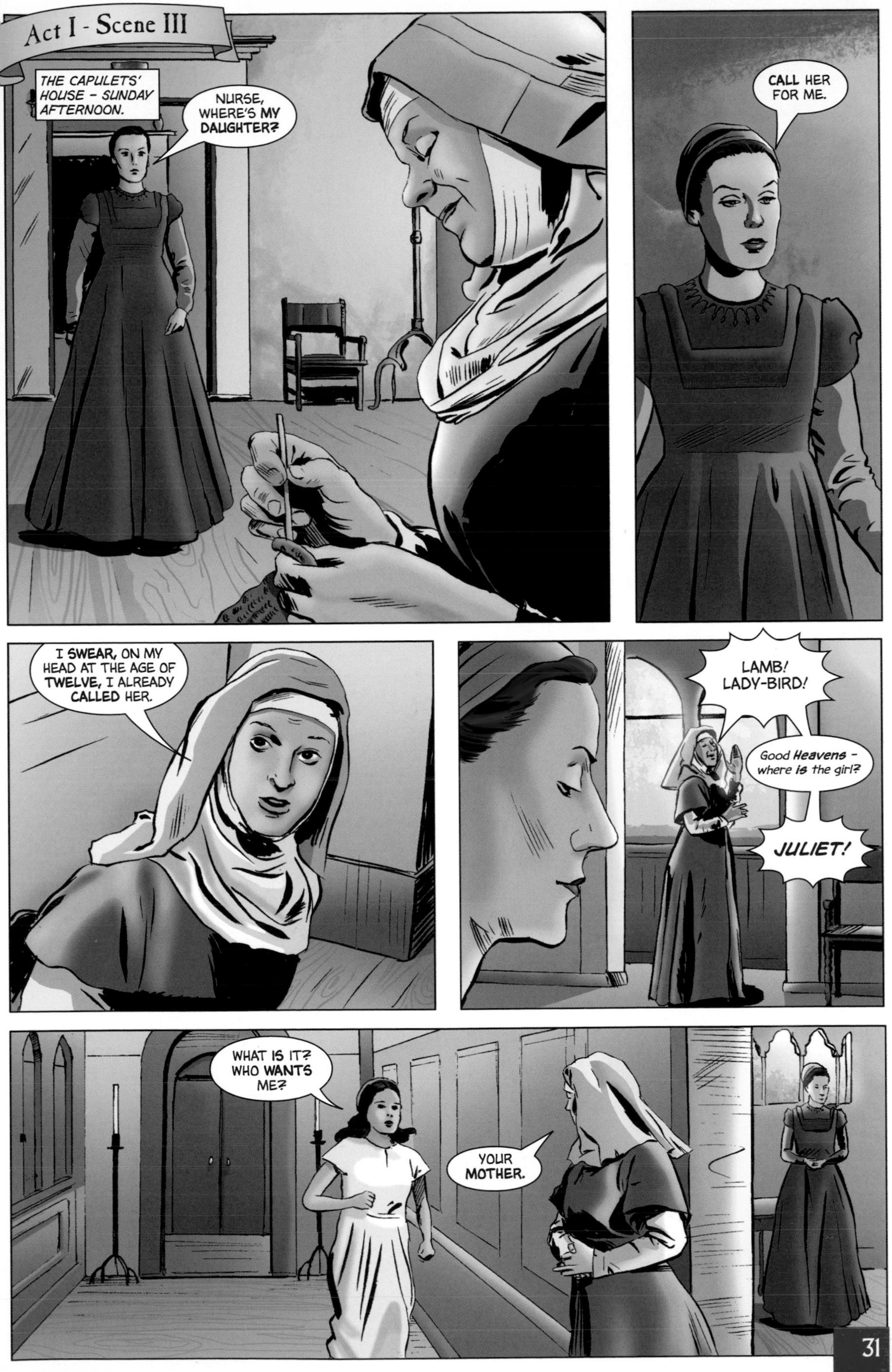

Act I - Scene III
THE CAPULETS' HOUSE – SUNDAY AFTERNOON.
NURSE, WHERE'S MY DAUGHTER?
CALL HER FOR ME.
I SWEAR, ON MY HEAD AT THE AGE OF TWELVE, I ALREADY CALLED HER.
LAMB! LADY-BIRD!
Good Heavens – where is the girl?
JULIET!
WHAT IS IT? WHO WANTS ME?
YOUR MOTHER.

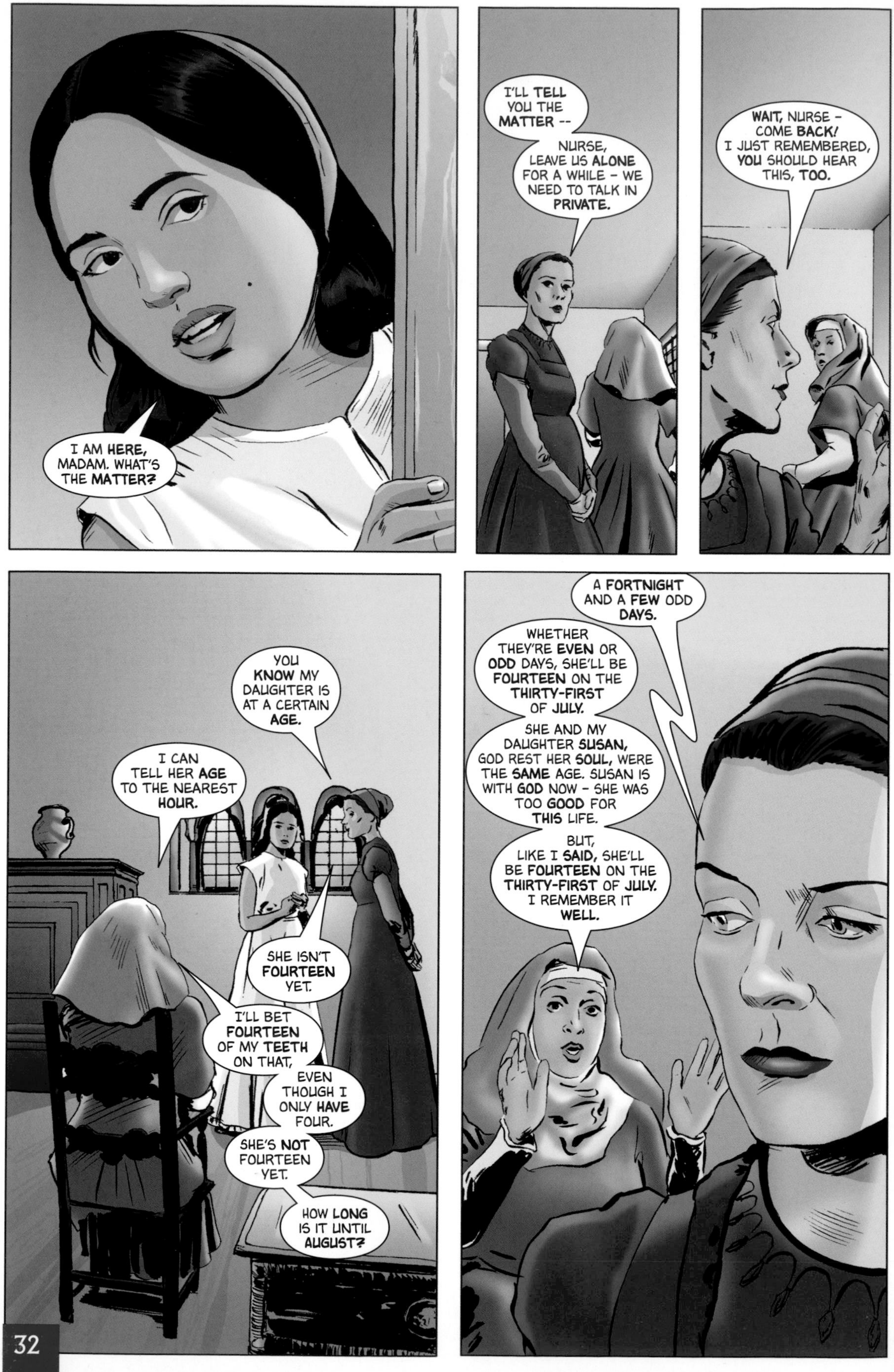
I AM HERE, MADAM. WHAT'S THE MATTER?
I'LL TELL YOU THE MATTER --
NURSE, LEAVE US ALONE FOR A WHILE - WE NEED TO TALK IN PRIVATE.
WAIT, NURSE - COME BACK! I JUST REMEMBERED, YOU SHOULD HEAR THIS, TOO.
YOU KNOW MY DAUGHTER IS AT A CERTAIN AGE.
I CAN TELL HER AGE TO THE NEAREST HOUR.
SHE ISN'T FOURTEEN YET.
I'LL BET FOURTEEN OF MY TEETH ON THAT,
EVEN THOUGH I ONLY HAVE FOUR.
SHE'S NOT FOURTEEN YET.
HOW LONG IS IT UNTIL AUGUST?
A FORTNIGHT AND A FEW ODD DAYS.
WHETHER THEY'RE EVEN OR ODD DAYS, SHE'LL BE FOURTEEN ON THE THIRTY-FIRST OF JULY.
SHE AND MY DAUGHTER SUSAN, GOD REST HER SOUL, WERE THE SAME AGE. SUSAN IS WITH GOD NOW - SHE WAS TOO GOOD FOR THIS LIFE.
BUT, LIKE I SAID, SHE'LL BE FOURTEEN ON THE THIRTY-FIRST OF JULY. I REMEMBER IT WELL.

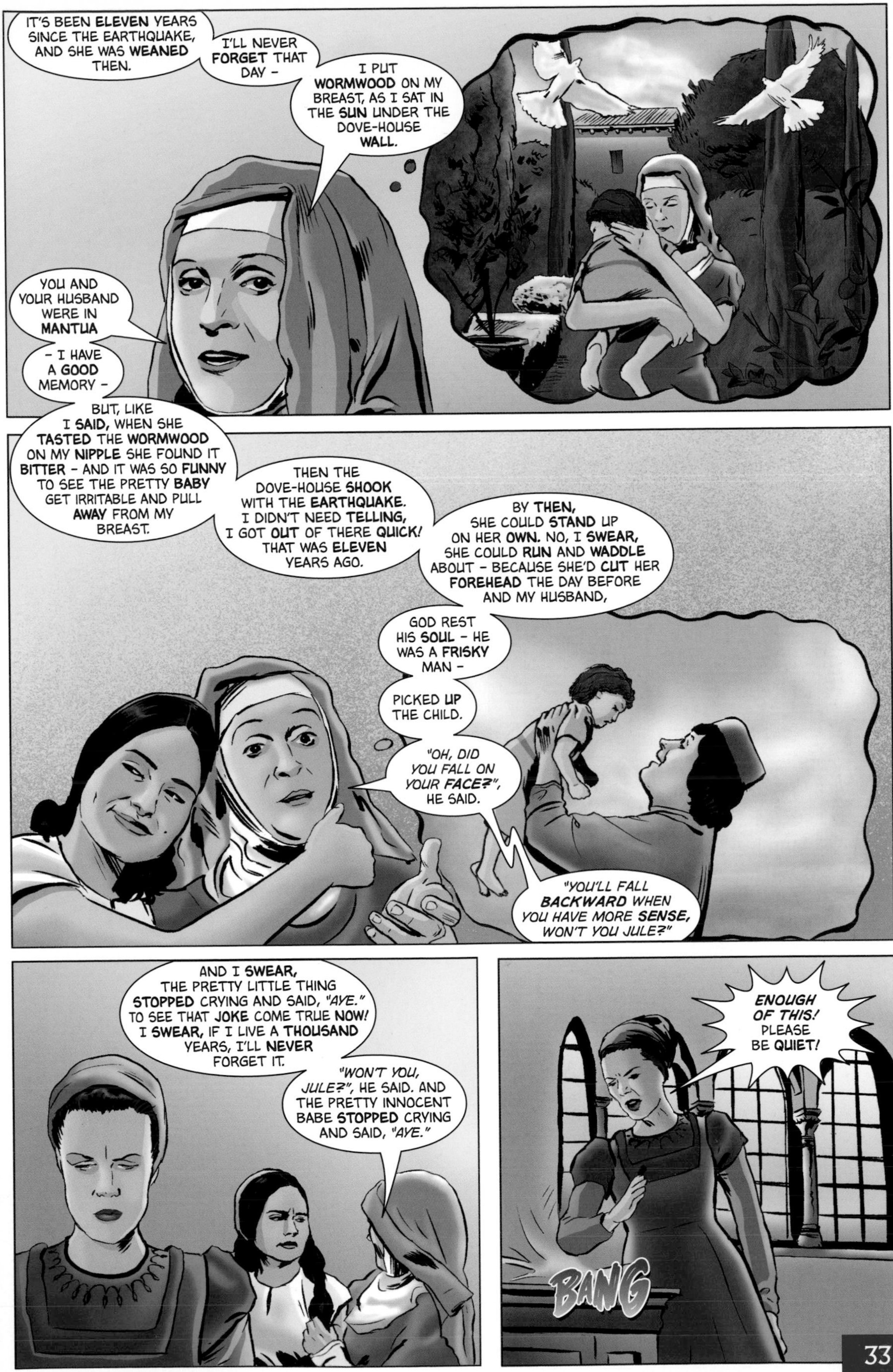
IT'S BEEN ELEVEN YEARS SINCE THE EARTHQUAKE, AND SHE WAS WEANED THEN.
I'LL NEVER FORGET THAT DAY -
I PUT WORMWOOD ON MY BREAST, AS I SAT IN THE SUN UNDER THE DOVE-HOUSE WALL.
YOU AND YOUR HUSBAND WERE IN MANTUA
- I HAVE A GOOD MEMORY -
BUT, LIKE I SAID, WHEN SHE TASTED THE WORMWOOD ON MY NIPPLE SHE FOUND IT BITTER - AND IT WAS SO FUNNY TO SEE THE PRETTY BABY GET IRRITABLE AND PULL AWAY FROM MY BREAST.
THEN THE DOVE-HOUSE SHOOK WITH THE EARTHQUAKE. I DIDN'T NEED TELLING, I GOT OUT OF THERE QUICK! THAT WAS ELEVEN YEARS AGO.
BY THEN, SHE COULD STAND UP ON HER OWN. NO, I SWEAR, SHE COULD RUN AND WADDLE ABOUT - BECAUSE SHE'D CUT HER FOREHEAD THE DAY BEFORE AND MY HUSBAND,
GOD REST HIS SOUL - HE WAS A FRISKY MAN -
PICKED UP THE CHILD.
"OH, DID YOU FALL ON YOUR FACE?", HE SAID.
"YOU'LL FALL BACKWARD WHEN YOU HAVE MORE SENSE, WON'T YOU JULE?"
AND I SWEAR, THE PRETTY LITTLE THING STOPPED CRYING AND SAID, "AYE." TO SEE THAT JOKE COME TRUE NOW! I SWEAR, IF I LIVE A THOUSAND YEARS, I'LL NEVER FORGET IT.
"WON'T YOU, JULE?", HE SAID. AND THE PRETTY INNOCENT BABE STOPPED CRYING AND SAID, "AYE."
ENOUGH OF THIS! PLEASE BE QUIET!
BANG

YES MADAM – BUT I CAN'T **HELP** LAUGHING WHEN I THINK HOW SHE **STOPPED** CRYING AND SAID, "AYE."

AND HER WITH A **BUMP** ON HER **FOREHEAD** AS BIG AS A YOUNG COCKEREL'S **STONE.**

IT WAS A **PAINFUL** BRUISE AND SHE CRIED **BITTERLY.**

"OH," SAID MY HUSBAND "DID YOU FALL ON YOUR **FACE?** YOU'LL FALL **BACKWARD** WHEN YOU'RE OLDER, WON'T YOU JULE?"

AND SHE **STOPPED** AND SAID, "AYE."

AND **YOU** STOP **TOO,** NURSE, PLEASE I SAY!

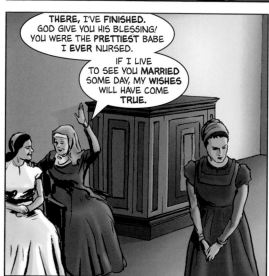

THERE, I'VE FINISHED. GOD GIVE YOU HIS BLESSING! YOU WERE THE **PRETTIEST** BABE I EVER NURSED.

IF I LIVE TO SEE YOU **MARRIED** SOME DAY, MY **WISHES** WILL HAVE COME **TRUE.**

WELL, **MARRIAGE** IS **EXACTLY** WHAT I'VE COME TO **TALK** TO YOU ABOUT.

TELL ME, JULIET, WOULD YOU **LIKE** TO GET **MARRIED?**

IT IS AN **HONOR** THAT I HAVEN'T **THOUGHT** MUCH **ABOUT.**

AN HONOR! IF I WASN'T YOUR **ONLY** NURSE, I'D SAY YOU **SUCKED** YOUR **WISDOM** FROM THE **BREAST!**

WELL, **START** THINKING ABOUT IT **NOW.**

YOUNGER GIRLS THAN **YOU,** FROM WELL **RESPECTED** FAMILIES IN VERONA, ALREADY HAVE **BABIES** OF THEIR **OWN.**

BY MY **RECKONING,** I HAD **YOU** WHEN I WAS ABOUT YOUR **AGE.**

I'LL BE **BRIEF:**

THE **HONORABLE PARIS** WISHES TO **MARRY** YOU.

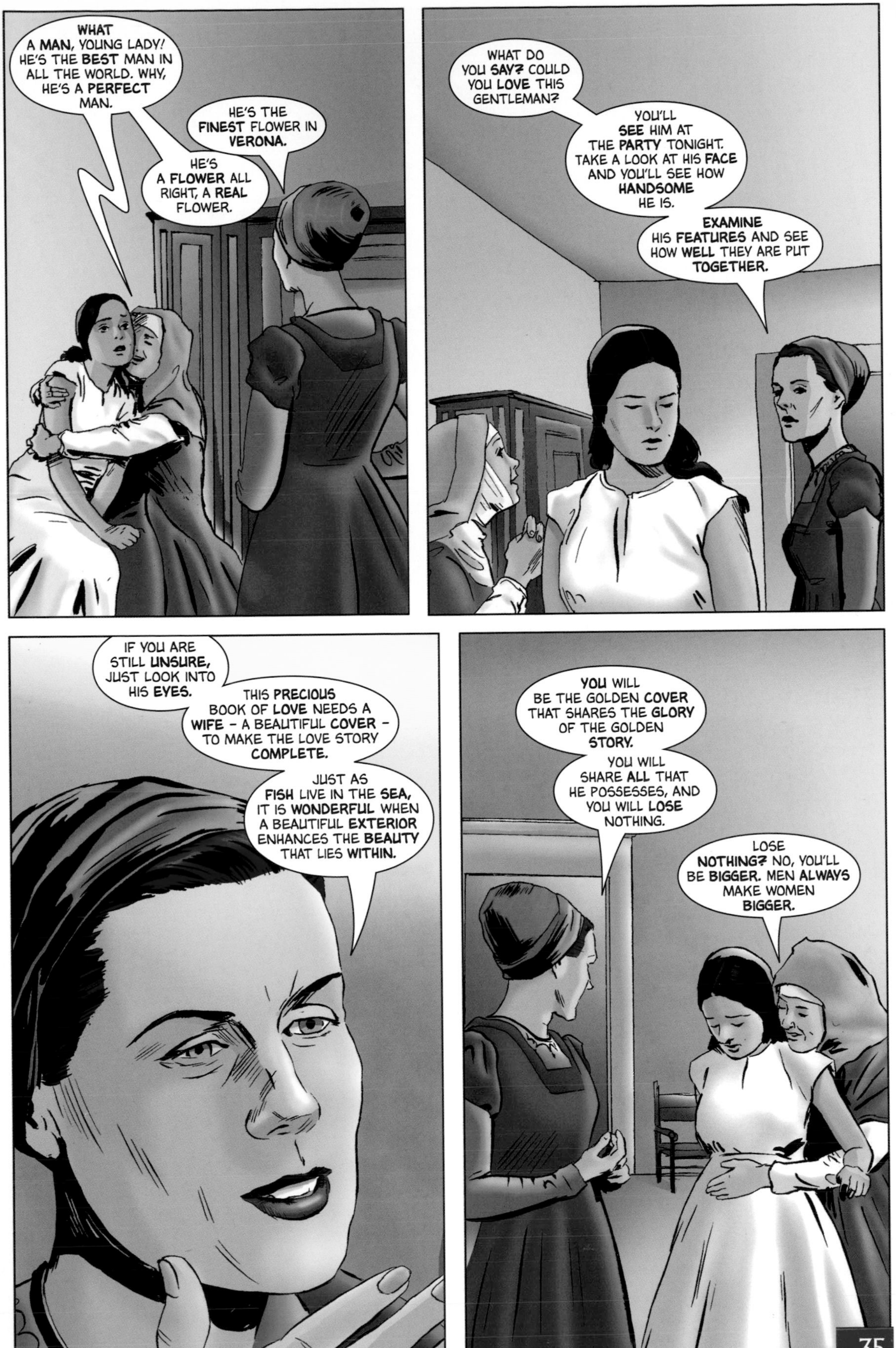
WHAT A MAN, YOUNG LADY! HE'S THE BEST MAN IN ALL THE WORLD. WHY, HE'S A PERFECT MAN.
HE'S THE FINEST FLOWER IN VERONA.
HE'S A FLOWER ALL RIGHT, A REAL FLOWER.
WHAT DO YOU SAY? COULD YOU LOVE THIS GENTLEMAN?
YOU'LL SEE HIM AT THE PARTY TONIGHT. TAKE A LOOK AT HIS FACE AND YOU'LL SEE HOW HANDSOME HE IS.
EXAMINE HIS FEATURES AND SEE HOW WELL THEY ARE PUT TOGETHER.
IF YOU ARE STILL UNSURE, JUST LOOK INTO HIS EYES.
THIS PRECIOUS BOOK OF LOVE NEEDS A WIFE – A BEAUTIFUL COVER – TO MAKE THE LOVE STORY COMPLETE.
JUST AS FISH LIVE IN THE SEA, IT IS WONDERFUL WHEN A BEAUTIFUL EXTERIOR ENHANCES THE BEAUTY THAT LIES WITHIN.
YOU WILL BE THE GOLDEN COVER THAT SHARES THE GLORY OF THE GOLDEN STORY.
YOU WILL SHARE ALL THAT HE POSSESSES, AND YOU WILL LOSE NOTHING.
LOSE NOTHING? NO, YOU'LL BE BIGGER. MEN ALWAYS MAKE WOMEN BIGGER.

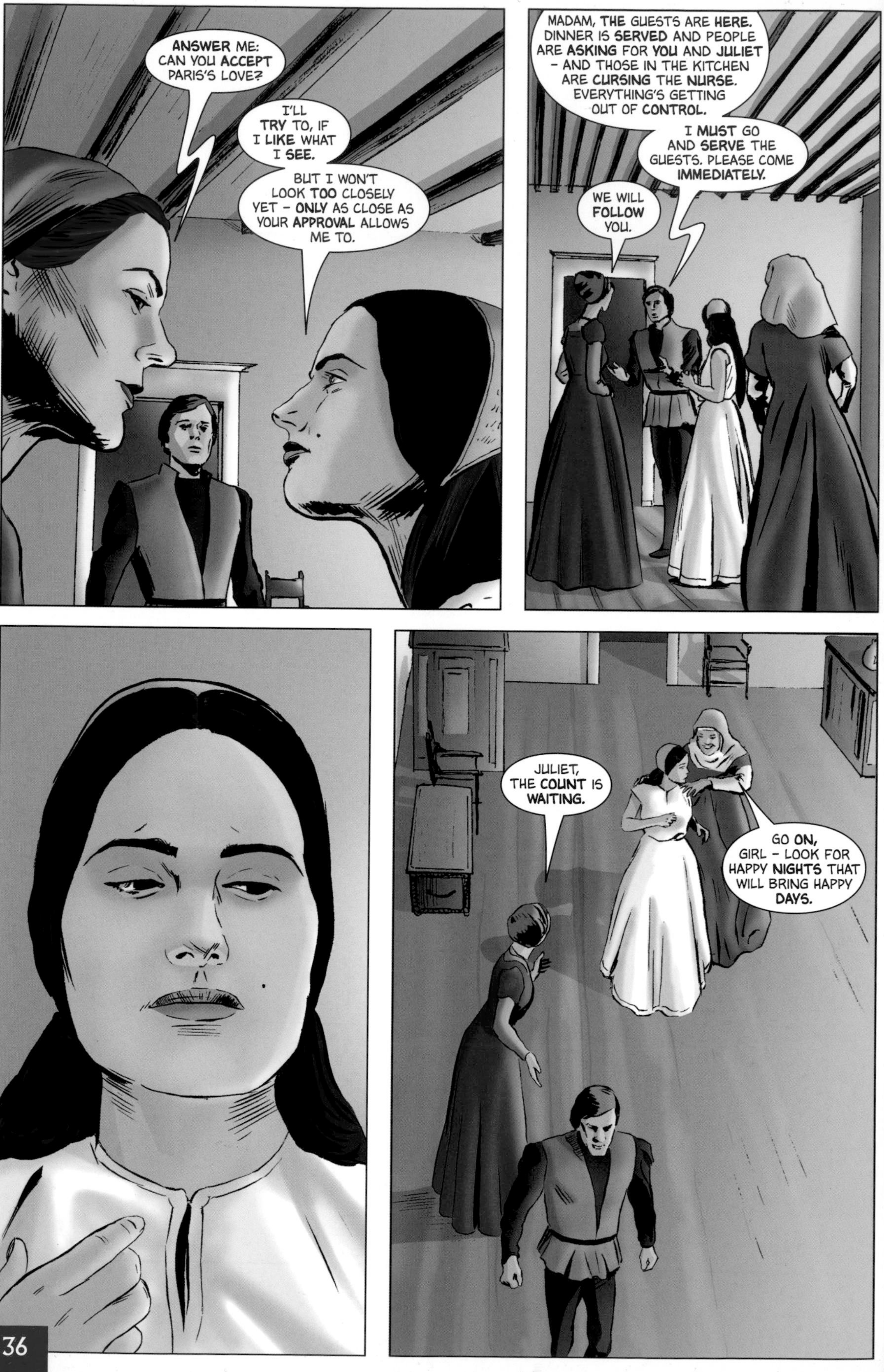
ANSWER ME: CAN YOU ACCEPT PARIS'S LOVE?
I'LL TRY TO, IF I LIKE WHAT I SEE.
BUT I WON'T LOOK TOO CLOSELY YET – ONLY AS CLOSE AS YOUR APPROVAL ALLOWS ME TO.
MADAM, THE GUESTS ARE HERE. DINNER IS SERVED AND PEOPLE ARE ASKING FOR YOU AND JULIET – AND THOSE IN THE KITCHEN ARE CURSING THE NURSE. EVERYTHING'S GETTING OUT OF CONTROL.
I MUST GO AND SERVE THE GUESTS. PLEASE COME IMMEDIATELY.
WE WILL FOLLOW YOU.
JULIET, THE COUNT IS WAITING.
GO ON, GIRL – LOOK FOR HAPPY NIGHTS THAT WILL BRING HAPPY DAYS.

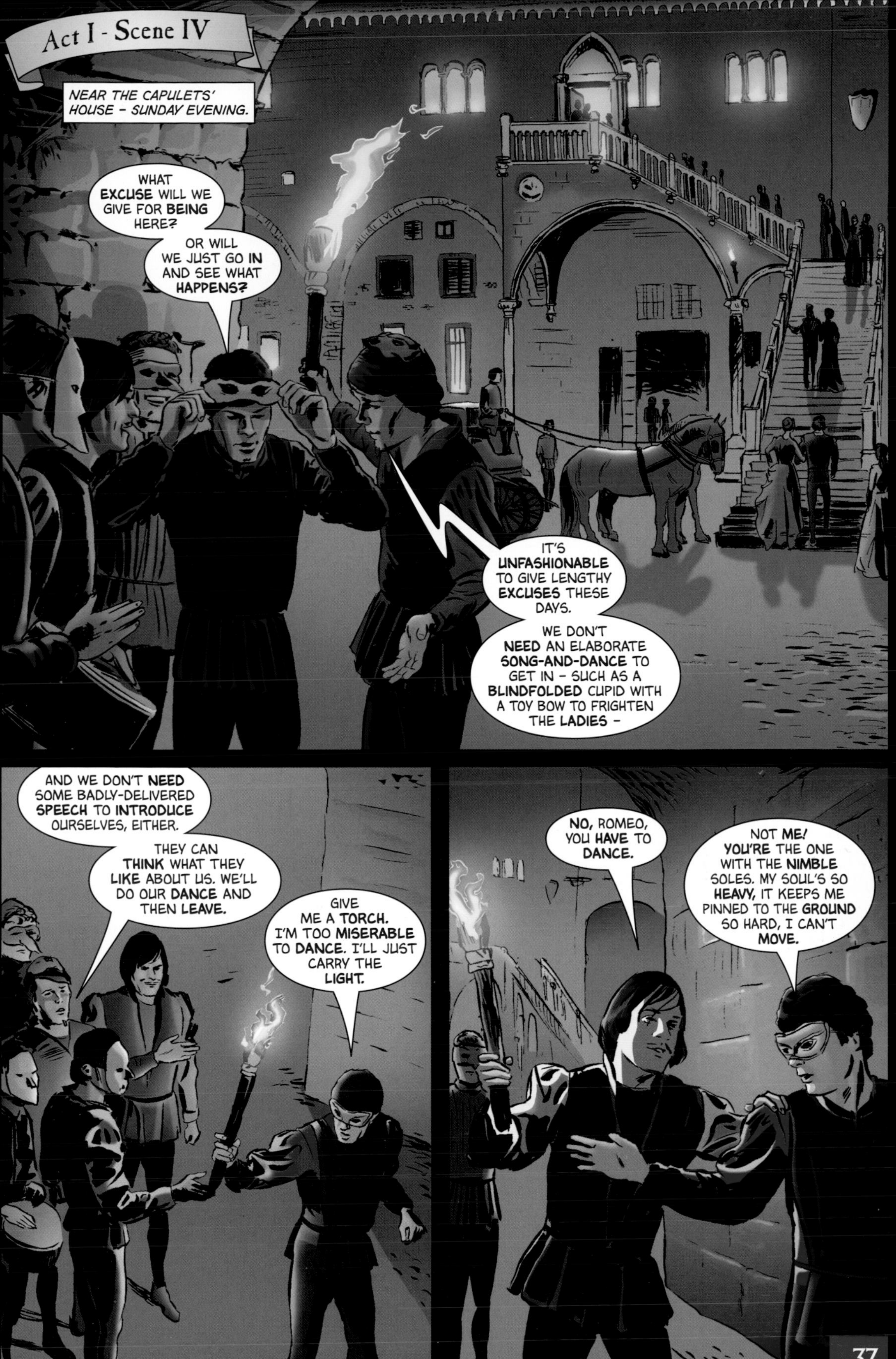
Act I - Scene IV
NEAR THE CAPULETS' HOUSE - SUNDAY EVENING.
WHAT EXCUSE WILL WE GIVE FOR BEING HERE?
OR WILL WE JUST GO IN AND SEE WHAT HAPPENS?
IT'S UNFASHIONABLE TO GIVE LENGTHY EXCUSES THESE DAYS.
WE DON'T NEED AN ELABORATE SONG-AND-DANCE TO GET IN - SUCH AS A BLINDFOLDED CUPID WITH A TOY BOW TO FRIGHTEN THE LADIES -
AND WE DON'T NEED SOME BADLY-DELIVERED SPEECH TO INTRODUCE OURSELVES, EITHER.
THEY CAN THINK WHAT THEY LIKE ABOUT US. WE'LL DO OUR DANCE AND THEN LEAVE.
GIVE ME A TORCH. I'M TOO MISERABLE TO DANCE. I'LL JUST CARRY THE LIGHT.
NO, ROMEO, YOU HAVE TO DANCE.
NOT ME! YOU'RE THE ONE WITH THE NIMBLE SOLES. MY SOUL'S SO HEAVY, IT KEEPS ME PINNED TO THE GROUND SO HARD, I CAN'T MOVE.

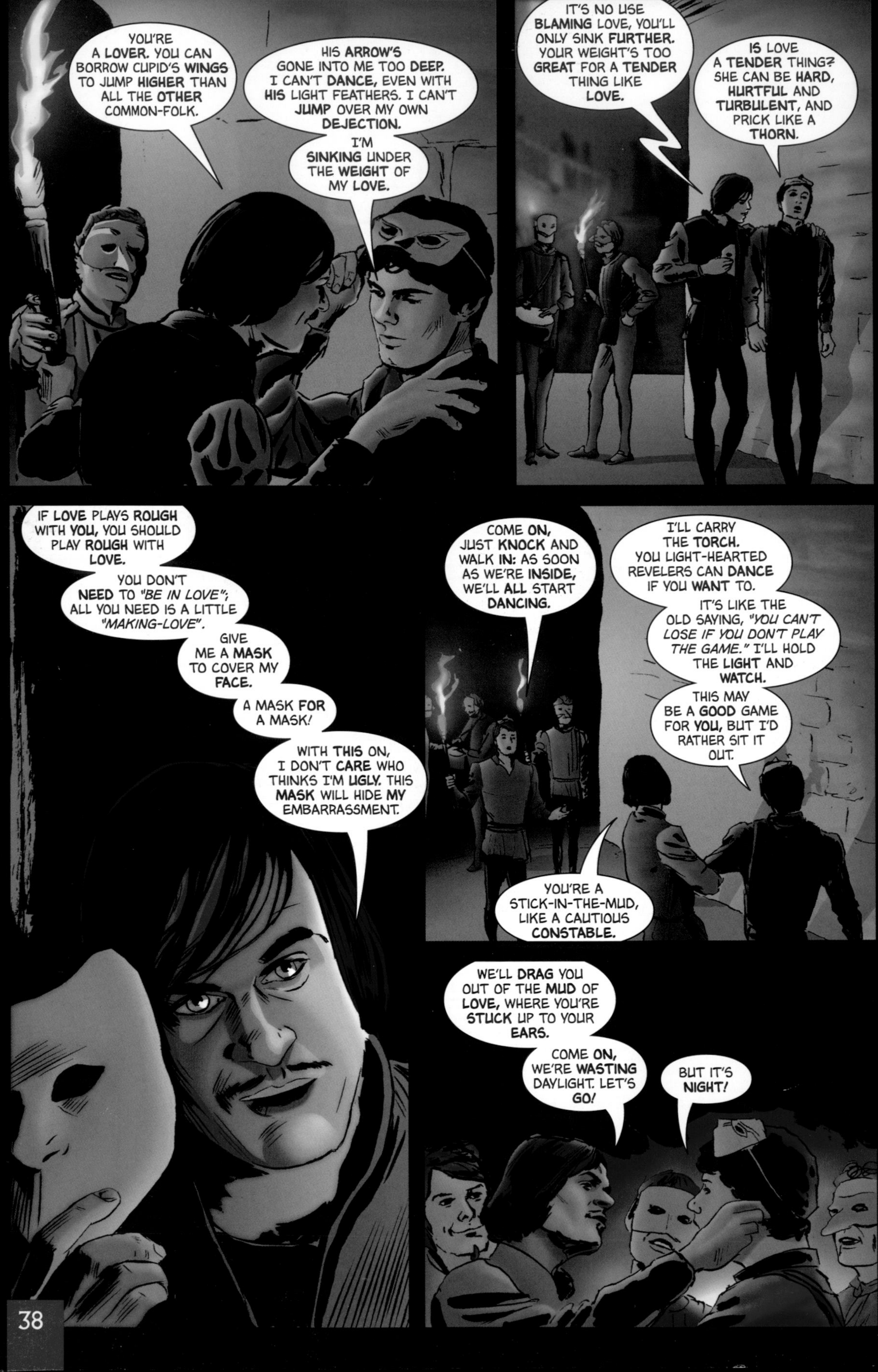
YOU'RE A LOVER. YOU CAN BORROW CUPID'S WINGS TO JUMP HIGHER THAN ALL THE OTHER COMMON-FOLK.
HIS ARROW'S GONE INTO ME TOO DEEP. I CAN'T DANCE, EVEN WITH HIS LIGHT FEATHERS. I CAN'T JUMP OVER MY OWN DEJECTION.
I'M SINKING UNDER THE WEIGHT OF MY LOVE.
IT'S NO USE BLAMING LOVE, YOU'LL ONLY SINK FURTHER. YOUR WEIGHT'S TOO GREAT FOR A TENDER THING LIKE LOVE.
IS LOVE A TENDER THING? SHE CAN BE HARD, HURTFUL AND TURBULENT, AND PRICK LIKE A THORN.
IF LOVE PLAYS ROUGH WITH YOU, YOU SHOULD PLAY ROUGH WITH LOVE.
YOU DON'T NEED TO *"BE IN LOVE"*; ALL YOU NEED IS A LITTLE *"MAKING-LOVE"*.
GIVE ME A MASK TO COVER MY FACE.
A MASK FOR A MASK!
WITH THIS ON, I DON'T CARE WHO THINKS I'M UGLY. THIS MASK WILL HIDE MY EMBARRASSMENT.
COME ON, JUST KNOCK AND WALK IN: AS SOON AS WE'RE INSIDE, WE'LL ALL START DANCING.
I'LL CARRY THE TORCH. YOU LIGHT-HEARTED REVELERS CAN DANCE IF YOU WANT TO.
IT'S LIKE THE OLD SAYING, *"YOU CAN'T LOSE IF YOU DON'T PLAY THE GAME."* I'LL HOLD THE LIGHT AND WATCH.
THIS MAY BE A GOOD GAME FOR YOU, BUT I'D RATHER SIT IT OUT.
YOU'RE A STICK-IN-THE-MUD, LIKE A CAUTIOUS CONSTABLE.
WE'LL DRAG YOU OUT OF THE MUD OF LOVE, WHERE YOU'RE STUCK UP TO YOUR EARS.
COME ON, WE'RE WASTING DAYLIGHT. LET'S GO!
BUT IT'S NIGHT!

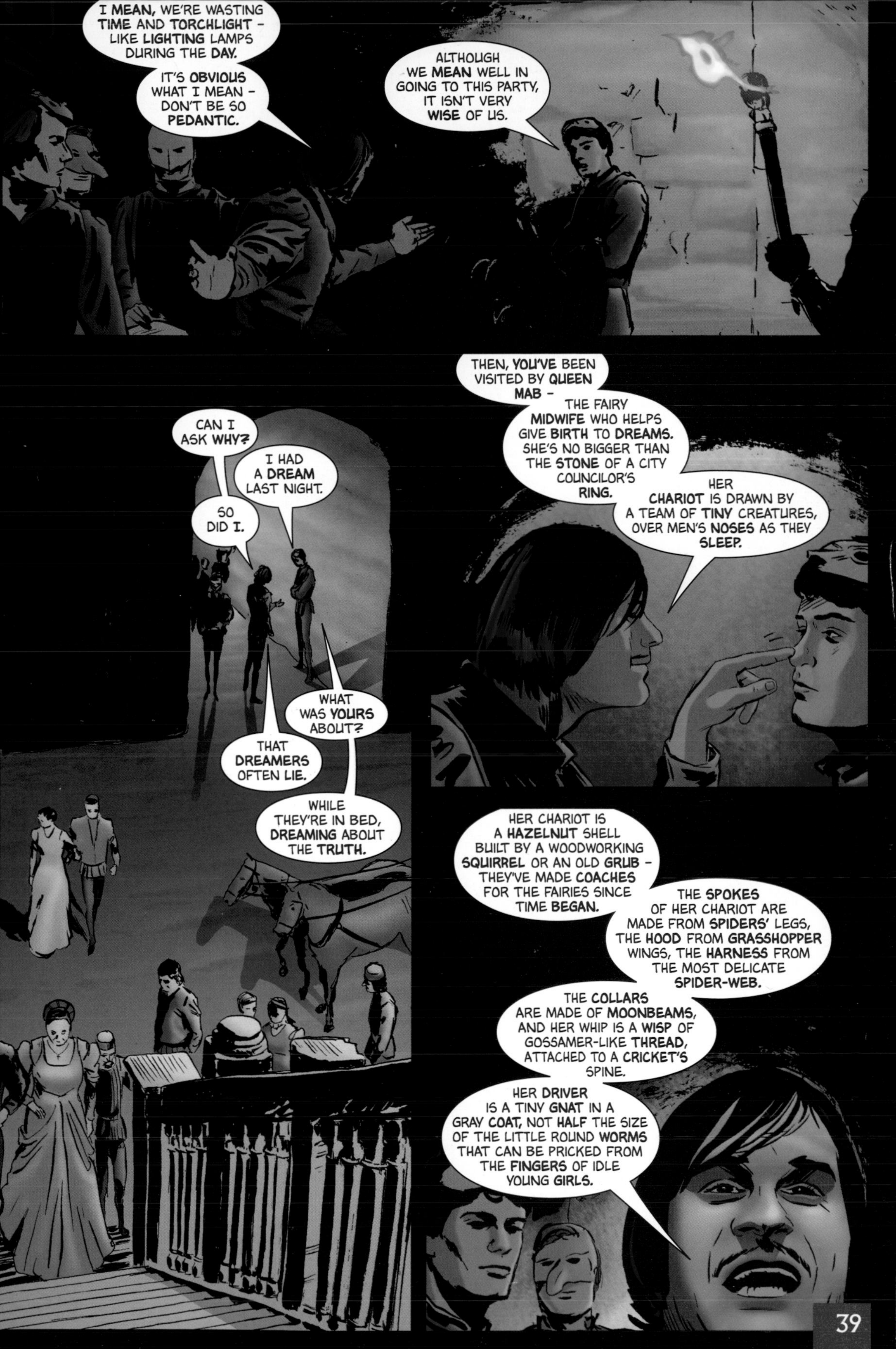

I MEAN, WE'RE WASTING TIME AND TORCHLIGHT - LIKE LIGHTING LAMPS DURING THE DAY.
IT'S OBVIOUS WHAT I MEAN - DON'T BE SO PEDANTIC.
ALTHOUGH WE MEAN WELL IN GOING TO THIS PARTY, IT ISN'T VERY WISE OF US.
CAN I ASK WHY?
I HAD A DREAM LAST NIGHT.
SO DID I.
WHAT WAS YOURS ABOUT?
THAT DREAMERS OFTEN LIE.
WHILE THEY'RE IN BED, DREAMING ABOUT THE TRUTH.
THEN, YOU'VE BEEN VISITED BY QUEEN MAB -
THE FAIRY MIDWIFE WHO HELPS GIVE BIRTH TO DREAMS. SHE'S NO BIGGER THAN THE STONE OF A CITY COUNCILOR'S RING.
HER CHARIOT IS DRAWN BY A TEAM OF TINY CREATURES, OVER MEN'S NOSES AS THEY SLEEP.
HER CHARIOT IS A HAZELNUT SHELL BUILT BY A WOODWORKING SQUIRREL OR AN OLD GRUB - THEY'VE MADE COACHES FOR THE FAIRIES SINCE TIME BEGAN.
THE SPOKES OF HER CHARIOT ARE MADE FROM SPIDERS' LEGS, THE HOOD FROM GRASSHOPPER WINGS, THE HARNESS FROM THE MOST DELICATE SPIDER-WEB.
THE COLLARS ARE MADE OF MOONBEAMS, AND HER WHIP IS A WISP OF GOSSAMER-LIKE THREAD, ATTACHED TO A CRICKET'S SPINE.
HER DRIVER IS A TINY GNAT IN A GRAY COAT, NOT HALF THE SIZE OF THE LITTLE ROUND WORMS THAT CAN BE PRICKED FROM THE FINGERS OF IDLE YOUNG GIRLS.

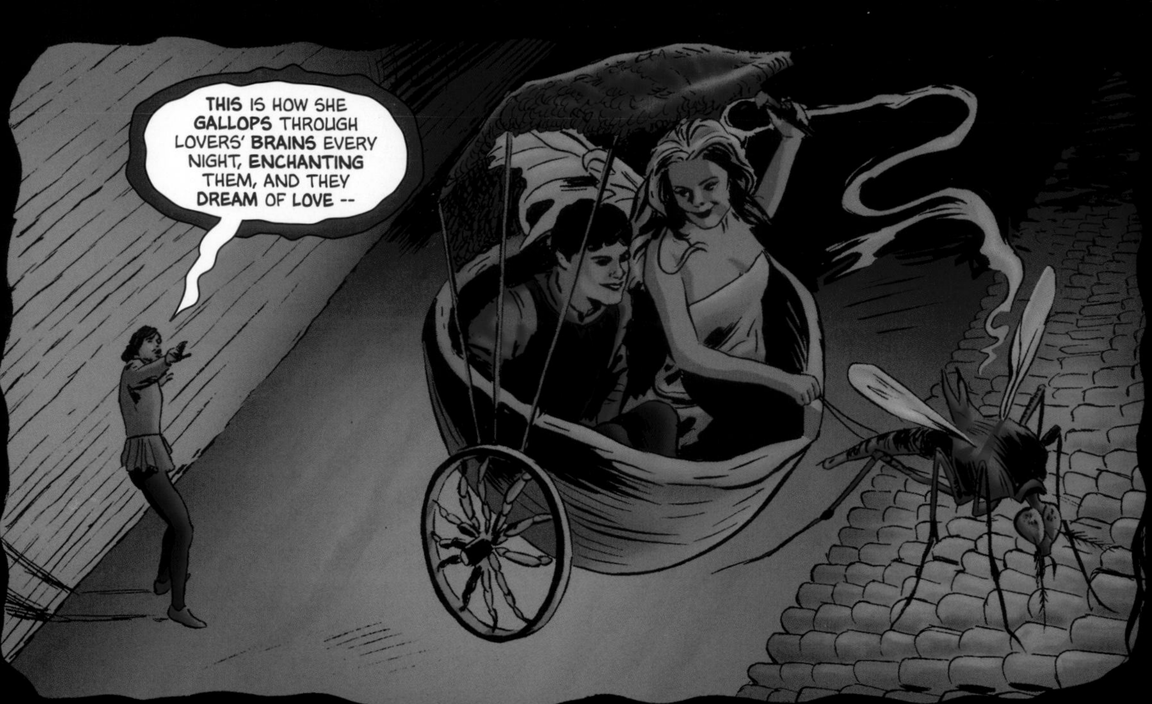
THIS IS HOW SHE GALLOPS THROUGH LOVERS' BRAINS EVERY NIGHT, ENCHANTING THEM, AND THEY DREAM OF LOVE --

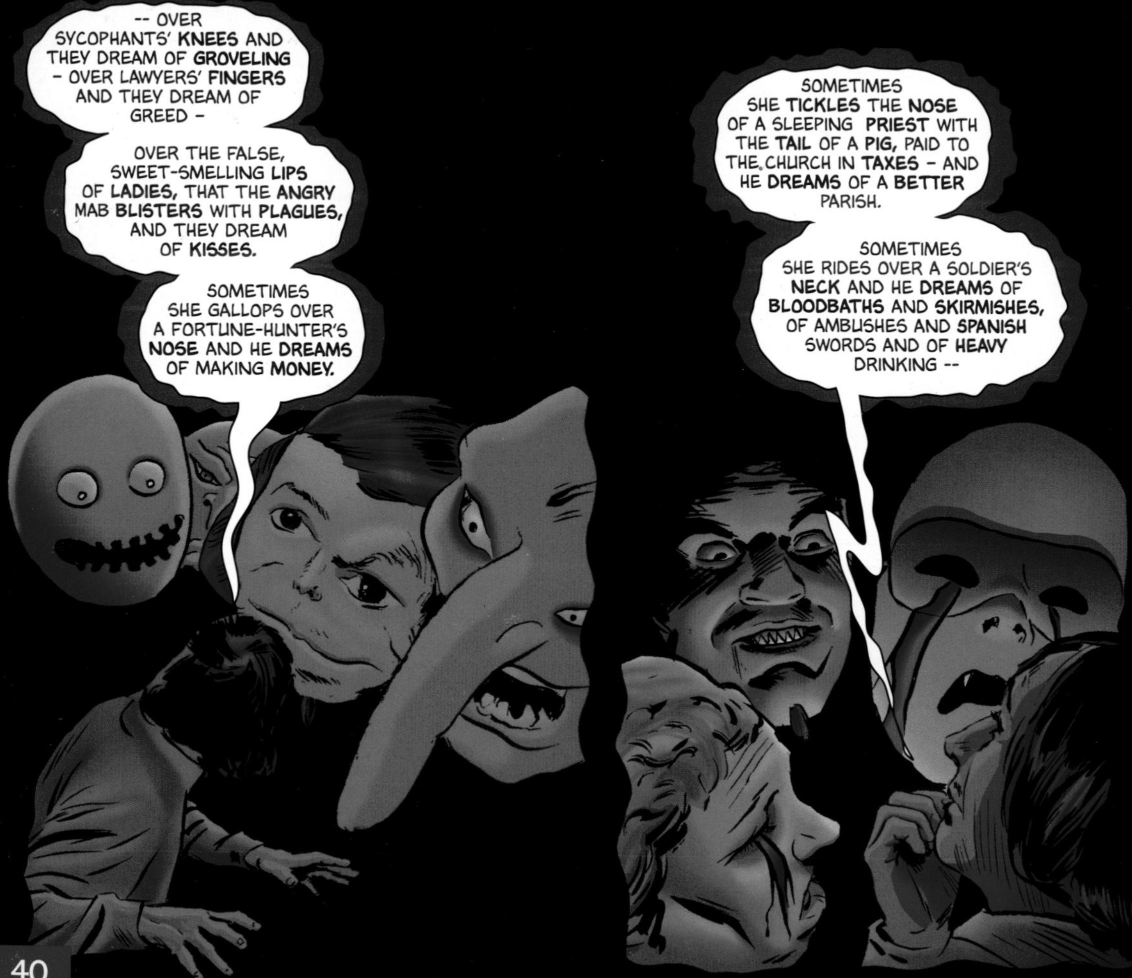
-- OVER SYCOPHANTS' KNEES AND THEY DREAM OF GROVELING - OVER LAWYERS' FINGERS AND THEY DREAM OF GREED -
OVER THE FALSE, SWEET-SMELLING LIPS OF LADIES, THAT THE ANGRY MAB BLISTERS WITH PLAGUES, AND THEY DREAM OF KISSES.
SOMETIMES SHE GALLOPS OVER A FORTUNE-HUNTER'S NOSE AND HE DREAMS OF MAKING MONEY.
SOMETIMES SHE TICKLES THE NOSE OF A SLEEPING PRIEST WITH THE TAIL OF A PIG, PAID TO THE CHURCH IN TAXES - AND HE DREAMS OF A BETTER PARISH.
SOMETIMES SHE RIDES OVER A SOLDIER'S NECK AND HE DREAMS OF BLOODBATHS AND SKIRMISHES, OF AMBUSHES AND SPANISH SWORDS AND OF HEAVY DRINKING --

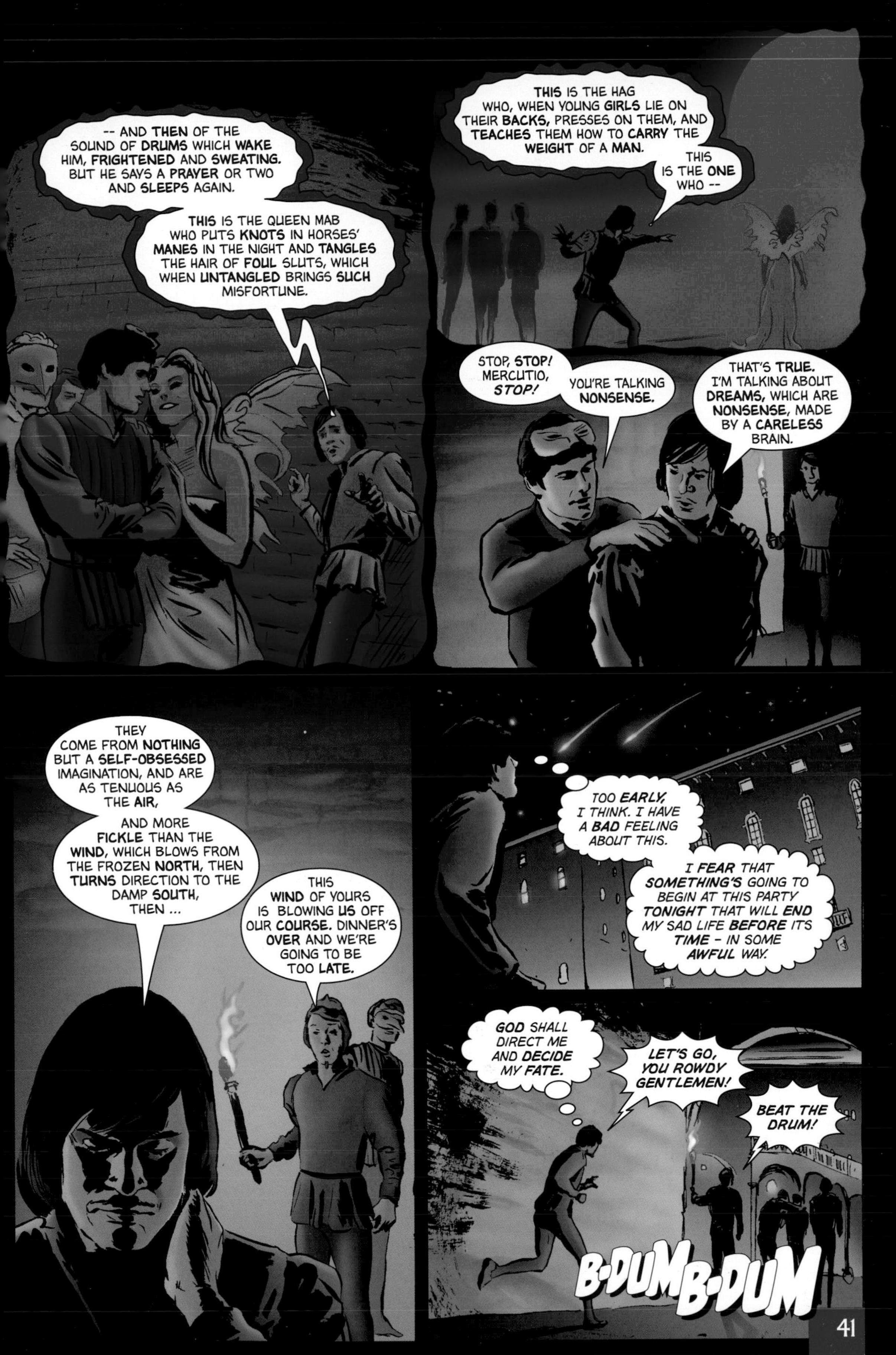
-- AND THEN OF THE SOUND OF DRUMS WHICH WAKE HIM, FRIGHTENED AND SWEATING. BUT HE SAYS A PRAYER OR TWO AND SLEEPS AGAIN.
THIS IS THE QUEEN MAB WHO PUTS KNOTS IN HORSES' MANES IN THE NIGHT AND TANGLES THE HAIR OF FOUL SLUTS, WHICH WHEN UNTANGLED BRINGS SUCH MISFORTUNE.
THIS IS THE HAG WHO, WHEN YOUNG GIRLS LIE ON THEIR BACKS, PRESSES ON THEM, AND TEACHES THEM HOW TO CARRY THE WEIGHT OF A MAN.
THIS IS THE ONE WHO --
STOP, STOP! MERCUTIO, STOP!
YOU'RE TALKING NONSENSE.
THAT'S TRUE. I'M TALKING ABOUT DREAMS, WHICH ARE NONSENSE, MADE BY A CARELESS BRAIN.
THEY COME FROM NOTHING BUT A SELF-OBSESSED IMAGINATION, AND ARE AS TENUOUS AS THE AIR,
AND MORE FICKLE THAN THE WIND, WHICH BLOWS FROM THE FROZEN NORTH, THEN TURNS DIRECTION TO THE DAMP SOUTH, THEN ...
THIS WIND OF YOURS IS BLOWING US OFF OUR COURSE. DINNER'S OVER AND WE'RE GOING TO BE TOO LATE.
TOO EARLY, I THINK. I HAVE A BAD FEELING ABOUT THIS.
I FEAR THAT SOMETHING'S GOING TO BEGIN AT THIS PARTY TONIGHT THAT WILL END MY SAD LIFE BEFORE ITS TIME - IN SOME AWFUL WAY.
GOD SHALL DIRECT ME AND DECIDE MY FATE.
LET'S GO, YOU ROWDY GENTLEMEN!
BEAT THE DRUM!
B-DUM B-DUM

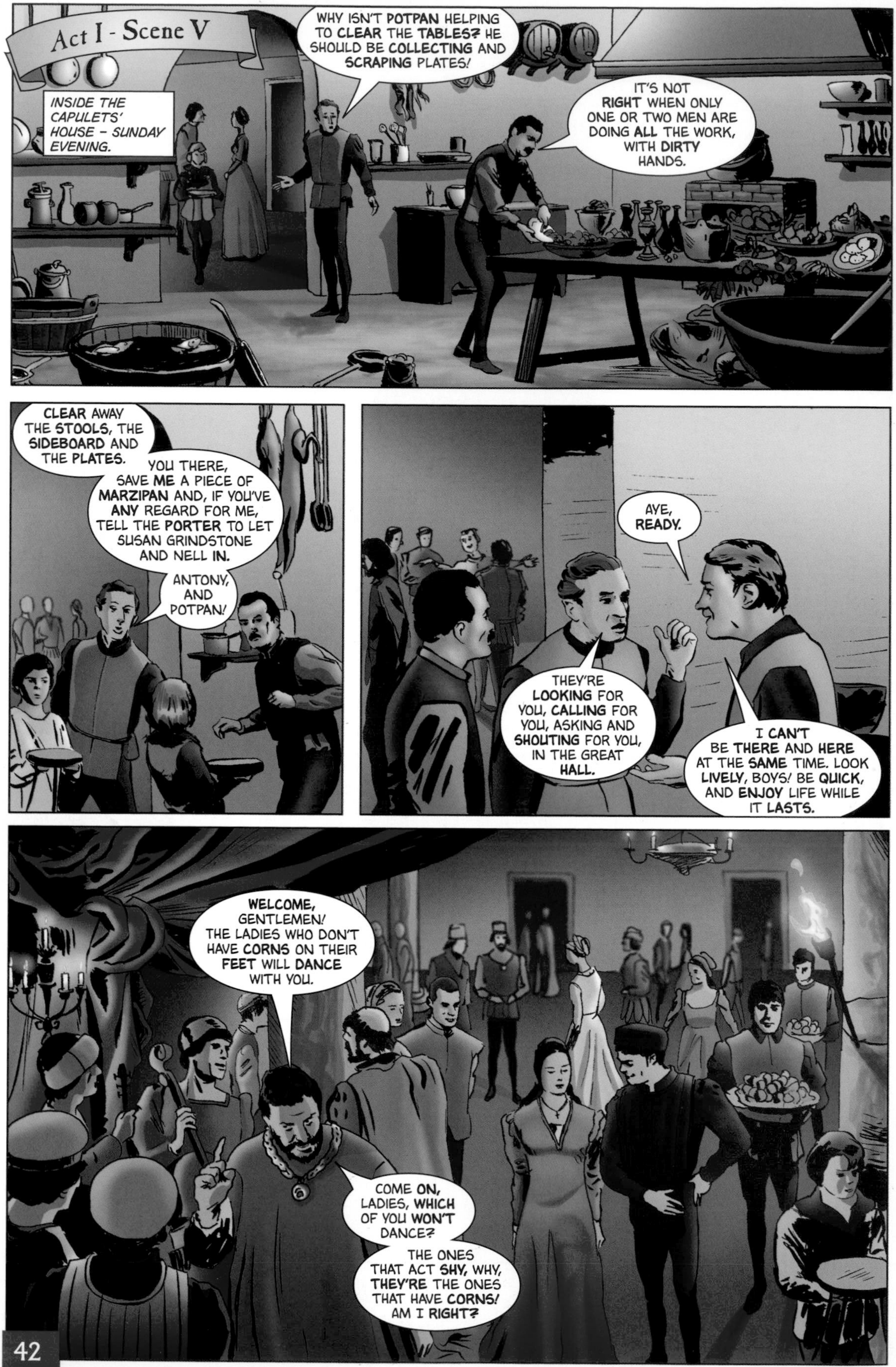
Act I - Scene V
INSIDE THE CAPULETS' HOUSE – SUNDAY EVENING.
WHY ISN'T POTPAN HELPING TO CLEAR THE TABLES? HE SHOULD BE COLLECTING AND SCRAPING PLATES!
IT'S NOT RIGHT WHEN ONLY ONE OR TWO MEN ARE DOING ALL THE WORK, WITH DIRTY HANDS.
CLEAR AWAY THE STOOLS, THE SIDEBOARD AND THE PLATES.
YOU THERE, SAVE ME A PIECE OF MARZIPAN AND, IF YOU'VE ANY REGARD FOR ME, TELL THE PORTER TO LET SUSAN GRINDSTONE AND NELL IN.
ANTONY, AND POTPAN!
AYE, READY.
THEY'RE LOOKING FOR YOU, CALLING FOR YOU, ASKING AND SHOUTING FOR YOU, IN THE GREAT HALL.
I CAN'T BE THERE AND HERE AT THE SAME TIME. LOOK LIVELY, BOYS! BE QUICK, AND ENJOY LIFE WHILE IT LASTS.
WELCOME, GENTLEMEN! THE LADIES WHO DON'T HAVE CORNS ON THEIR FEET WILL DANCE WITH YOU.
COME ON, LADIES, WHICH OF YOU WON'T DANCE?
THE ONES THAT ACT SHY, WHY, THEY'RE THE ONES THAT HAVE CORNS! AM I RIGHT?

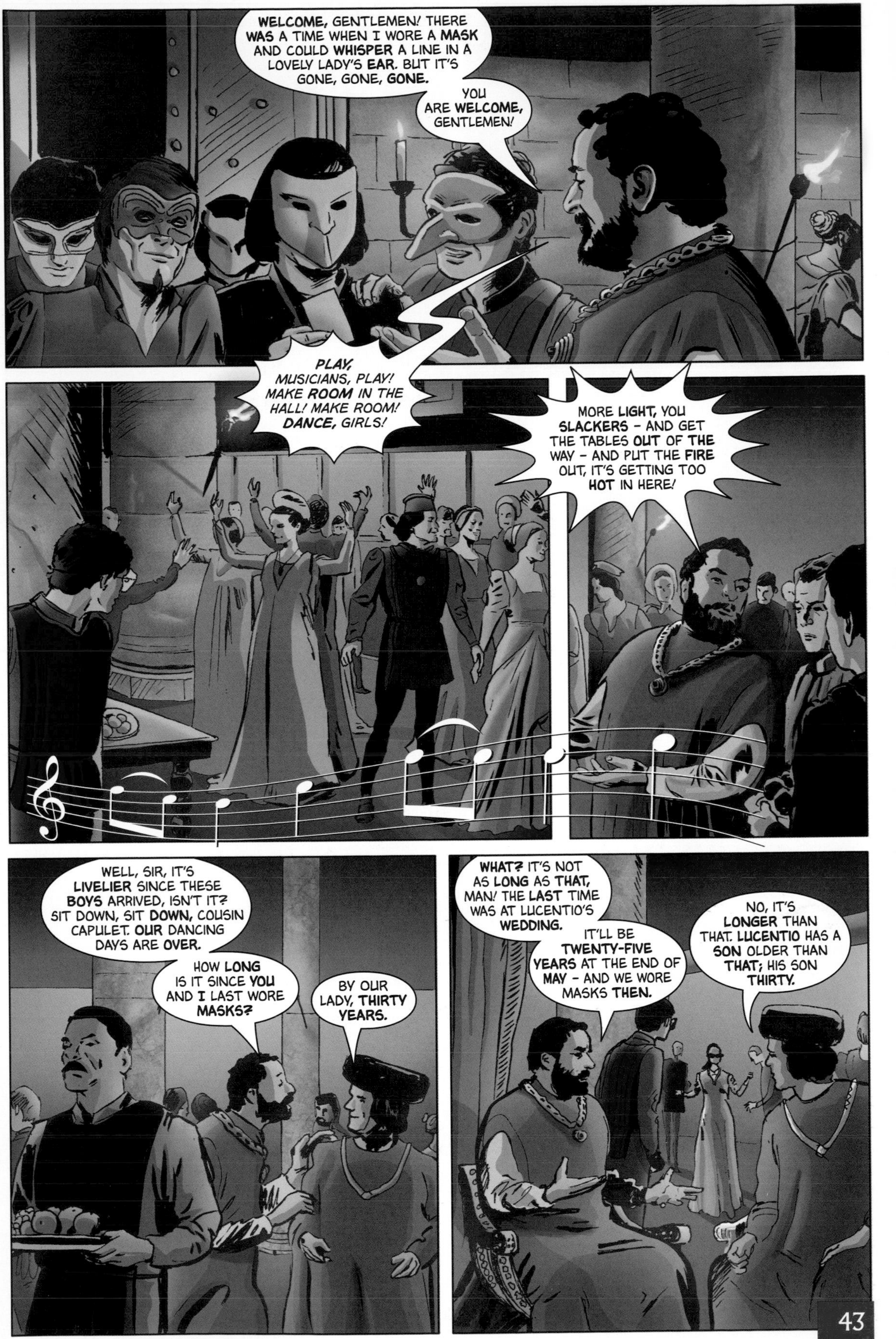
WELCOME, GENTLEMEN! THERE WAS A TIME WHEN I WORE A MASK AND COULD WHISPER A LINE IN A LOVELY LADY'S EAR. BUT IT'S GONE, GONE, GONE.
YOU ARE WELCOME, GENTLEMEN!
PLAY, MUSICIANS, PLAY! MAKE ROOM IN THE HALL! MAKE ROOM! DANCE, GIRLS!
MORE LIGHT, YOU SLACKERS - AND GET THE TABLES OUT OF THE WAY - AND PUT THE FIRE OUT, IT'S GETTING TOO HOT IN HERE!
WELL, SIR, IT'S LIVELIER SINCE THESE BOYS ARRIVED, ISN'T IT? SIT DOWN, SIT DOWN, COUSIN CAPULET. OUR DANCING DAYS ARE OVER.
HOW LONG IS IT SINCE YOU AND I LAST WORE MASKS?
BY OUR LADY, THIRTY YEARS.
WHAT? IT'S NOT AS LONG AS THAT, MAN! THE LAST TIME WAS AT LUCENTIO'S WEDDING.
IT'LL BE TWENTY-FIVE YEARS AT THE END OF MAY - AND WE WORE MASKS THEN.
NO, IT'S LONGER THAN THAT. LUCENTIO HAS A SON OLDER THAN THAT; HIS SON THIRTY.

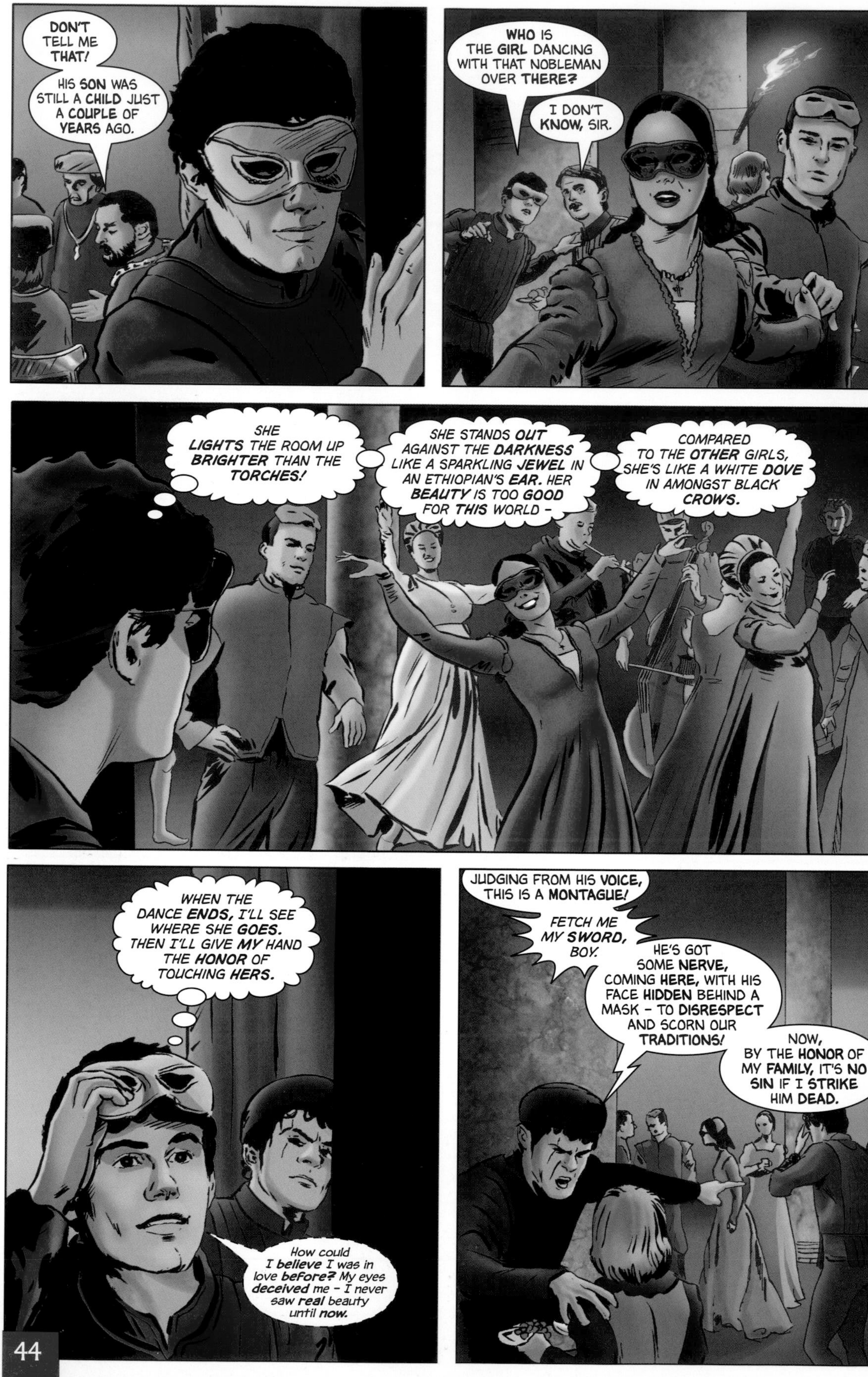
DON'T TELL ME THAT!
HIS SON WAS STILL A CHILD JUST A COUPLE OF YEARS AGO.
WHO IS THE GIRL DANCING WITH THAT NOBLEMAN OVER THERE?
I DON'T KNOW, SIR.
SHE LIGHTS THE ROOM UP BRIGHTER THAN THE TORCHES!
SHE STANDS OUT AGAINST THE DARKNESS LIKE A SPARKLING JEWEL IN AN ETHIOPIAN'S EAR. HER BEAUTY IS TOO GOOD FOR THIS WORLD –
COMPARED TO THE OTHER GIRLS, SHE'S LIKE A WHITE DOVE IN AMONGST BLACK CROWS.
WHEN THE DANCE ENDS, I'LL SEE WHERE SHE GOES. THEN I'LL GIVE MY HAND THE HONOR OF TOUCHING HERS.
How could I believe I was in love before? My eyes deceived me – I never saw real beauty until now.
JUDGING FROM HIS VOICE, THIS IS A MONTAGUE!
FETCH ME MY SWORD, BOY.
HE'S GOT SOME NERVE, COMING HERE, WITH HIS FACE HIDDEN BEHIND A MASK – TO DISRESPECT AND SCORN OUR TRADITIONS!
NOW, BY THE HONOR OF MY FAMILY, IT'S NO SIN IF I STRIKE HIM DEAD.

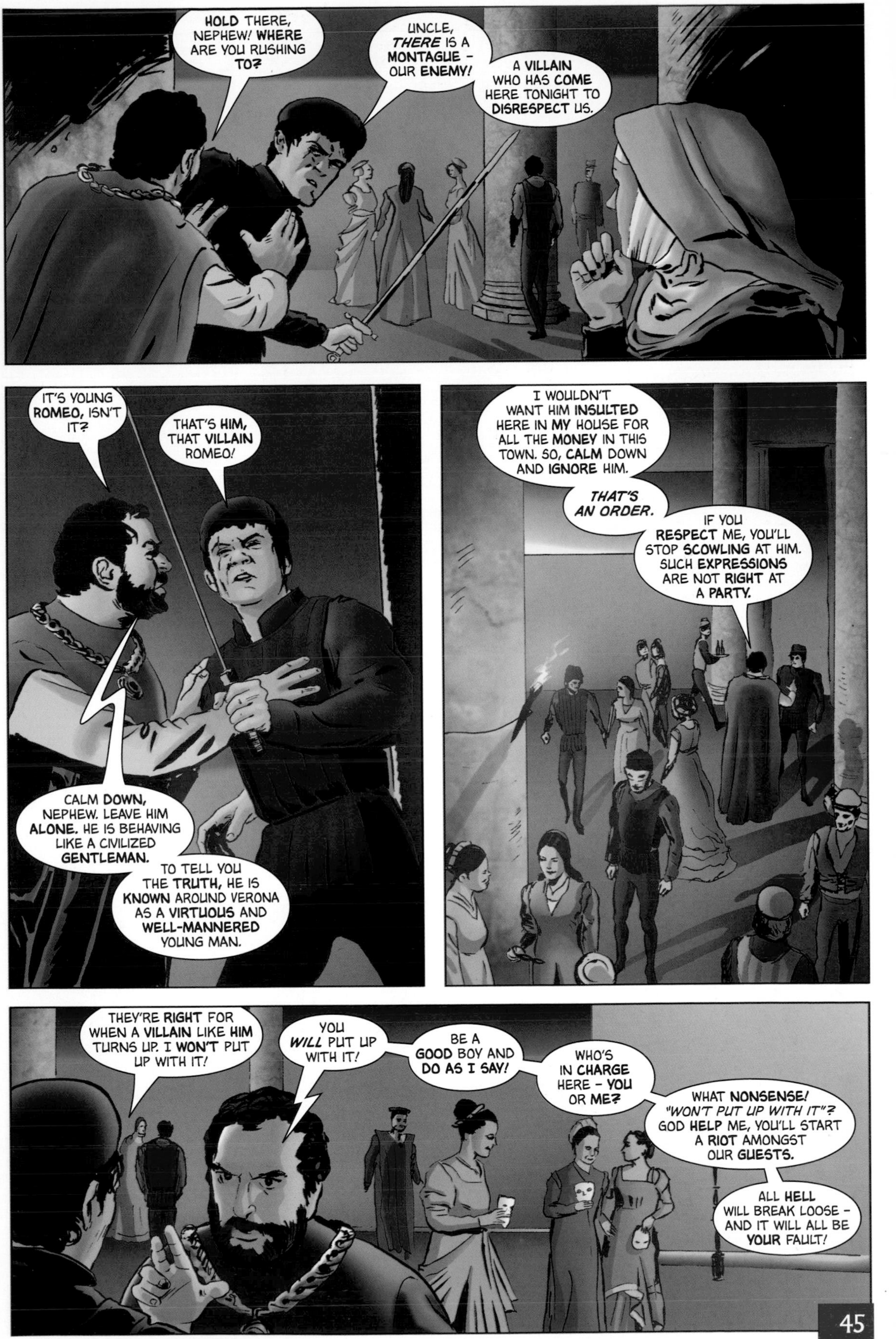
HOLD THERE, NEPHEW! WHERE ARE YOU RUSHING TO?
UNCLE, THERE IS A MONTAGUE - OUR ENEMY!
A VILLAIN WHO HAS COME HERE TONIGHT TO DISRESPECT US.
IT'S YOUNG ROMEO, ISN'T IT?
THAT'S HIM, THAT VILLAIN ROMEO!
CALM DOWN, NEPHEW. LEAVE HIM ALONE. HE IS BEHAVING LIKE A CIVILIZED GENTLEMAN.
TO TELL YOU THE TRUTH, HE IS KNOWN AROUND VERONA AS A VIRTUOUS AND WELL-MANNERED YOUNG MAN.
I WOULDN'T WANT HIM INSULTED HERE IN MY HOUSE FOR ALL THE MONEY IN THIS TOWN. SO, CALM DOWN AND IGNORE HIM.
THAT'S AN ORDER.
IF YOU RESPECT ME, YOU'LL STOP SCOWLING AT HIM. SUCH EXPRESSIONS ARE NOT RIGHT AT A PARTY.
THEY'RE RIGHT FOR WHEN A VILLAIN LIKE HIM TURNS UP. I WON'T PUT UP WITH IT!
YOU WILL PUT UP WITH IT!
BE A GOOD BOY AND DO AS I SAY!
WHO'S IN CHARGE HERE - YOU OR ME?
WHAT NONSENSE! "WON'T PUT UP WITH IT"? GOD HELP ME, YOU'LL START A RIOT AMONGST OUR GUESTS.
ALL HELL WILL BREAK LOOSE - AND IT WILL ALL BE YOUR FAULT!

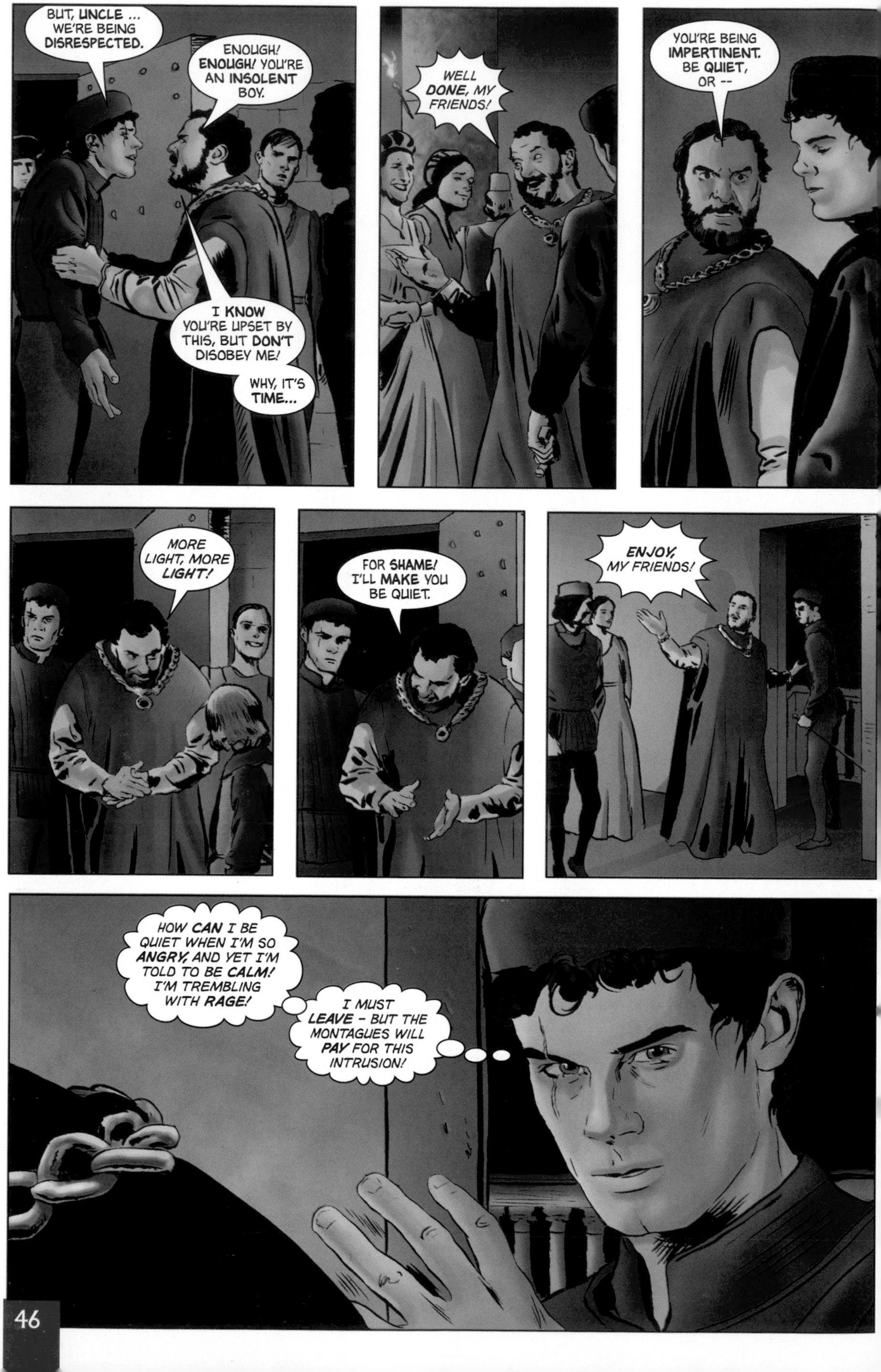

BUT, UNCLE ... WE'RE BEING DISRESPECTED.
ENOUGH! ENOUGH! YOU'RE AN INSOLENT BOY.
I KNOW YOU'RE UPSET BY THIS, BUT DON'T DISOBEY ME!
WHY, IT'S TIME...
WELL DONE, MY FRIENDS!
YOU'RE BEING IMPERTINENT. BE QUIET, OR --
MORE LIGHT, MORE LIGHT!
FOR SHAME! I'LL MAKE YOU BE QUIET.
ENJOY, MY FRIENDS!
HOW CAN I BE QUIET WHEN I'M SO ANGRY, AND YET I'M TOLD TO BE CALM! I'M TREMBLING WITH RAGE!
I MUST LEAVE - BUT THE MONTAGUES WILL PAY FOR THIS INTRUSION!

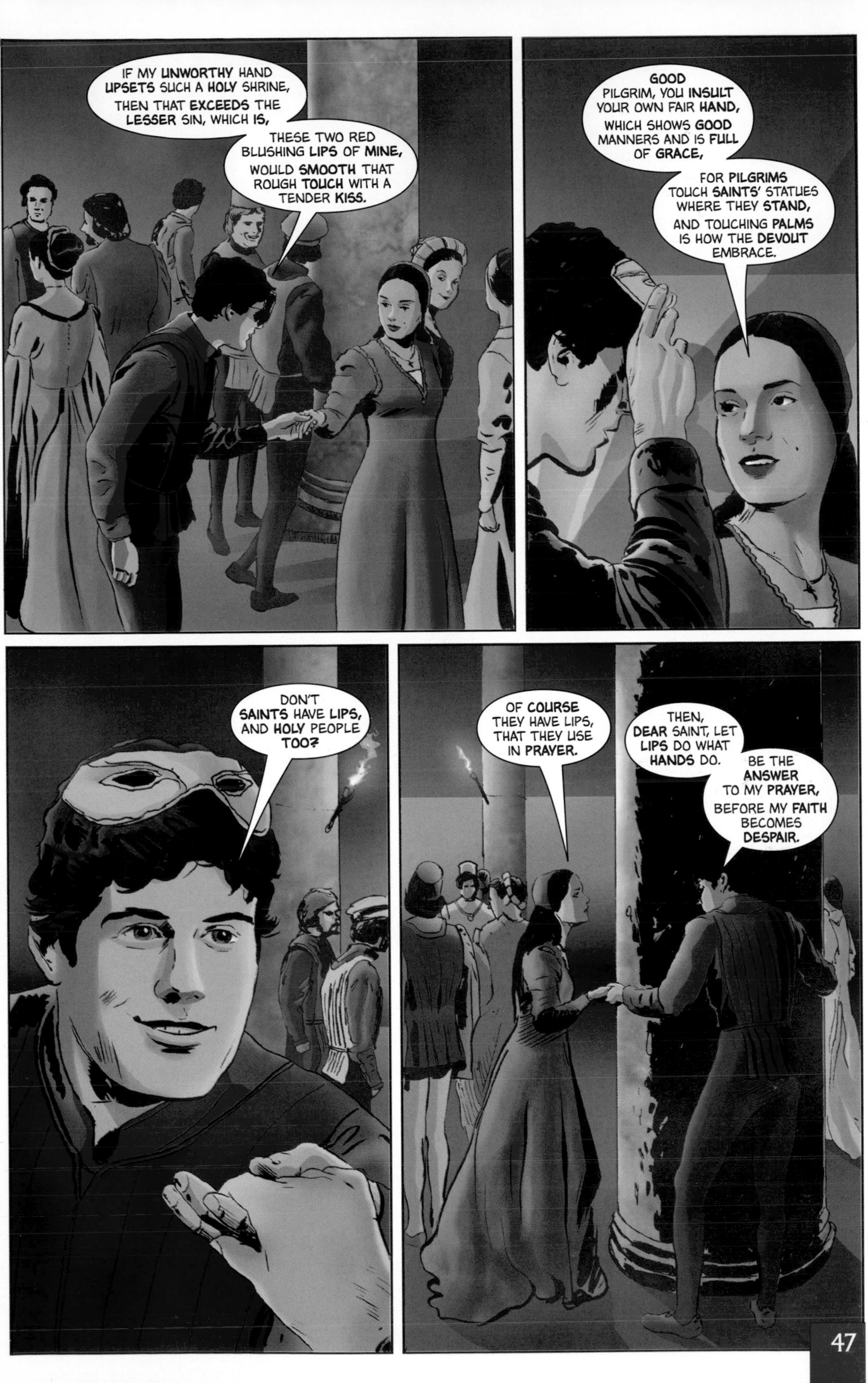
IF MY UNWORTHY HAND UPSETS SUCH A HOLY SHRINE, THEN THAT EXCEEDS THE LESSER SIN, WHICH IS,
THESE TWO RED BLUSHING LIPS OF MINE, WOULD SMOOTH THAT ROUGH TOUCH WITH A TENDER KISS.
GOOD PILGRIM, YOU INSULT YOUR OWN FAIR HAND, WHICH SHOWS GOOD MANNERS AND IS FULL OF GRACE,
FOR PILGRIMS TOUCH SAINTS' STATUES WHERE THEY STAND, AND TOUCHING PALMS IS HOW THE DEVOUT EMBRACE.
DON'T SAINTS HAVE LIPS, AND HOLY PEOPLE TOO?
OF COURSE THEY HAVE LIPS, THAT THEY USE IN PRAYER.
THEN, DEAR SAINT, LET LIPS DO WHAT HANDS DO.
BE THE ANSWER TO MY PRAYER, BEFORE MY FAITH BECOMES DESPAIR.

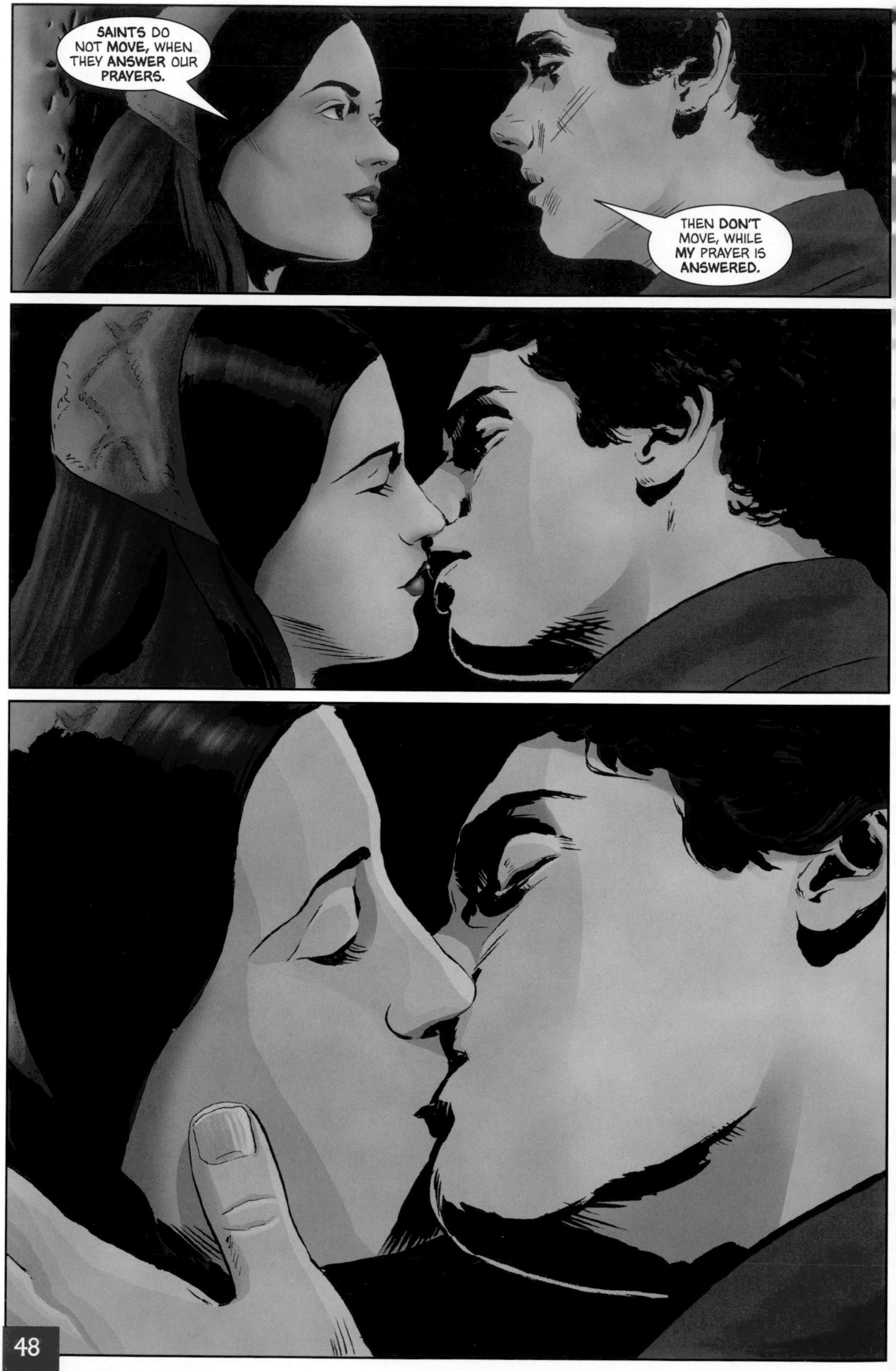
SAINTS DO NOT MOVE, WHEN THEY ANSWER OUR PRAYERS.
THEN DON'T MOVE, WHILE MY PRAYER IS ANSWERED.

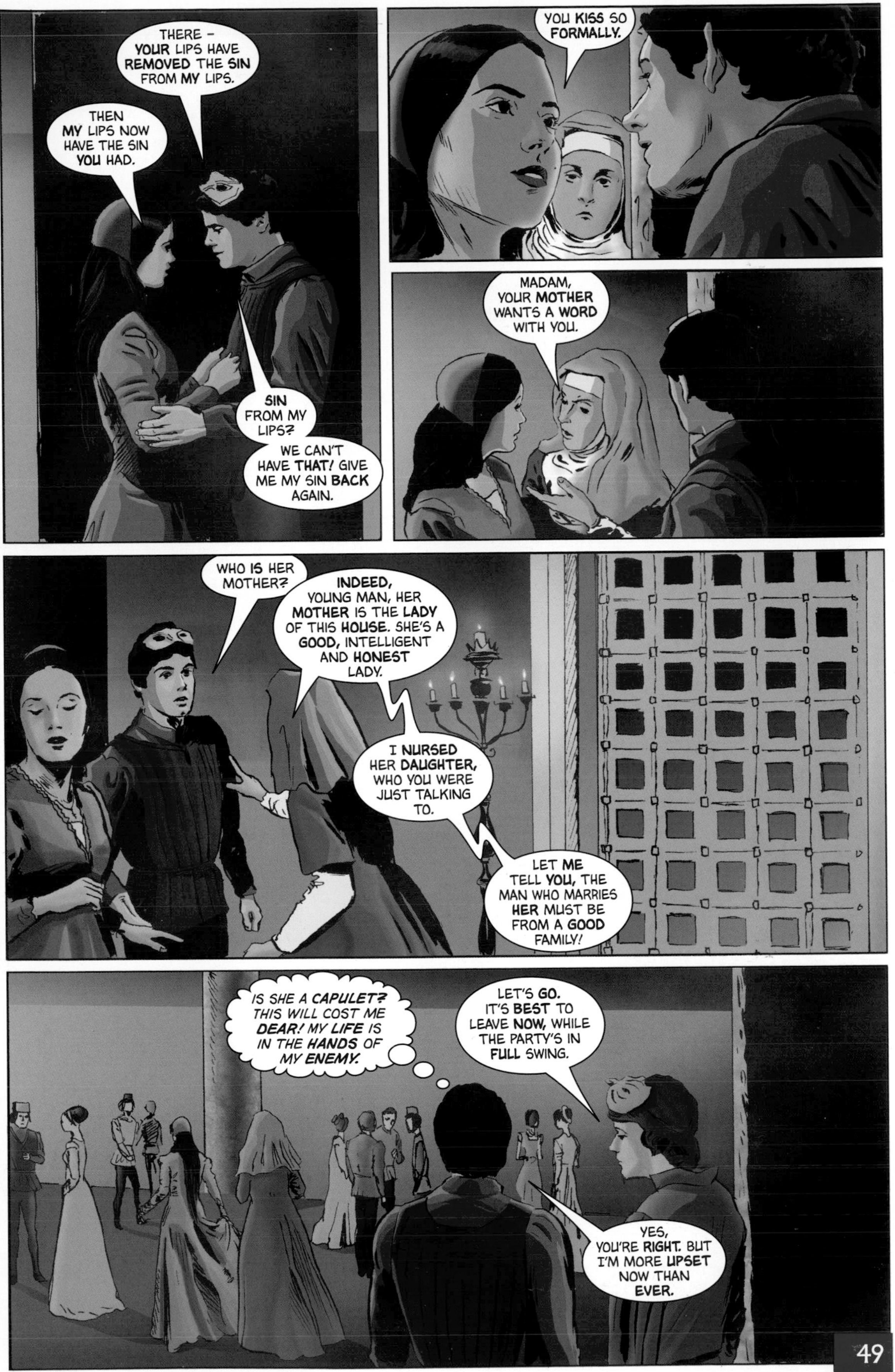
THERE – YOUR LIPS HAVE REMOVED THE SIN FROM MY LIPS.
THEN MY LIPS NOW HAVE THE SIN YOU HAD.
SIN FROM MY LIPS?
WE CAN'T HAVE THAT! GIVE ME MY SIN BACK AGAIN.
YOU KISS SO FORMALLY.
MADAM, YOUR MOTHER WANTS A WORD WITH YOU.
WHO IS HER MOTHER?
INDEED, YOUNG MAN, HER MOTHER IS THE LADY OF THIS HOUSE. SHE'S A GOOD, INTELLIGENT AND HONEST LADY.
I NURSED HER DAUGHTER, WHO YOU WERE JUST TALKING TO.
LET ME TELL YOU, THE MAN WHO MARRIES HER MUST BE FROM A GOOD FAMILY!
IS SHE A CAPULET? THIS WILL COST ME DEAR! MY LIFE IS IN THE HANDS OF MY ENEMY.
LET'S GO. IT'S BEST TO LEAVE NOW, WHILE THE PARTY'S IN FULL SWING.
YES, YOU'RE RIGHT. BUT I'M MORE UPSET NOW THAN EVER.

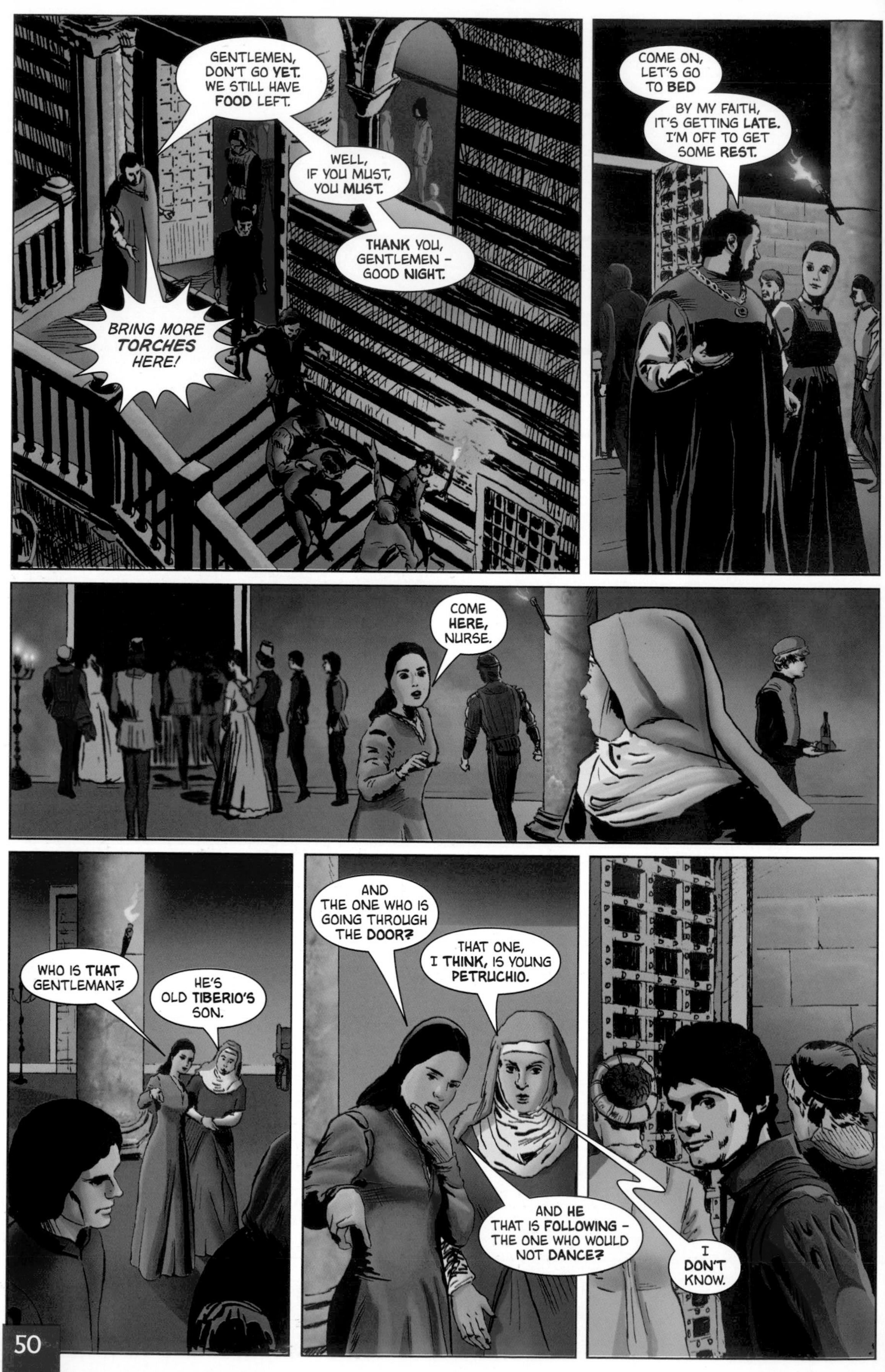
GENTLEMEN, DON'T GO YET. WE STILL HAVE FOOD LEFT.
WELL, IF YOU MUST, YOU MUST.
THANK YOU, GENTLEMEN – GOOD NIGHT.
BRING MORE TORCHES HERE!
COME ON, LET'S GO TO BED
BY MY FAITH, IT'S GETTING LATE. I'M OFF TO GET SOME REST.
COME HERE, NURSE.
WHO IS THAT GENTLEMAN?
HE'S OLD TIBERIO'S SON.
AND THE ONE WHO IS GOING THROUGH THE DOOR?
THAT ONE, I THINK, IS YOUNG PETRUCHIO.
AND HE THAT IS FOLLOWING – THE ONE WHO WOULD NOT DANCE?
I DON'T KNOW.

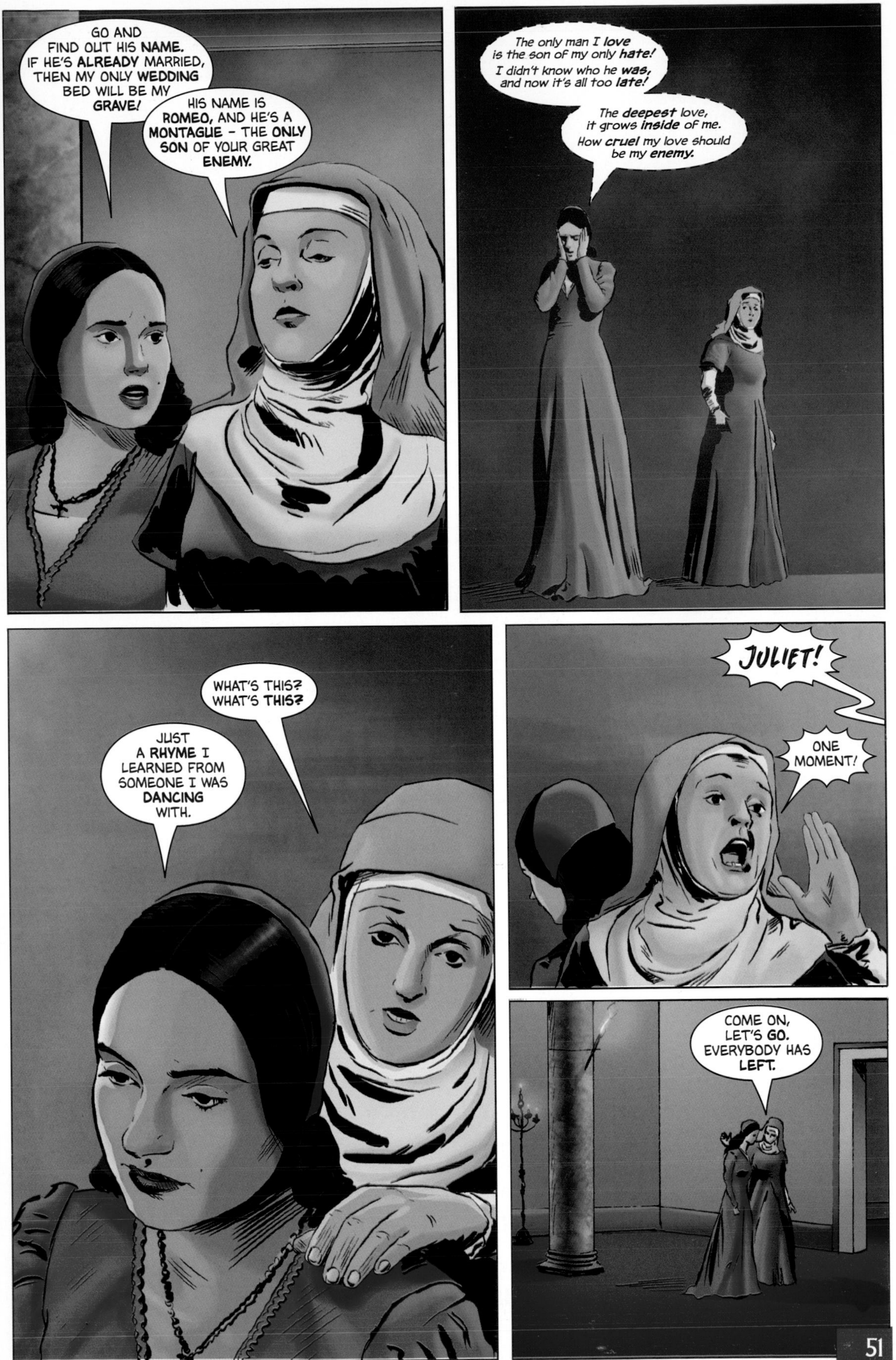

GO AND FIND OUT HIS NAME. IF HE'S ALREADY MARRIED, THEN MY ONLY WEDDING BED WILL BE MY GRAVE!
HIS NAME IS ROMEO, AND HE'S A MONTAGUE – THE ONLY SON OF YOUR GREAT ENEMY.
The only man I love is the son of my only hate! I didn't know who he was, and now it's all too late!
The deepest love, it grows inside of me. How cruel my love should be my enemy.
WHAT'S THIS? WHAT'S THIS?
JUST A RHYME I LEARNED FROM SOMEONE I WAS DANCING WITH.
JULIET!
ONE MOMENT!
COME ON, LET'S GO. EVERYBODY HAS LEFT.

Act II - Prologue

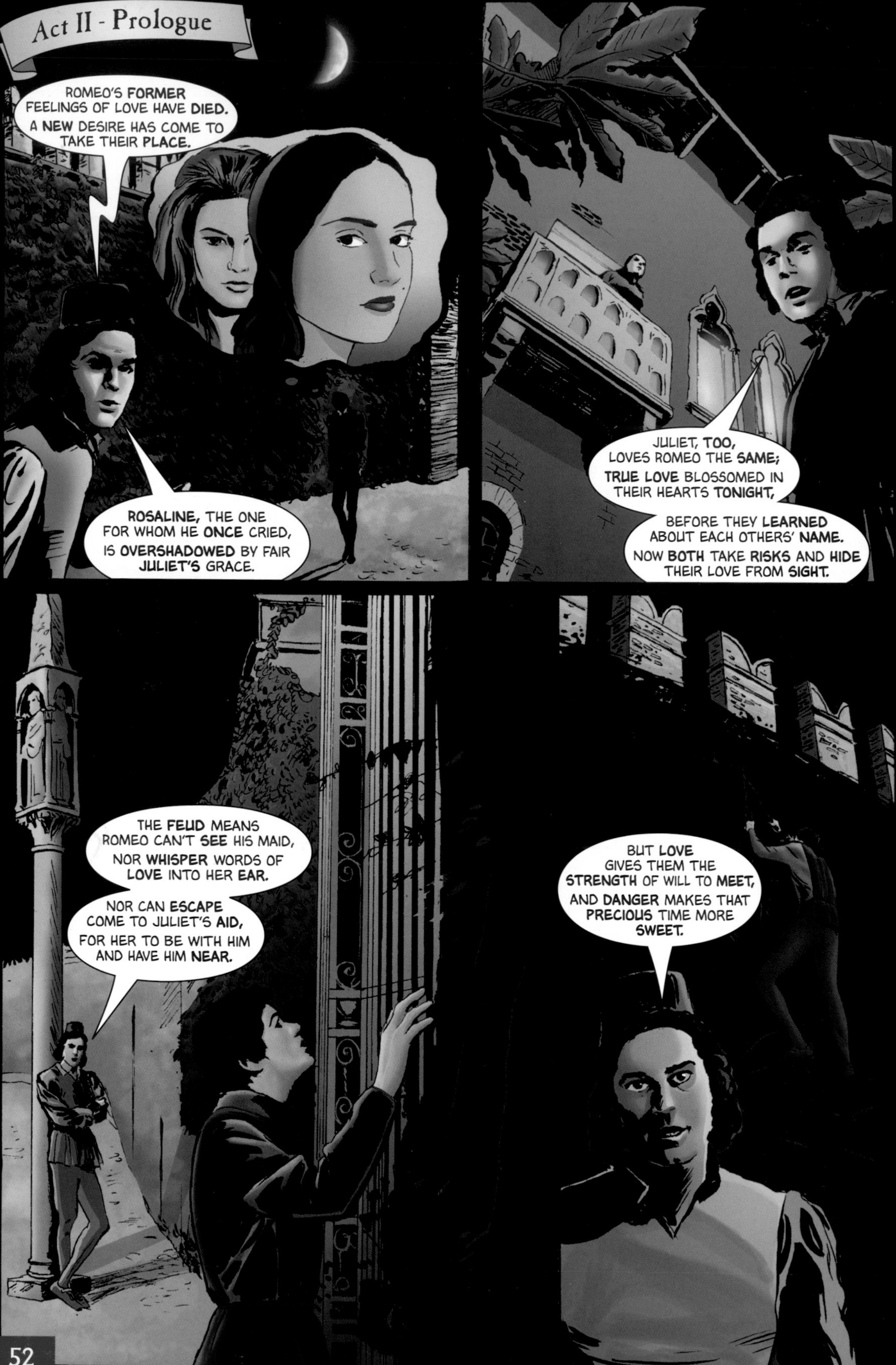

ROMEO'S FORMER FEELINGS OF LOVE HAVE DIED. A NEW DESIRE HAS COME TO TAKE THEIR PLACE.
ROSALINE, THE ONE FOR WHOM HE ONCE CRIED, IS OVERSHADOWED BY FAIR JULIET'S GRACE.
JULIET, TOO, LOVES ROMEO THE SAME; TRUE LOVE BLOSSOMED IN THEIR HEARTS TONIGHT,
BEFORE THEY LEARNED ABOUT EACH OTHERS' NAME. NOW BOTH TAKE RISKS AND HIDE THEIR LOVE FROM SIGHT.
THE FEUD MEANS ROMEO CAN'T SEE HIS MAID, NOR WHISPER WORDS OF LOVE INTO HER EAR.
NOR CAN ESCAPE COME TO JULIET'S AID, FOR HER TO BE WITH HIM AND HAVE HIM NEAR.
BUT LOVE GIVES THEM THE STRENGTH OF WILL TO MEET, AND DANGER MAKES THAT PRECIOUS TIME MORE SWEET.

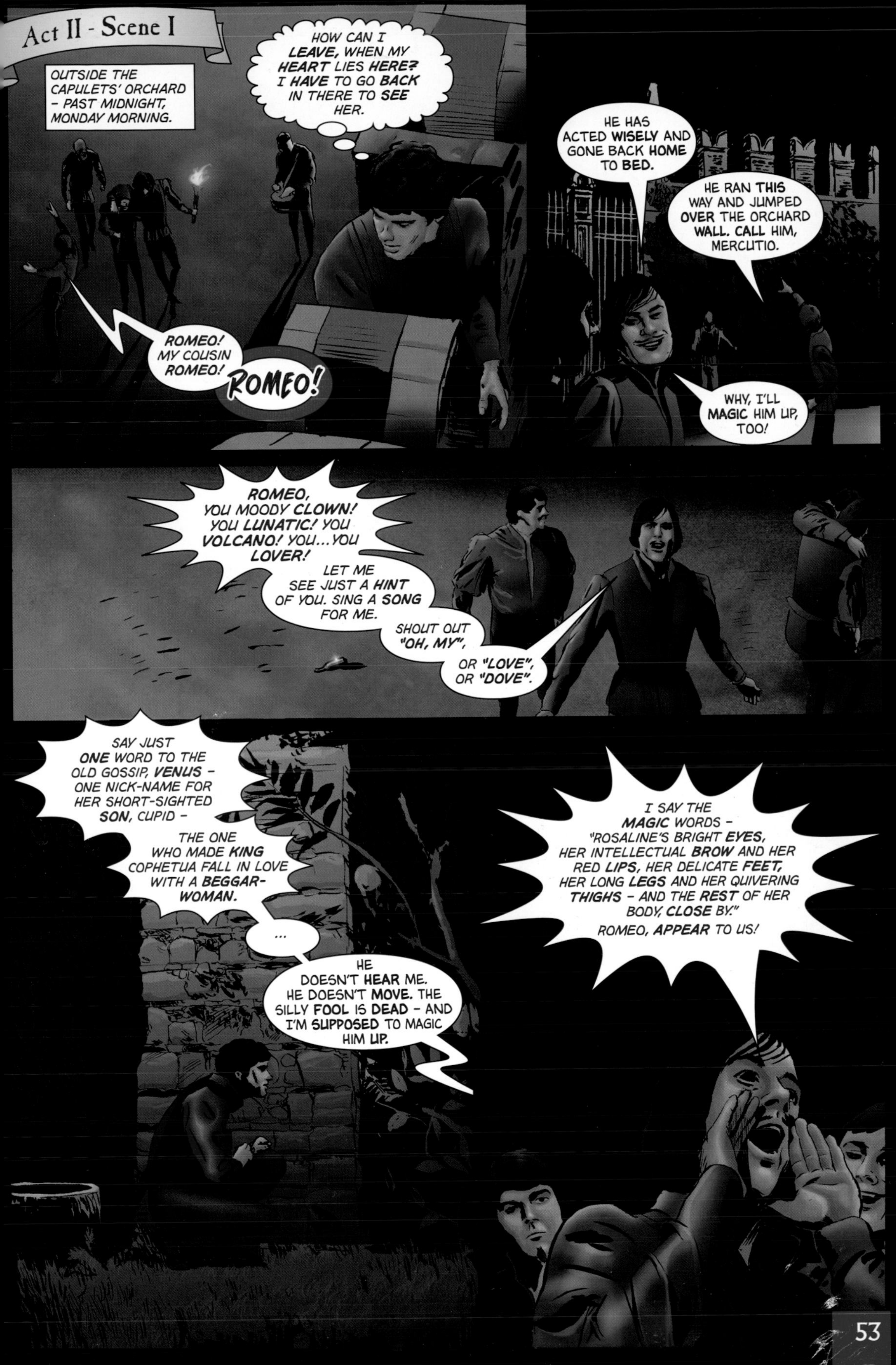
Act II - Scene I
OUTSIDE THE CAPULETS' ORCHARD – PAST MIDNIGHT, MONDAY MORNING.
HOW CAN I LEAVE, WHEN MY HEART LIES HERE? I HAVE TO GO BACK IN THERE TO SEE HER.
ROMEO! MY COUSIN ROMEO!
ROMEO!
HE HAS ACTED WISELY AND GONE BACK HOME TO BED.
HE RAN THIS WAY AND JUMPED OVER THE ORCHARD WALL. CALL HIM, MERCUTIO.
WHY, I'LL MAGIC HIM UP, TOO!
ROMEO, YOU MOODY CLOWN! YOU LUNATIC! YOU VOLCANO! YOU...YOU LOVER!
LET ME SEE JUST A HINT OF YOU. SING A SONG FOR ME.
SHOUT OUT "OH, MY",
OR "LOVE", OR "DOVE".
SAY JUST ONE WORD TO THE OLD GOSSIP, VENUS – ONE NICK-NAME FOR HER SHORT-SIGHTED SON, CUPID –
THE ONE WHO MADE KING COPHETUA FALL IN LOVE WITH A BEGGAR-WOMAN.
...
HE DOESN'T HEAR ME. HE DOESN'T MOVE. THE SILLY FOOL IS DEAD – AND I'M SUPPOSED TO MAGIC HIM UP.
I SAY THE MAGIC WORDS – "ROSALINE'S BRIGHT EYES, HER INTELLECTUAL BROW AND HER RED LIPS, HER DELICATE FEET, HER LONG LEGS AND HER QUIVERING THIGHS – AND THE REST OF HER BODY, CLOSE BY."
ROMEO, APPEAR TO US!

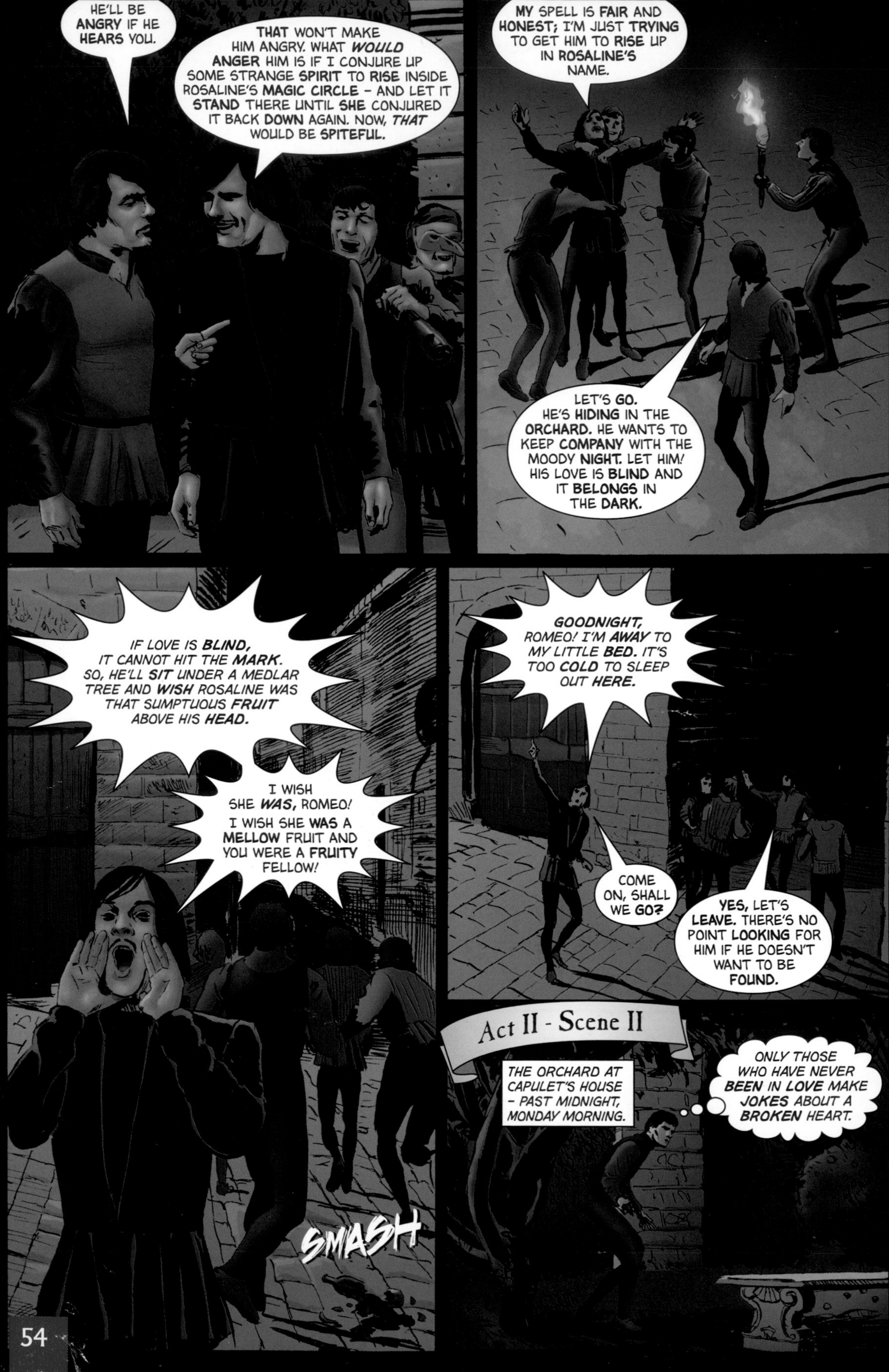

HE'LL BE ANGRY IF HE HEARS YOU.
THAT WON'T MAKE HIM ANGRY. WHAT WOULD ANGER HIM IS IF I CONJURE UP SOME STRANGE SPIRIT TO RISE INSIDE ROSALINE'S MAGIC CIRCLE – AND LET IT STAND THERE UNTIL SHE CONJURED IT BACK DOWN AGAIN. NOW, THAT WOULD BE SPITEFUL.
MY SPELL IS FAIR AND HONEST; I'M JUST TRYING TO GET HIM TO RISE UP IN ROSALINE'S NAME.
LET'S GO. HE'S HIDING IN THE ORCHARD. HE WANTS TO KEEP COMPANY WITH THE MOODY NIGHT. LET HIM! HIS LOVE IS BLIND AND IT BELONGS IN THE DARK.
IF LOVE IS BLIND, IT CANNOT HIT THE MARK. SO, HE'LL SIT UNDER A MEDLAR TREE AND WISH ROSALINE WAS THAT SUMPTUOUS FRUIT ABOVE HIS HEAD.
I WISH SHE WAS, ROMEO! I WISH SHE WAS A MELLOW FRUIT AND YOU WERE A FRUITY FELLOW!
SMASH
GOODNIGHT, ROMEO! I'M AWAY TO MY LITTLE BED. IT'S TOO COLD TO SLEEP OUT HERE.
COME ON, SHALL WE GO?
YES, LET'S LEAVE. THERE'S NO POINT LOOKING FOR HIM IF HE DOESN'T WANT TO BE FOUND.
Act II - Scene II
THE ORCHARD AT CAPULET'S HOUSE – PAST MIDNIGHT, MONDAY MORNING.
ONLY THOSE WHO HAVE NEVER BEEN IN LOVE MAKE JOKES ABOUT A BROKEN HEART.

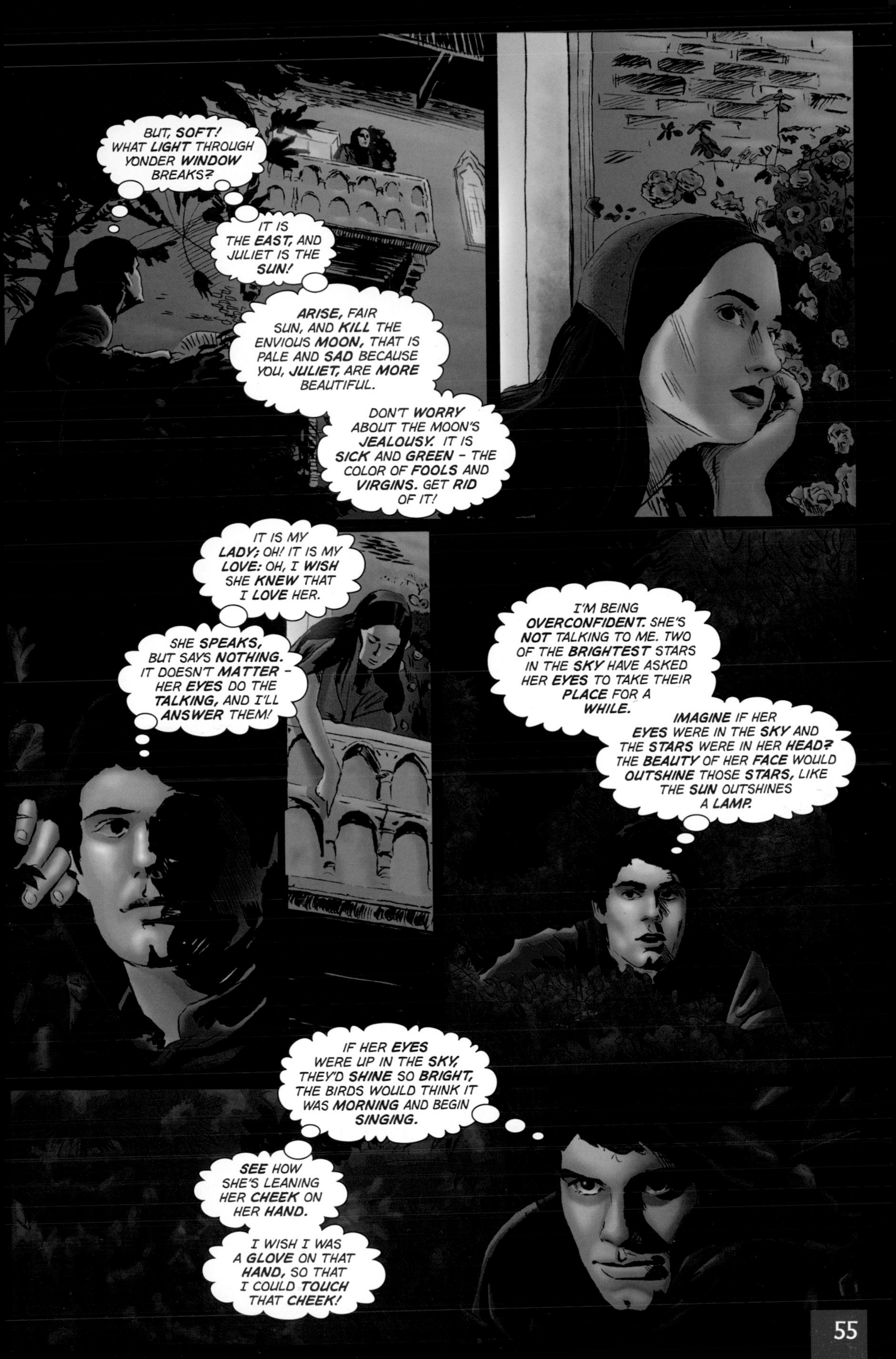
BUT, SOFT! WHAT LIGHT THROUGH YONDER WINDOW BREAKS?
IT IS THE EAST, AND JULIET IS THE SUN!
ARISE, FAIR SUN, AND KILL THE ENVIOUS MOON, THAT IS PALE AND SAD BECAUSE YOU, JULIET, ARE MORE BEAUTIFUL.
DON'T WORRY ABOUT THE MOON'S JEALOUSY. IT IS SICK AND GREEN - THE COLOR OF FOOLS AND VIRGINS. GET RID OF IT!
IT IS MY LADY; OH! IT IS MY LOVE: OH, I WISH SHE KNEW THAT I LOVE HER.
SHE SPEAKS, BUT SAYS NOTHING. IT DOESN'T MATTER - HER EYES DO THE TALKING, AND I'LL ANSWER THEM!
I'M BEING OVERCONFIDENT. SHE'S NOT TALKING TO ME. TWO OF THE BRIGHTEST STARS IN THE SKY HAVE ASKED HER EYES TO TAKE THEIR PLACE FOR A WHILE.
IMAGINE IF HER EYES WERE IN THE SKY AND THE STARS WERE IN HER HEAD? THE BEAUTY OF HER FACE WOULD OUTSHINE THOSE STARS, LIKE THE SUN OUTSHINES A LAMP.
IF HER EYES WERE UP IN THE SKY, THEY'D SHINE SO BRIGHT, THE BIRDS WOULD THINK IT WAS MORNING AND BEGIN SINGING.
SEE HOW SHE'S LEANING HER CHEEK ON HER HAND.
I WISH I WAS A GLOVE ON THAT HAND, SO THAT I COULD TOUCH THAT CHEEK!

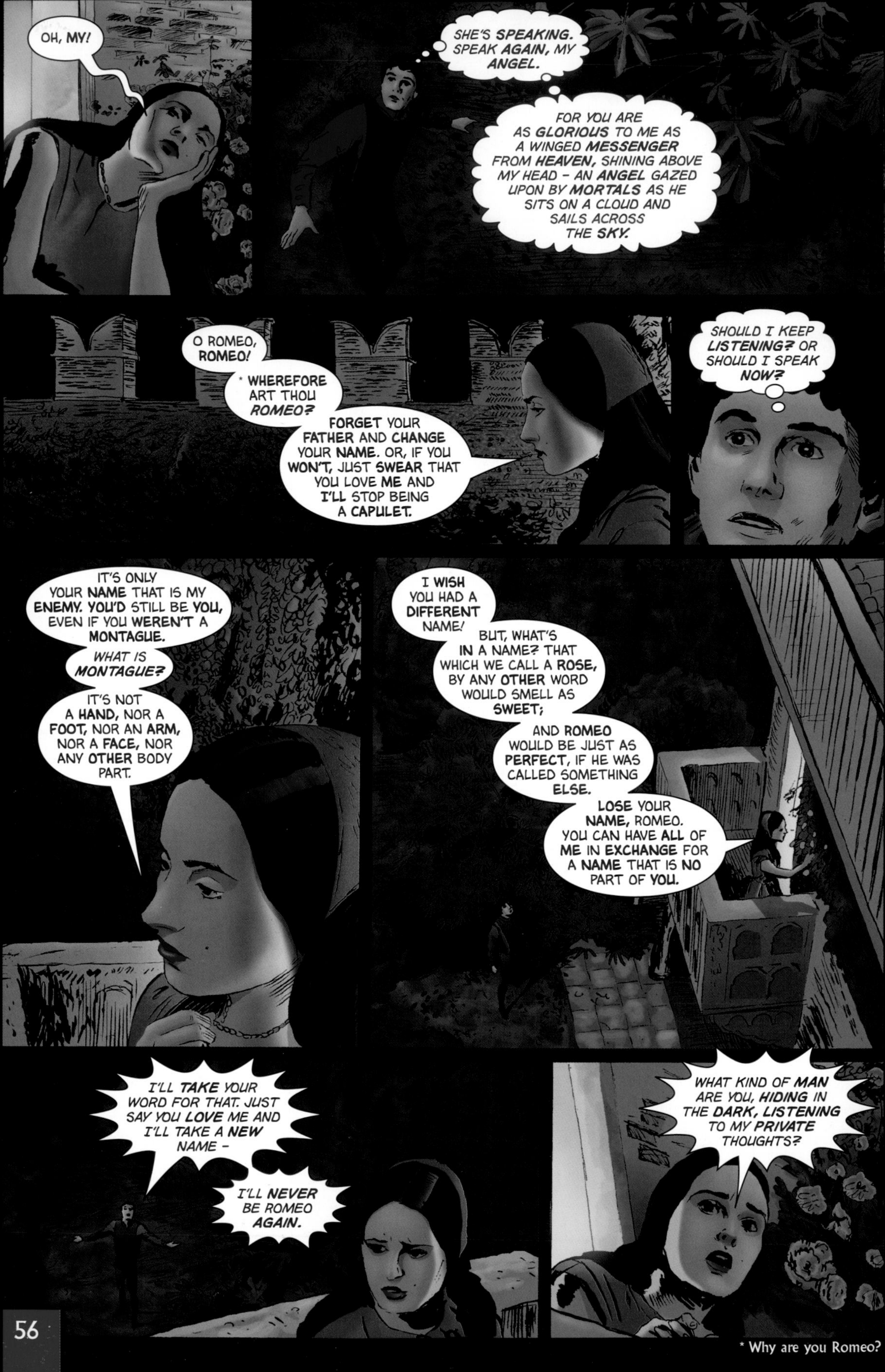
OH, MY!
SHE'S SPEAKING. SPEAK AGAIN, MY ANGEL.
FOR YOU ARE AS GLORIOUS TO ME AS A WINGED MESSENGER FROM HEAVEN, SHINING ABOVE MY HEAD – AN ANGEL GAZED UPON BY MORTALS AS HE SITS ON A CLOUD AND SAILS ACROSS THE SKY.
O ROMEO, ROMEO!
* WHEREFORE ART THOU ROMEO?
FORGET YOUR FATHER AND CHANGE YOUR NAME. OR, IF YOU WON'T, JUST SWEAR THAT YOU LOVE ME AND I'LL STOP BEING A CAPULET.
SHOULD I KEEP LISTENING? OR SHOULD I SPEAK NOW?
IT'S ONLY YOUR NAME THAT IS MY ENEMY. YOU'D STILL BE YOU, EVEN IF YOU WEREN'T A MONTAGUE.
WHAT IS MONTAGUE?
IT'S NOT A HAND, NOR A FOOT, NOR AN ARM, NOR A FACE, NOR ANY OTHER BODY PART.
I WISH YOU HAD A DIFFERENT NAME!
BUT, WHAT'S IN A NAME? THAT WHICH WE CALL A ROSE, BY ANY OTHER WORD WOULD SMELL AS SWEET;
AND ROMEO WOULD BE JUST AS PERFECT, IF HE WAS CALLED SOMETHING ELSE.
LOSE YOUR NAME, ROMEO. YOU CAN HAVE ALL OF ME IN EXCHANGE FOR A NAME THAT IS NO PART OF YOU.
I'LL TAKE YOUR WORD FOR THAT. JUST SAY YOU LOVE ME AND I'LL TAKE A NEW NAME –
I'LL NEVER BE ROMEO AGAIN.
WHAT KIND OF MAN ARE YOU, HIDING IN THE DARK, LISTENING TO MY PRIVATE THOUGHTS?

* Why are you Romeo?

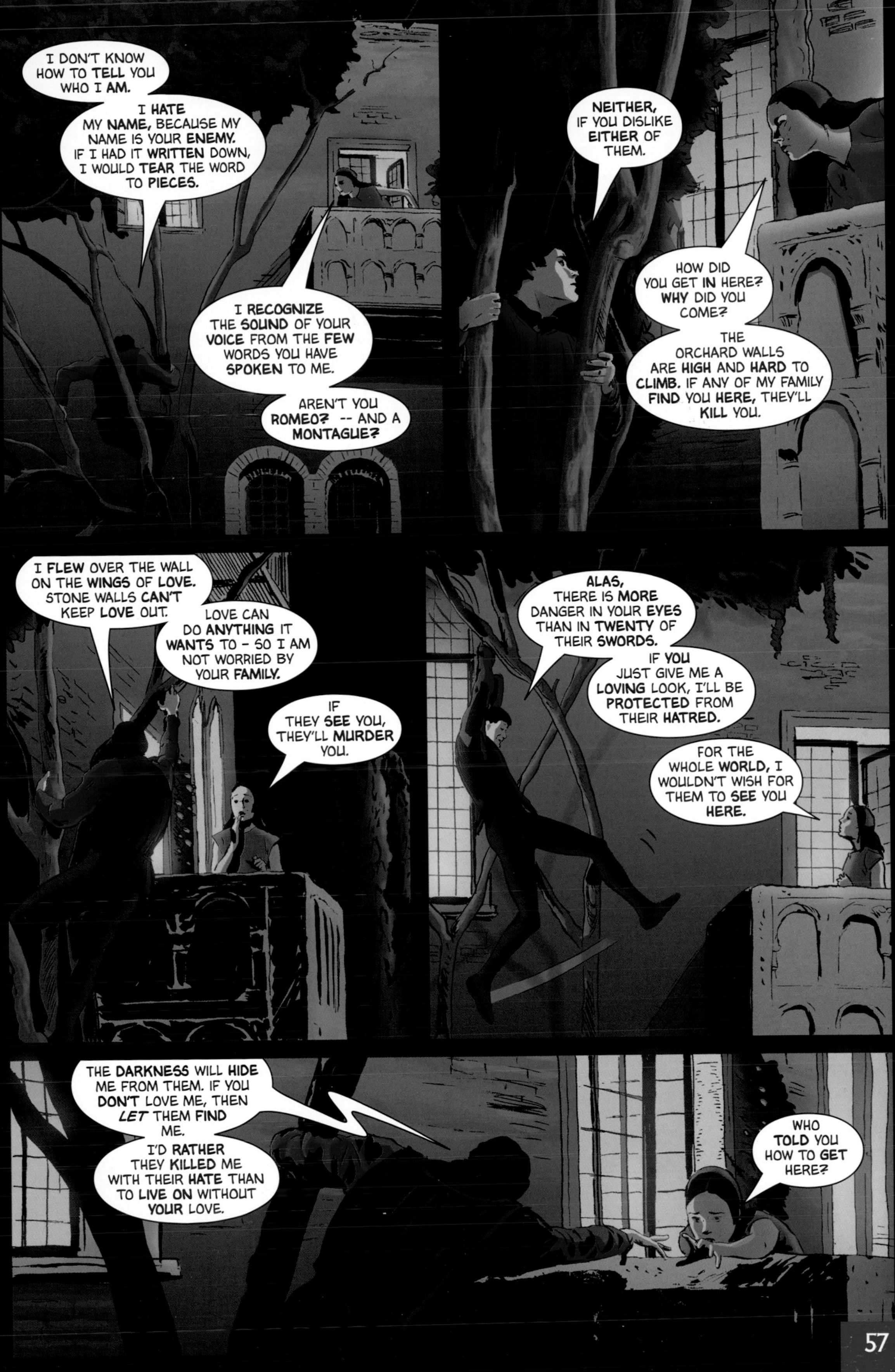
I DON'T KNOW HOW TO TELL YOU WHO I AM.
I HATE MY NAME, BECAUSE MY NAME IS YOUR ENEMY. IF I HAD IT WRITTEN DOWN, I WOULD TEAR THE WORD TO PIECES.
I RECOGNIZE THE SOUND OF YOUR VOICE FROM THE FEW WORDS YOU HAVE SPOKEN TO ME.
AREN'T YOU ROMEO? -- AND A MONTAGUE?
NEITHER, IF YOU DISLIKE EITHER OF THEM.
HOW DID YOU GET IN HERE? WHY DID YOU COME?
THE ORCHARD WALLS ARE HIGH AND HARD TO CLIMB. IF ANY OF MY FAMILY FIND YOU HERE, THEY'LL KILL YOU.
I FLEW OVER THE WALL ON THE WINGS OF LOVE. STONE WALLS CAN'T KEEP LOVE OUT.
LOVE CAN DO ANYTHING IT WANTS TO - SO I AM NOT WORRIED BY YOUR FAMILY.
IF THEY SEE YOU, THEY'LL MURDER YOU.
ALAS, THERE IS MORE DANGER IN YOUR EYES THAN IN TWENTY OF THEIR SWORDS.
IF YOU JUST GIVE ME A LOVING LOOK, I'LL BE PROTECTED FROM THEIR HATRED.
FOR THE WHOLE WORLD, I WOULDN'T WISH FOR THEM TO SEE YOU HERE.
THE DARKNESS WILL HIDE ME FROM THEM. IF YOU DON'T LOVE ME, THEN LET THEM FIND ME.
I'D RATHER THEY KILLED ME WITH THEIR HATE THAN TO LIVE ON WITHOUT YOUR LOVE.
WHO TOLD YOU HOW TO GET HERE?

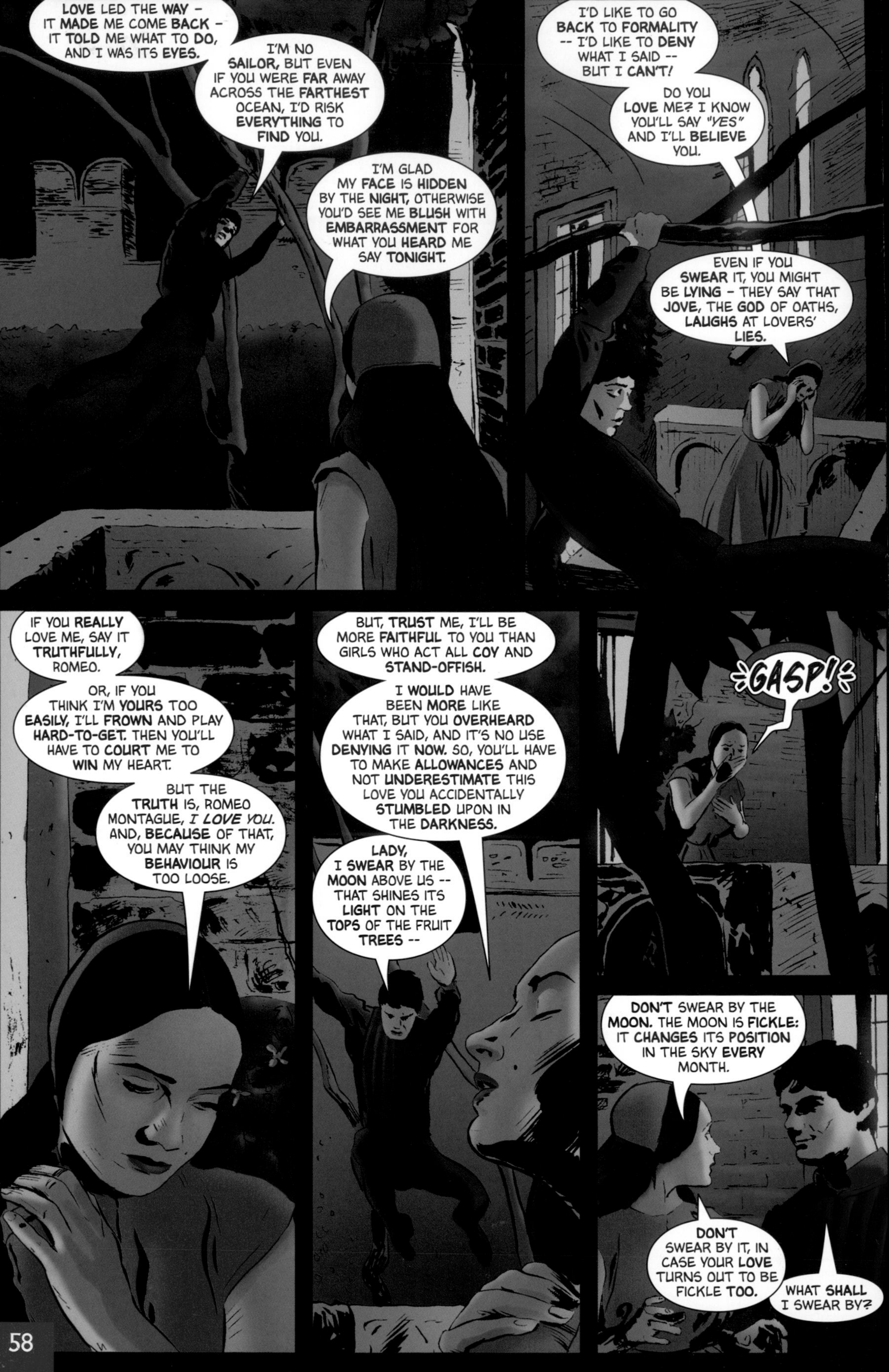
LOVE LED THE WAY – IT MADE ME COME BACK – IT TOLD ME WHAT TO DO, AND I WAS ITS EYES.
I'M NO SAILOR, BUT EVEN IF YOU WERE FAR AWAY ACROSS THE FARTHEST OCEAN, I'D RISK EVERYTHING TO FIND YOU.
I'M GLAD MY FACE IS HIDDEN BY THE NIGHT, OTHERWISE YOU'D SEE ME BLUSH WITH EMBARRASSMENT FOR WHAT YOU HEARD ME SAY TONIGHT.
I'D LIKE TO GO BACK TO FORMALITY -- I'D LIKE TO DENY WHAT I SAID -- BUT I CAN'T!
DO YOU LOVE ME? I KNOW YOU'LL SAY "YES" AND I'LL BELIEVE YOU.
EVEN IF YOU SWEAR IT, YOU MIGHT BE LYING – THEY SAY THAT JOVE, THE GOD OF OATHS, LAUGHS AT LOVERS' LIES.
IF YOU REALLY LOVE ME, SAY IT TRUTHFULLY, ROMEO.
OR, IF YOU THINK I'M YOURS TOO EASILY, I'LL FROWN AND PLAY HARD-TO-GET. THEN YOU'LL HAVE TO COURT ME TO WIN MY HEART.
BUT THE TRUTH IS, ROMEO MONTAGUE, I LOVE YOU. AND, BECAUSE OF THAT, YOU MAY THINK MY BEHAVIOUR IS TOO LOOSE.
BUT, TRUST ME, I'LL BE MORE FAITHFUL TO YOU THAN GIRLS WHO ACT ALL COY AND STAND-OFFISH.
I WOULD HAVE BEEN MORE LIKE THAT, BUT YOU OVERHEARD WHAT I SAID, AND IT'S NO USE DENYING IT NOW. SO, YOU'LL HAVE TO MAKE ALLOWANCES AND NOT UNDERESTIMATE THIS LOVE YOU ACCIDENTALLY STUMBLED UPON IN THE DARKNESS.
LADY, I SWEAR BY THE MOON ABOVE US -- THAT SHINES ITS LIGHT ON THE TOPS OF THE FRUIT TREES --
GASP!
DON'T SWEAR BY THE MOON. THE MOON IS FICKLE: IT CHANGES ITS POSITION IN THE SKY EVERY MONTH.
DON'T SWEAR BY IT, IN CASE YOUR LOVE TURNS OUT TO BE FICKLE TOO.
WHAT SHALL I SWEAR BY?

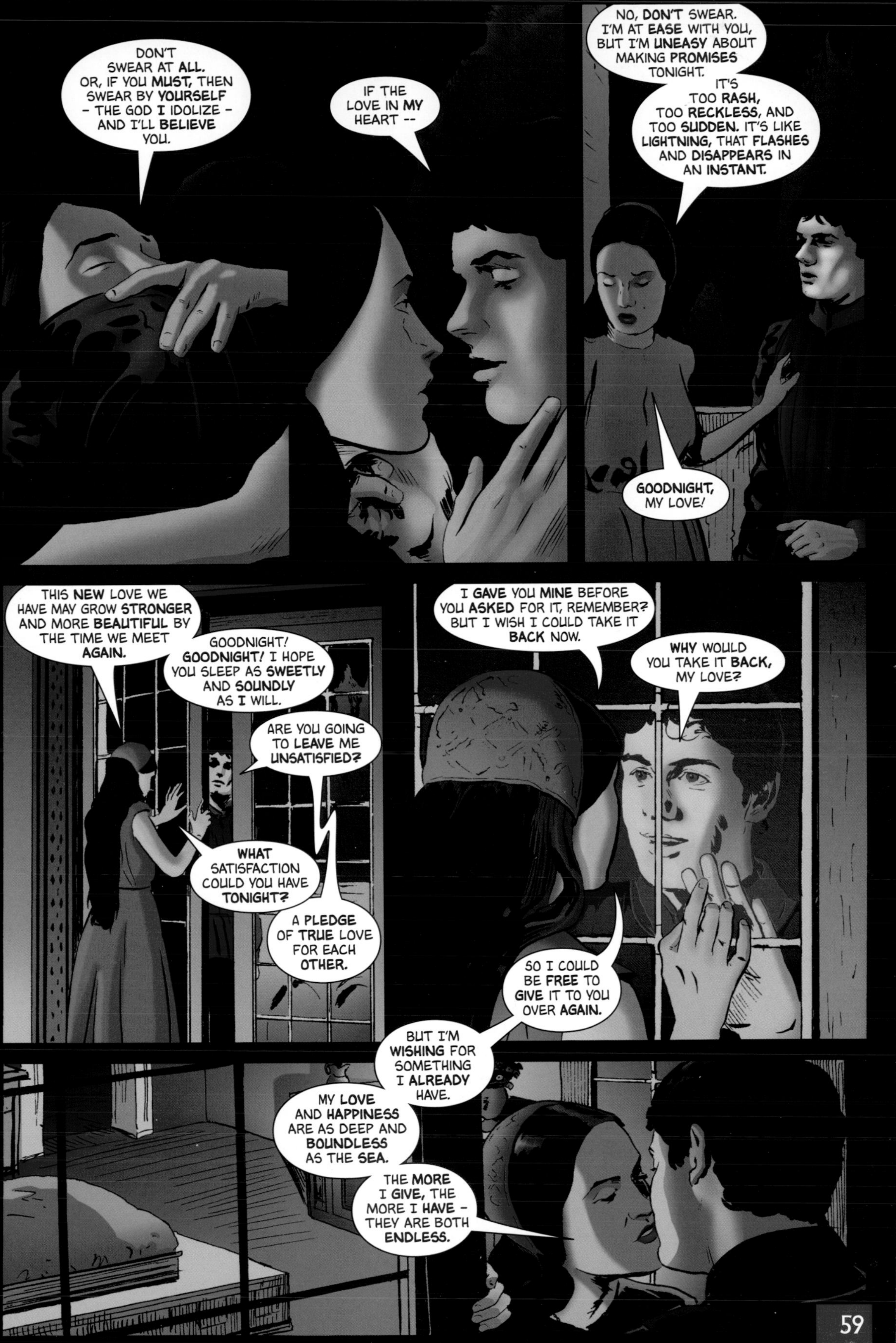

DON'T SWEAR AT ALL. OR, IF YOU MUST, THEN SWEAR BY YOURSELF - THE GOD I IDOLIZE - AND I'LL BELIEVE YOU.
IF THE LOVE IN MY HEART --
NO, DON'T SWEAR. I'M AT EASE WITH YOU, BUT I'M UNEASY ABOUT MAKING PROMISES TONIGHT.
IT'S TOO RASH, TOO RECKLESS, AND TOO SUDDEN. IT'S LIKE LIGHTNING, THAT FLASHES AND DISAPPEARS IN AN INSTANT.
GOODNIGHT, MY LOVE!
THIS NEW LOVE WE HAVE MAY GROW STRONGER AND MORE BEAUTIFUL BY THE TIME WE MEET AGAIN.
GOODNIGHT! GOODNIGHT! I HOPE YOU SLEEP AS SWEETLY AND SOUNDLY AS I WILL.
ARE YOU GOING TO LEAVE ME UNSATISFIED?
WHAT SATISFACTION COULD YOU HAVE TONIGHT?
A PLEDGE OF TRUE LOVE FOR EACH OTHER.
I GAVE YOU MINE BEFORE YOU ASKED FOR IT, REMEMBER? BUT I WISH I COULD TAKE IT BACK NOW.
WHY WOULD YOU TAKE IT BACK, MY LOVE?
SO I COULD BE FREE TO GIVE IT TO YOU OVER AGAIN.
BUT I'M WISHING FOR SOMETHING I ALREADY HAVE.
MY LOVE AND HAPPINESS ARE AS DEEP AND BOUNDLESS AS THE SEA.
THE MORE I GIVE, THE MORE I HAVE - THEY ARE BOTH ENDLESS.

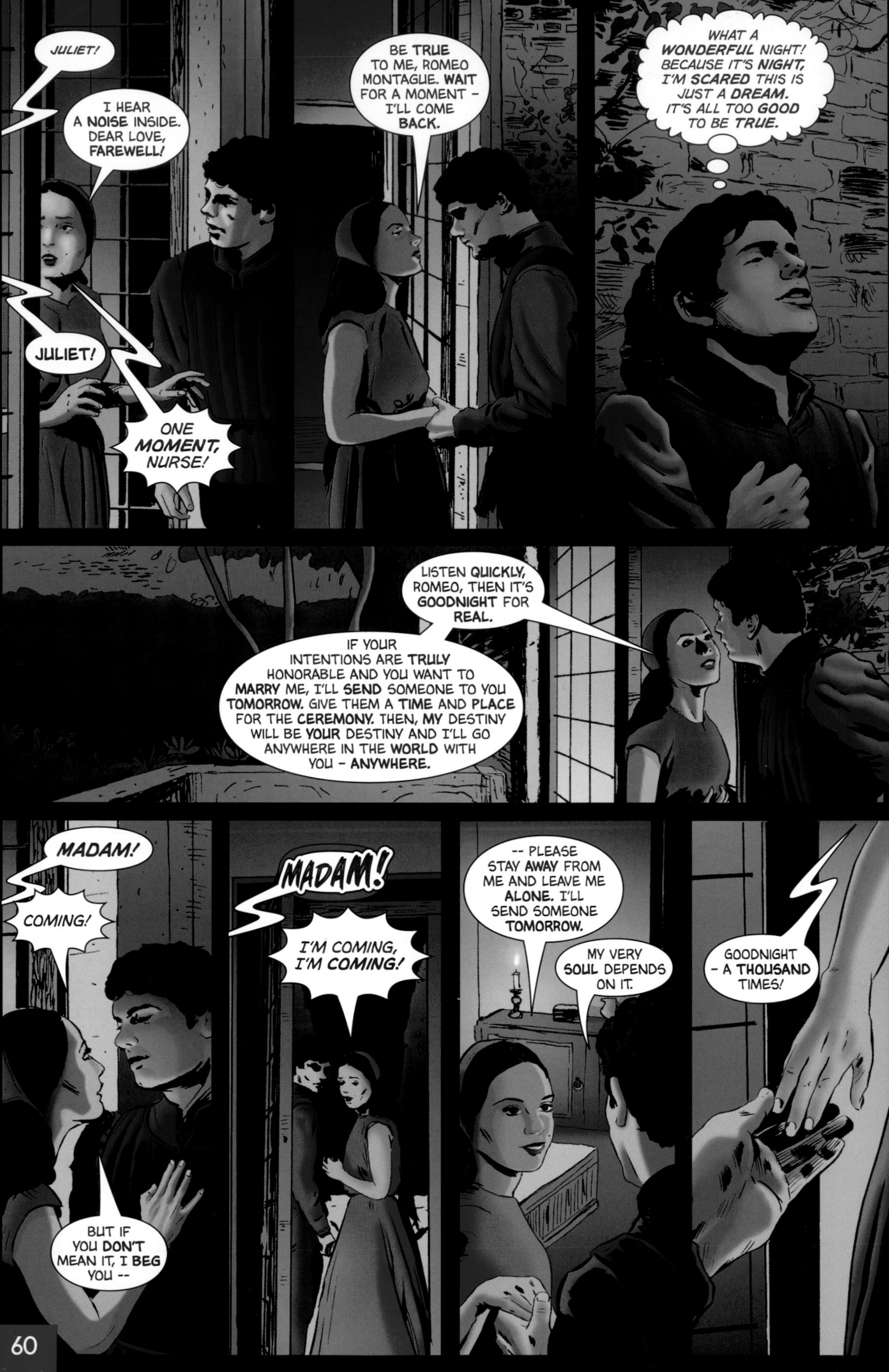
JULIET!
I HEAR A NOISE INSIDE. DEAR LOVE, FAREWELL!
JULIET!
ONE MOMENT, NURSE!
BE TRUE TO ME, ROMEO MONTAGUE. WAIT FOR A MOMENT - I'LL COME BACK.
WHAT A WONDERFUL NIGHT! BECAUSE IT'S NIGHT, I'M SCARED THIS IS JUST A DREAM. IT'S ALL TOO GOOD TO BE TRUE.
LISTEN QUICKLY, ROMEO, THEN IT'S GOODNIGHT FOR REAL.
IF YOUR INTENTIONS ARE TRULY HONORABLE AND YOU WANT TO MARRY ME, I'LL SEND SOMEONE TO YOU TOMORROW. GIVE THEM A TIME AND PLACE FOR THE CEREMONY. THEN, MY DESTINY WILL BE YOUR DESTINY AND I'LL GO ANYWHERE IN THE WORLD WITH YOU - ANYWHERE.
MADAM!
COMING!
BUT IF YOU DON'T MEAN IT, I BEG YOU --
MADAM!
I'M COMING, I'M COMING!
-- PLEASE STAY AWAY FROM ME AND LEAVE ME ALONE. I'LL SEND SOMEONE TOMORROW.
MY VERY SOUL DEPENDS ON IT.
GOODNIGHT - A THOUSAND TIMES!

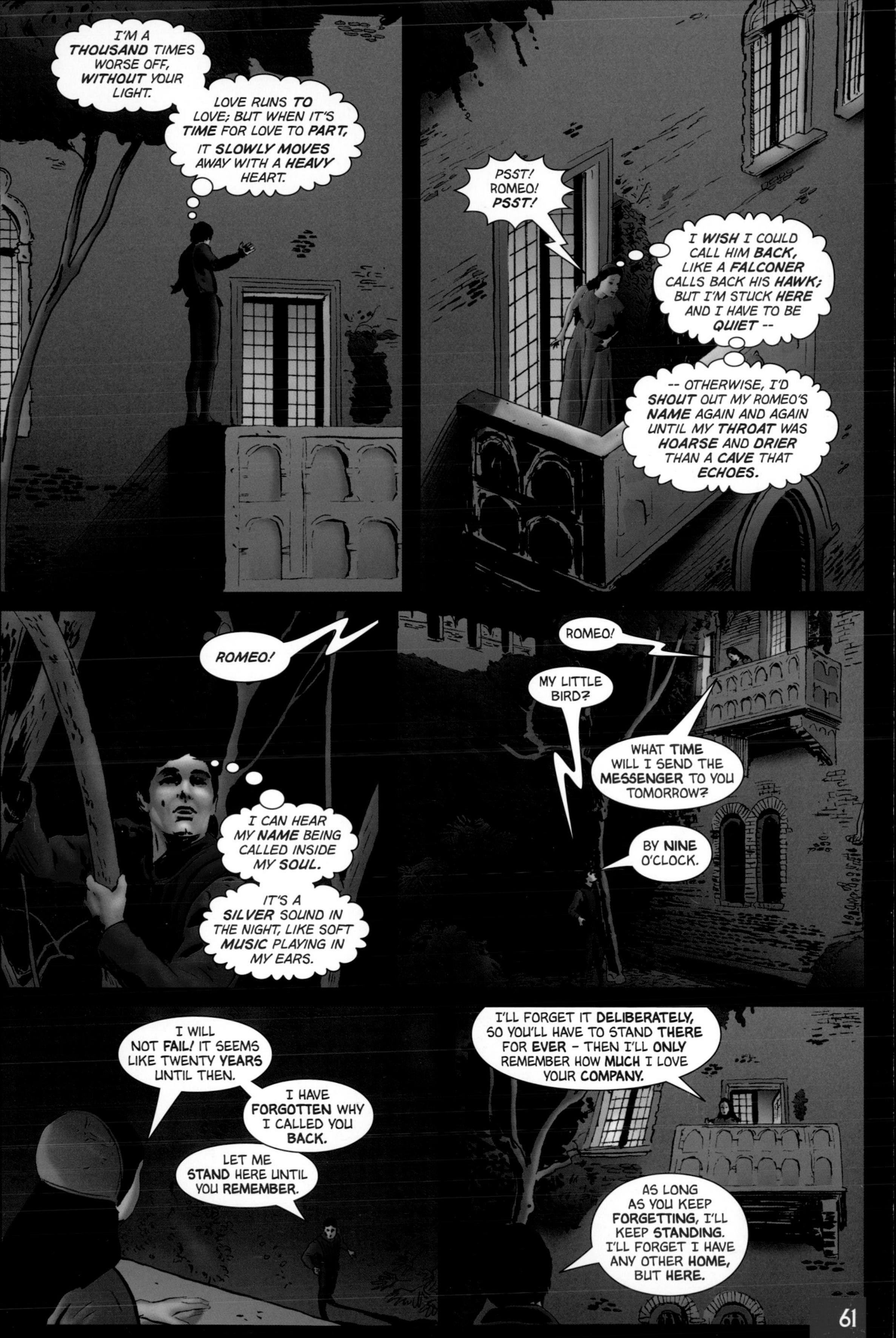
I'M A THOUSAND TIMES WORSE OFF, WITHOUT YOUR LIGHT.
LOVE RUNS TO LOVE; BUT WHEN IT'S TIME FOR LOVE TO PART, IT SLOWLY MOVES AWAY WITH A HEAVY HEART.
PSST! ROMEO! PSST!
I WISH I COULD CALL HIM BACK, LIKE A FALCONER CALLS BACK HIS HAWK; BUT I'M STUCK HERE AND I HAVE TO BE QUIET --
-- OTHERWISE, I'D SHOUT OUT MY ROMEO'S NAME AGAIN AND AGAIN UNTIL MY THROAT WAS HOARSE AND DRIER THAN A CAVE THAT ECHOES.
ROMEO!
I CAN HEAR MY NAME BEING CALLED INSIDE MY SOUL.
IT'S A SILVER SOUND IN THE NIGHT, LIKE SOFT MUSIC PLAYING IN MY EARS.
ROMEO!
MY LITTLE BIRD?
WHAT TIME WILL I SEND THE MESSENGER TO YOU TOMORROW?
BY NINE O'CLOCK.
I WILL NOT FAIL! IT SEEMS LIKE TWENTY YEARS UNTIL THEN.
I HAVE FORGOTTEN WHY I CALLED YOU BACK.
LET ME STAND HERE UNTIL YOU REMEMBER.
I'LL FORGET IT DELIBERATELY, SO YOU'LL HAVE TO STAND THERE FOR EVER - THEN I'LL ONLY REMEMBER HOW MUCH I LOVE YOUR COMPANY.
AS LONG AS YOU KEEP FORGETTING, I'LL KEEP STANDING. I'LL FORGET I HAVE ANY OTHER HOME, BUT HERE.

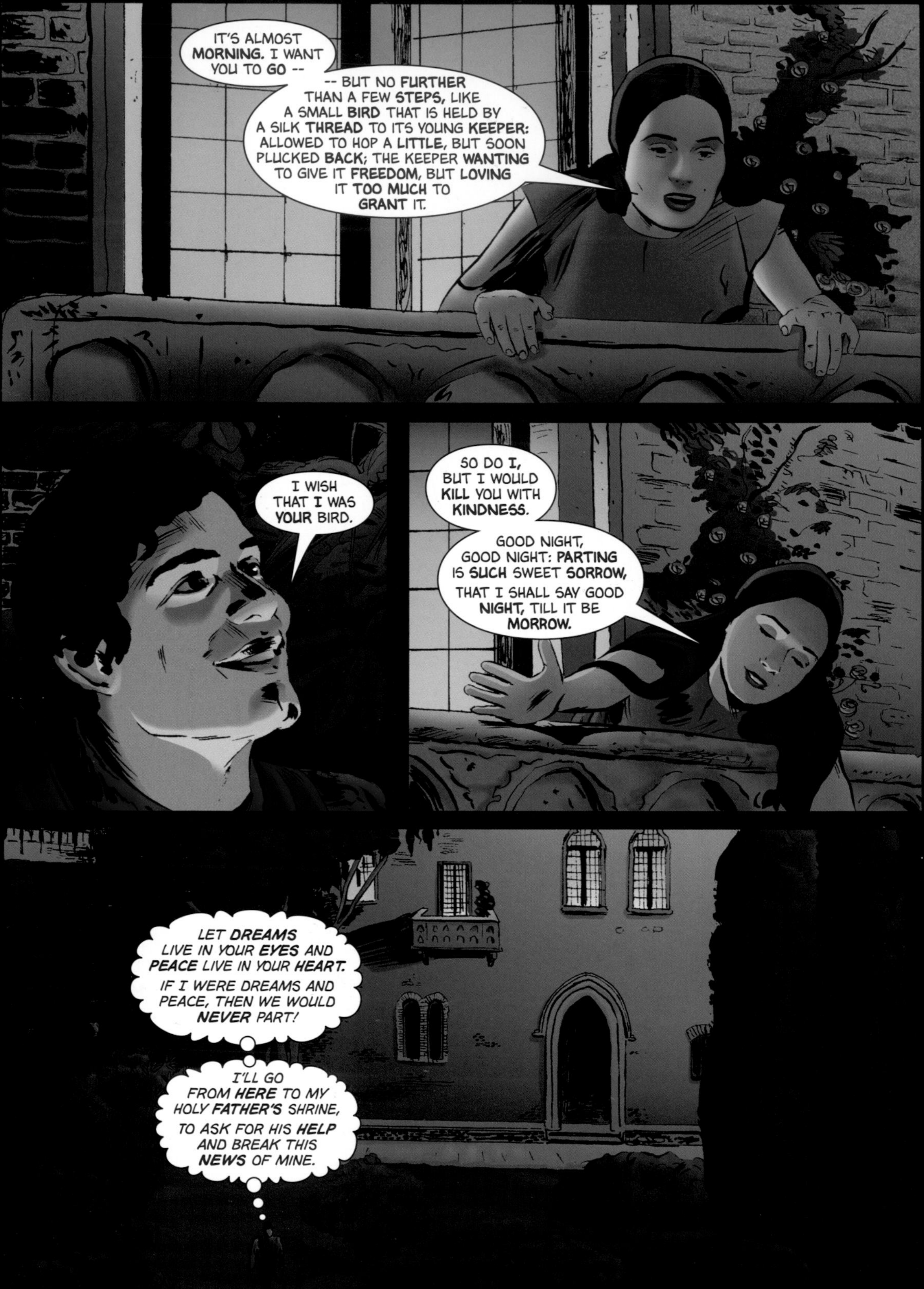
IT'S ALMOST MORNING. I WANT YOU TO GO --
-- BUT NO FURTHER THAN A FEW STEPS, LIKE A SMALL BIRD THAT IS HELD BY A SILK THREAD TO ITS YOUNG KEEPER: ALLOWED TO HOP A LITTLE, BUT SOON PLUCKED BACK; THE KEEPER WANTING TO GIVE IT FREEDOM, BUT LOVING IT TOO MUCH TO GRANT IT.
I WISH THAT I WAS YOUR BIRD.
SO DO I, BUT I WOULD KILL YOU WITH KINDNESS.
GOOD NIGHT, GOOD NIGHT: PARTING IS SUCH SWEET SORROW, THAT I SHALL SAY GOOD NIGHT, TILL IT BE MORROW.
LET DREAMS LIVE IN YOUR EYES AND PEACE LIVE IN YOUR HEART. IF I WERE DREAMS AND PEACE, THEN WE WOULD NEVER PART!
I'LL GO FROM HERE TO MY HOLY FATHER'S SHRINE, TO ASK FOR HIS HELP AND BREAK THIS NEWS OF MINE.

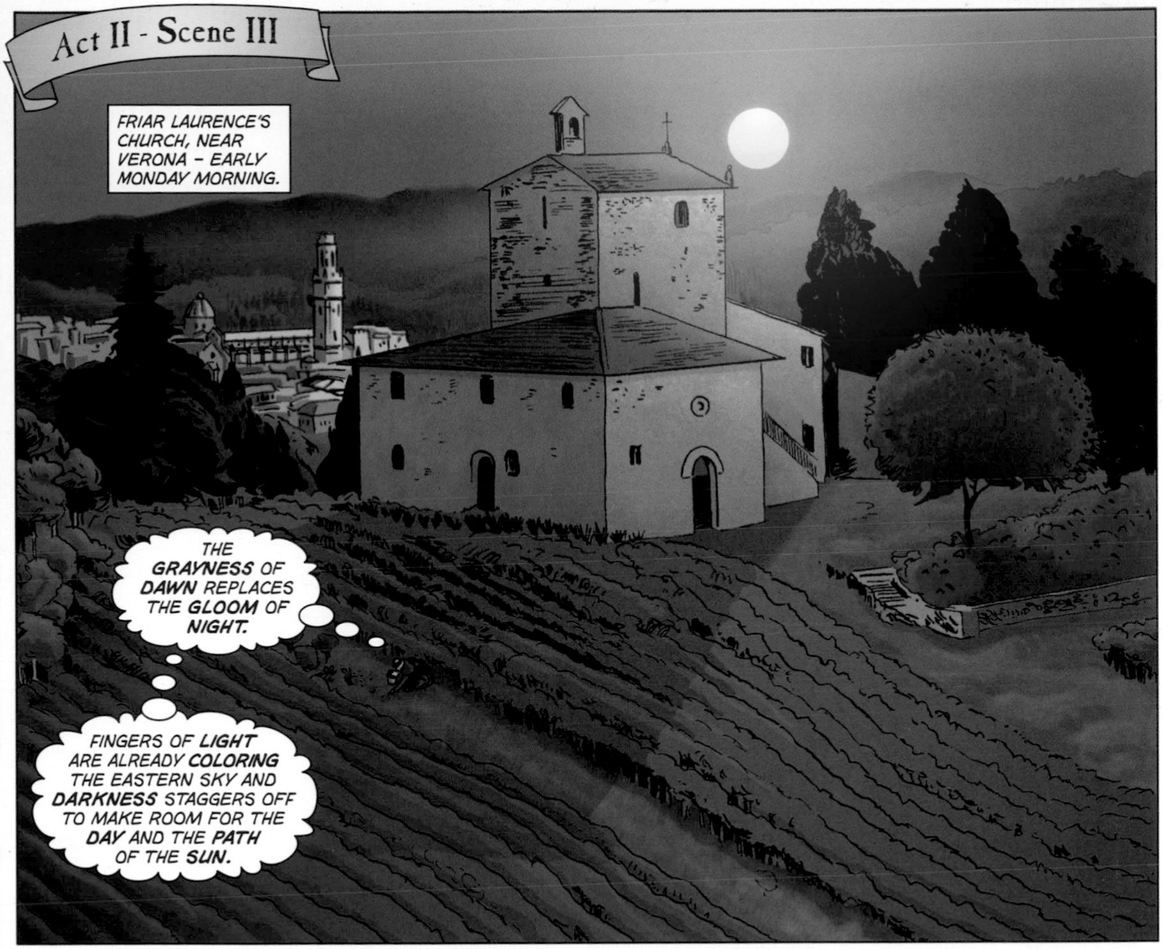

Act II - Scene III
FRIAR LAURENCE'S CHURCH, NEAR VERONA – EARLY MONDAY MORNING.
THE GRAYNESS OF DAWN REPLACES THE GLOOM OF NIGHT.
FINGERS OF LIGHT ARE ALREADY COLORING THE EASTERN SKY AND DARKNESS STAGGERS OFF TO MAKE ROOM FOR THE DAY AND THE PATH OF THE SUN.

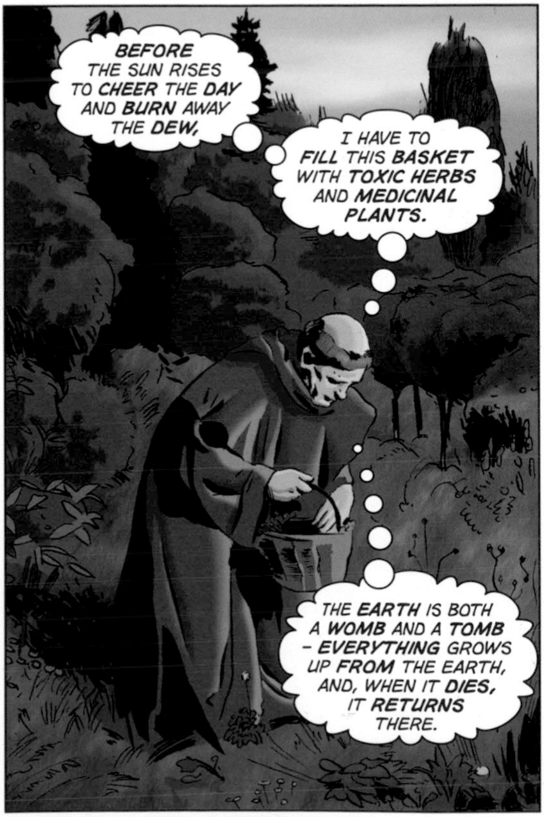

BEFORE THE SUN RISES TO CHEER THE DAY AND BURN AWAY THE DEW,
I HAVE TO FILL THIS BASKET WITH TOXIC HERBS AND MEDICINAL PLANTS.
THE EARTH IS BOTH A WOMB AND A TOMB – EVERYTHING GROWS UP FROM THE EARTH, AND, WHEN IT DIES, IT RETURNS THERE.

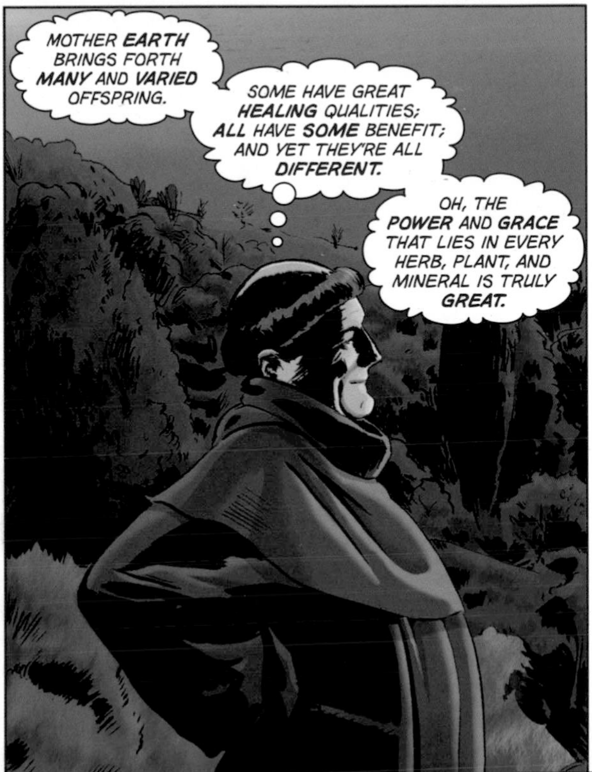

MOTHER EARTH BRINGS FORTH MANY AND VARIED OFFSPRING.
SOME HAVE GREAT HEALING QUALITIES; ALL HAVE SOME BENEFIT; AND YET THEY'RE ALL DIFFERENT.
OH, THE POWER AND GRACE THAT LIES IN EVERY HERB, PLANT, AND MINERAL IS TRULY GREAT.

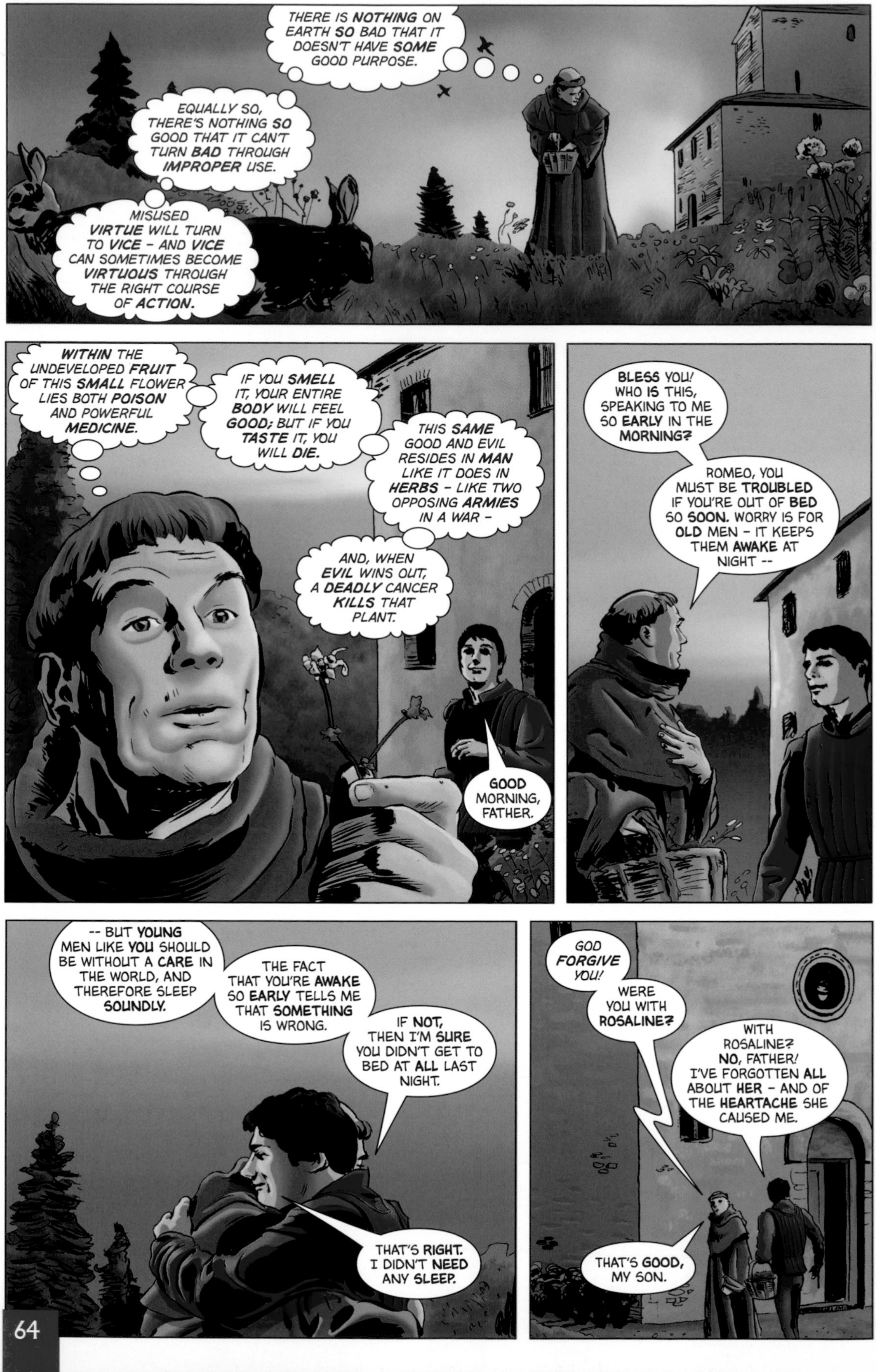
THERE IS NOTHING ON EARTH SO BAD THAT IT DOESN'T HAVE SOME GOOD PURPOSE.
EQUALLY SO, THERE'S NOTHING SO GOOD THAT IT CAN'T TURN BAD THROUGH IMPROPER USE.
MISUSED VIRTUE WILL TURN TO VICE - AND VICE CAN SOMETIMES BECOME VIRTUOUS THROUGH THE RIGHT COURSE OF ACTION.
WITHIN THE UNDEVELOPED FRUIT OF THIS SMALL FLOWER LIES BOTH POISON AND POWERFUL MEDICINE.
IF YOU SMELL IT, YOUR ENTIRE BODY WILL FEEL GOOD; BUT IF YOU TASTE IT, YOU WILL DIE.
THIS SAME GOOD AND EVIL RESIDES IN MAN LIKE IT DOES IN HERBS - LIKE TWO OPPOSING ARMIES IN A WAR -
AND, WHEN EVIL WINS OUT, A DEADLY CANCER KILLS THAT PLANT.
GOOD MORNING, FATHER.
BLESS YOU! WHO IS THIS, SPEAKING TO ME SO EARLY IN THE MORNING?
ROMEO, YOU MUST BE TROUBLED IF YOU'RE OUT OF BED SO SOON. WORRY IS FOR OLD MEN - IT KEEPS THEM AWAKE AT NIGHT --
-- BUT YOUNG MEN LIKE YOU SHOULD BE WITHOUT A CARE IN THE WORLD, AND THEREFORE SLEEP SOUNDLY.
THE FACT THAT YOU'RE AWAKE SO EARLY TELLS ME THAT SOMETHING IS WRONG.
IF NOT, THEN I'M SURE YOU DIDN'T GET TO BED AT ALL LAST NIGHT.
THAT'S RIGHT. I DIDN'T NEED ANY SLEEP.
GOD FORGIVE YOU!
WERE YOU WITH ROSALINE?
WITH ROSALINE? NO, FATHER! I'VE FORGOTTEN ALL ABOUT HER - AND OF THE HEARTACHE SHE CAUSED ME.
THAT'S GOOD, MY SON.

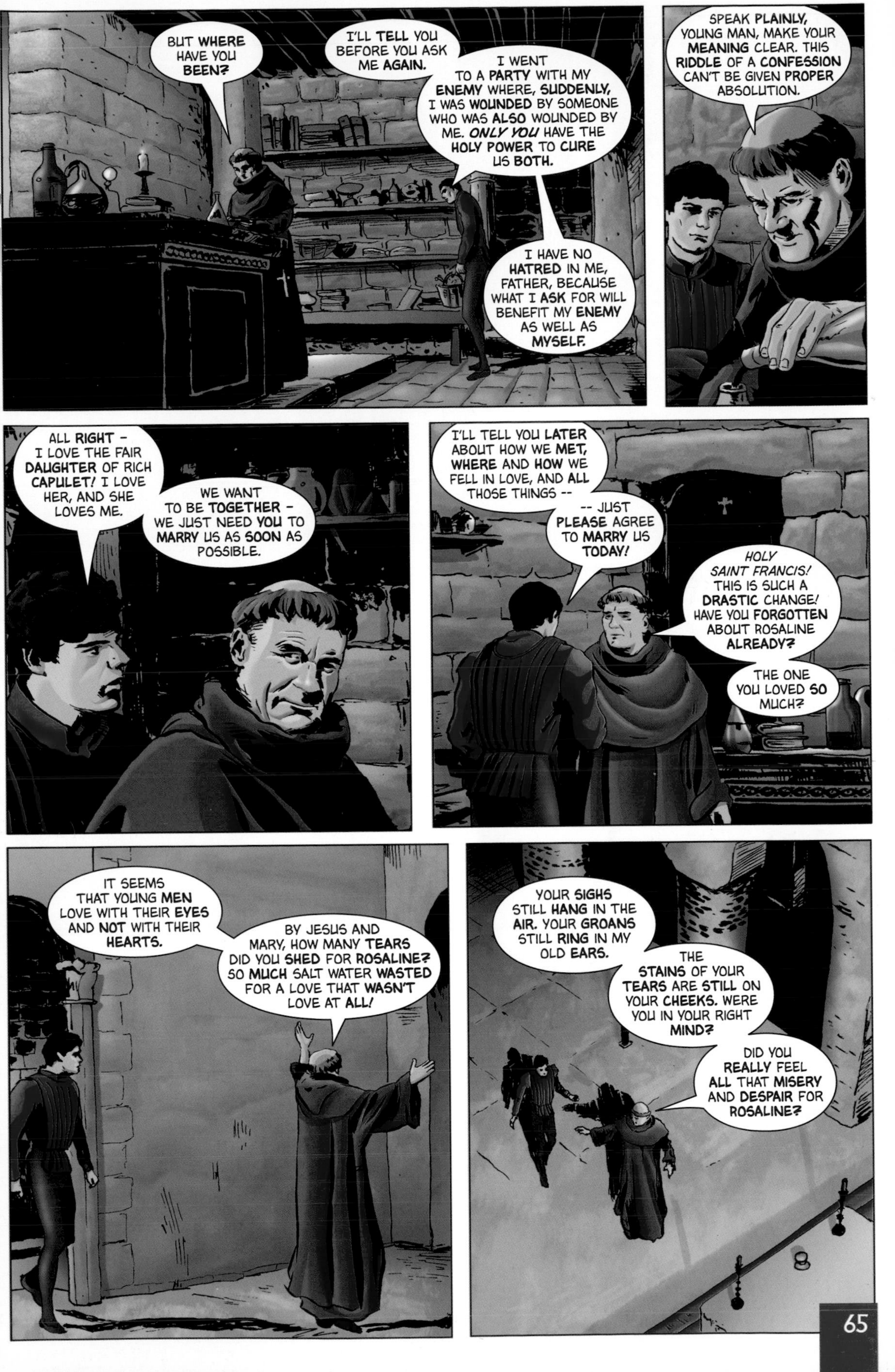
BUT WHERE HAVE YOU BEEN?
I'LL TELL YOU BEFORE YOU ASK ME AGAIN.
I WENT TO A PARTY WITH MY ENEMY WHERE, SUDDENLY, I WAS WOUNDED BY SOMEONE WHO WAS ALSO WOUNDED BY ME. ONLY YOU HAVE THE HOLY POWER TO CURE US BOTH.
I HAVE NO HATRED IN ME, FATHER, BECAUSE WHAT I ASK FOR WILL BENEFIT MY ENEMY AS WELL AS MYSELF.
SPEAK PLAINLY, YOUNG MAN, MAKE YOUR MEANING CLEAR. THIS RIDDLE OF A CONFESSION CAN'T BE GIVEN PROPER ABSOLUTION.
ALL RIGHT – I LOVE THE FAIR DAUGHTER OF RICH CAPULET! I LOVE HER, AND SHE LOVES ME.
WE WANT TO BE TOGETHER – WE JUST NEED YOU TO MARRY US AS SOON AS POSSIBLE.
I'LL TELL YOU LATER ABOUT HOW WE MET, WHERE AND HOW WE FELL IN LOVE, AND ALL THOSE THINGS --
-- JUST PLEASE AGREE TO MARRY US TODAY!
HOLY SAINT FRANCIS! THIS IS SUCH A DRASTIC CHANGE! HAVE YOU FORGOTTEN ABOUT ROSALINE ALREADY?
THE ONE YOU LOVED SO MUCH?
IT SEEMS THAT YOUNG MEN LOVE WITH THEIR EYES AND NOT WITH THEIR HEARTS.
BY JESUS AND MARY, HOW MANY TEARS DID YOU SHED FOR ROSALINE? SO MUCH SALT WATER WASTED FOR A LOVE THAT WASN'T LOVE AT ALL!
YOUR SIGHS STILL HANG IN THE AIR. YOUR GROANS STILL RING IN MY OLD EARS.
THE STAINS OF YOUR TEARS ARE STILL ON YOUR CHEEKS. WERE YOU IN YOUR RIGHT MIND?
DID YOU REALLY FEEL ALL THAT MISERY AND DESPAIR FOR ROSALINE?

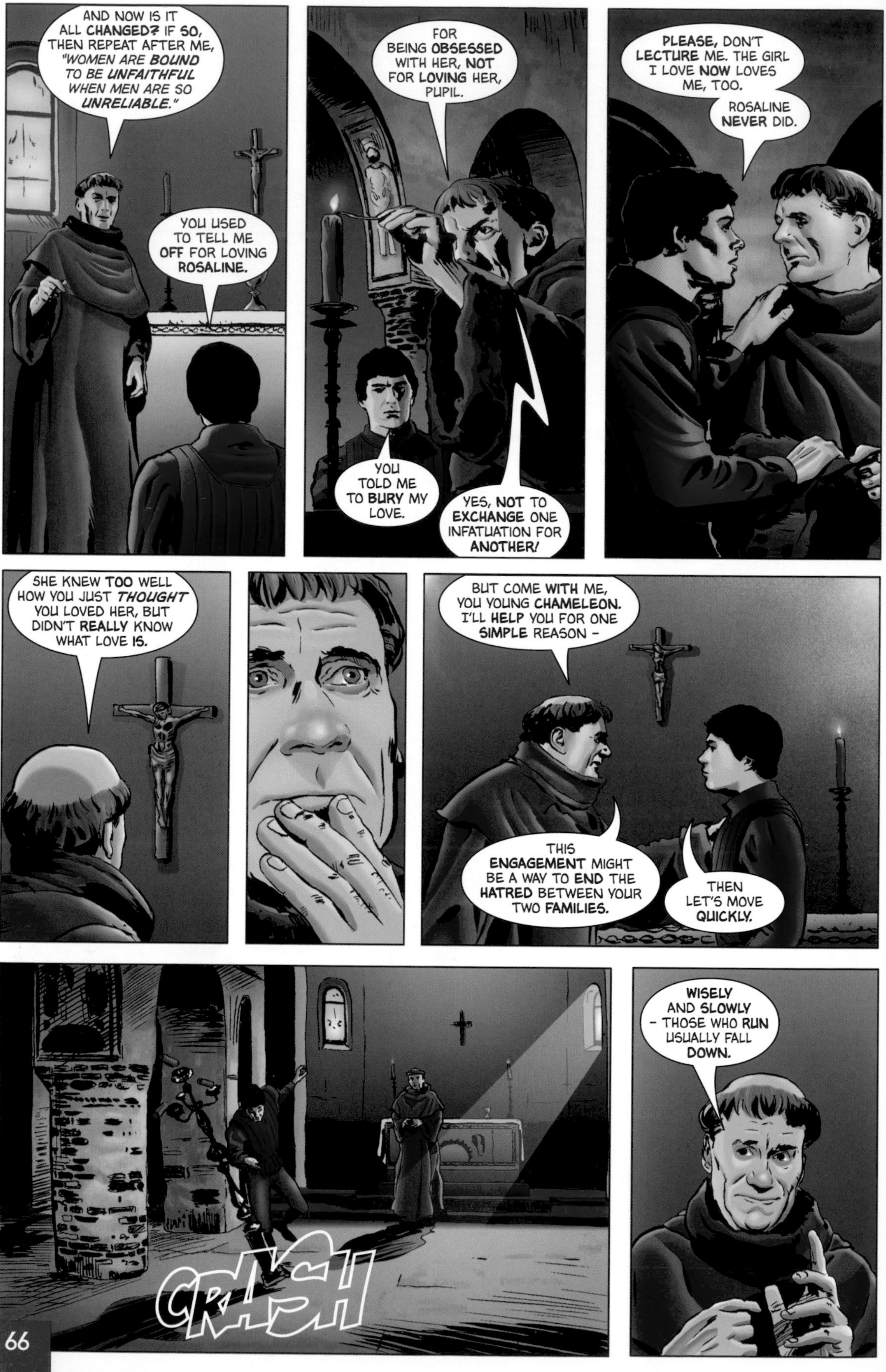
AND NOW IS IT ALL CHANGED? IF SO, THEN REPEAT AFTER ME, "WOMEN ARE BOUND TO BE UNFAITHFUL WHEN MEN ARE SO UNRELIABLE."
YOU USED TO TELL ME OFF FOR LOVING ROSALINE.
FOR BEING OBSESSED WITH HER, NOT FOR LOVING HER, PUPIL.
YOU TOLD ME TO BURY MY LOVE.
YES, NOT TO EXCHANGE ONE INFATUATION FOR ANOTHER!
PLEASE, DON'T LECTURE ME. THE GIRL I LOVE NOW LOVES ME, TOO.
ROSALINE NEVER DID.
SHE KNEW TOO WELL HOW YOU JUST THOUGHT YOU LOVED HER, BUT DIDN'T REALLY KNOW WHAT LOVE IS.
BUT COME WITH ME, YOU YOUNG CHAMELEON. I'LL HELP YOU FOR ONE SIMPLE REASON –
THIS ENGAGEMENT MIGHT BE A WAY TO END THE HATRED BETWEEN YOUR TWO FAMILIES.
THEN LET'S MOVE QUICKLY.
CRASH
WISELY AND SLOWLY – THOSE WHO RUN USUALLY FALL DOWN.

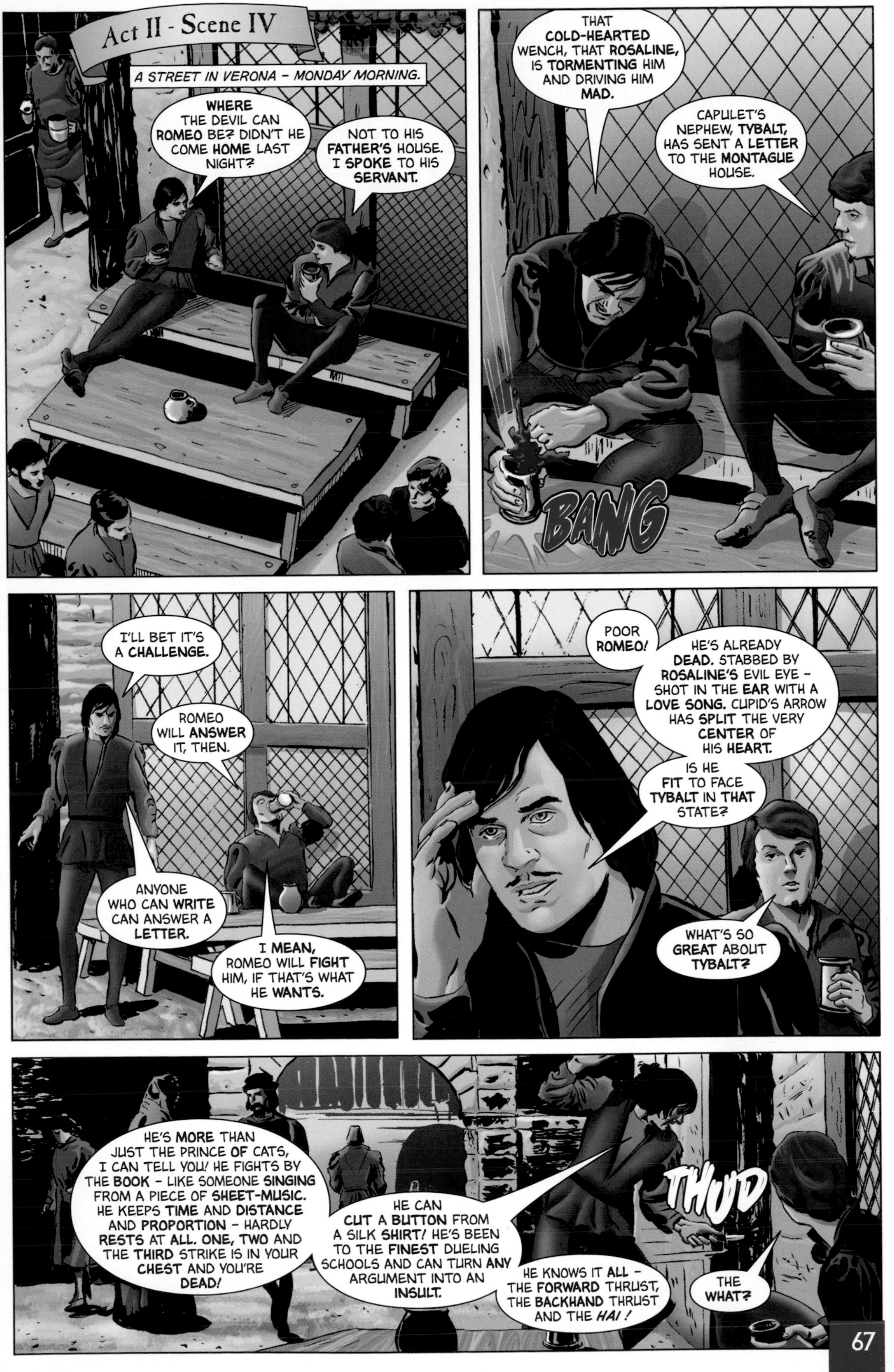
Act II - Scene IV
A STREET IN VERONA – MONDAY MORNING.
WHERE THE DEVIL CAN ROMEO BE? DIDN'T HE COME HOME LAST NIGHT?
NOT TO HIS FATHER'S HOUSE. I SPOKE TO HIS SERVANT.
THAT COLD-HEARTED WENCH, THAT ROSALINE, IS TORMENTING HIM AND DRIVING HIM MAD.
CAPULET'S NEPHEW, TYBALT, HAS SENT A LETTER TO THE MONTAGUE HOUSE.
BANG
I'LL BET IT'S A CHALLENGE.
ROMEO WILL ANSWER IT, THEN.
ANYONE WHO CAN WRITE CAN ANSWER A LETTER.
I MEAN, ROMEO WILL FIGHT HIM, IF THAT'S WHAT HE WANTS.
POOR ROMEO!
HE'S ALREADY DEAD. STABBED BY ROSALINE'S EVIL EYE – SHOT IN THE EAR WITH A LOVE SONG. CUPID'S ARROW HAS SPLIT THE VERY CENTER OF HIS HEART.
IS HE FIT TO FACE TYBALT IN THAT STATE?
WHAT'S SO GREAT ABOUT TYBALT?
HE'S MORE THAN JUST THE PRINCE OF CATS, I CAN TELL YOU! HE FIGHTS BY THE BOOK – LIKE SOMEONE SINGING FROM A PIECE OF SHEET-MUSIC. HE KEEPS TIME AND DISTANCE AND PROPORTION – HARDLY RESTS AT ALL. ONE, TWO AND THE THIRD STRIKE IS IN YOUR CHEST AND YOU'RE DEAD!
HE CAN CUT A BUTTON FROM A SILK SHIRT! HE'S BEEN TO THE FINEST DUELING SCHOOLS AND CAN TURN ANY ARGUMENT INTO AN INSULT.
HE KNOWS IT ALL – THE FORWARD THRUST, THE BACKHAND THRUST AND THE HAI !
THUD
THE WHAT?

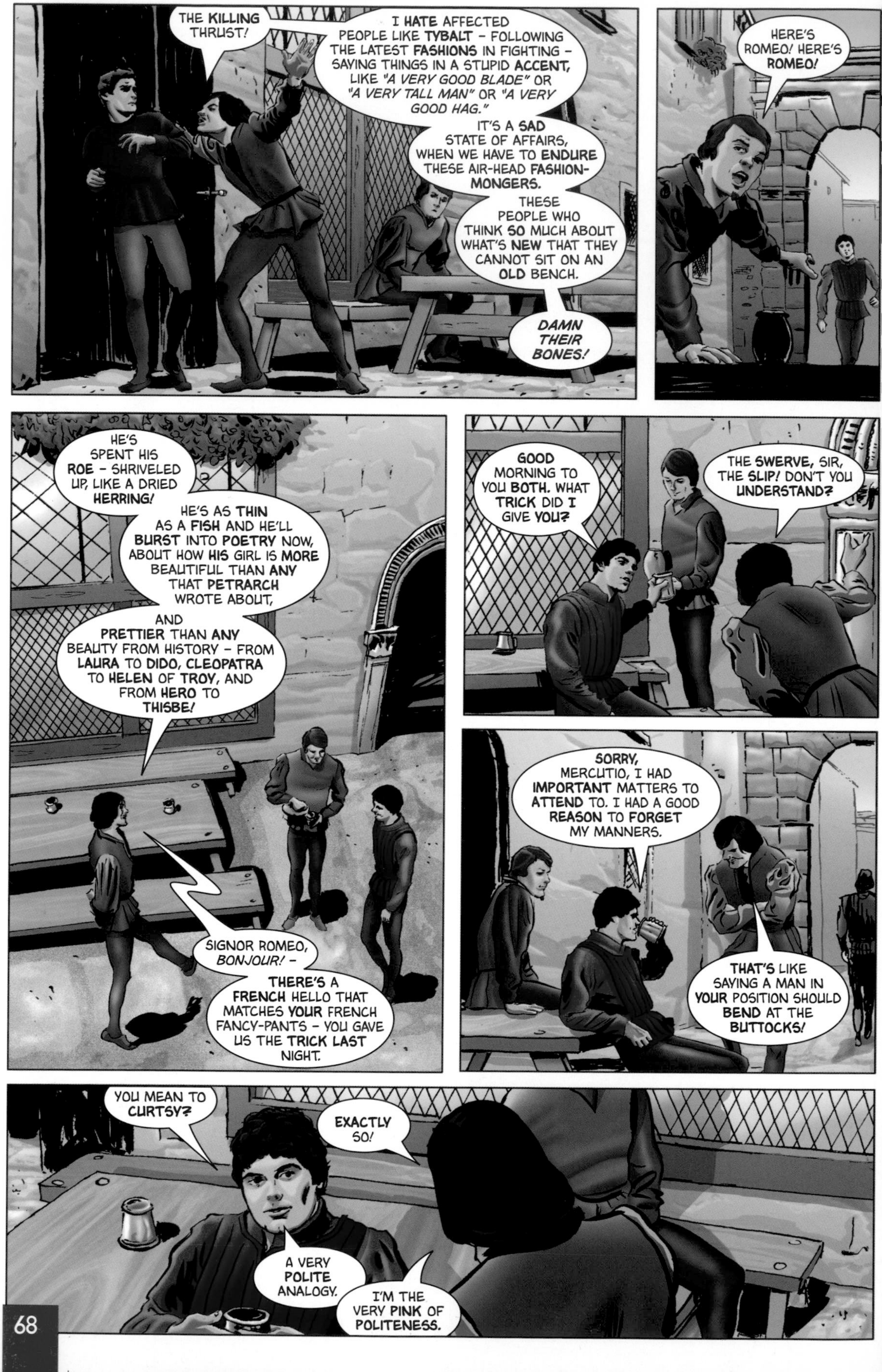

THE KILLING THRUST!
I HATE AFFECTED PEOPLE LIKE TYBALT – FOLLOWING THE LATEST FASHIONS IN FIGHTING – SAYING THINGS IN A STUPID ACCENT, LIKE "A VERY GOOD BLADE" OR "A VERY TALL MAN" OR "A VERY GOOD HAG."
IT'S A SAD STATE OF AFFAIRS, WHEN WE HAVE TO ENDURE THESE AIR-HEAD FASHION-MONGERS.
THESE PEOPLE WHO THINK SO MUCH ABOUT WHAT'S NEW THAT THEY CANNOT SIT ON AN OLD BENCH.
DAMN THEIR BONES!
HERE'S ROMEO! HERE'S ROMEO!
HE'S SPENT HIS ROE – SHRIVELED UP, LIKE A DRIED HERRING!
HE'S AS THIN AS A FISH AND HE'LL BURST INTO POETRY NOW, ABOUT HOW HIS GIRL IS MORE BEAUTIFUL THAN ANY THAT PETRARCH WROTE ABOUT,
AND PRETTIER THAN ANY BEAUTY FROM HISTORY – FROM LAURA TO DIDO, CLEOPATRA TO HELEN OF TROY, AND FROM HERO TO THISBE!
SIGNOR ROMEO, BONJOUR! –
THERE'S A FRENCH HELLO THAT MATCHES YOUR FRENCH FANCY-PANTS – YOU GAVE US THE TRICK LAST NIGHT.
GOOD MORNING TO YOU BOTH. WHAT TRICK DID I GIVE YOU?
THE SWERVE, SIR, THE SLIP! DON'T YOU UNDERSTAND?
SORRY, MERCUTIO, I HAD IMPORTANT MATTERS TO ATTEND TO. I HAD A GOOD REASON TO FORGET MY MANNERS.
THAT'S LIKE SAYING A MAN IN YOUR POSITION SHOULD BEND AT THE BUTTOCKS!
YOU MEAN TO CURTSY?
EXACTLY SO!
A VERY POLITE ANALOGY.
I'M THE VERY PINK OF POLITENESS.

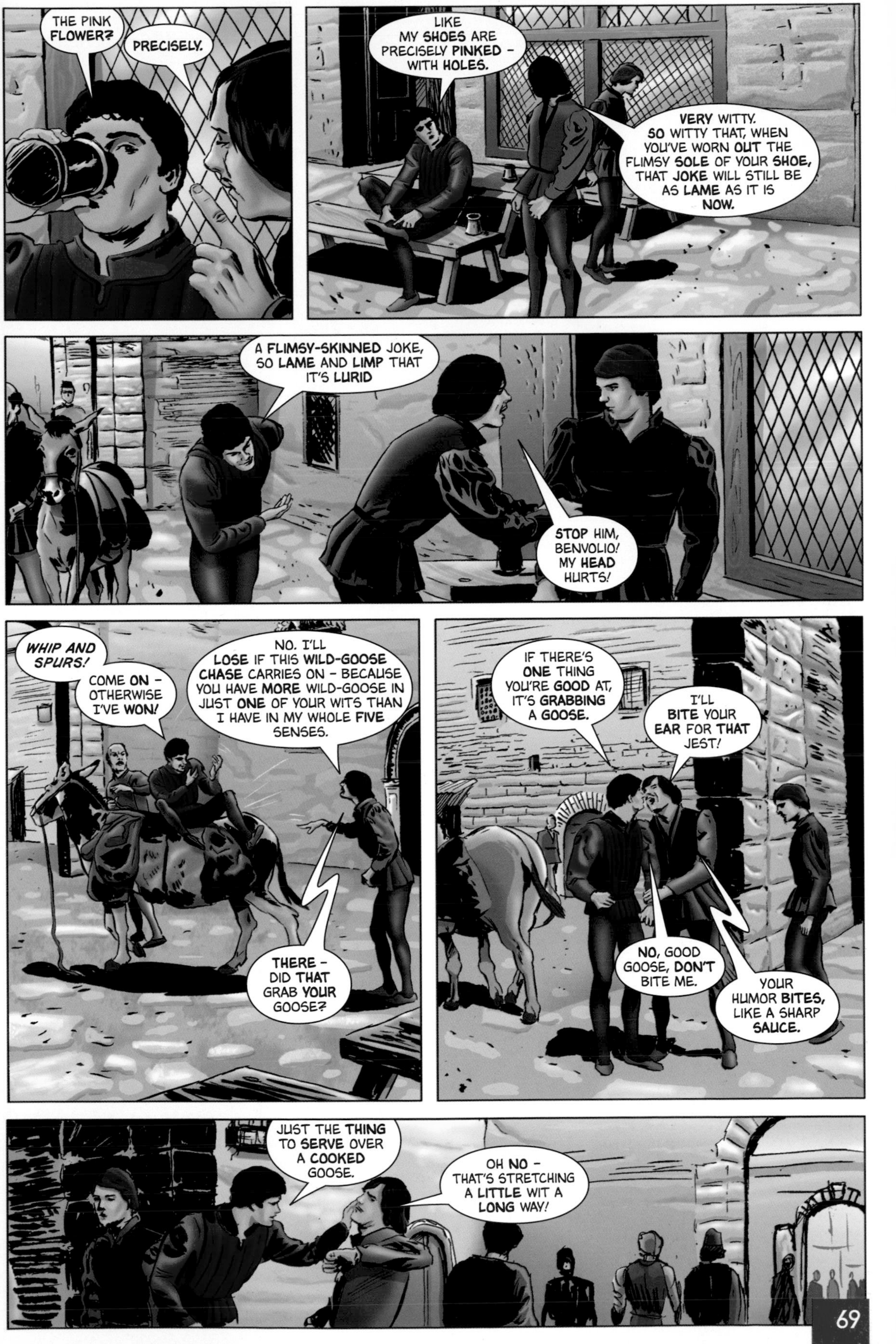
THE PINK FLOWER?
PRECISELY.
LIKE MY SHOES ARE PRECISELY PINKED – WITH HOLES.
VERY WITTY. SO WITTY THAT, WHEN YOU'VE WORN OUT THE FLIMSY SOLE OF YOUR SHOE, THAT JOKE WILL STILL BE AS LAME AS IT IS NOW.
A FLIMSY-SKINNED JOKE, SO LAME AND LIMP THAT IT'S LURID
STOP HIM, BENVOLIO! MY HEAD HURTS!
WHIP AND SPURS!
COME ON – OTHERWISE I'VE WON!
NO. I'LL LOSE IF THIS WILD-GOOSE CHASE CARRIES ON – BECAUSE YOU HAVE MORE WILD-GOOSE IN JUST ONE OF YOUR WITS THAN I HAVE IN MY WHOLE FIVE SENSES.
THERE – DID THAT GRAB YOUR GOOSE?
IF THERE'S ONE THING YOU'RE GOOD AT, IT'S GRABBING A GOOSE.
I'LL BITE YOUR EAR FOR THAT JEST!
NO, GOOD GOOSE, DON'T BITE ME.
YOUR HUMOR BITES, LIKE A SHARP SAUCE.
JUST THE THING TO SERVE OVER A COOKED GOOSE.
OH NO – THAT'S STRETCHING A LITTLE WIT A LONG WAY!

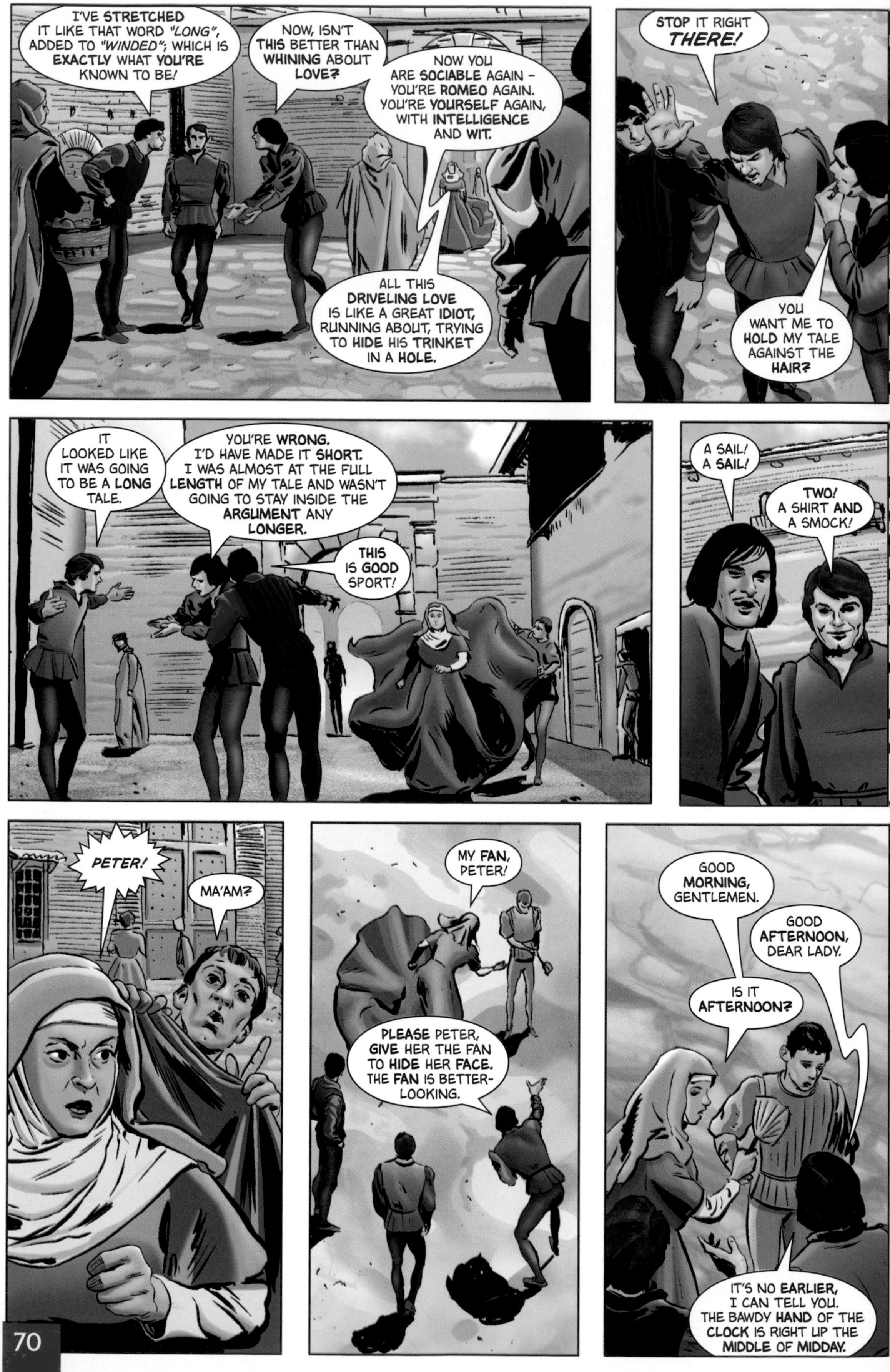
I'VE STRETCHED IT LIKE THAT WORD "LONG", ADDED TO "WINDED"; WHICH IS EXACTLY WHAT YOU'RE KNOWN TO BE!
NOW, ISN'T THIS BETTER THAN WHINING ABOUT LOVE?
NOW YOU ARE SOCIABLE AGAIN - YOU'RE ROMEO AGAIN. YOU'RE YOURSELF AGAIN, WITH INTELLIGENCE AND WIT.
ALL THIS DRIVELING LOVE IS LIKE A GREAT IDIOT, RUNNING ABOUT, TRYING TO HIDE HIS TRINKET IN A HOLE.
STOP IT RIGHT THERE!
YOU WANT ME TO HOLD MY TALE AGAINST THE HAIR?
IT LOOKED LIKE IT WAS GOING TO BE A LONG TALE.
YOU'RE WRONG. I'D HAVE MADE IT SHORT. I WAS ALMOST AT THE FULL LENGTH OF MY TALE AND WASN'T GOING TO STAY INSIDE THE ARGUMENT ANY LONGER.
THIS IS GOOD SPORT!
A SAIL! A SAIL!
TWO! A SHIRT AND A SMOCK!
PETER!
MA'AM?
MY FAN, PETER!
PLEASE PETER, GIVE HER THE FAN TO HIDE HER FACE. THE FAN IS BETTER-LOOKING.
GOOD MORNING, GENTLEMEN.
GOOD AFTERNOON, DEAR LADY.
IS IT AFTERNOON?
IT'S NO EARLIER, I CAN TELL YOU. THE BAWDY HAND OF THE CLOCK IS RIGHT UP THE MIDDLE OF MIDDAY.

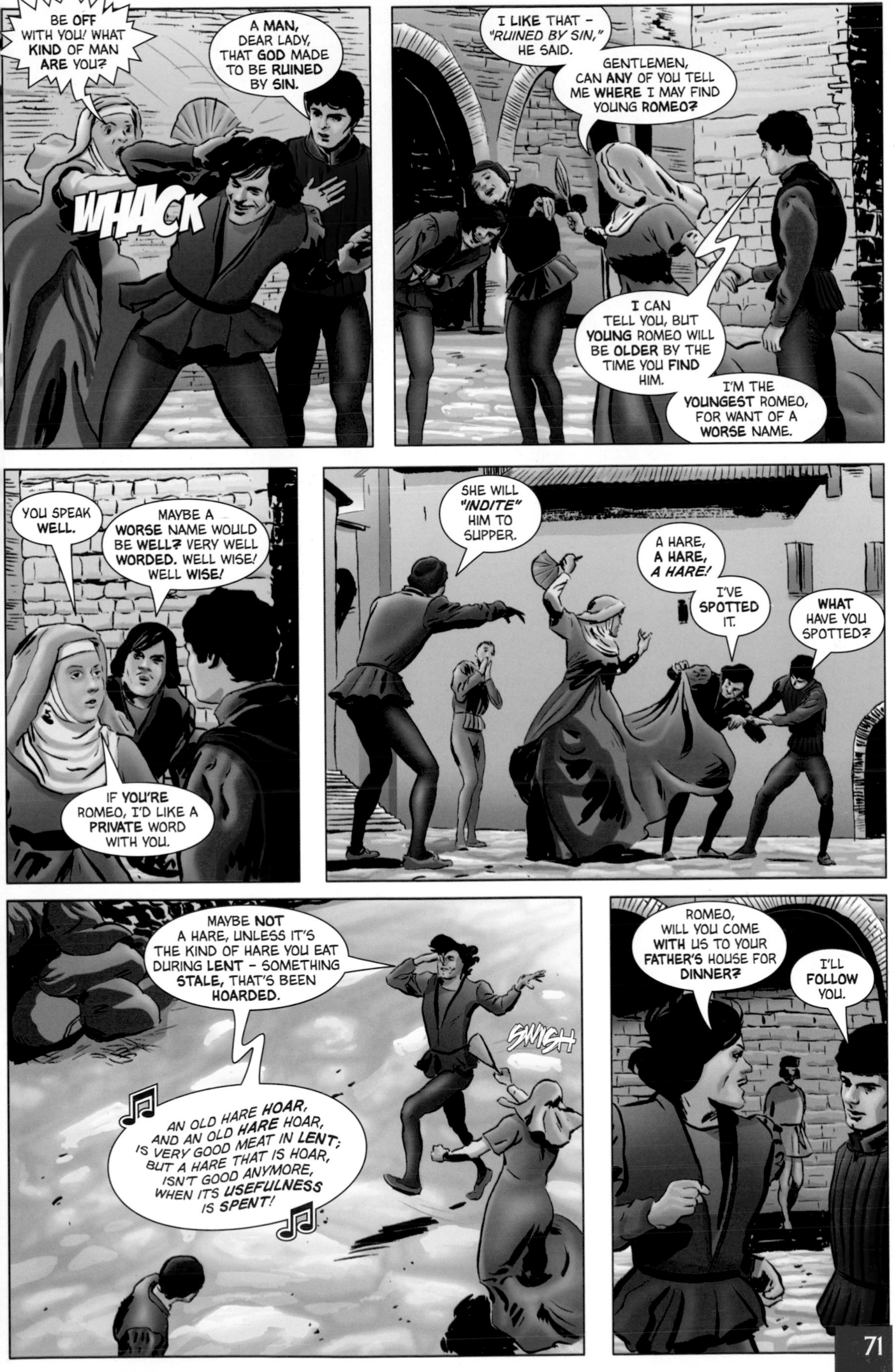
BE OFF WITH YOU! WHAT KIND OF MAN ARE YOU?
A MAN, DEAR LADY, THAT GOD MADE TO BE RUINED BY SIN.
WHACK
I LIKE THAT – "RUINED BY SIN," HE SAID.
GENTLEMEN, CAN ANY OF YOU TELL ME WHERE I MAY FIND YOUNG ROMEO?
I CAN TELL YOU, BUT YOUNG ROMEO WILL BE OLDER BY THE TIME YOU FIND HIM.
I'M THE YOUNGEST ROMEO, FOR WANT OF A WORSE NAME.
YOU SPEAK WELL.
MAYBE A WORSE NAME WOULD BE WELL? VERY WELL WORDED. WELL WISE! WELL WISE!
IF YOU'RE ROMEO, I'D LIKE A PRIVATE WORD WITH YOU.
SHE WILL "INDITE" HIM TO SUPPER.
A HARE, A HARE, A HARE!
I'VE SPOTTED IT.
WHAT HAVE YOU SPOTTED?
MAYBE NOT A HARE, UNLESS IT'S THE KIND OF HARE YOU EAT DURING LENT – SOMETHING STALE, THAT'S BEEN HOARDED.
SWISH
AN OLD HARE HOAR, AND AN OLD HARE HOAR, IS VERY GOOD MEAT IN LENT; BUT A HARE THAT IS HOAR, ISN'T GOOD ANYMORE, WHEN ITS USEFULNESS IS SPENT!
ROMEO, WILL YOU COME WITH US TO YOUR FATHER'S HOUSE FOR DINNER?
I'LL FOLLOW YOU.

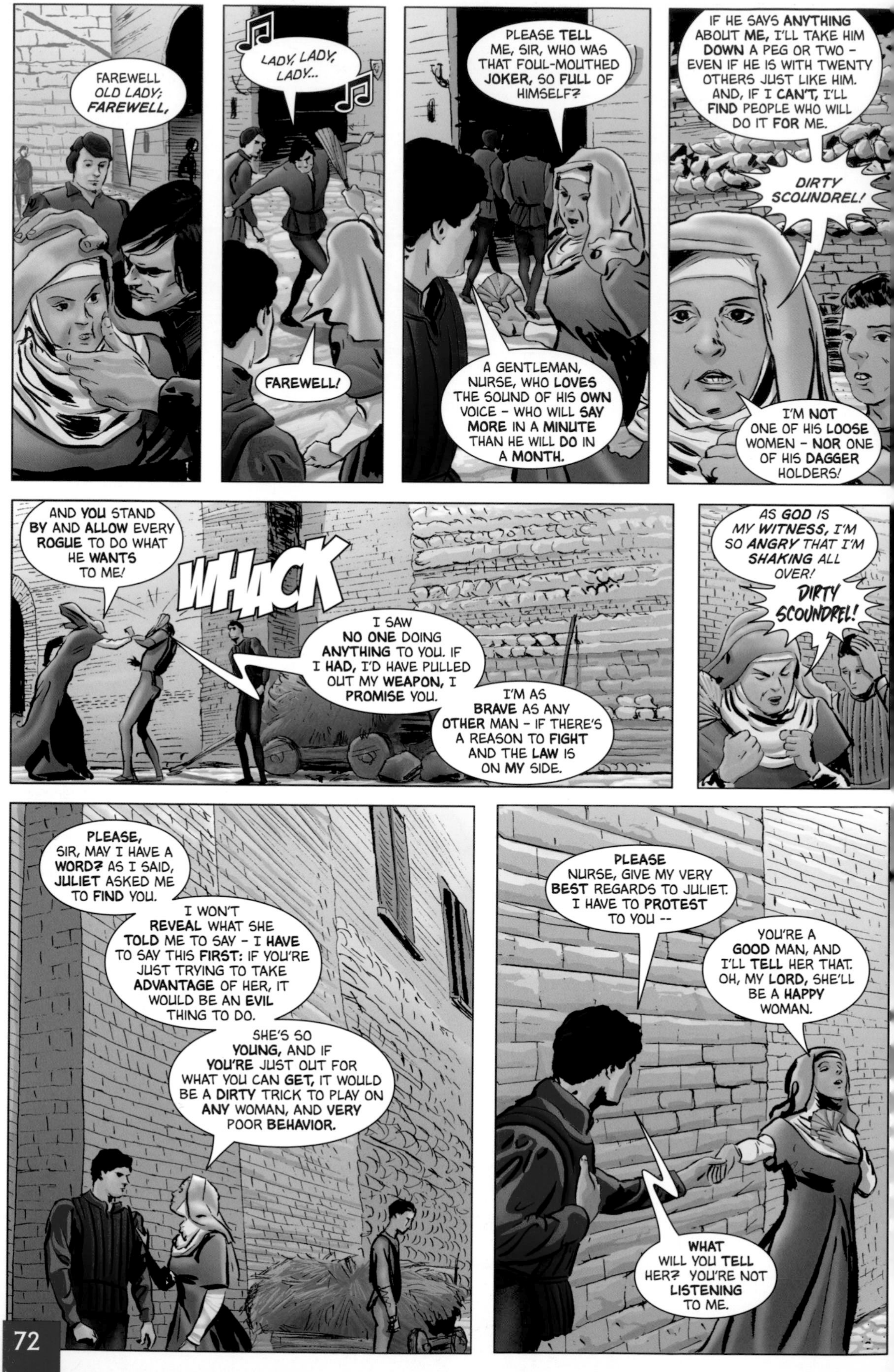
FAREWELL OLD LADY; FAREWELL,
LADY, LADY, LADY...
FAREWELL!
PLEASE TELL ME, SIR, WHO WAS THAT FOUL-MOUTHED JOKER, SO FULL OF HIMSELF?
A GENTLEMAN, NURSE, WHO LOVES THE SOUND OF HIS OWN VOICE - WHO WILL SAY MORE IN A MINUTE THAN HE WILL DO IN A MONTH.
IF HE SAYS ANYTHING ABOUT ME, I'LL TAKE HIM DOWN A PEG OR TWO - EVEN IF HE IS WITH TWENTY OTHERS JUST LIKE HIM. AND, IF I CAN'T, I'LL FIND PEOPLE WHO WILL DO IT FOR ME.
DIRTY SCOUNDREL!
I'M NOT ONE OF HIS LOOSE WOMEN - NOR ONE OF HIS DAGGER HOLDERS!
AND YOU STAND BY AND ALLOW EVERY ROGUE TO DO WHAT HE WANTS TO ME!
WHACK
I SAW NO ONE DOING ANYTHING TO YOU. IF I HAD, I'D HAVE PULLED OUT MY WEAPON, I PROMISE YOU.
I'M AS BRAVE AS ANY OTHER MAN - IF THERE'S A REASON TO FIGHT AND THE LAW IS ON MY SIDE.
AS GOD IS MY WITNESS, I'M SO ANGRY THAT I'M SHAKING ALL OVER!
DIRTY SCOUNDREL!
PLEASE, SIR, MAY I HAVE A WORD? AS I SAID, JULIET ASKED ME TO FIND YOU.
I WON'T REVEAL WHAT SHE TOLD ME TO SAY - I HAVE TO SAY THIS FIRST: IF YOU'RE JUST TRYING TO TAKE ADVANTAGE OF HER, IT WOULD BE AN EVIL THING TO DO.
SHE'S SO YOUNG, AND IF YOU'RE JUST OUT FOR WHAT YOU CAN GET, IT WOULD BE A DIRTY TRICK TO PLAY ON ANY WOMAN, AND VERY POOR BEHAVIOR.
PLEASE NURSE, GIVE MY VERY BEST REGARDS TO JULIET. I HAVE TO PROTEST TO YOU --
YOU'RE A GOOD MAN, AND I'LL TELL HER THAT. OH, MY LORD, SHE'LL BE A HAPPY WOMAN.
WHAT WILL YOU TELL HER? YOU'RE NOT LISTENING TO ME.

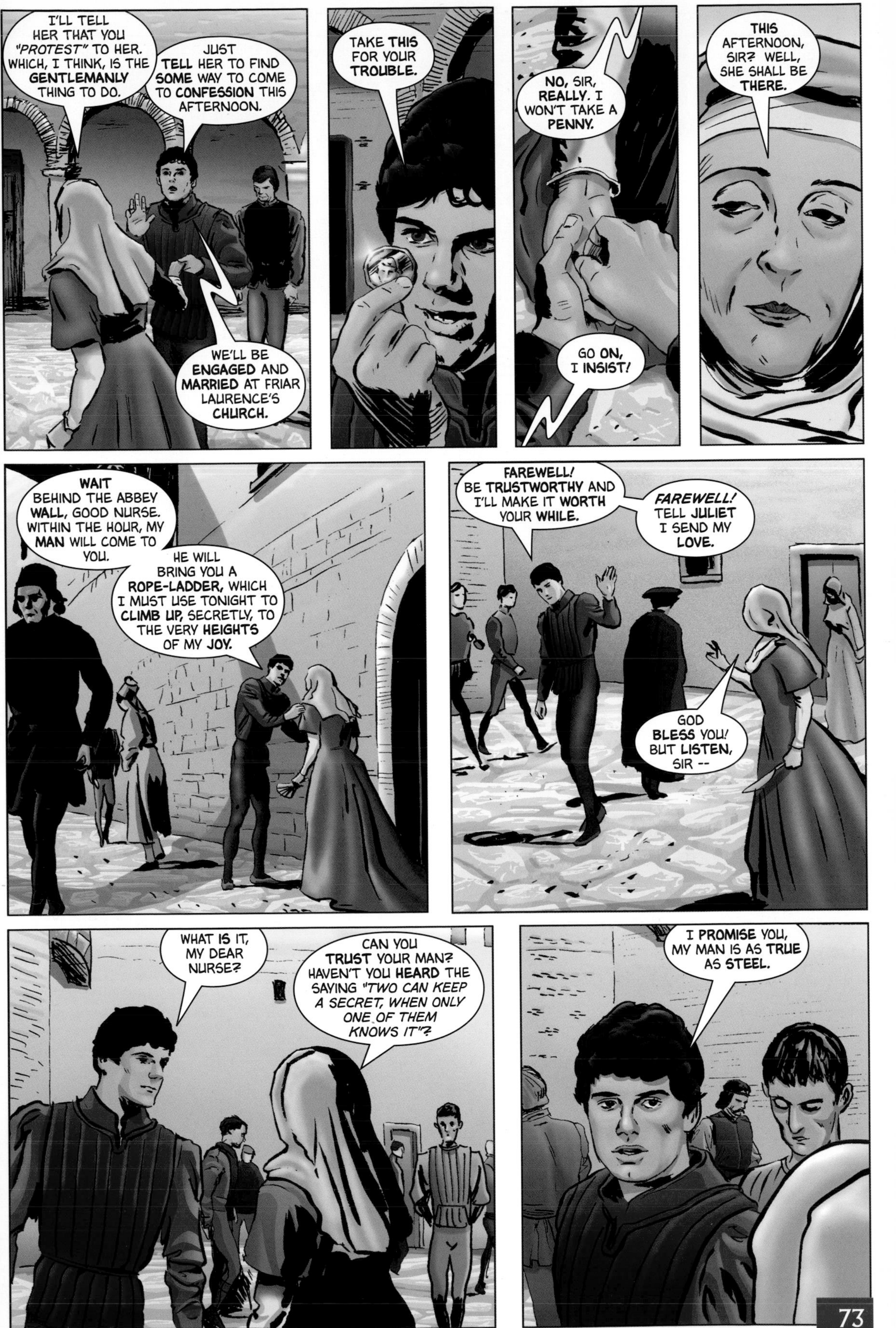

I'LL TELL HER THAT YOU "PROTEST" TO HER. WHICH, I THINK, IS THE GENTLEMANLY THING TO DO.
JUST TELL HER TO FIND SOME WAY TO COME TO CONFESSION THIS AFTERNOON.
WE'LL BE ENGAGED AND MARRIED AT FRIAR LAURENCE'S CHURCH.
TAKE THIS FOR YOUR TROUBLE.
NO, SIR, REALLY. I WON'T TAKE A PENNY.
GO ON, I INSIST!
THIS AFTERNOON, SIR? WELL, SHE SHALL BE THERE.
WAIT BEHIND THE ABBEY WALL, GOOD NURSE. WITHIN THE HOUR, MY MAN WILL COME TO YOU.
HE WILL BRING YOU A ROPE-LADDER, WHICH I MUST USE TONIGHT TO CLIMB UP, SECRETLY, TO THE VERY HEIGHTS OF MY JOY.
FAREWELL! BE TRUSTWORTHY AND I'LL MAKE IT WORTH YOUR WHILE.
FAREWELL! TELL JULIET I SEND MY LOVE.
GOD BLESS YOU! BUT LISTEN, SIR --
WHAT IS IT, MY DEAR NURSE?
CAN YOU TRUST YOUR MAN? HAVEN'T YOU HEARD THE SAYING "TWO CAN KEEP A SECRET, WHEN ONLY ONE OF THEM KNOWS IT"?
I PROMISE YOU, MY MAN IS AS TRUE AS STEEL.

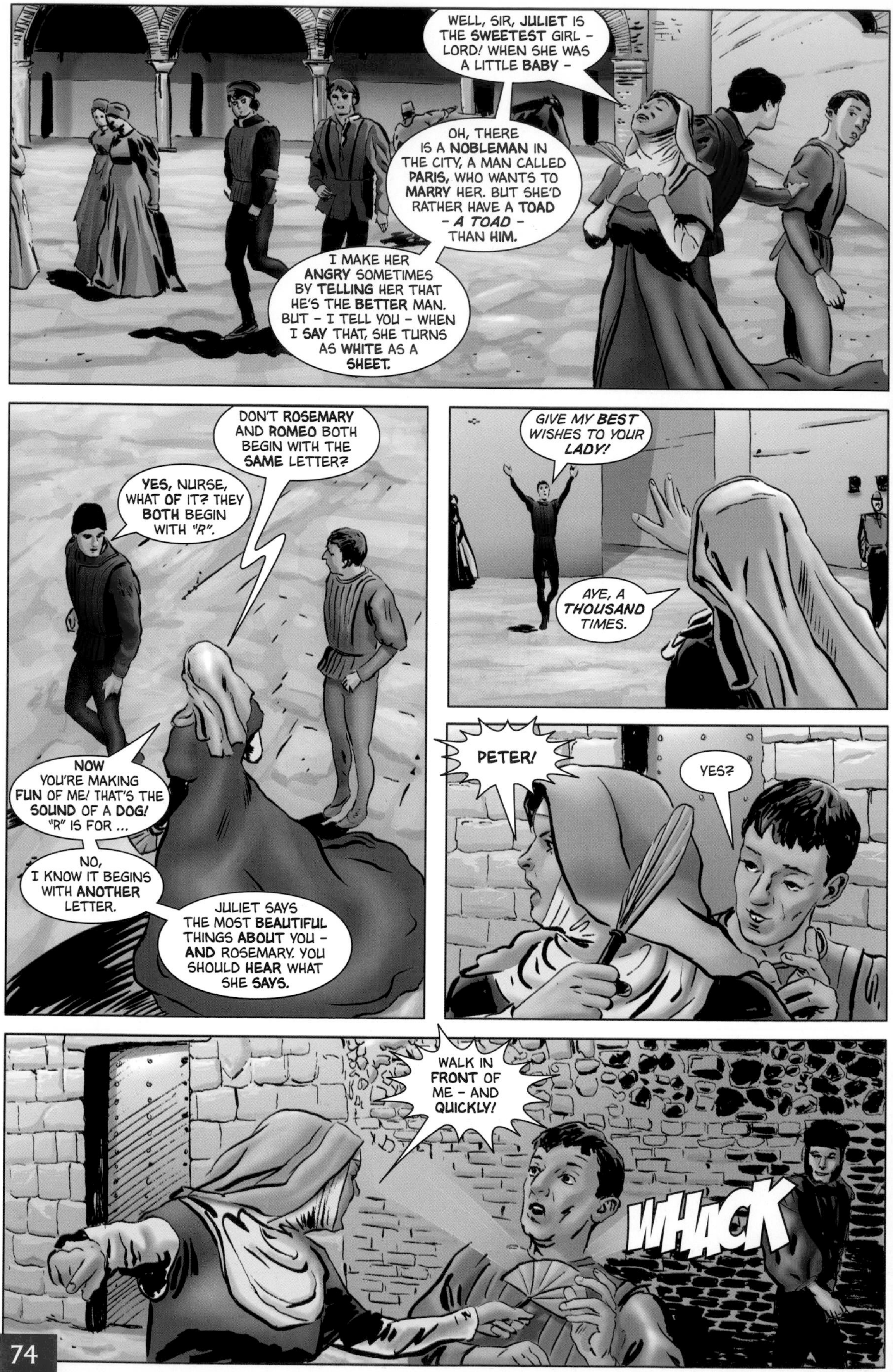
WELL, SIR, JULIET IS THE SWEETEST GIRL – LORD! WHEN SHE WAS A LITTLE BABY –
OH, THERE IS A NOBLEMAN IN THE CITY, A MAN CALLED PARIS, WHO WANTS TO MARRY HER. BUT SHE'D RATHER HAVE A TOAD – A TOAD – THAN HIM.
I MAKE HER ANGRY SOMETIMES BY TELLING HER THAT HE'S THE BETTER MAN. BUT – I TELL YOU – WHEN I SAY THAT, SHE TURNS AS WHITE AS A SHEET.
DON'T ROSEMARY AND ROMEO BOTH BEGIN WITH THE SAME LETTER?
YES, NURSE, WHAT OF IT? THEY BOTH BEGIN WITH "R".
NOW YOU'RE MAKING FUN OF ME! THAT'S THE SOUND OF A DOG! "R" IS FOR ...
NO, I KNOW IT BEGINS WITH ANOTHER LETTER.
JULIET SAYS THE MOST BEAUTIFUL THINGS ABOUT YOU – AND ROSEMARY. YOU SHOULD HEAR WHAT SHE SAYS.
GIVE MY BEST WISHES TO YOUR LADY!
AYE, A THOUSAND TIMES.
PETER!
YES?
WALK IN FRONT OF ME – AND QUICKLY!
WHACK

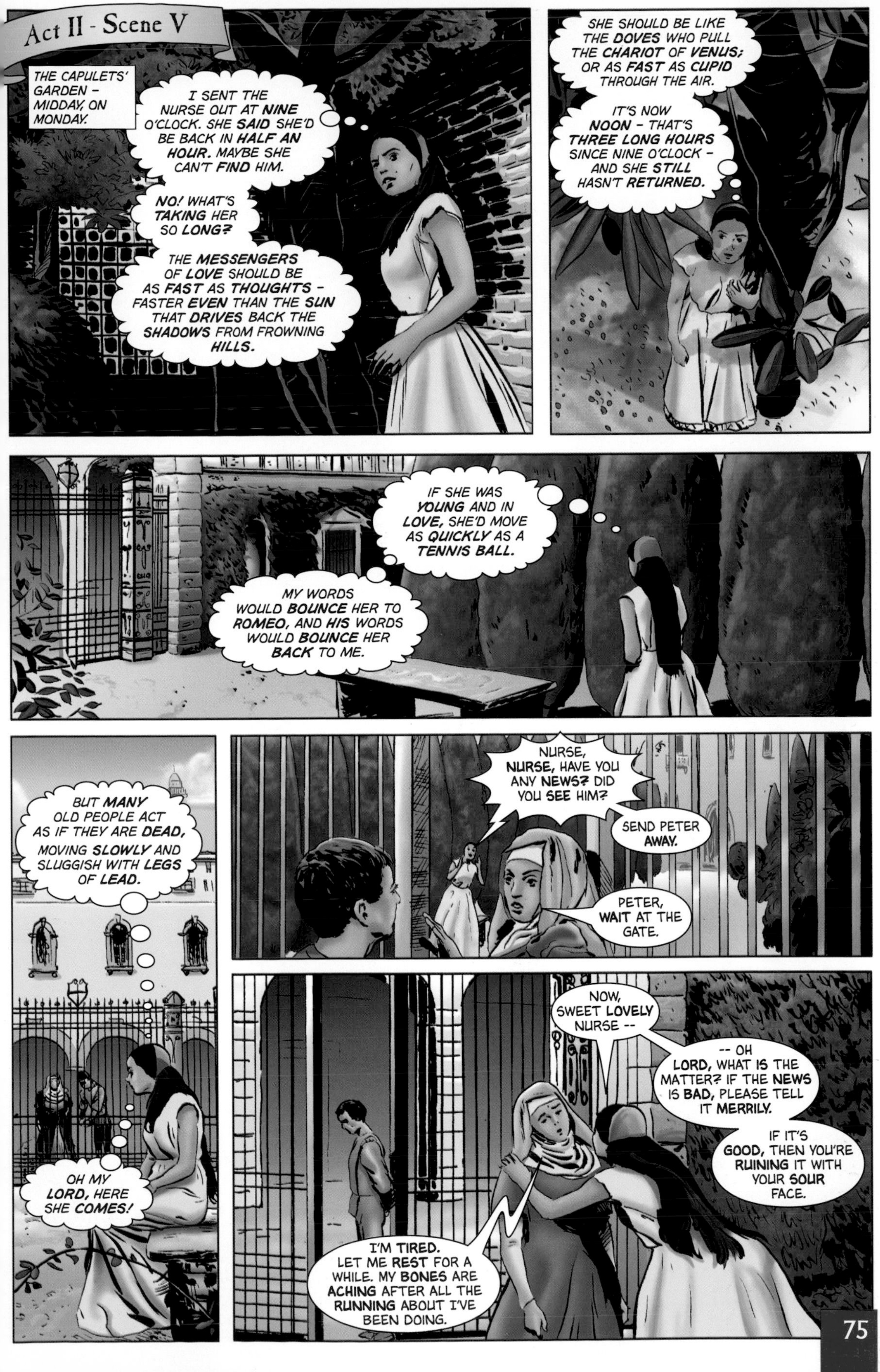

Act II - Scene V
THE CAPULETS' GARDEN – MIDDAY, ON MONDAY.
I SENT THE NURSE OUT AT NINE O'CLOCK. SHE SAID SHE'D BE BACK IN HALF AN HOUR. MAYBE SHE CAN'T FIND HIM.
NO! WHAT'S TAKING HER SO LONG?
THE MESSENGERS OF LOVE SHOULD BE AS FAST AS THOUGHTS – FASTER EVEN THAN THE SUN THAT DRIVES BACK THE SHADOWS FROM FROWNING HILLS.
SHE SHOULD BE LIKE THE DOVES WHO PULL THE CHARIOT OF VENUS; OR AS FAST AS CUPID THROUGH THE AIR.
IT'S NOW NOON – THAT'S THREE LONG HOURS SINCE NINE O'CLOCK – AND SHE STILL HASN'T RETURNED.
IF SHE WAS YOUNG AND IN LOVE, SHE'D MOVE AS QUICKLY AS A TENNIS BALL.
MY WORDS WOULD BOUNCE HER TO ROMEO, AND HIS WORDS WOULD BOUNCE HER BACK TO ME.
BUT MANY OLD PEOPLE ACT AS IF THEY ARE DEAD, MOVING SLOWLY AND SLUGGISH WITH LEGS OF LEAD.
OH MY LORD, HERE SHE COMES!
NURSE, NURSE, HAVE YOU ANY NEWS? DID YOU SEE HIM?
SEND PETER AWAY.
PETER, WAIT AT THE GATE.
NOW, SWEET LOVELY NURSE --
-- OH LORD, WHAT IS THE MATTER? IF THE NEWS IS BAD, PLEASE TELL IT MERRILY.
IF IT'S GOOD, THEN YOU'RE RUINING IT WITH YOUR SOUR FACE.
I'M TIRED. LET ME REST FOR A WHILE. MY BONES ARE ACHING AFTER ALL THE RUNNING ABOUT I'VE BEEN DOING.

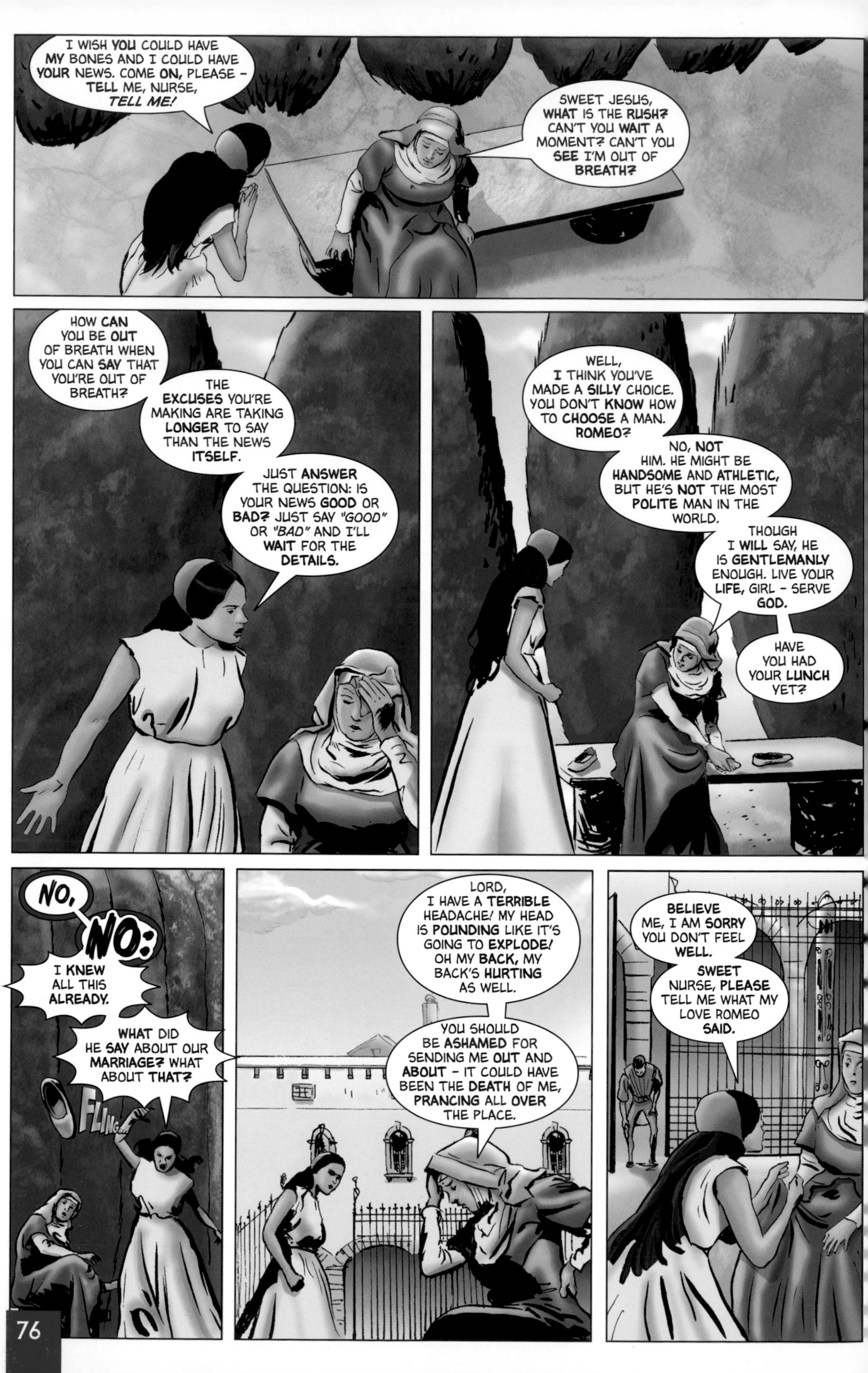
I WISH YOU COULD HAVE MY BONES AND I COULD HAVE YOUR NEWS. COME ON, PLEASE - TELL ME, NURSE, TELL ME!
SWEET JESUS, WHAT IS THE RUSH? CAN'T YOU WAIT A MOMENT? CAN'T YOU SEE I'M OUT OF BREATH?
HOW CAN YOU BE OUT OF BREATH WHEN YOU CAN SAY THAT YOU'RE OUT OF BREATH?
THE EXCUSES YOU'RE MAKING ARE TAKING LONGER TO SAY THAN THE NEWS ITSELF.
JUST ANSWER THE QUESTION: IS YOUR NEWS GOOD OR BAD? JUST SAY "GOOD" OR "BAD" AND I'LL WAIT FOR THE DETAILS.
WELL, I THINK YOU'VE MADE A SILLY CHOICE. YOU DON'T KNOW HOW TO CHOOSE A MAN. ROMEO?
NO, NOT HIM. HE MIGHT BE HANDSOME AND ATHLETIC, BUT HE'S NOT THE MOST POLITE MAN IN THE WORLD.
THOUGH I WILL SAY, HE IS GENTLEMANLY ENOUGH. LIVE YOUR LIFE, GIRL - SERVE GOD.
HAVE YOU HAD YOUR LUNCH YET?
NO, NO!
I KNEW ALL THIS ALREADY.
WHAT DID HE SAY ABOUT OUR MARRIAGE? WHAT ABOUT THAT?
FLING
LORD, I HAVE A TERRIBLE HEADACHE! MY HEAD IS POUNDING LIKE IT'S GOING TO EXPLODE! OH MY BACK, MY BACK'S HURTING AS WELL.
YOU SHOULD BE ASHAMED FOR SENDING ME OUT AND ABOUT - IT COULD HAVE BEEN THE DEATH OF ME, PRANCING ALL OVER THE PLACE.
BELIEVE ME, I AM SORRY YOU DON'T FEEL WELL.
SWEET NURSE, PLEASE TELL ME WHAT MY LOVE ROMEO SAID.

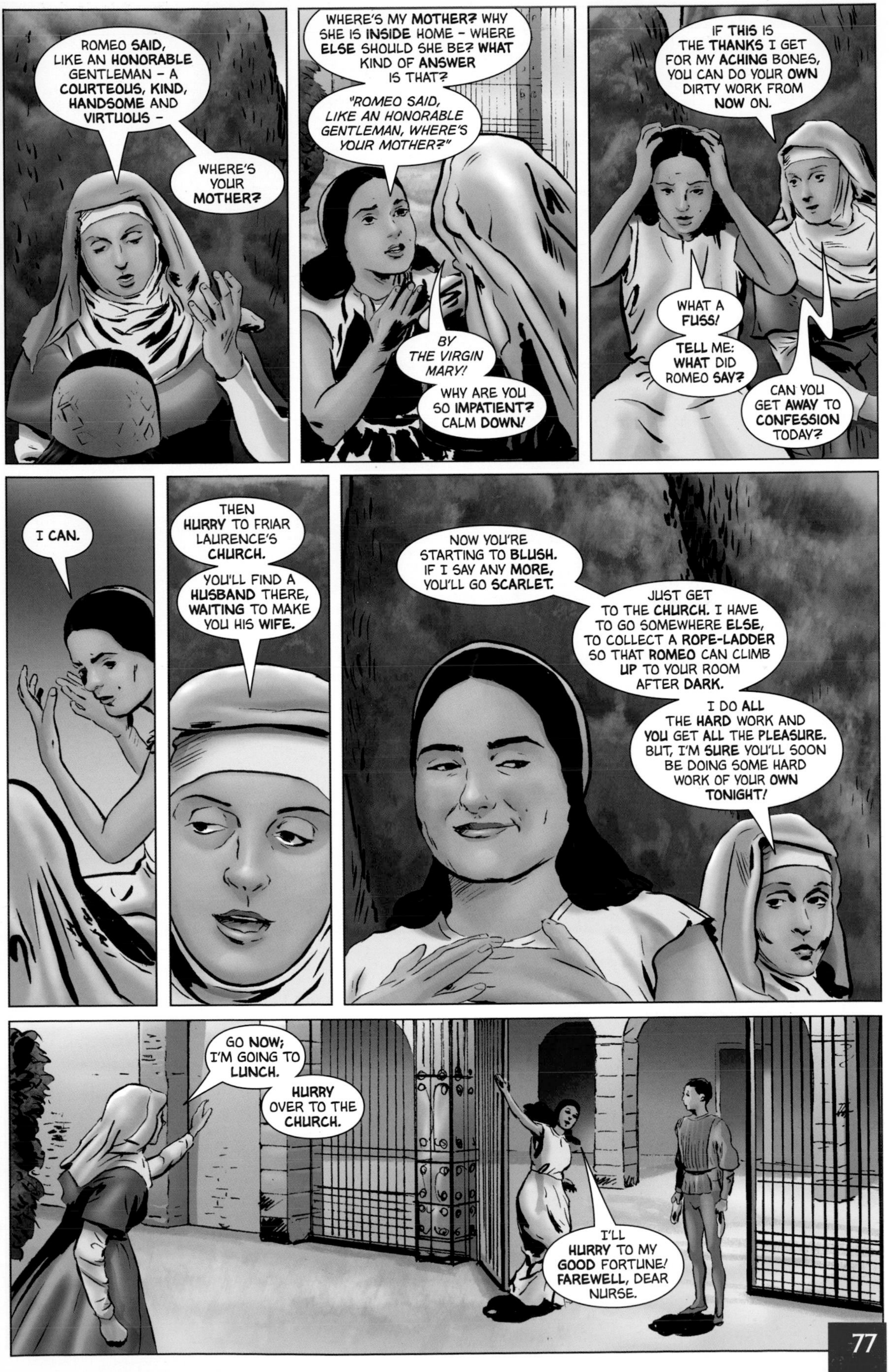
ROMEO SAID, LIKE AN HONORABLE GENTLEMAN – A COURTEOUS, KIND, HANDSOME AND VIRTUOUS –
WHERE'S YOUR MOTHER?
WHERE'S MY MOTHER? WHY SHE IS INSIDE HOME – WHERE ELSE SHOULD SHE BE? WHAT KIND OF ANSWER IS THAT?
"ROMEO SAID, LIKE AN HONORABLE GENTLEMAN, WHERE'S YOUR MOTHER?"
BY THE VIRGIN MARY!
WHY ARE YOU SO IMPATIENT? CALM DOWN!
IF THIS IS THE THANKS I GET FOR MY ACHING BONES, YOU CAN DO YOUR OWN DIRTY WORK FROM NOW ON.
WHAT A FUSS!
TELL ME: WHAT DID ROMEO SAY?
CAN YOU GET AWAY TO CONFESSION TODAY?
I CAN.
THEN HURRY TO FRIAR LAURENCE'S CHURCH.
YOU'LL FIND A HUSBAND THERE, WAITING TO MAKE YOU HIS WIFE.
NOW YOU'RE STARTING TO BLUSH. IF I SAY ANY MORE, YOU'LL GO SCARLET.
JUST GET TO THE CHURCH. I HAVE TO GO SOMEWHERE ELSE, TO COLLECT A ROPE-LADDER SO THAT ROMEO CAN CLIMB UP TO YOUR ROOM AFTER DARK.
I DO ALL THE HARD WORK AND YOU GET ALL THE PLEASURE. BUT, I'M SURE YOU'LL SOON BE DOING SOME HARD WORK OF YOUR OWN TONIGHT!
GO NOW; I'M GOING TO LUNCH.
HURRY OVER TO THE CHURCH.
I'LL HURRY TO MY GOOD FORTUNE! FAREWELL, DEAR NURSE.

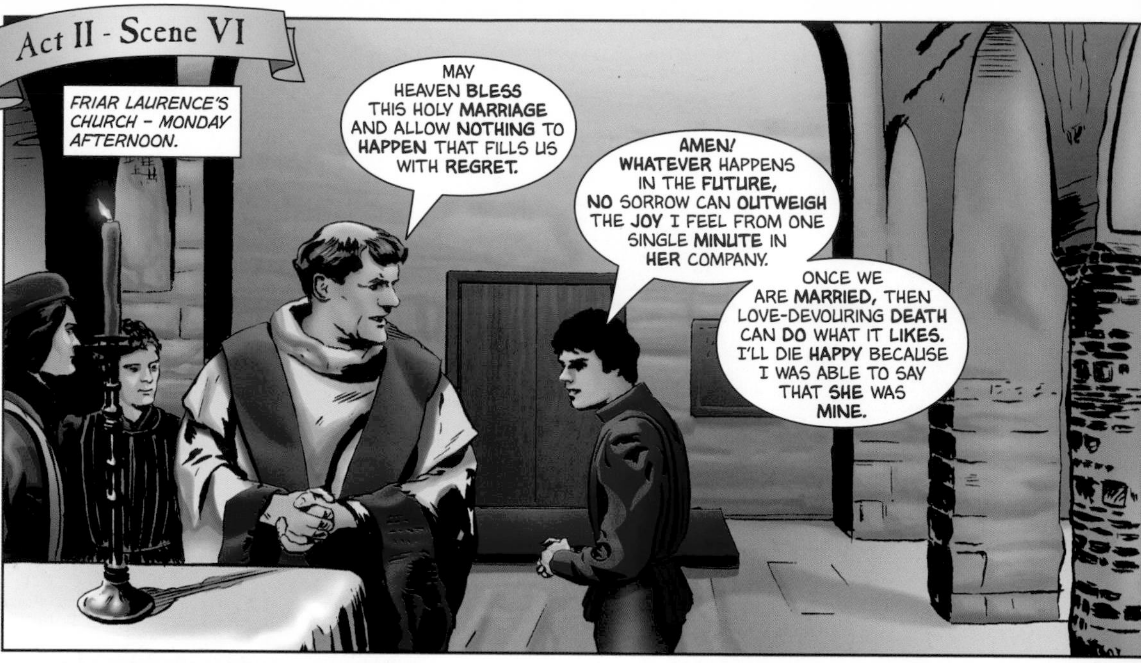
Act II - Scene VI
FRIAR LAURENCE'S CHURCH – MONDAY AFTERNOON.
MAY HEAVEN BLESS THIS HOLY MARRIAGE AND ALLOW NOTHING TO HAPPEN THAT FILLS US WITH REGRET.
AMEN! WHATEVER HAPPENS IN THE FUTURE, NO SORROW CAN OUTWEIGH THE JOY I FEEL FROM ONE SINGLE MINUTE IN HER COMPANY.
ONCE WE ARE MARRIED, THEN LOVE-DEVOURING DEATH CAN DO WHAT IT LIKES. I'LL DIE HAPPY BECAUSE I WAS ABLE TO SAY THAT SHE WAS MINE.

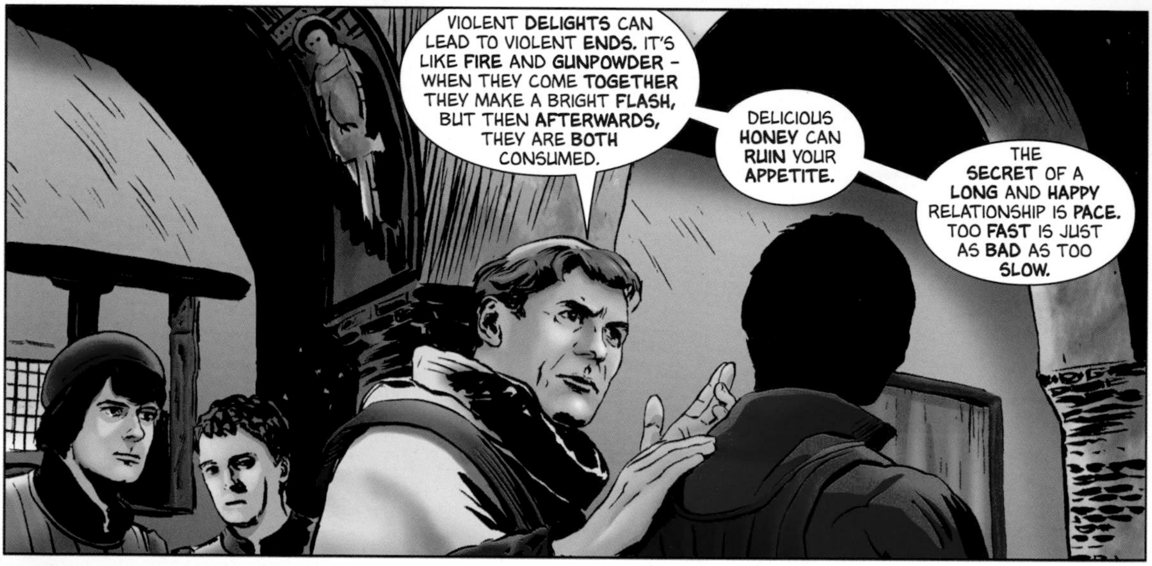
VIOLENT DELIGHTS CAN LEAD TO VIOLENT ENDS. IT'S LIKE FIRE AND GUNPOWDER – WHEN THEY COME TOGETHER THEY MAKE A BRIGHT FLASH, BUT THEN AFTERWARDS, THEY ARE BOTH CONSUMED.
DELICIOUS HONEY CAN RUIN YOUR APPETITE.
THE SECRET OF A LONG AND HAPPY RELATIONSHIP IS PACE. TOO FAST IS JUST AS BAD AS TOO SLOW.

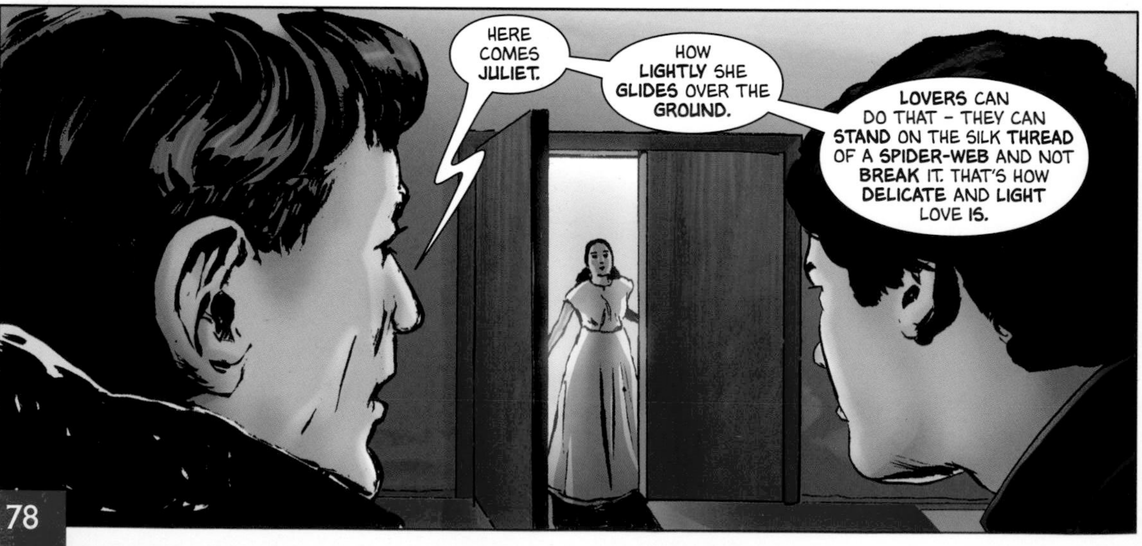
HERE COMES JULIET.
HOW LIGHTLY SHE GLIDES OVER THE GROUND.
LOVERS CAN DO THAT – THEY CAN STAND ON THE SILK THREAD OF A SPIDER-WEB AND NOT BREAK IT. THAT'S HOW DELICATE AND LIGHT LOVE IS.

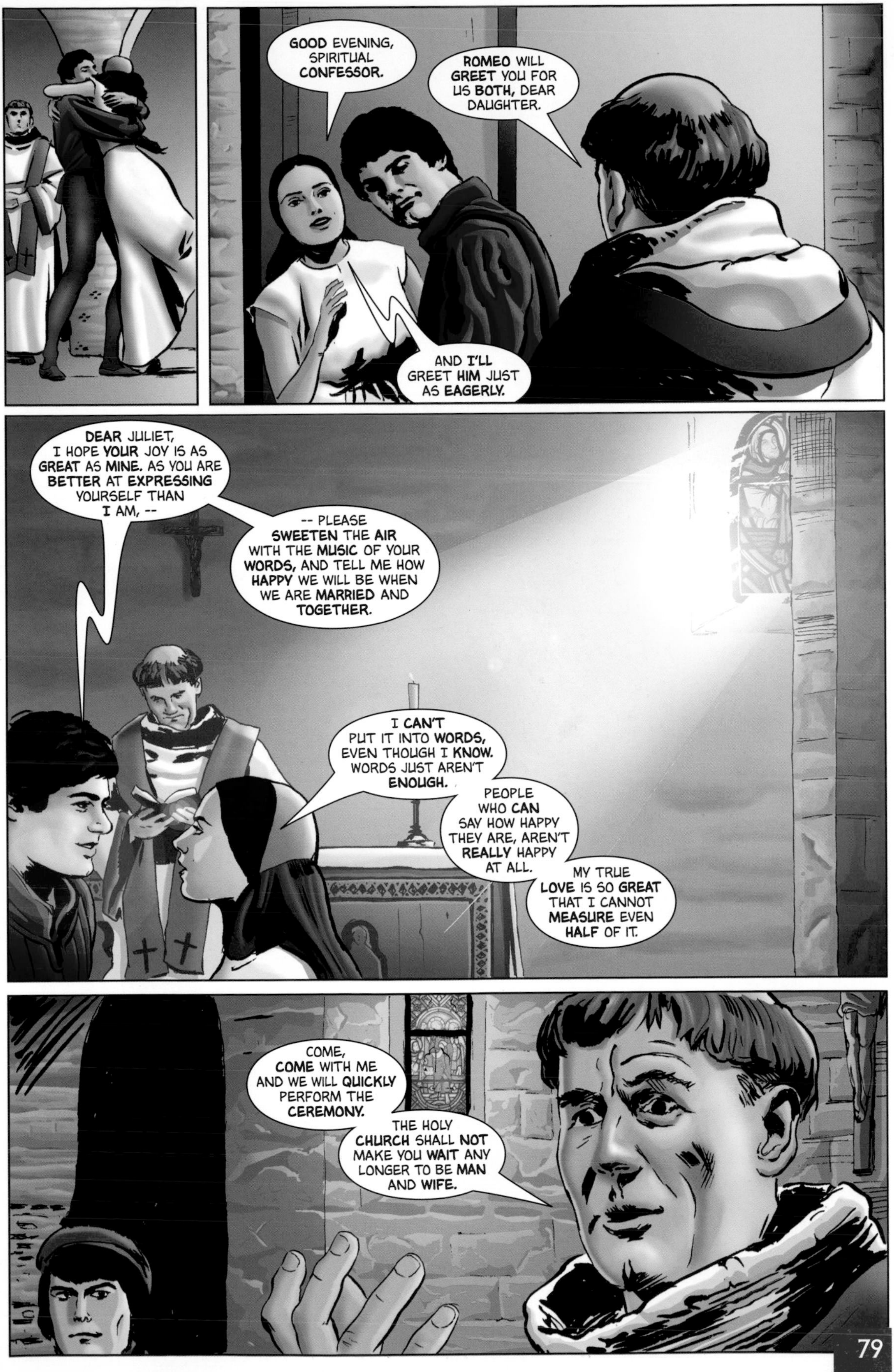
GOOD EVENING, SPIRITUAL CONFESSOR.
ROMEO WILL GREET YOU FOR US BOTH, DEAR DAUGHTER.
AND I'LL GREET HIM JUST AS EAGERLY.
DEAR JULIET, I HOPE YOUR JOY IS AS GREAT AS MINE. AS YOU ARE BETTER AT EXPRESSING YOURSELF THAN I AM, --
-- PLEASE SWEETEN THE AIR WITH THE MUSIC OF YOUR WORDS, AND TELL ME HOW HAPPY WE WILL BE WHEN WE ARE MARRIED AND TOGETHER.
I CAN'T PUT IT INTO WORDS, EVEN THOUGH I KNOW. WORDS JUST AREN'T ENOUGH.
PEOPLE WHO CAN SAY HOW HAPPY THEY ARE, AREN'T REALLY HAPPY AT ALL.
MY TRUE LOVE IS SO GREAT THAT I CANNOT MEASURE EVEN HALF OF IT.
COME, COME WITH ME AND WE WILL QUICKLY PERFORM THE CEREMONY.
THE HOLY CHURCH SHALL NOT MAKE YOU WAIT ANY LONGER TO BE MAN AND WIFE.

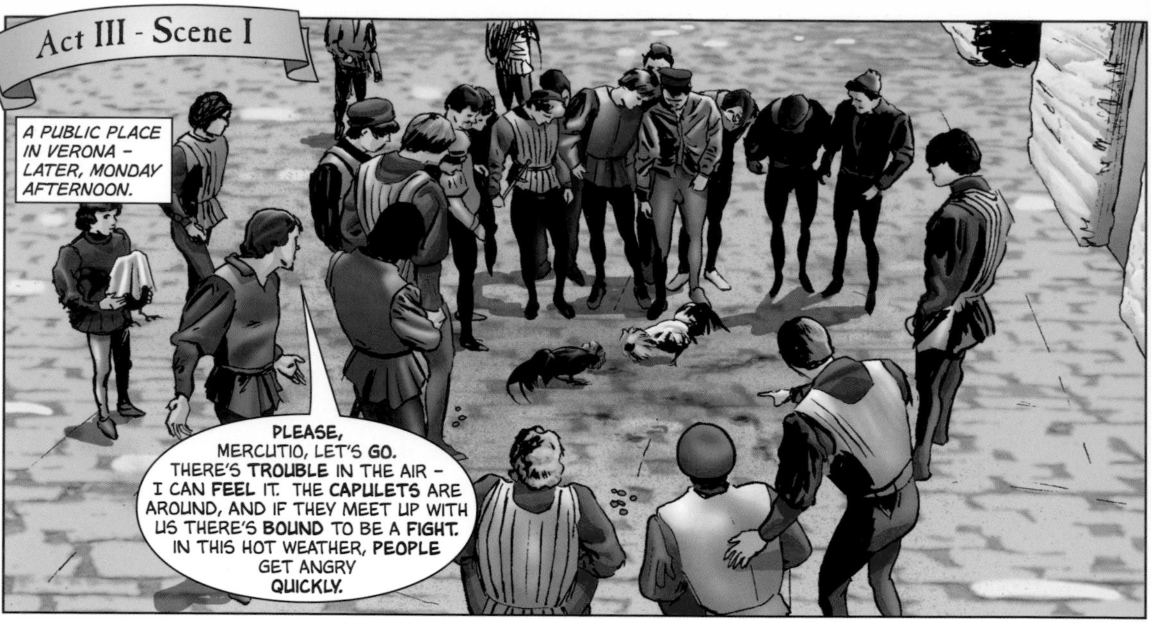
Act III - Scene I
A PUBLIC PLACE IN VERONA – LATER, MONDAY AFTERNOON.
PLEASE, MERCUTIO, LET'S GO. THERE'S TROUBLE IN THE AIR – I CAN FEEL IT. THE CAPULETS ARE AROUND, AND IF THEY MEET UP WITH US THERE'S BOUND TO BE A FIGHT. IN THIS HOT WEATHER, PEOPLE GET ANGRY QUICKLY.

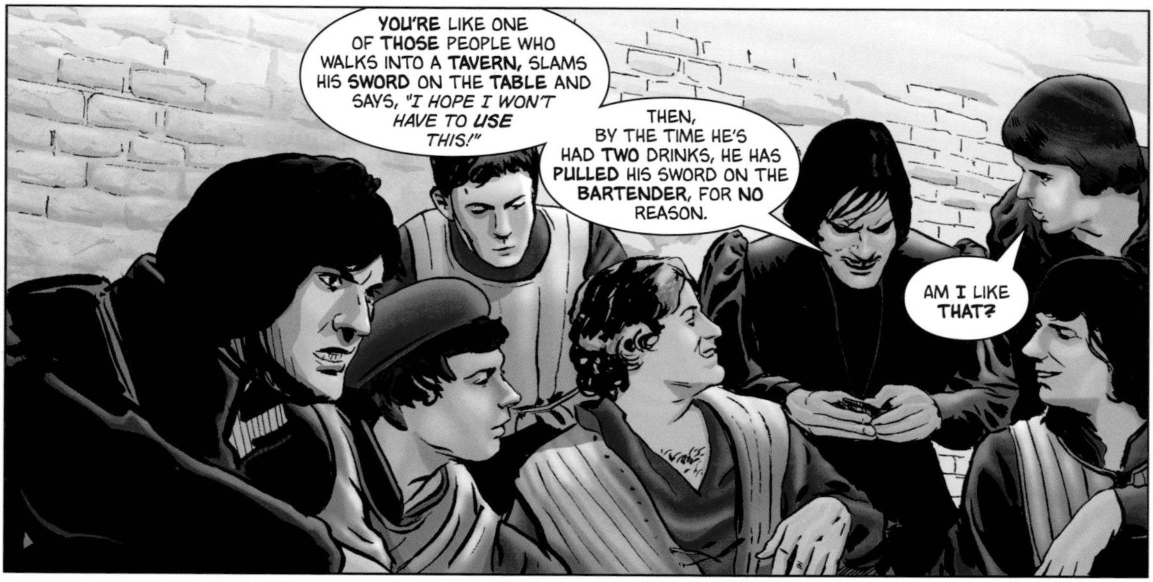
YOU'RE LIKE ONE OF THOSE PEOPLE WHO WALKS INTO A TAVERN, SLAMS HIS SWORD ON THE TABLE AND SAYS, "I HOPE I WON'T HAVE TO USE THIS!"
THEN, BY THE TIME HE'S HAD TWO DRINKS, HE HAS PULLED HIS SWORD ON THE BARTENDER, FOR NO REASON.
AM I LIKE THAT?

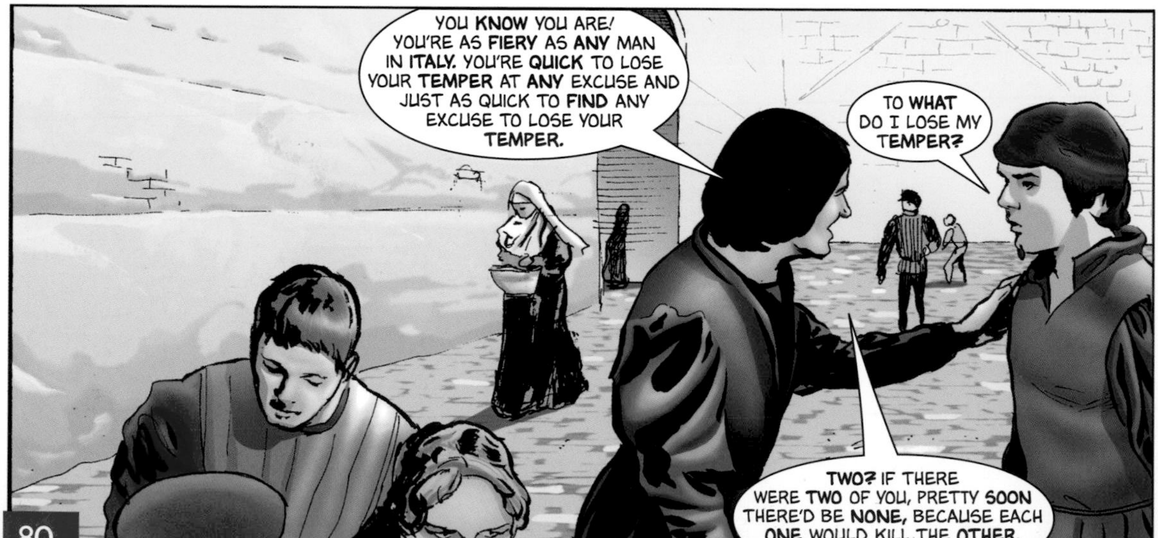
YOU KNOW YOU ARE! YOU'RE AS FIERY AS ANY MAN IN ITALY. YOU'RE QUICK TO LOSE YOUR TEMPER AT ANY EXCUSE AND JUST AS QUICK TO FIND ANY EXCUSE TO LOSE YOUR TEMPER.
TO WHAT DO I LOSE MY TEMPER?
TWO? IF THERE WERE TWO OF YOU, PRETTY SOON THERE'D BE NONE, BECAUSE EACH ONE WOULD KILL THE OTHER.

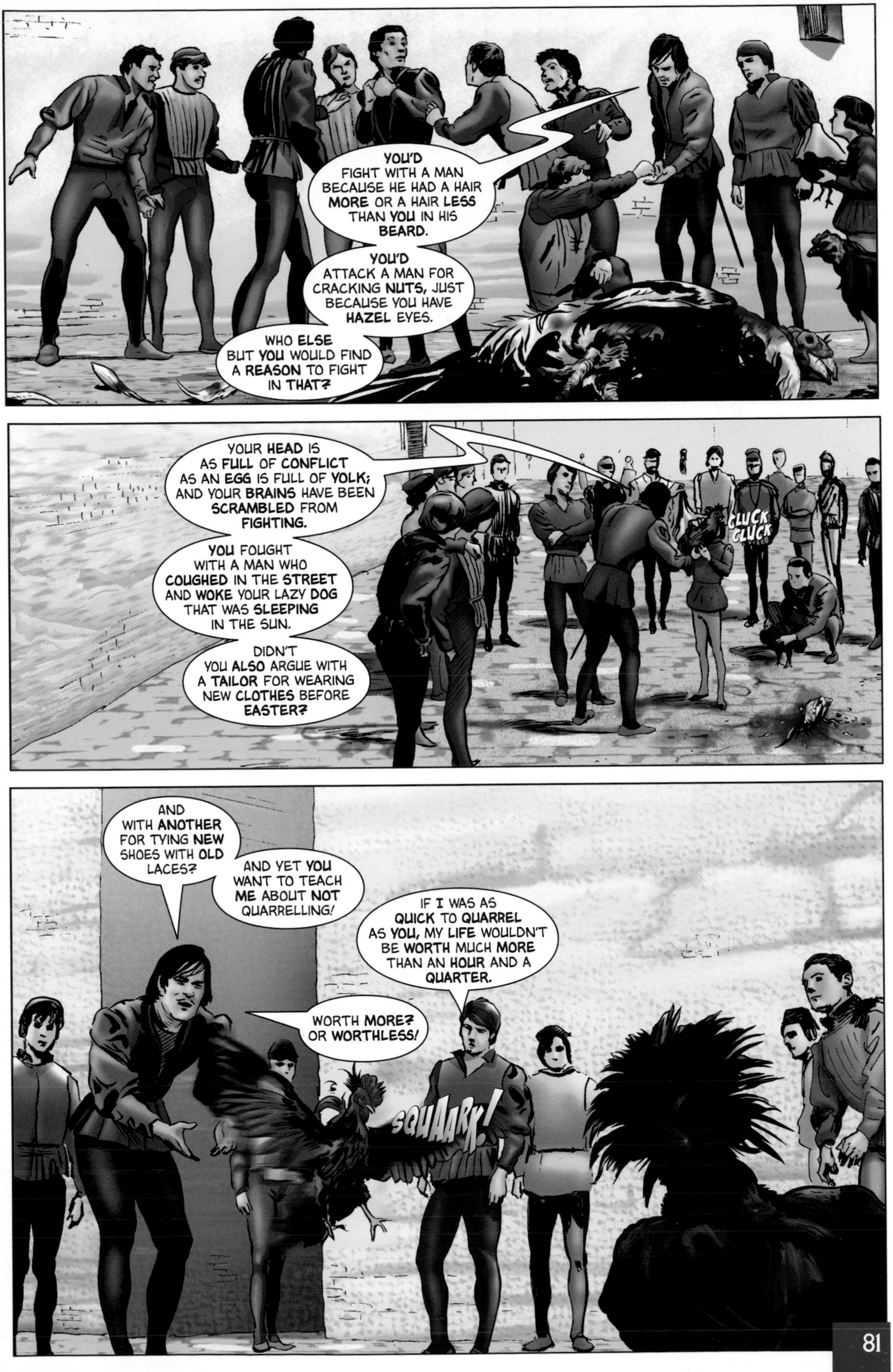
YOU'D FIGHT WITH A MAN BECAUSE HE HAD A HAIR MORE OR A HAIR LESS THAN YOU IN HIS BEARD.
YOU'D ATTACK A MAN FOR CRACKING NUTS, JUST BECAUSE YOU HAVE HAZEL EYES.
WHO ELSE BUT YOU WOULD FIND A REASON TO FIGHT IN THAT?
YOUR HEAD IS AS FULL OF CONFLICT AS AN EGG IS FULL OF YOLK; AND YOUR BRAINS HAVE BEEN SCRAMBLED FROM FIGHTING.
YOU FOUGHT WITH A MAN WHO COUGHED IN THE STREET AND WOKE YOUR LAZY DOG THAT WAS SLEEPING IN THE SUN.
DIDN'T YOU ALSO ARGUE WITH A TAILOR FOR WEARING NEW CLOTHES BEFORE EASTER?
CLUCK CLUCK
AND WITH ANOTHER FOR TYING NEW SHOES WITH OLD LACES?
AND YET YOU WANT TO TEACH ME ABOUT NOT QUARRELLING!
IF I WAS AS QUICK TO QUARREL AS YOU, MY LIFE WOULDN'T BE WORTH MUCH MORE THAN AN HOUR AND A QUARTER.
WORTH MORE? OR WORTHLESS!
SQUAARK!

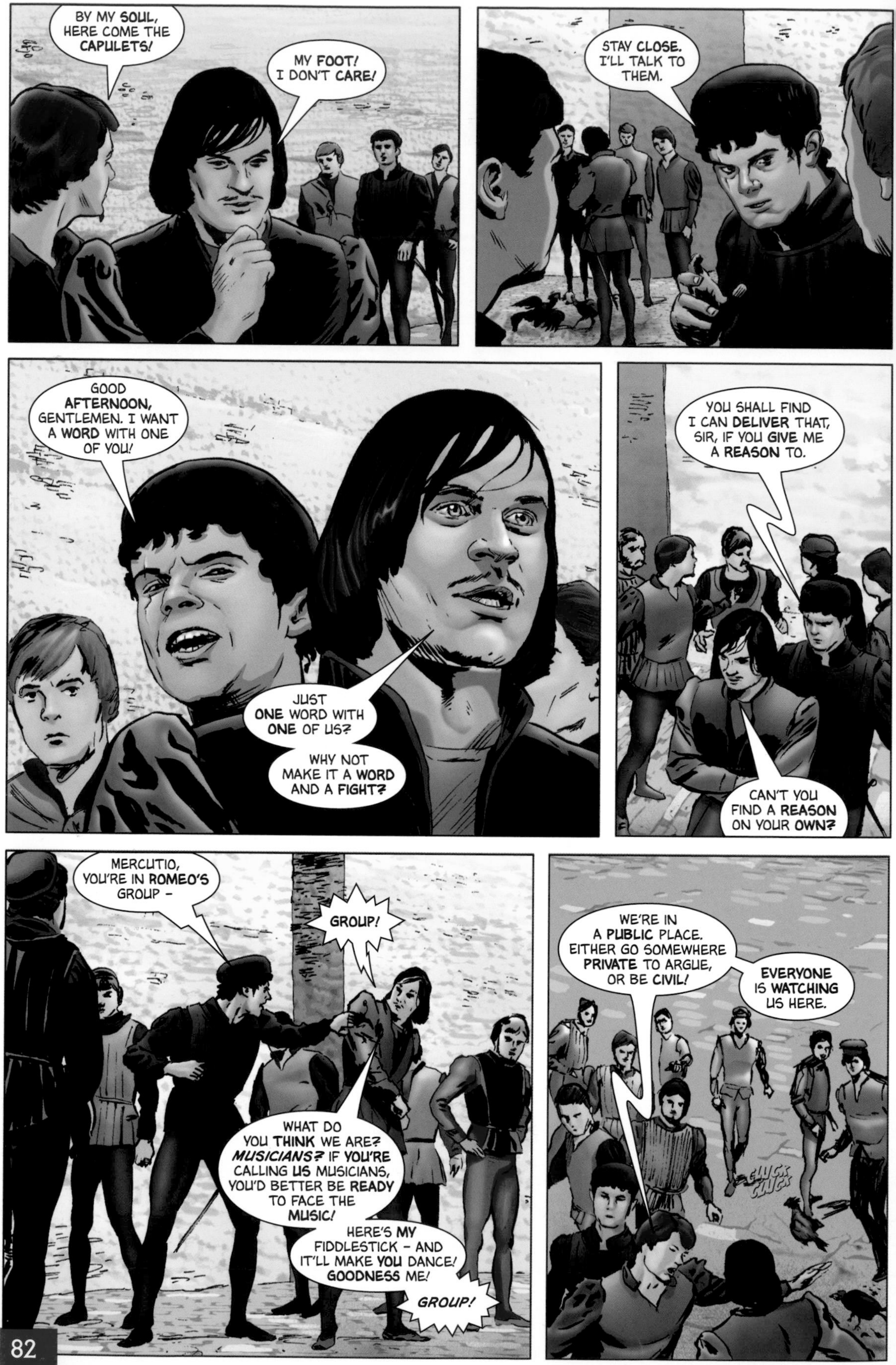

BY MY SOUL, HERE COME THE CAPULETS!
MY FOOT! I DON'T CARE!
STAY CLOSE. I'LL TALK TO THEM.
GOOD AFTERNOON, GENTLEMEN. I WANT A WORD WITH ONE OF YOU!
JUST ONE WORD WITH ONE OF US?
WHY NOT MAKE IT A WORD AND A FIGHT?
YOU SHALL FIND I CAN DELIVER THAT, SIR, IF YOU GIVE ME A REASON TO.
CAN'T YOU FIND A REASON ON YOUR OWN?
MERCUTIO, YOU'RE IN ROMEO'S GROUP –
GROUP!
WHAT DO YOU THINK WE ARE? MUSICIANS? IF YOU'RE CALLING US MUSICIANS, YOU'D BETTER BE READY TO FACE THE MUSIC!
HERE'S MY FIDDLESTICK – AND IT'LL MAKE YOU DANCE! GOODNESS ME!
GROUP!
WE'RE IN A PUBLIC PLACE. EITHER GO SOMEWHERE PRIVATE TO ARGUE, OR BE CIVIL!
EVERYONE IS WATCHING US HERE.
CLUCK CLUCK

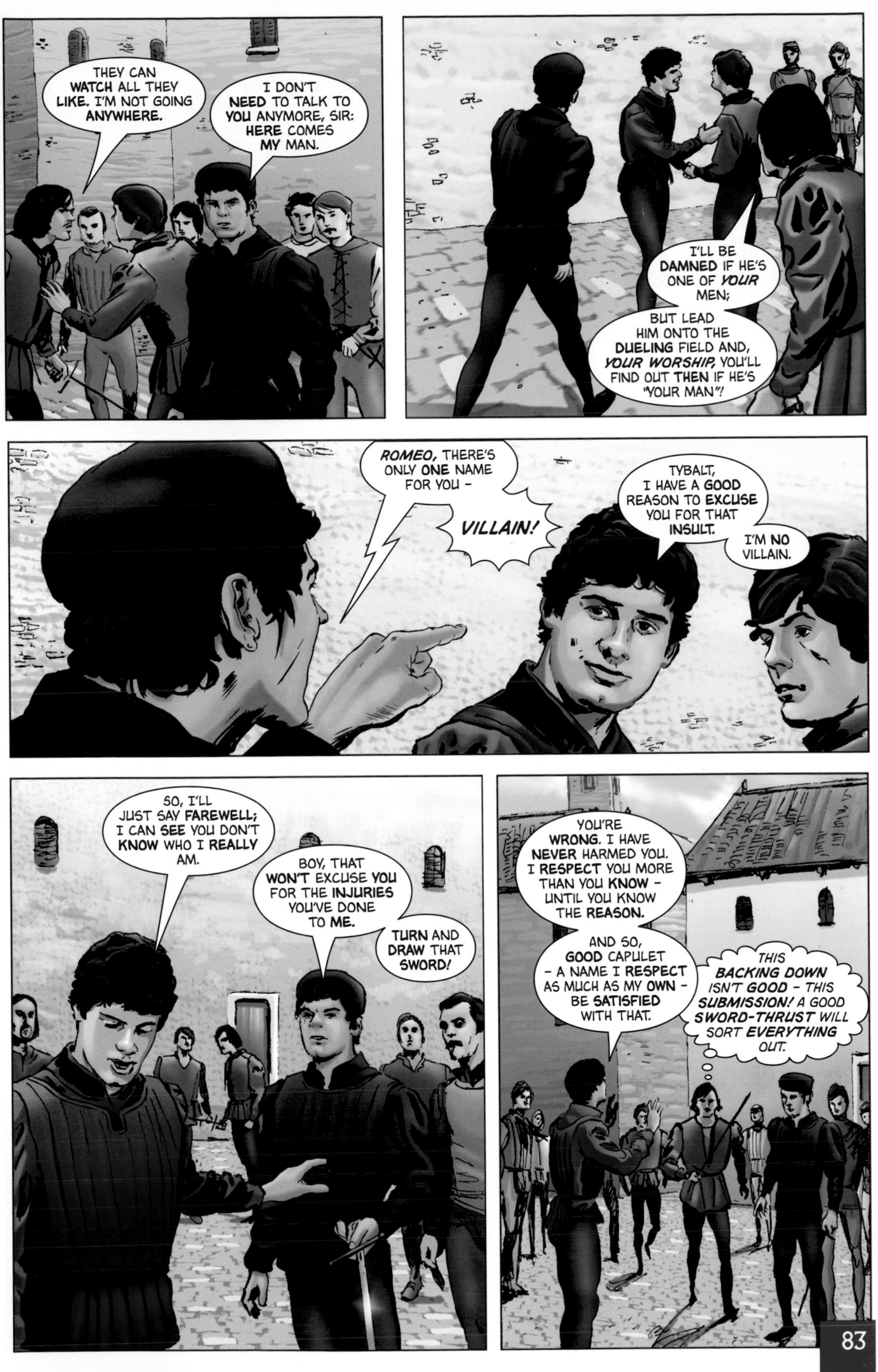
THEY CAN WATCH ALL THEY LIKE. I'M NOT GOING ANYWHERE.
I DON'T NEED TO TALK TO YOU ANYMORE, SIR: HERE COMES MY MAN.
I'LL BE DAMNED IF HE'S ONE OF YOUR MEN;
BUT LEAD HIM ONTO THE DUELING FIELD AND, YOUR WORSHIP, YOU'LL FIND OUT THEN IF HE'S "YOUR MAN"!
ROMEO, THERE'S ONLY ONE NAME FOR YOU -
VILLAIN!
TYBALT, I HAVE A GOOD REASON TO EXCUSE YOU FOR THAT INSULT.
I'M NO VILLAIN.
SO, I'LL JUST SAY FAREWELL; I CAN SEE YOU DON'T KNOW WHO I REALLY AM.
BOY, THAT WON'T EXCUSE YOU FOR THE INJURIES YOU'VE DONE TO ME.
TURN AND DRAW THAT SWORD!
YOU'RE WRONG. I HAVE NEVER HARMED YOU. I RESPECT YOU MORE THAN YOU KNOW - UNTIL YOU KNOW THE REASON.
AND SO, GOOD CAPULET - A NAME I RESPECT AS MUCH AS MY OWN - BE SATISFIED WITH THAT.
THIS BACKING DOWN ISN'T GOOD - THIS SUBMISSION! A GOOD SWORD-THRUST WILL SORT EVERYTHING OUT.

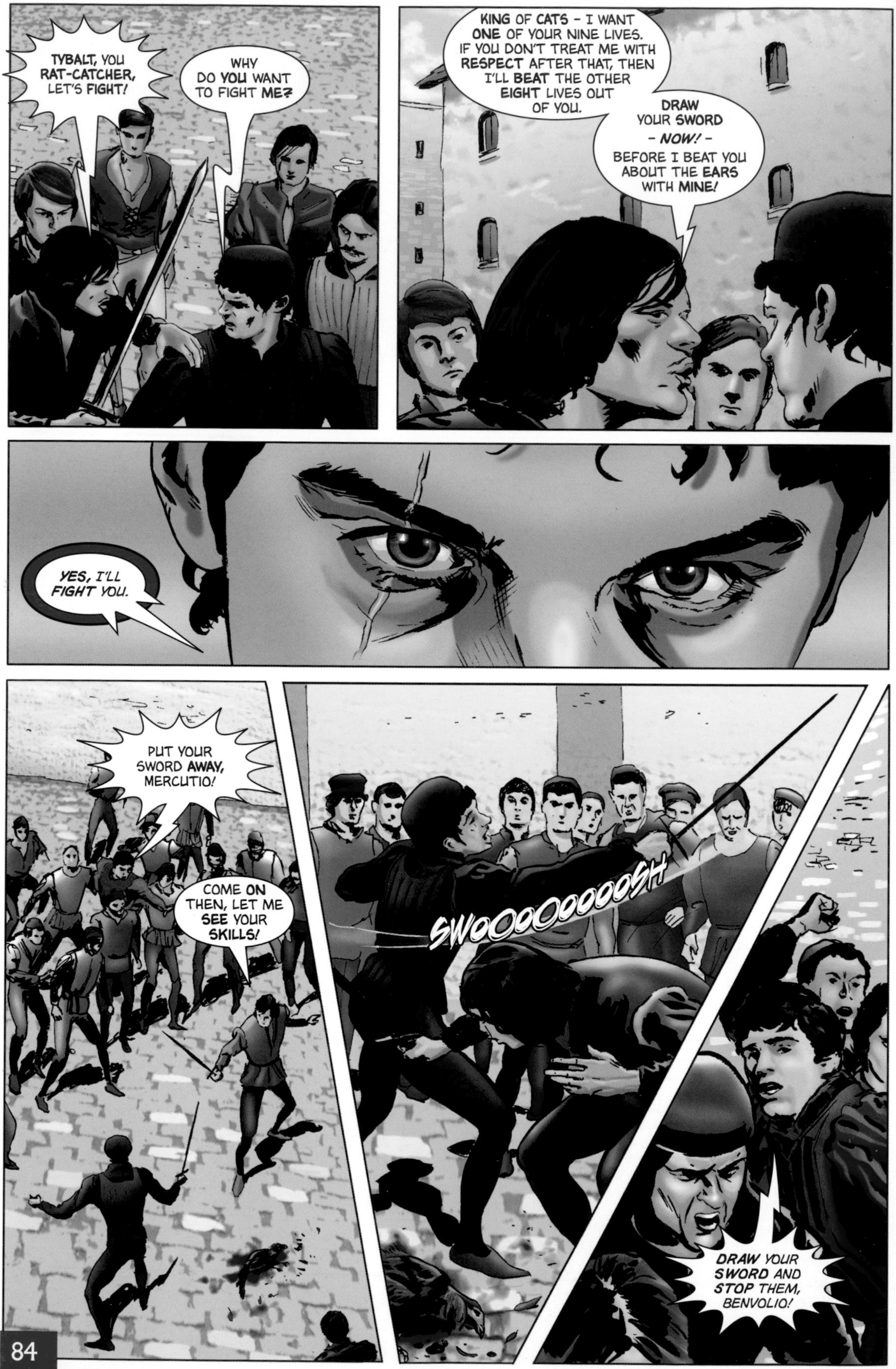
TYBALT, YOU RAT-CATCHER, LET'S FIGHT!
WHY DO YOU WANT TO FIGHT ME?
KING OF CATS – I WANT ONE OF YOUR NINE LIVES. IF YOU DON'T TREAT ME WITH RESPECT AFTER THAT, THEN I'LL BEAT THE OTHER EIGHT LIVES OUT OF YOU.
DRAW YOUR SWORD – NOW! – BEFORE I BEAT YOU ABOUT THE EARS WITH MINE!
YES, I'LL FIGHT YOU.
PUT YOUR SWORD AWAY, MERCUTIO!
COME ON THEN, LET ME SEE YOUR SKILLS!
SWOOOOOOOOOSH
DRAW YOUR SWORD AND STOP THEM, BENVOLIO!

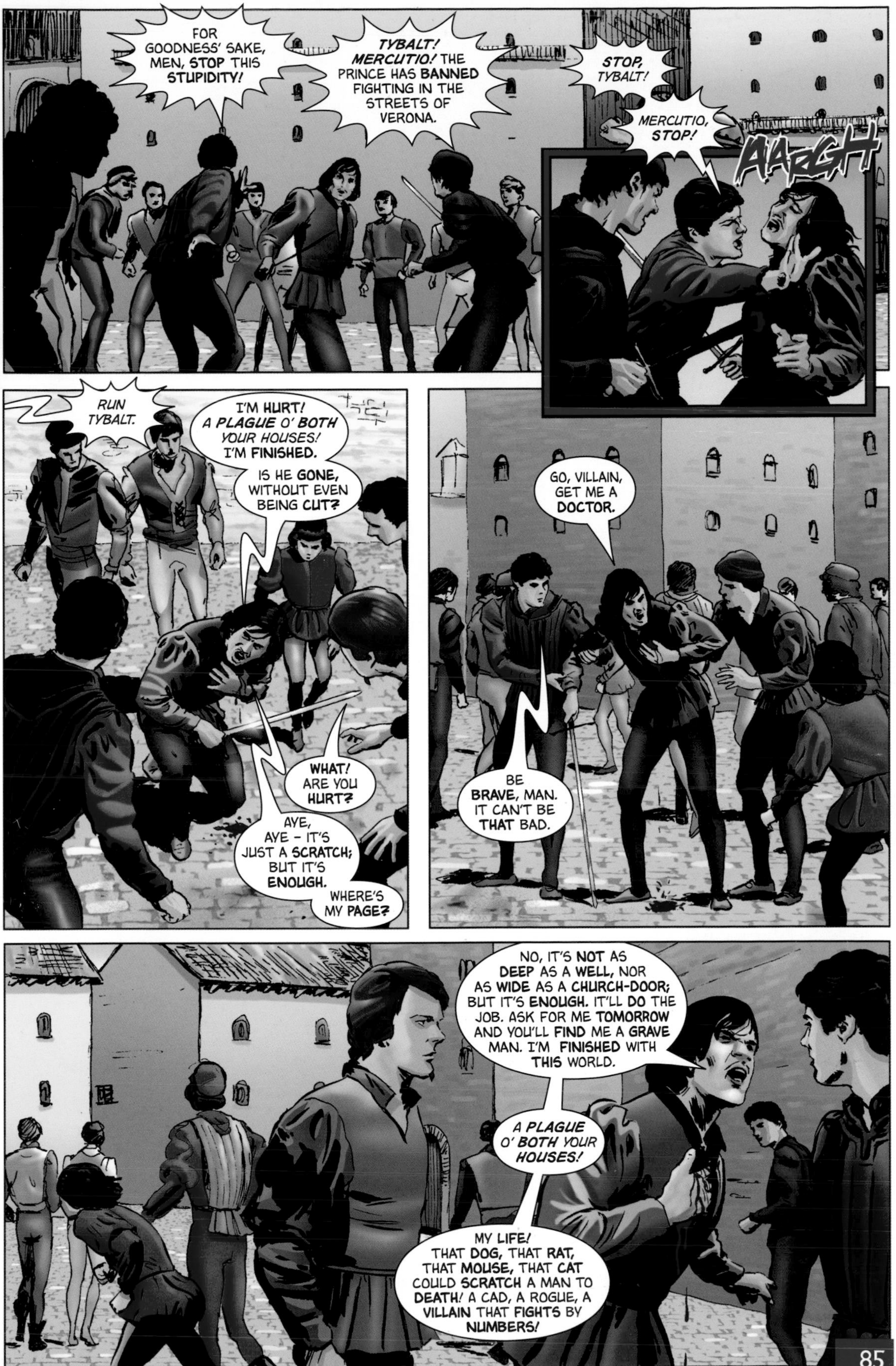
FOR GOODNESS' SAKE, MEN, STOP THIS STUPIDITY!
TYBALT! MERCUTIO! THE PRINCE HAS BANNED FIGHTING IN THE STREETS OF VERONA.
STOP, TYBALT!
MERCUTIO, STOP!
AARGH
RUN TYBALT.
I'M HURT! A PLAGUE O' BOTH YOUR HOUSES! I'M FINISHED.
IS HE GONE, WITHOUT EVEN BEING CUT?
WHAT! ARE YOU HURT?
AYE, AYE – IT'S JUST A SCRATCH; BUT IT'S ENOUGH.
WHERE'S MY PAGE?
GO, VILLAIN, GET ME A DOCTOR.
BE BRAVE, MAN. IT CAN'T BE THAT BAD.
NO, IT'S NOT AS DEEP AS A WELL, NOR AS WIDE AS A CHURCH-DOOR; BUT IT'S ENOUGH. IT'LL DO THE JOB. ASK FOR ME TOMORROW AND YOU'LL FIND ME A GRAVE MAN. I'M FINISHED WITH THIS WORLD.
A PLAGUE O' BOTH YOUR HOUSES!
MY LIFE! THAT DOG, THAT RAT, THAT MOUSE, THAT CAT COULD SCRATCH A MAN TO DEATH! A CAD, A ROGUE, A VILLAIN THAT FIGHTS BY NUMBERS!

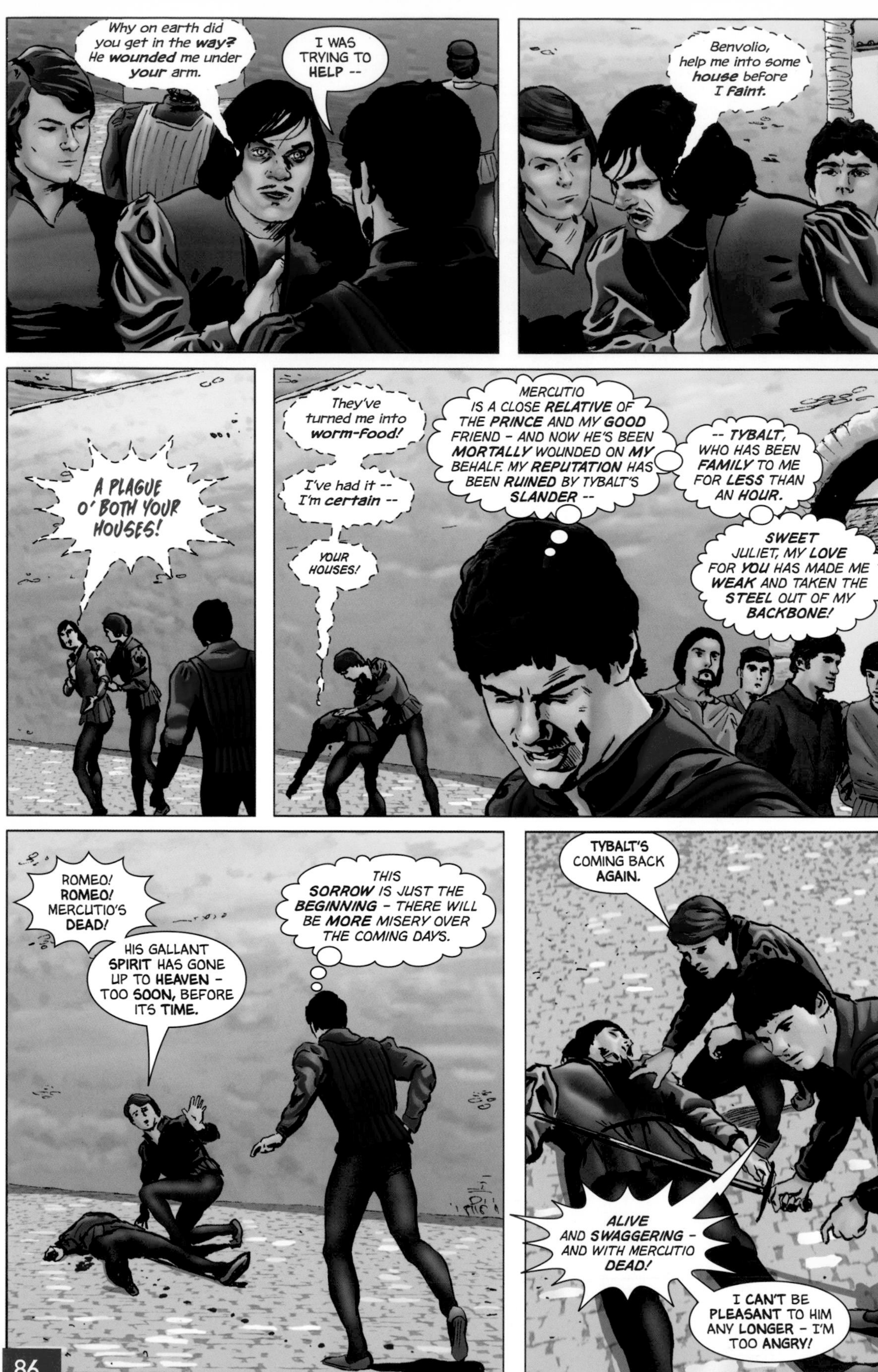

Why on earth did you get in the **way?** He **wounded** me under **your** arm.
I WAS TRYING TO **HELP** --
Benvolio, help me into some **house** before I **faint.**
A PLAGUE O' BOTH YOUR HOUSES!
They've turned me into **worm-food!**
I've had it -- I'm **certain** --
YOUR HOUSES!
MERCUTIO IS A CLOSE **RELATIVE** OF THE **PRINCE** AND MY **GOOD** FRIEND – AND NOW HE'S BEEN **MORTALLY** WOUNDED ON **MY** BEHALF. MY **REPUTATION** HAS BEEN **RUINED** BY TYBALT'S **SLANDER** --
-- **TYBALT,** WHO HAS BEEN **FAMILY** TO ME FOR **LESS** THAN AN **HOUR.**
SWEET JULIET, MY **LOVE** FOR **YOU** HAS MADE ME **WEAK** AND TAKEN THE **STEEL** OUT OF MY **BACKBONE!**
ROMEO! **ROMEO!** MERCUTIO'S **DEAD!**
HIS GALLANT **SPIRIT** HAS GONE UP TO **HEAVEN** – TOO **SOON,** BEFORE ITS **TIME.**
THIS **SORROW** IS JUST THE **BEGINNING** – THERE WILL BE **MORE** MISERY OVER THE COMING DAYS.
TYBALT'S COMING BACK **AGAIN.**
ALIVE AND **SWAGGERING** – AND WITH MERCUTIO **DEAD!**
I **CAN'T** BE **PLEASANT** TO HIM ANY **LONGER** – I'M TOO **ANGRY!**

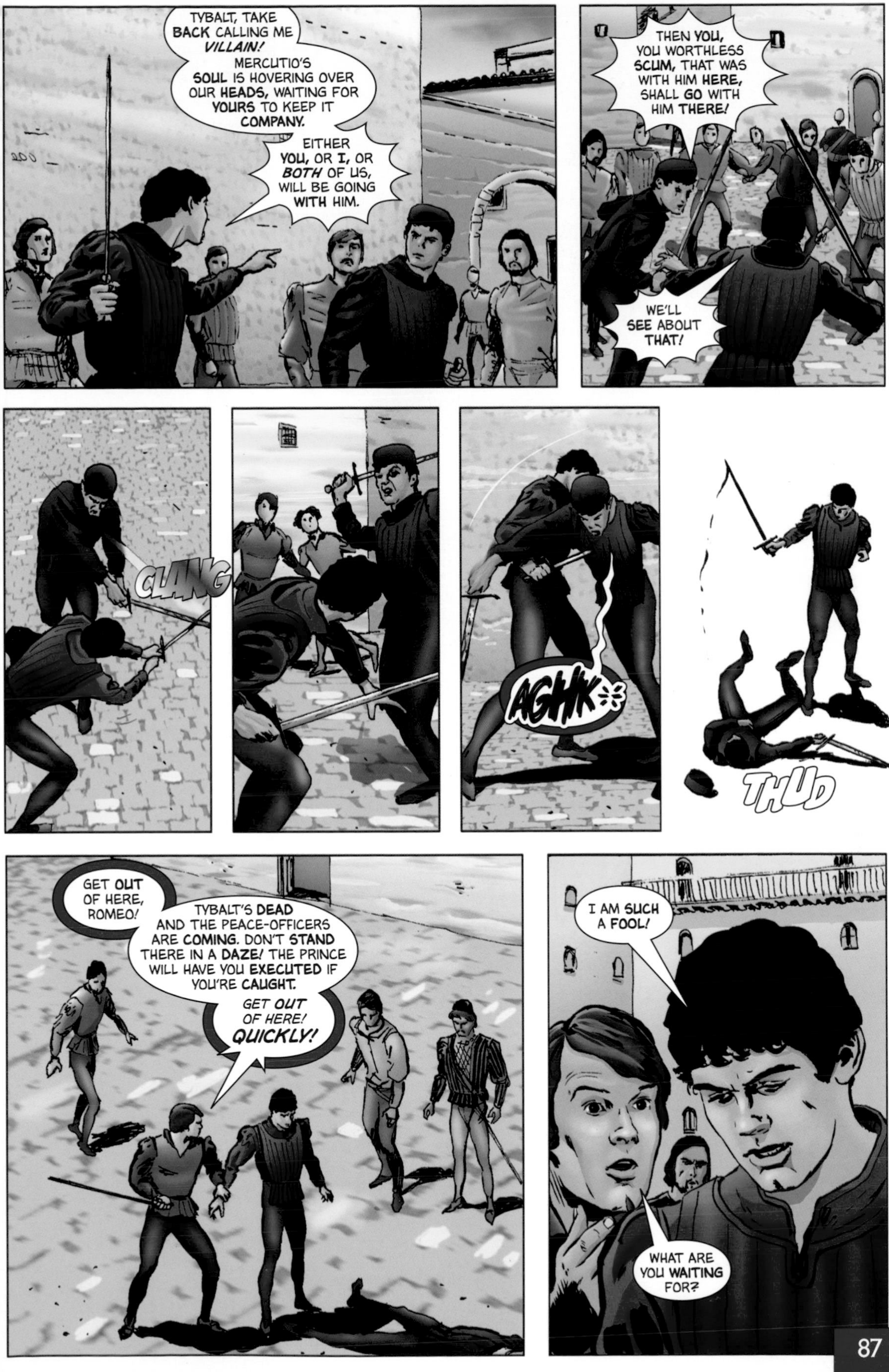
TYBALT, TAKE BACK CALLING ME VILLAIN!
MERCUTIO'S SOUL IS HOVERING OVER OUR HEADS, WAITING FOR YOURS TO KEEP IT COMPANY.
EITHER YOU, OR I, OR BOTH OF US, WILL BE GOING WITH HIM.
THEN YOU, YOU WORTHLESS SCUM, THAT WAS WITH HIM HERE, SHALL GO WITH HIM THERE!
WE'LL SEE ABOUT THAT!
CLANG
AGHK
THUD
GET OUT OF HERE, ROMEO!
TYBALT'S DEAD AND THE PEACE-OFFICERS ARE COMING. DON'T STAND THERE IN A DAZE! THE PRINCE WILL HAVE YOU EXECUTED IF YOU'RE CAUGHT.
GET OUT OF HERE! QUICKLY!
I AM SUCH A FOOL!
WHAT ARE YOU WAITING FOR?

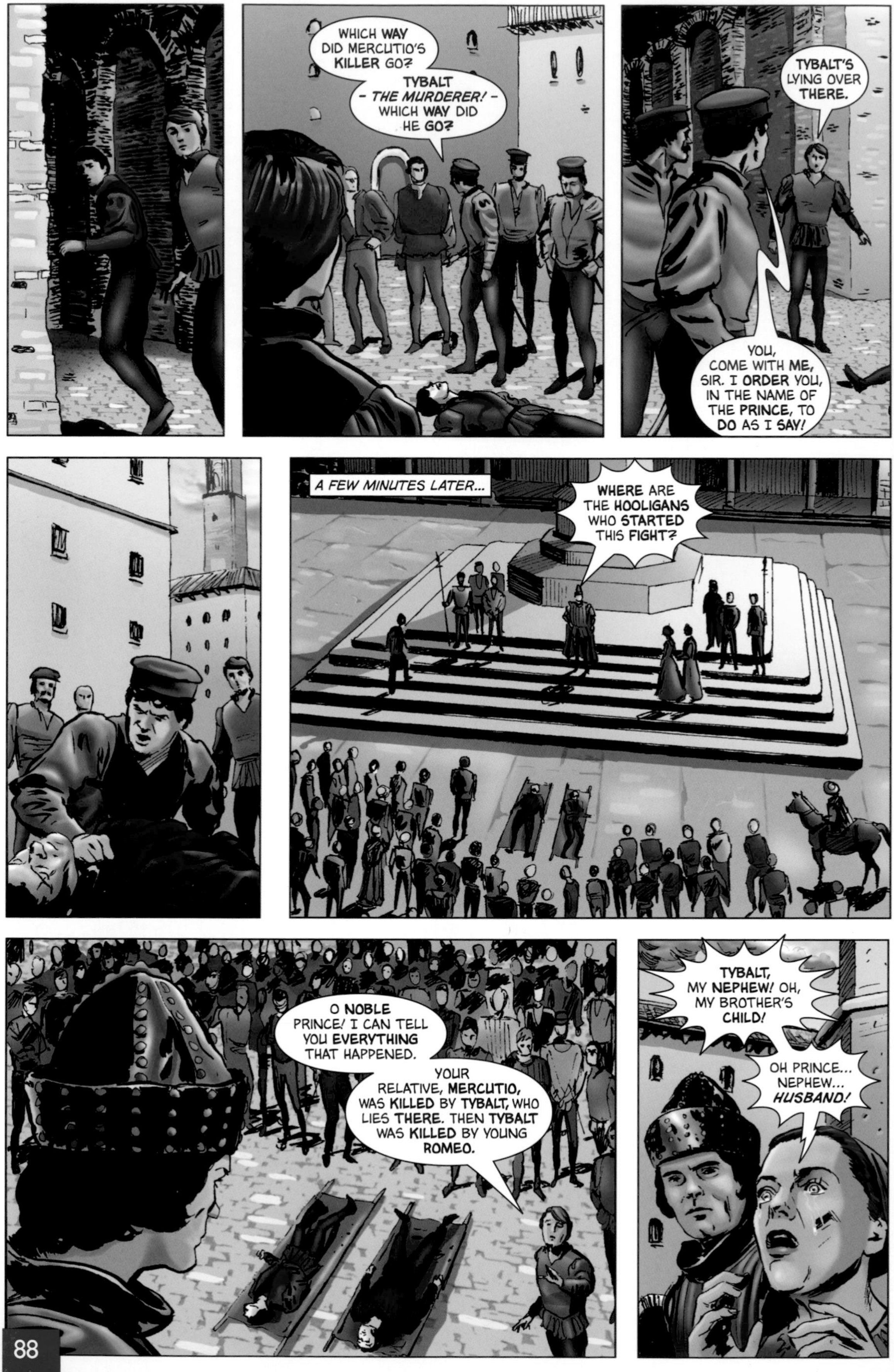

WHICH WAY DID MERCUTIO'S KILLER GO?
TYBALT - THE MURDERER! - WHICH WAY DID HE GO?
TYBALT'S LYING OVER THERE.
YOU, COME WITH ME, SIR. I ORDER YOU, IN THE NAME OF THE PRINCE, TO DO AS I SAY!
A FEW MINUTES LATER...
WHERE ARE THE HOOLIGANS WHO STARTED THIS FIGHT?
O NOBLE PRINCE! I CAN TELL YOU EVERYTHING THAT HAPPENED.
YOUR RELATIVE, MERCUTIO, WAS KILLED BY TYBALT, WHO LIES THERE. THEN TYBALT WAS KILLED BY YOUNG ROMEO.
TYBALT, MY NEPHEW! OH, MY BROTHER'S CHILD!
OH PRINCE... NEPHEW... HUSBAND!

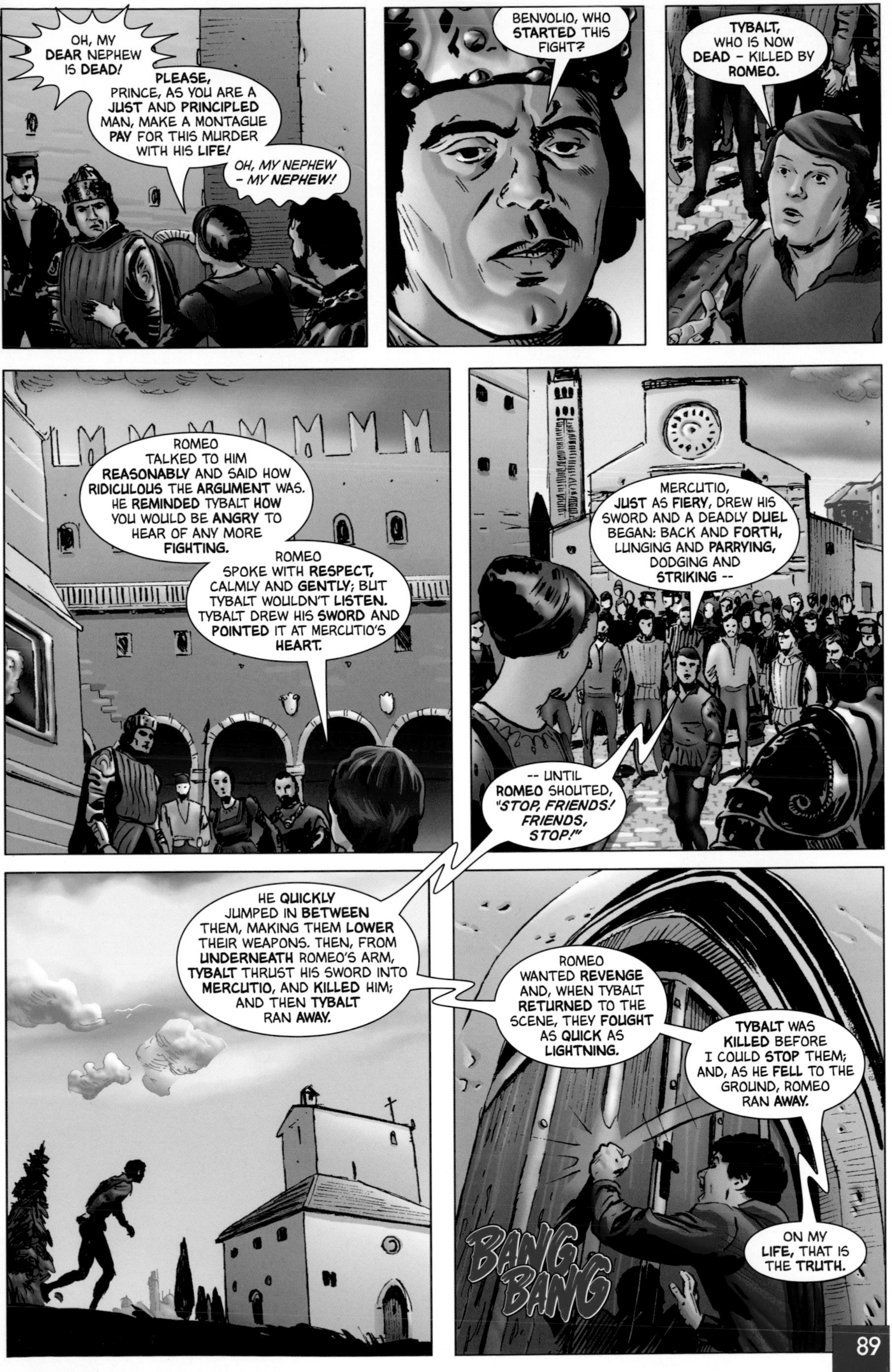
OH, MY DEAR NEPHEW IS DEAD!
PLEASE, PRINCE, AS YOU ARE A JUST AND PRINCIPLED MAN, MAKE A MONTAGUE PAY FOR THIS MURDER WITH HIS LIFE!
OH, MY NEPHEW – MY NEPHEW!
BENVOLIO, WHO STARTED THIS FIGHT?
TYBALT, WHO IS NOW DEAD – KILLED BY ROMEO.
ROMEO TALKED TO HIM REASONABLY AND SAID HOW RIDICULOUS THE ARGUMENT WAS. HE REMINDED TYBALT HOW YOU WOULD BE ANGRY TO HEAR OF ANY MORE FIGHTING.
ROMEO SPOKE WITH RESPECT, CALMLY AND GENTLY; BUT TYBALT WOULDN'T LISTEN. TYBALT DREW HIS SWORD AND POINTED IT AT MERCUTIO'S HEART.
MERCUTIO, JUST AS FIERY, DREW HIS SWORD AND A DEADLY DUEL BEGAN: BACK AND FORTH, LUNGING AND PARRYING, DODGING AND STRIKING --
-- UNTIL ROMEO SHOUTED, "STOP, FRIENDS! FRIENDS, STOP!"
HE QUICKLY JUMPED IN BETWEEN THEM, MAKING THEM LOWER THEIR WEAPONS. THEN, FROM UNDERNEATH ROMEO'S ARM, TYBALT THRUST HIS SWORD INTO MERCUTIO, AND KILLED HIM; AND THEN TYBALT RAN AWAY.
ROMEO WANTED REVENGE AND, WHEN TYBALT RETURNED TO THE SCENE, THEY FOUGHT AS QUICK AS LIGHTNING.
TYBALT WAS KILLED BEFORE I COULD STOP THEM; AND, AS HE FELL TO THE GROUND, ROMEO RAN AWAY.
BANG BANG
ON MY LIFE, THAT IS THE TRUTH.

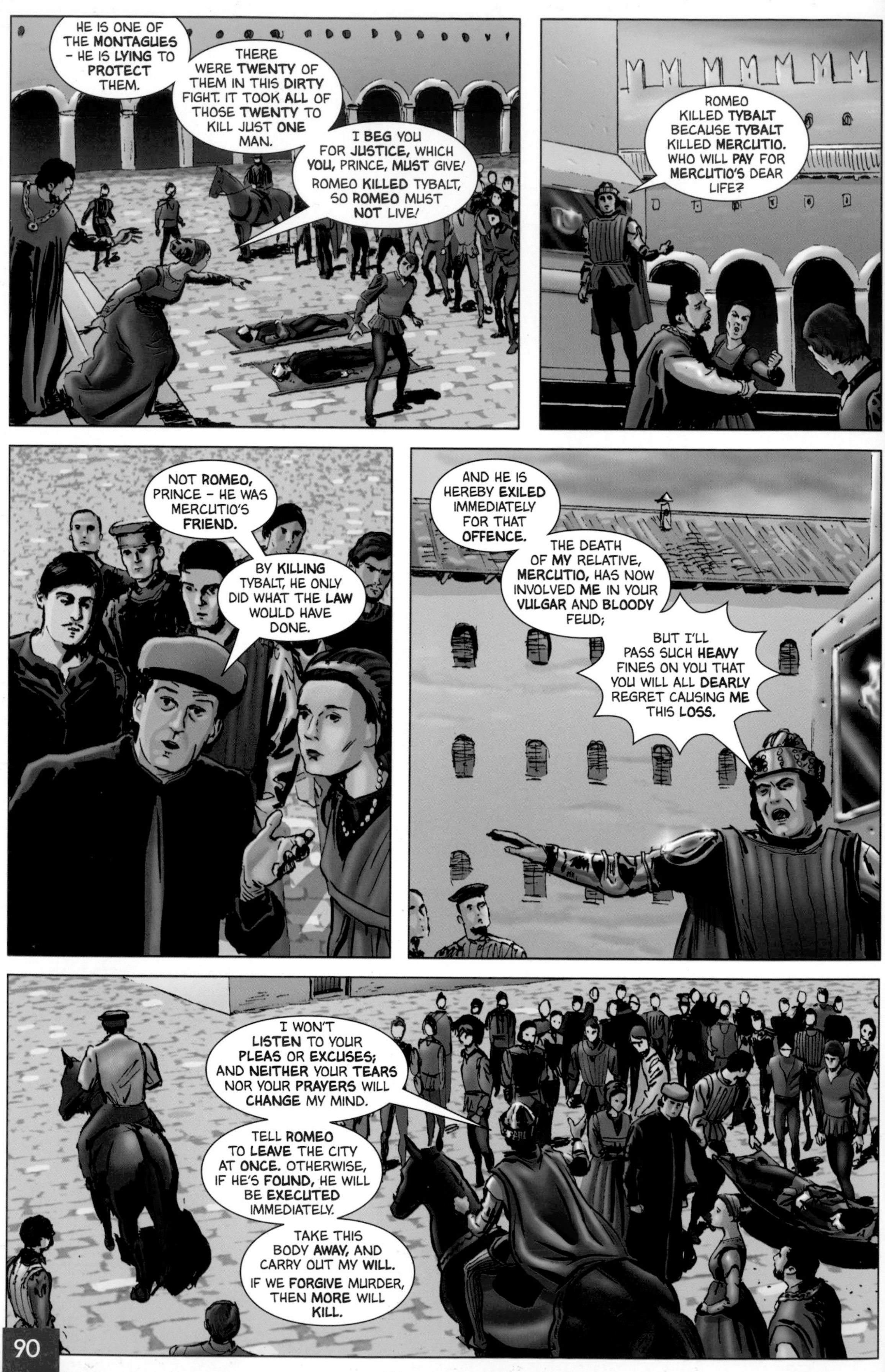
HE IS ONE OF THE MONTAGUES – HE IS LYING TO PROTECT THEM.
THERE WERE TWENTY OF THEM IN THIS DIRTY FIGHT. IT TOOK ALL OF THOSE TWENTY TO KILL JUST ONE MAN.
I BEG YOU FOR JUSTICE, WHICH YOU, PRINCE, MUST GIVE!
ROMEO KILLED TYBALT, SO ROMEO MUST NOT LIVE!
ROMEO KILLED TYBALT BECAUSE TYBALT KILLED MERCUTIO. WHO WILL PAY FOR MERCUTIO'S DEAR LIFE?
NOT ROMEO, PRINCE – HE WAS MERCUTIO'S FRIEND.
BY KILLING TYBALT, HE ONLY DID WHAT THE LAW WOULD HAVE DONE.
AND HE IS HEREBY EXILED IMMEDIATELY FOR THAT OFFENCE.
THE DEATH OF MY RELATIVE, MERCUTIO, HAS NOW INVOLVED ME IN YOUR VULGAR AND BLOODY FEUD;
BUT I'LL PASS SUCH HEAVY FINES ON YOU THAT YOU WILL ALL DEARLY REGRET CAUSING ME THIS LOSS.
I WON'T LISTEN TO YOUR PLEAS OR EXCUSES; AND NEITHER YOUR TEARS NOR YOUR PRAYERS WILL CHANGE MY MIND.
TELL ROMEO TO LEAVE THE CITY AT ONCE. OTHERWISE, IF HE'S FOUND, HE WILL BE EXECUTED IMMEDIATELY.
TAKE THIS BODY AWAY, AND CARRY OUT MY WILL.
IF WE FORGIVE MURDER, THEN MORE WILL KILL.

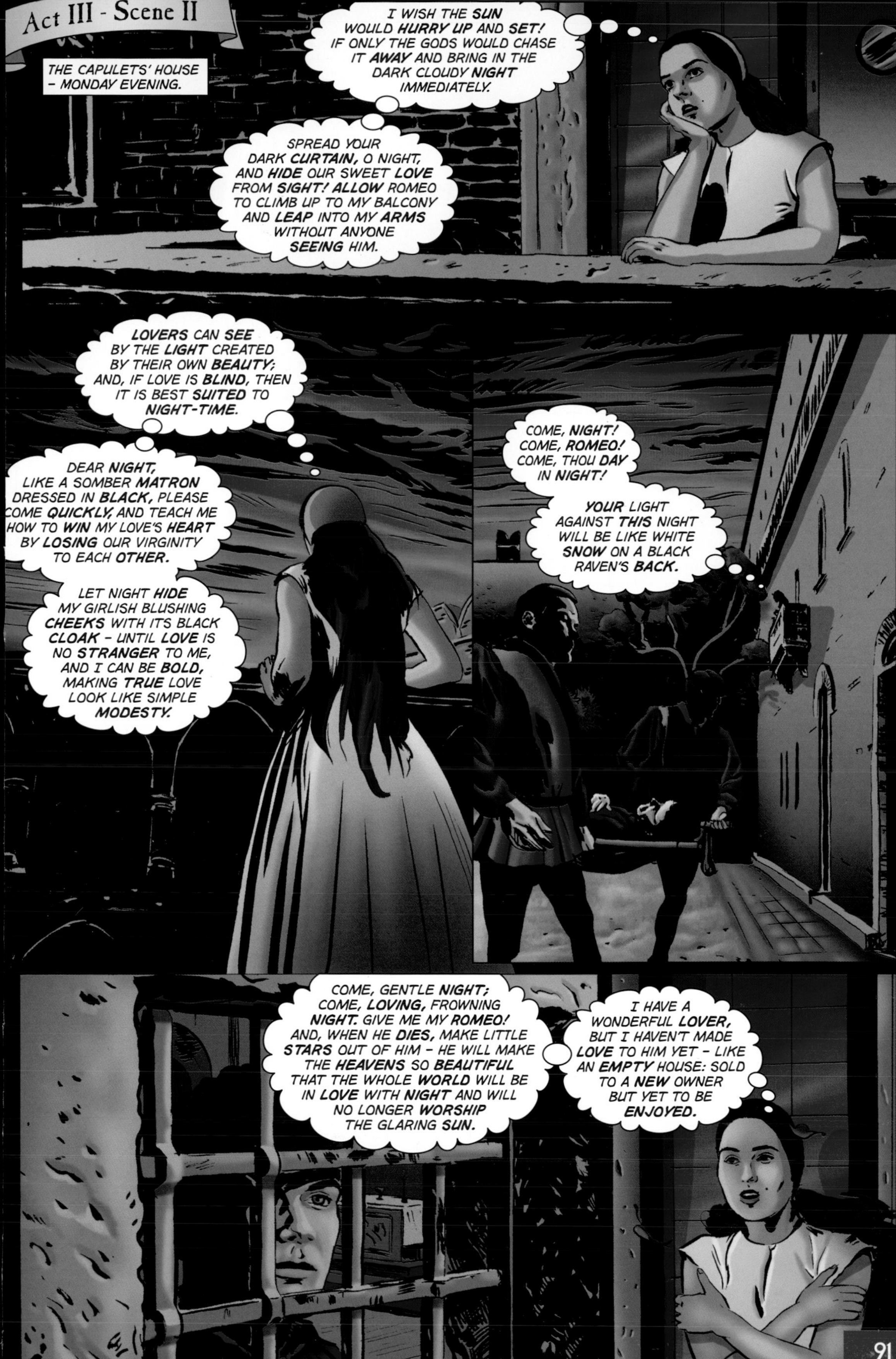

Act III - Scene II
THE CAPULETS' HOUSE - MONDAY EVENING.
I WISH THE SUN WOULD HURRY UP AND SET! IF ONLY THE GODS WOULD CHASE IT AWAY AND BRING IN THE DARK CLOUDY NIGHT IMMEDIATELY.
SPREAD YOUR DARK CURTAIN, O NIGHT, AND HIDE OUR SWEET LOVE FROM SIGHT! ALLOW ROMEO TO CLIMB UP TO MY BALCONY AND LEAP INTO MY ARMS WITHOUT ANYONE SEEING HIM.
LOVERS CAN SEE BY THE LIGHT CREATED BY THEIR OWN BEAUTY; AND, IF LOVE IS BLIND, THEN IT IS BEST SUITED TO NIGHT-TIME.
DEAR NIGHT, LIKE A SOMBER MATRON DRESSED IN BLACK, PLEASE COME QUICKLY, AND TEACH ME HOW TO WIN MY LOVE'S HEART BY LOSING OUR VIRGINITY TO EACH OTHER.
LET NIGHT HIDE MY GIRLISH BLUSHING CHEEKS WITH ITS BLACK CLOAK - UNTIL LOVE IS NO STRANGER TO ME, AND I CAN BE BOLD, MAKING TRUE LOVE LOOK LIKE SIMPLE MODESTY.
COME, NIGHT! COME, ROMEO! COME, THOU DAY IN NIGHT!
YOUR LIGHT AGAINST THIS NIGHT WILL BE LIKE WHITE SNOW ON A BLACK RAVEN'S BACK.
COME, GENTLE NIGHT; COME, LOVING, FROWNING NIGHT. GIVE ME MY ROMEO! AND, WHEN HE DIES, MAKE LITTLE STARS OUT OF HIM - HE WILL MAKE THE HEAVENS SO BEAUTIFUL THAT THE WHOLE WORLD WILL BE IN LOVE WITH NIGHT AND WILL NO LONGER WORSHIP THE GLARING SUN.
I HAVE A WONDERFUL LOVER, BUT I HAVEN'T MADE LOVE TO HIM YET - LIKE AN EMPTY HOUSE: SOLD TO A NEW OWNER BUT YET TO BE ENJOYED.

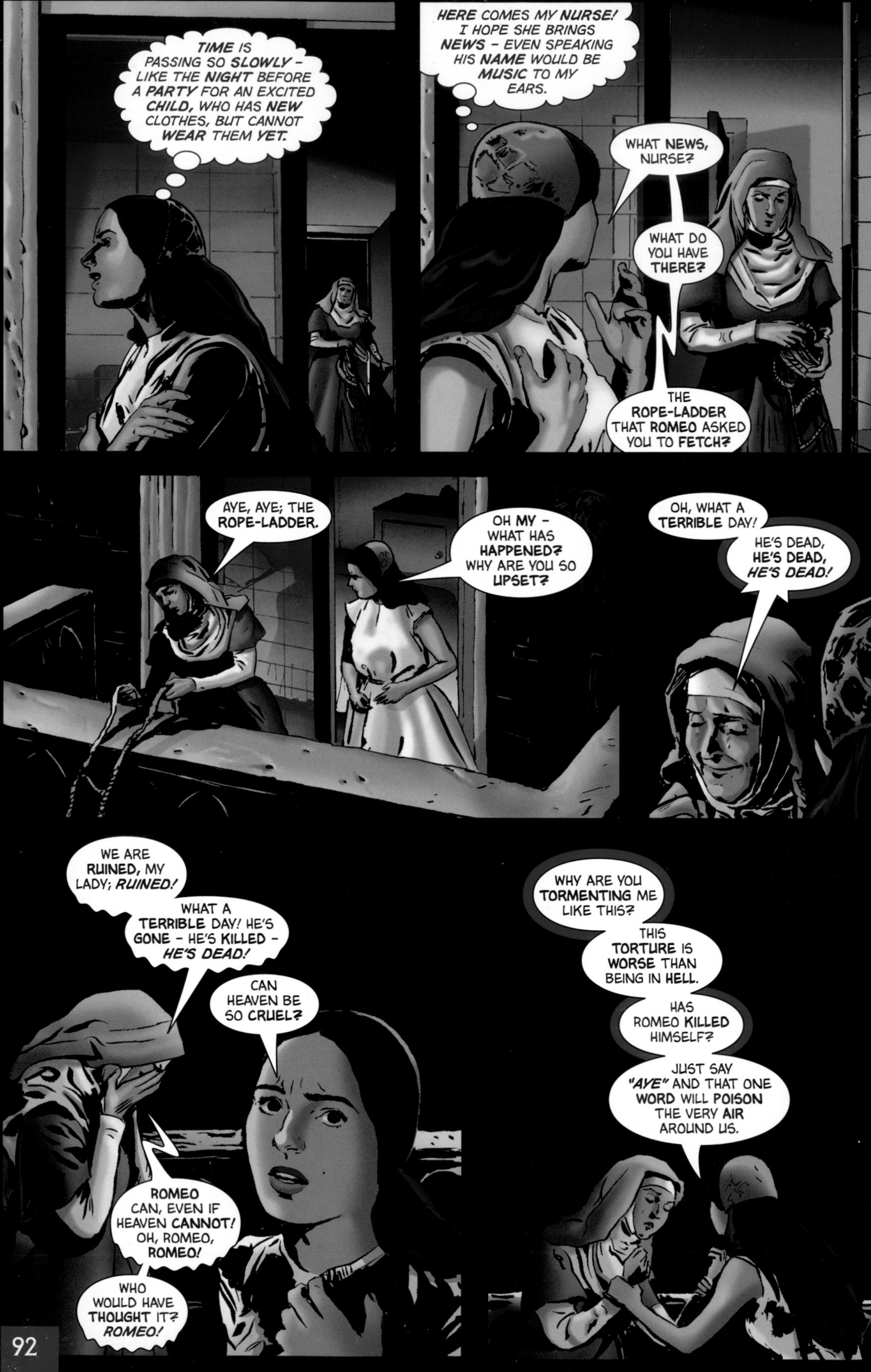
TIME IS PASSING SO SLOWLY – LIKE THE NIGHT BEFORE A PARTY FOR AN EXCITED CHILD, WHO HAS NEW CLOTHES, BUT CANNOT WEAR THEM YET.
HERE COMES MY NURSE! I HOPE SHE BRINGS NEWS – EVEN SPEAKING HIS NAME WOULD BE MUSIC TO MY EARS.
WHAT NEWS, NURSE?
WHAT DO YOU HAVE THERE?
THE ROPE-LADDER THAT ROMEO ASKED YOU TO FETCH?
AYE, AYE; THE ROPE-LADDER.
OH MY – WHAT HAS HAPPENED? WHY ARE YOU SO UPSET?
OH, WHAT A TERRIBLE DAY!
HE'S DEAD, HE'S DEAD, HE'S DEAD!
WE ARE RUINED, MY LADY; RUINED!
WHAT A TERRIBLE DAY! HE'S GONE – HE'S KILLED – HE'S DEAD!
CAN HEAVEN BE SO CRUEL?
ROMEO CAN, EVEN IF HEAVEN CANNOT! OH, ROMEO, ROMEO!
WHO WOULD HAVE THOUGHT IT? ROMEO!
WHY ARE YOU TORMENTING ME LIKE THIS?
THIS TORTURE IS WORSE THAN BEING IN HELL.
HAS ROMEO KILLED HIMSELF?
JUST SAY "AYE" AND THAT ONE WORD WILL POISON THE VERY AIR AROUND US.

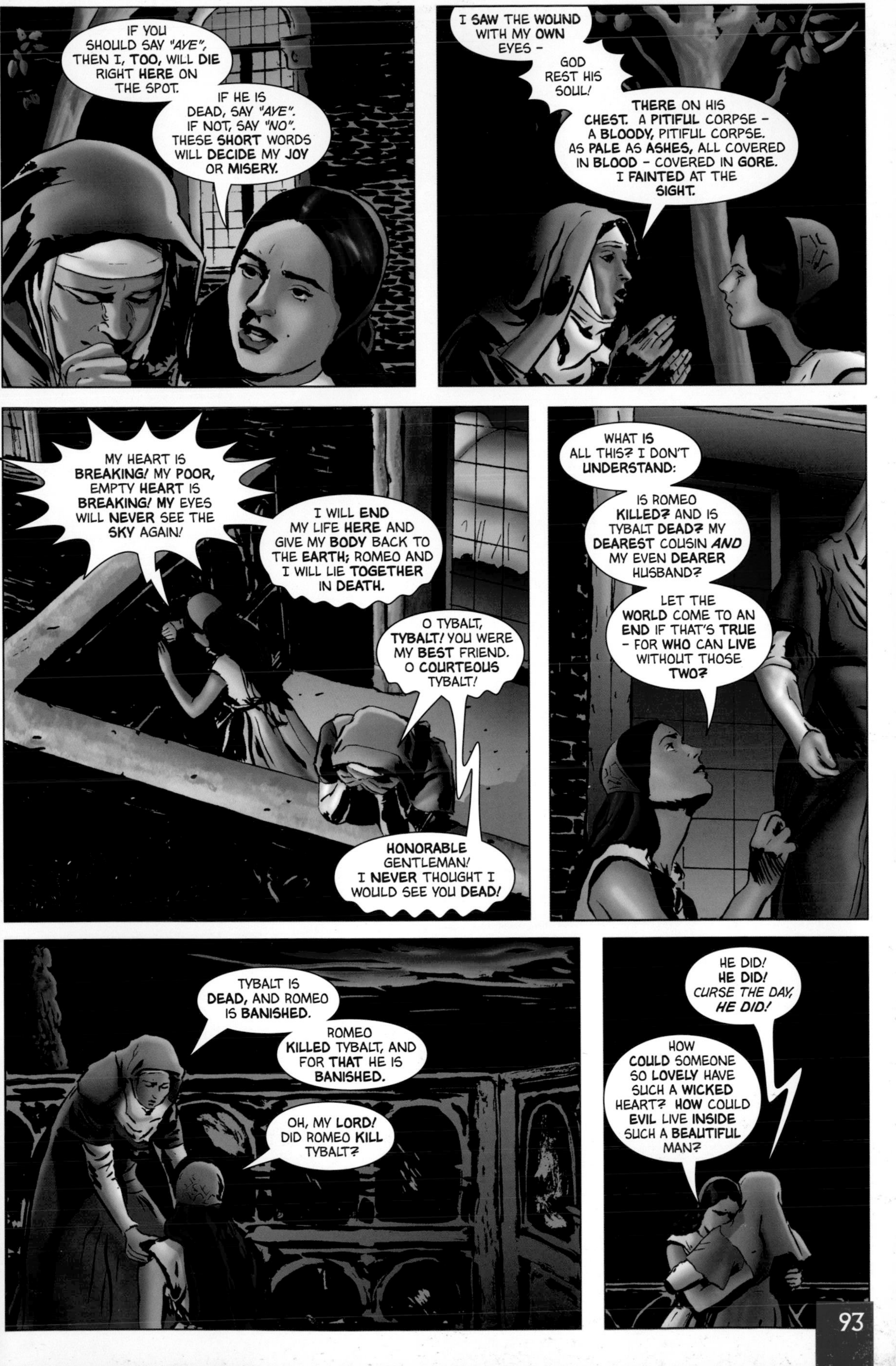

IF YOU SHOULD SAY "AYE", THEN I, TOO, WILL DIE RIGHT HERE ON THE SPOT.
IF HE IS DEAD, SAY "AYE". IF NOT, SAY "NO". THESE SHORT WORDS WILL DECIDE MY JOY OR MISERY.
I SAW THE WOUND WITH MY OWN EYES -
GOD REST HIS SOUL!
THERE ON HIS CHEST. A PITIFUL CORPSE - A BLOODY, PITIFUL CORPSE. AS PALE AS ASHES, ALL COVERED IN BLOOD - COVERED IN GORE. I FAINTED AT THE SIGHT.
MY HEART IS BREAKING! MY POOR, EMPTY HEART IS BREAKING! MY EYES WILL NEVER SEE THE SKY AGAIN!
I WILL END MY LIFE HERE AND GIVE MY BODY BACK TO THE EARTH; ROMEO AND I WILL LIE TOGETHER IN DEATH.
O TYBALT, TYBALT! YOU WERE MY BEST FRIEND. O COURTEOUS TYBALT!
HONORABLE GENTLEMAN! I NEVER THOUGHT I WOULD SEE YOU DEAD!
WHAT IS ALL THIS? I DON'T UNDERSTAND:
IS ROMEO KILLED? AND IS TYBALT DEAD? MY DEAREST COUSIN AND MY EVEN DEARER HUSBAND?
LET THE WORLD COME TO AN END IF THAT'S TRUE - FOR WHO CAN LIVE WITHOUT THOSE TWO?
TYBALT IS DEAD, AND ROMEO IS BANISHED.
ROMEO KILLED TYBALT, AND FOR THAT HE IS BANISHED.
OH, MY LORD! DID ROMEO KILL TYBALT?
HE DID! HE DID! CURSE THE DAY, HE DID!
HOW COULD SOMEONE SO LOVELY HAVE SUCH A WICKED HEART? HOW COULD EVIL LIVE INSIDE SUCH A BEAUTIFUL MAN?

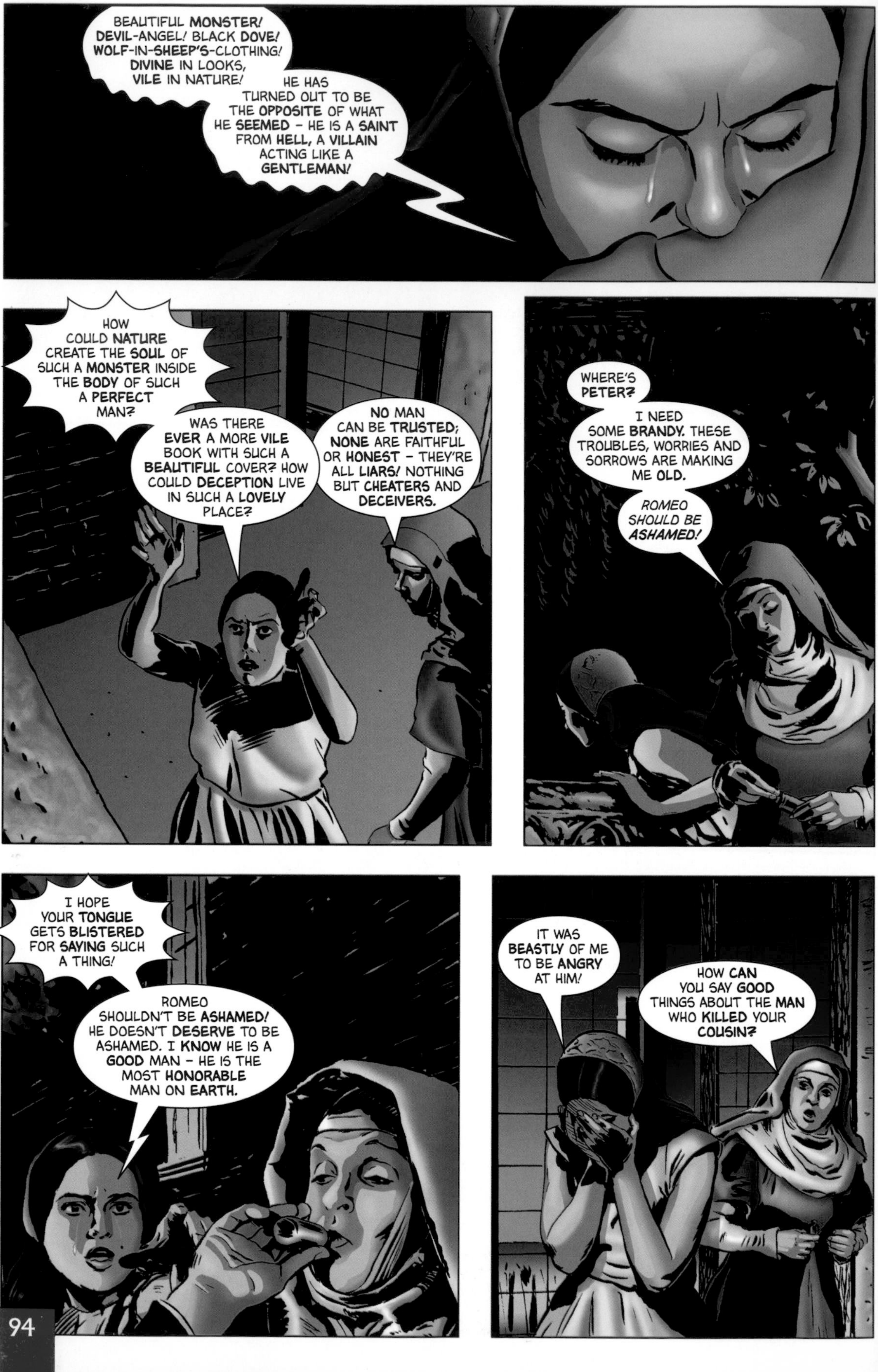
BEAUTIFUL MONSTER! DEVIL-ANGEL! BLACK DOVE! WOLF-IN-SHEEP'S-CLOTHING! DIVINE IN LOOKS, VILE IN NATURE!
HE HAS TURNED OUT TO BE THE OPPOSITE OF WHAT HE SEEMED – HE IS A SAINT FROM HELL, A VILLAIN ACTING LIKE A GENTLEMAN!
HOW COULD NATURE CREATE THE SOUL OF SUCH A MONSTER INSIDE THE BODY OF SUCH A PERFECT MAN?
WAS THERE EVER A MORE VILE BOOK WITH SUCH A BEAUTIFUL COVER? HOW COULD DECEPTION LIVE IN SUCH A LOVELY PLACE?
NO MAN CAN BE TRUSTED; NONE ARE FAITHFUL OR HONEST – THEY'RE ALL LIARS! NOTHING BUT CHEATERS AND DECEIVERS.
WHERE'S PETER?
I NEED SOME BRANDY. THESE TROUBLES, WORRIES AND SORROWS ARE MAKING ME OLD.
ROMEO SHOULD BE ASHAMED!
I HOPE YOUR TONGUE GETS BLISTERED FOR SAYING SUCH A THING!
ROMEO SHOULDN'T BE ASHAMED! HE DOESN'T DESERVE TO BE ASHAMED. I KNOW HE IS A GOOD MAN – HE IS THE MOST HONORABLE MAN ON EARTH.
IT WAS BEASTLY OF ME TO BE ANGRY AT HIM!
HOW CAN YOU SAY GOOD THINGS ABOUT THE MAN WHO KILLED YOUR COUSIN?

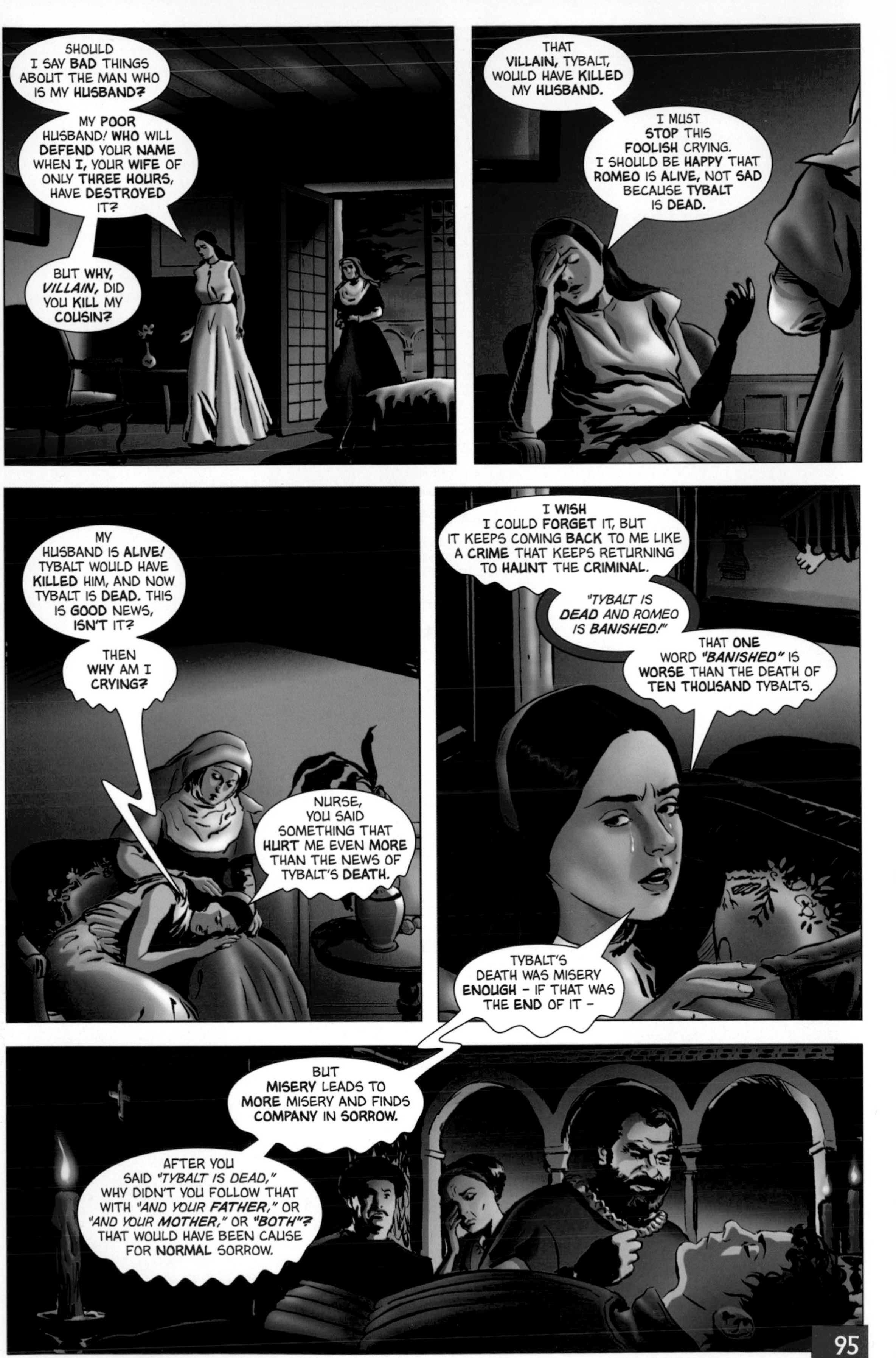
SHOULD I SAY BAD THINGS ABOUT THE MAN WHO IS MY HUSBAND?
MY POOR HUSBAND! WHO WILL DEFEND YOUR NAME WHEN I, YOUR WIFE OF ONLY THREE HOURS, HAVE DESTROYED IT?
BUT WHY, VILLAIN, DID YOU KILL MY COUSIN?
THAT VILLAIN, TYBALT, WOULD HAVE KILLED MY HUSBAND.
I MUST STOP THIS FOOLISH CRYING. I SHOULD BE HAPPY THAT ROMEO IS ALIVE, NOT SAD BECAUSE TYBALT IS DEAD.
MY HUSBAND IS ALIVE! TYBALT WOULD HAVE KILLED HIM, AND NOW TYBALT IS DEAD. THIS IS GOOD NEWS, ISN'T IT?
THEN WHY AM I CRYING?
NURSE, YOU SAID SOMETHING THAT HURT ME EVEN MORE THAN THE NEWS OF TYBALT'S DEATH.
I WISH I COULD FORGET IT, BUT IT KEEPS COMING BACK TO ME LIKE A CRIME THAT KEEPS RETURNING TO HAUNT THE CRIMINAL.
"TYBALT IS DEAD AND ROMEO IS BANISHED!"
THAT ONE WORD "BANISHED" IS WORSE THAN THE DEATH OF TEN THOUSAND TYBALTS.
TYBALT'S DEATH WAS MISERY ENOUGH – IF THAT WAS THE END OF IT –
BUT MISERY LEADS TO MORE MISERY AND FINDS COMPANY IN SORROW.
AFTER YOU SAID "TYBALT IS DEAD," WHY DIDN'T YOU FOLLOW THAT WITH "AND YOUR FATHER," OR "AND YOUR MOTHER," OR "BOTH"? THAT WOULD HAVE BEEN CAUSE FOR NORMAL SORROW.

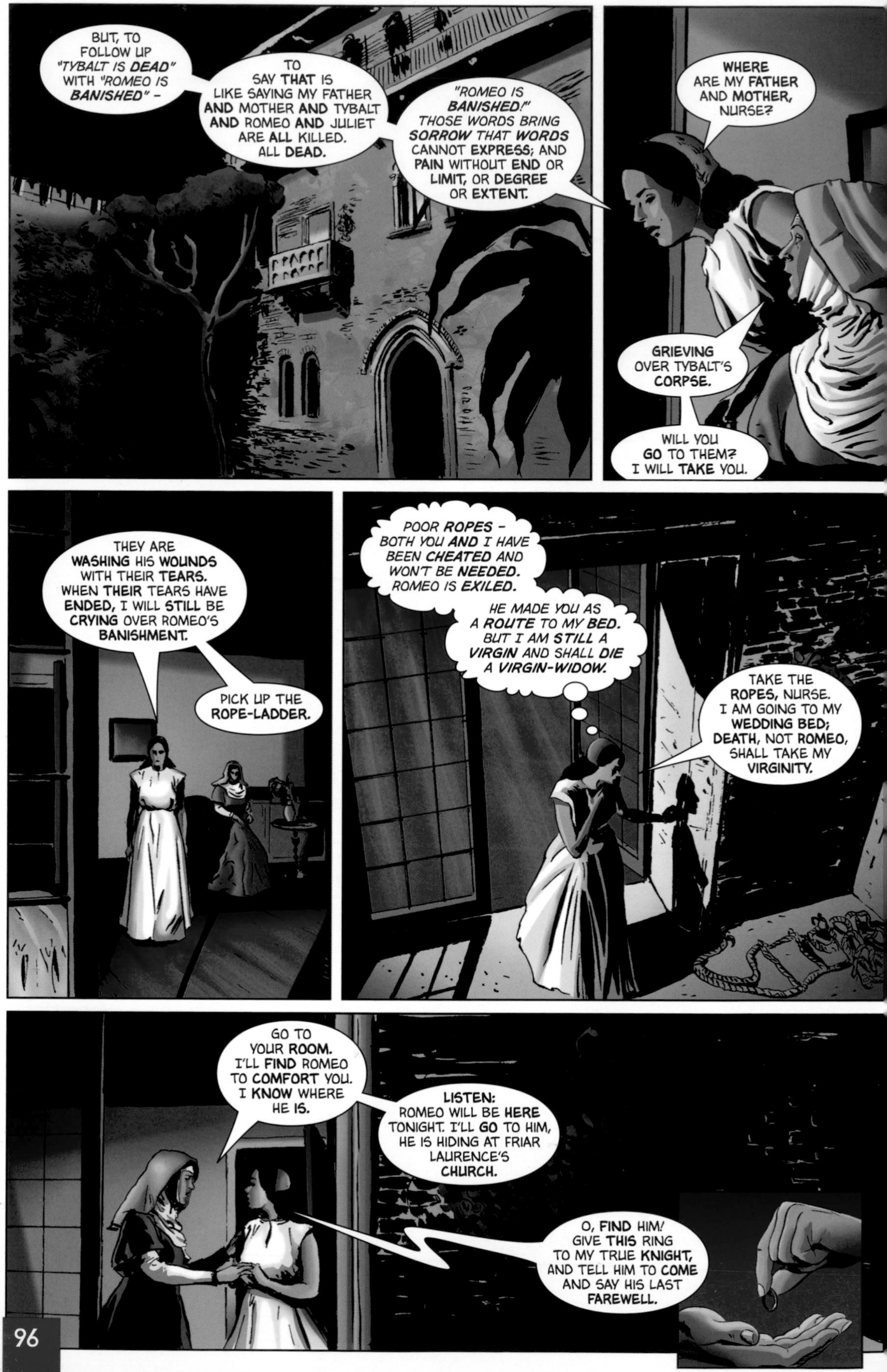
BUT, TO FOLLOW UP "TYBALT IS DEAD" WITH "ROMEO IS BANISHED" -
TO SAY THAT IS LIKE SAYING MY FATHER AND MOTHER AND TYBALT AND ROMEO AND JULIET ARE ALL KILLED. ALL DEAD.
"ROMEO IS BANISHED!" THOSE WORDS BRING SORROW THAT WORDS CANNOT EXPRESS; AND PAIN WITHOUT END OR LIMIT, OR DEGREE OR EXTENT.
WHERE ARE MY FATHER AND MOTHER, NURSE?
GRIEVING OVER TYBALT'S CORPSE.
WILL YOU GO TO THEM? I WILL TAKE YOU.
THEY ARE WASHING HIS WOUNDS WITH THEIR TEARS. WHEN THEIR TEARS HAVE ENDED, I WILL STILL BE CRYING OVER ROMEO'S BANISHMENT.
PICK UP THE ROPE-LADDER.
POOR ROPES - BOTH YOU AND I HAVE BEEN CHEATED AND WON'T BE NEEDED. ROMEO IS EXILED.
HE MADE YOU AS A ROUTE TO MY BED. BUT I AM STILL A VIRGIN AND SHALL DIE A VIRGIN-WIDOW.
TAKE THE ROPES, NURSE. I AM GOING TO MY WEDDING BED; DEATH, NOT ROMEO, SHALL TAKE MY VIRGINITY.
GO TO YOUR ROOM. I'LL FIND ROMEO TO COMFORT YOU. I KNOW WHERE HE IS.
LISTEN: ROMEO WILL BE HERE TONIGHT. I'LL GO TO HIM, HE IS HIDING AT FRIAR LAURENCE'S CHURCH.
O, FIND HIM! GIVE THIS RING TO MY TRUE KNIGHT, AND TELL HIM TO COME AND SAY HIS LAST FAREWELL.

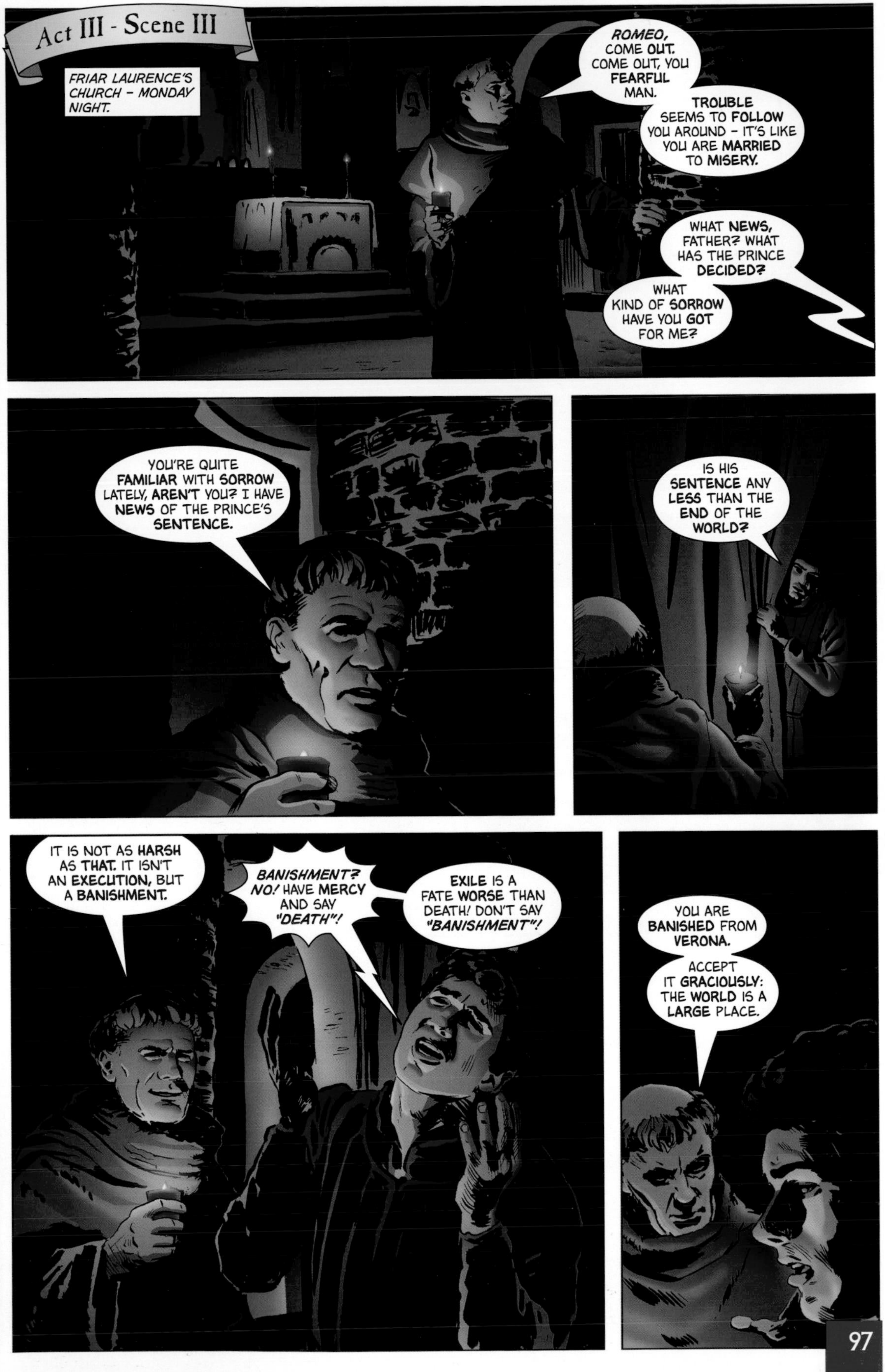
Act III - Scene III
FRIAR LAURENCE'S CHURCH – MONDAY NIGHT.
ROMEO, COME OUT. COME OUT, YOU FEARFUL MAN.
TROUBLE SEEMS TO FOLLOW YOU AROUND – IT'S LIKE YOU ARE MARRIED TO MISERY.
WHAT NEWS, FATHER? WHAT HAS THE PRINCE DECIDED?
WHAT KIND OF SORROW HAVE YOU GOT FOR ME?
YOU'RE QUITE FAMILIAR WITH SORROW LATELY, AREN'T YOU? I HAVE NEWS OF THE PRINCE'S SENTENCE.
IS HIS SENTENCE ANY LESS THAN THE END OF THE WORLD?
IT IS NOT AS HARSH AS THAT. IT ISN'T AN EXECUTION, BUT A BANISHMENT.
BANISHMENT? NO! HAVE MERCY AND SAY "DEATH"!
EXILE IS A FATE WORSE THAN DEATH! DON'T SAY "BANISHMENT"!
YOU ARE BANISHED FROM VERONA.
ACCEPT IT GRACIOUSLY: THE WORLD IS A LARGE PLACE.

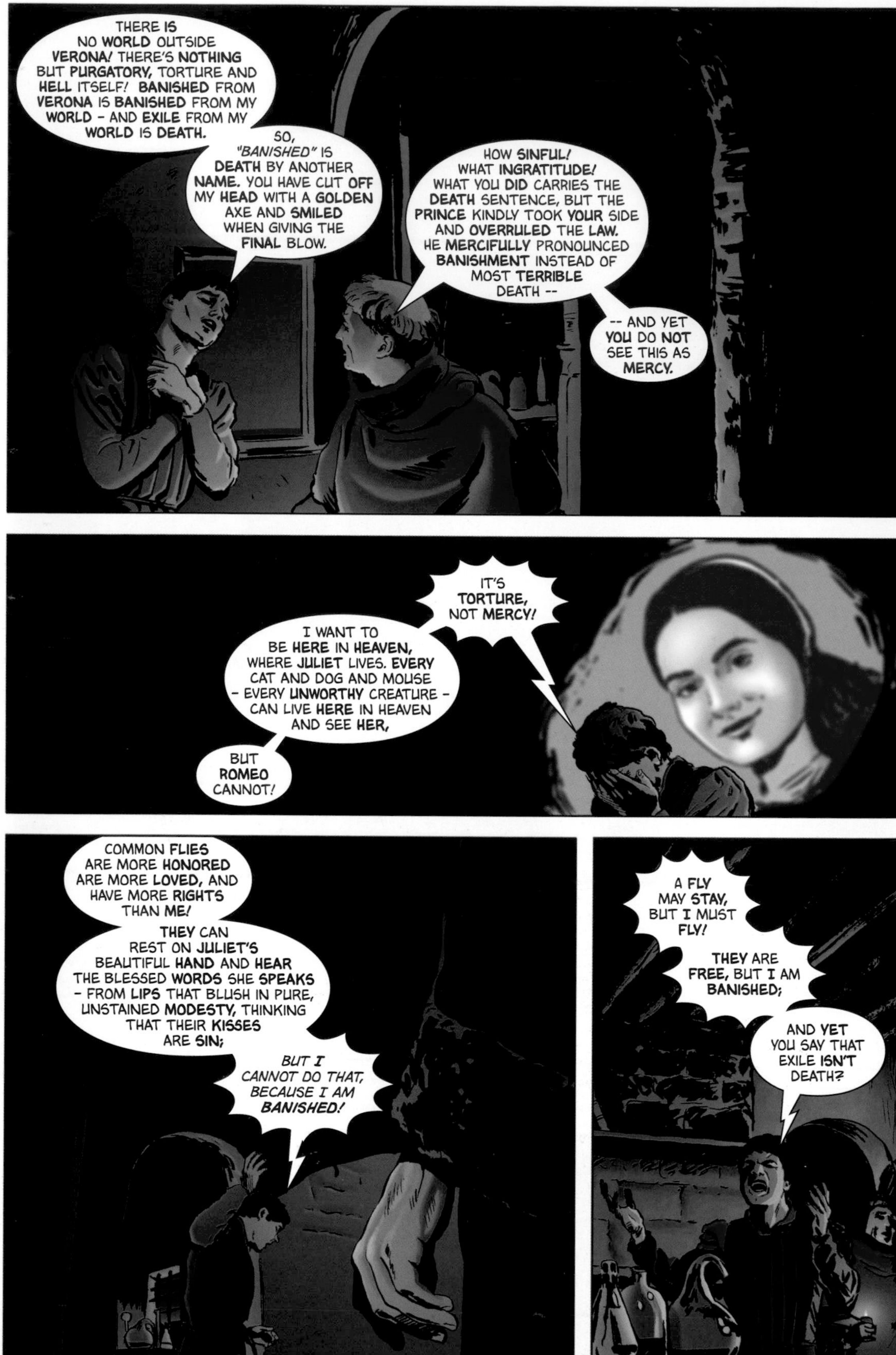
THERE IS NO WORLD OUTSIDE VERONA! THERE'S NOTHING BUT PURGATORY, TORTURE AND HELL ITSELF! BANISHED FROM VERONA IS BANISHED FROM MY WORLD - AND EXILE FROM MY WORLD IS DEATH.
SO, "BANISHED" IS DEATH BY ANOTHER NAME. YOU HAVE CUT OFF MY HEAD WITH A GOLDEN AXE AND SMILED WHEN GIVING THE FINAL BLOW.
HOW SINFUL! WHAT INGRATITUDE! WHAT YOU DID CARRIES THE DEATH SENTENCE, BUT THE PRINCE KINDLY TOOK YOUR SIDE AND OVERRULED THE LAW. HE MERCIFULLY PRONOUNCED BANISHMENT INSTEAD OF MOST TERRIBLE DEATH --
-- AND YET YOU DO NOT SEE THIS AS MERCY.
IT'S TORTURE, NOT MERCY!
I WANT TO BE HERE IN HEAVEN, WHERE JULIET LIVES. EVERY CAT AND DOG AND MOUSE - EVERY UNWORTHY CREATURE - CAN LIVE HERE IN HEAVEN AND SEE HER,
BUT ROMEO CANNOT!
COMMON FLIES ARE MORE HONORED ARE MORE LOVED, AND HAVE MORE RIGHTS THAN ME!
THEY CAN REST ON JULIET'S BEAUTIFUL HAND AND HEAR THE BLESSED WORDS SHE SPEAKS - FROM LIPS THAT BLUSH IN PURE, UNSTAINED MODESTY, THINKING THAT THEIR KISSES ARE SIN;
BUT I CANNOT DO THAT, BECAUSE I AM BANISHED!
A FLY MAY STAY, BUT I MUST FLY!
THEY ARE FREE, BUT I AM BANISHED;
AND YET YOU SAY THAT EXILE ISN'T DEATH?

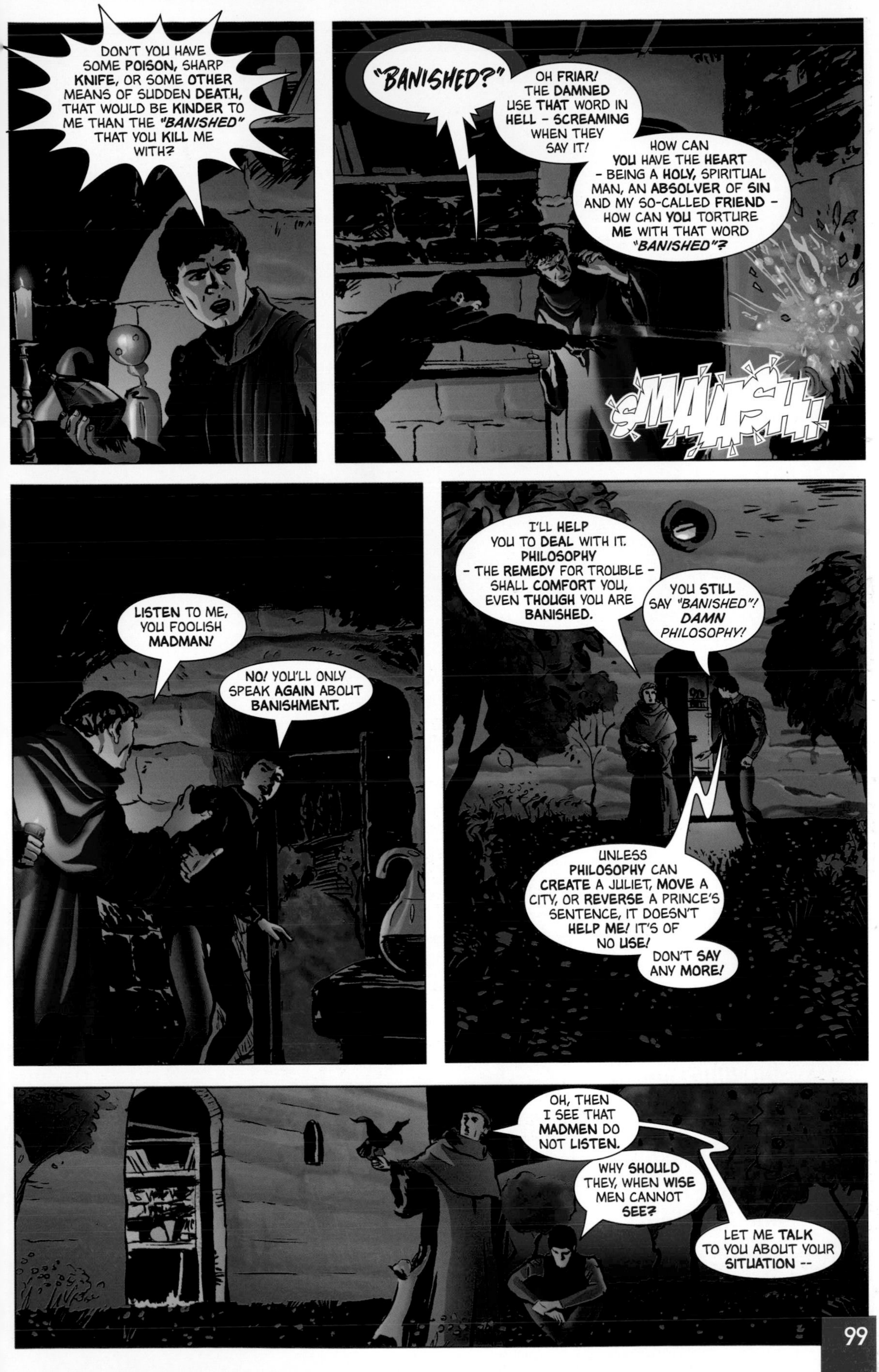

DON'T YOU HAVE SOME POISON, SHARP KNIFE, OR SOME OTHER MEANS OF SUDDEN DEATH, THAT WOULD BE KINDER TO ME THAN THE "BANISHED" THAT YOU KILL ME WITH?
"BANISHED?"
OH FRIAR! THE DAMNED USE THAT WORD IN HELL - SCREAMING WHEN THEY SAY IT!
HOW CAN YOU HAVE THE HEART - BEING A HOLY, SPIRITUAL MAN, AN ABSOLVER OF SIN AND MY SO-CALLED FRIEND - HOW CAN YOU TORTURE ME WITH THAT WORD "BANISHED"?
SMAAASH
LISTEN TO ME, YOU FOOLISH MADMAN!
NO! YOU'LL ONLY SPEAK AGAIN ABOUT BANISHMENT.
I'LL HELP YOU TO DEAL WITH IT. PHILOSOPHY - THE REMEDY FOR TROUBLE - SHALL COMFORT YOU, EVEN THOUGH YOU ARE BANISHED.
YOU STILL SAY "BANISHED"! DAMN PHILOSOPHY!
UNLESS PHILOSOPHY CAN CREATE A JULIET, MOVE A CITY, OR REVERSE A PRINCE'S SENTENCE, IT DOESN'T HELP ME! IT'S OF NO USE!
DON'T SAY ANY MORE!
OH, THEN I SEE THAT MADMEN DO NOT LISTEN.
WHY SHOULD THEY, WHEN WISE MEN CANNOT SEE?
LET ME TALK TO YOU ABOUT YOUR SITUATION --

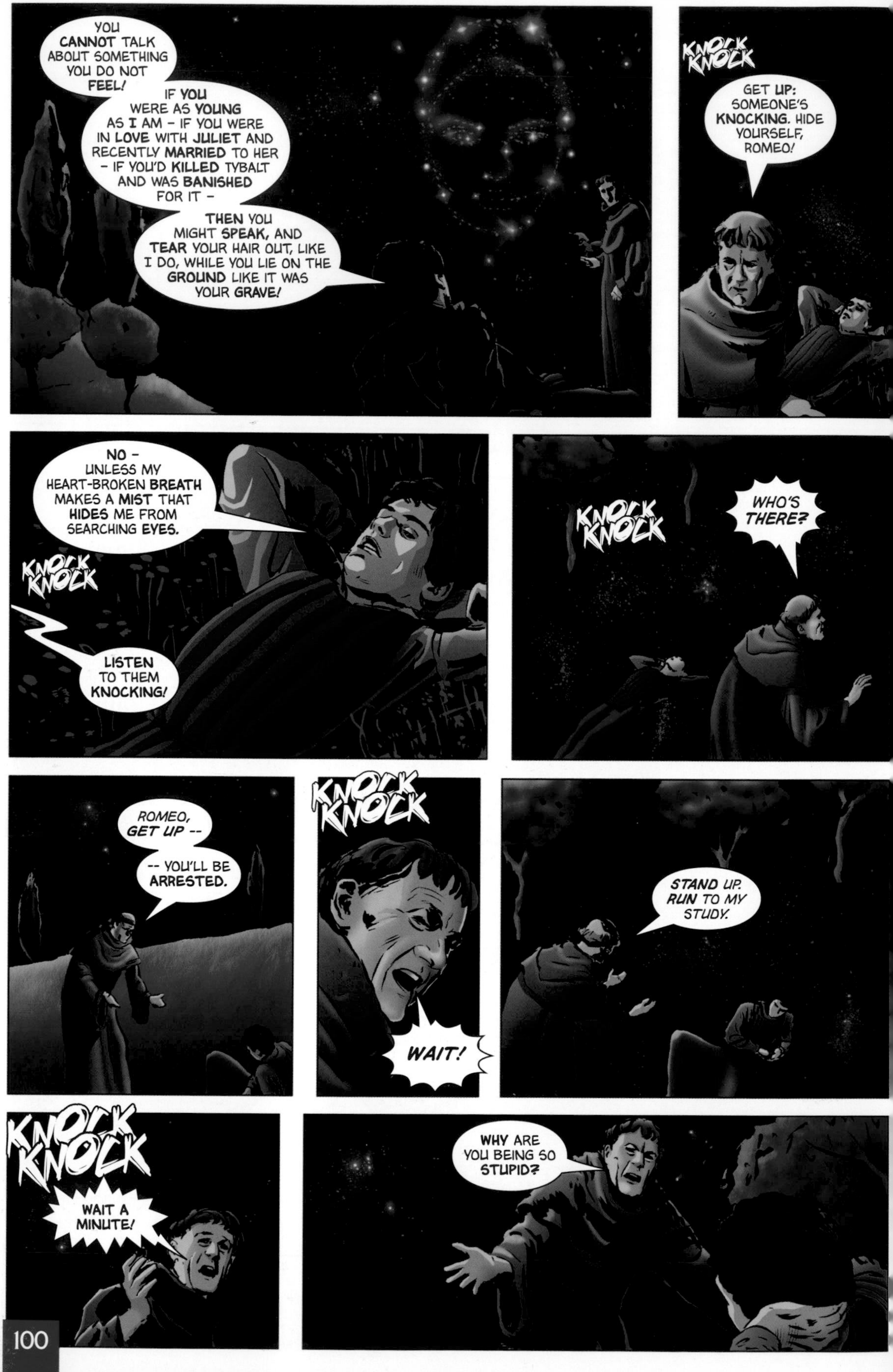

YOU CANNOT TALK ABOUT SOMETHING YOU DO NOT FEEL!
IF YOU WERE AS YOUNG AS I AM – IF YOU WERE IN LOVE WITH JULIET AND RECENTLY MARRIED TO HER – IF YOU'D KILLED TYBALT AND WAS BANISHED FOR IT –
THEN YOU MIGHT SPEAK, AND TEAR YOUR HAIR OUT, LIKE I DO, WHILE YOU LIE ON THE GROUND LIKE IT WAS YOUR GRAVE!
KNOCK KNOCK
GET UP: SOMEONE'S KNOCKING. HIDE YOURSELF, ROMEO!
NO – UNLESS MY HEART-BROKEN BREATH MAKES A MIST THAT HIDES ME FROM SEARCHING EYES.
KNOCK KNOCK
LISTEN TO THEM KNOCKING!
KNOCK KNOCK
WHO'S THERE?
ROMEO, GET UP --
-- YOU'LL BE ARRESTED.
KNOCK KNOCK
WAIT!
STAND UP. RUN TO MY STUDY.
KNOCK KNOCK
WAIT A MINUTE!
WHY ARE YOU BEING SO STUPID?

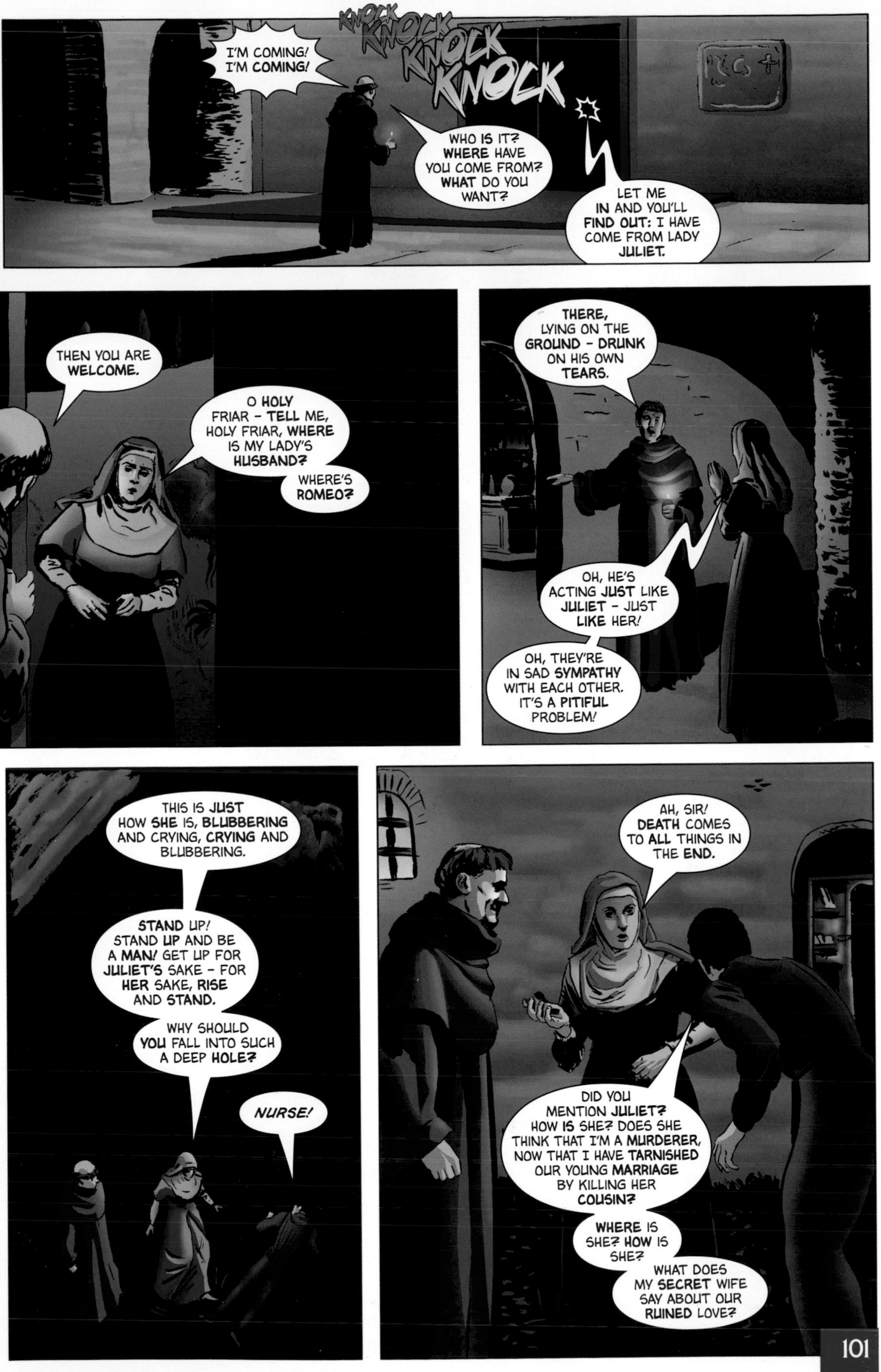
KNOCK KNOCK KNOCK KNOCK
I'M COMING! I'M COMING!
WHO IS IT? WHERE HAVE YOU COME FROM? WHAT DO YOU WANT?
LET ME IN AND YOU'LL FIND OUT: I HAVE COME FROM LADY JULIET.
THEN YOU ARE WELCOME.
O HOLY FRIAR – TELL ME, HOLY FRIAR, WHERE IS MY LADY'S HUSBAND?
WHERE'S ROMEO?
THERE, LYING ON THE GROUND – DRUNK ON HIS OWN TEARS.
OH, HE'S ACTING JUST LIKE JULIET – JUST LIKE HER!
OH, THEY'RE IN SAD SYMPATHY WITH EACH OTHER. IT'S A PITIFUL PROBLEM!
THIS IS JUST HOW SHE IS, BLUBBERING AND CRYING, CRYING AND BLUBBERING.
STAND UP! STAND UP AND BE A MAN! GET UP FOR JULIET'S SAKE – FOR HER SAKE, RISE AND STAND.
WHY SHOULD YOU FALL INTO SUCH A DEEP HOLE?
NURSE!
AH, SIR! DEATH COMES TO ALL THINGS IN THE END.
DID YOU MENTION JULIET? HOW IS SHE? DOES SHE THINK THAT I'M A MURDERER, NOW THAT I HAVE TARNISHED OUR YOUNG MARRIAGE BY KILLING HER COUSIN?
WHERE IS SHE? HOW IS SHE?
WHAT DOES MY SECRET WIFE SAY ABOUT OUR RUINED LOVE?

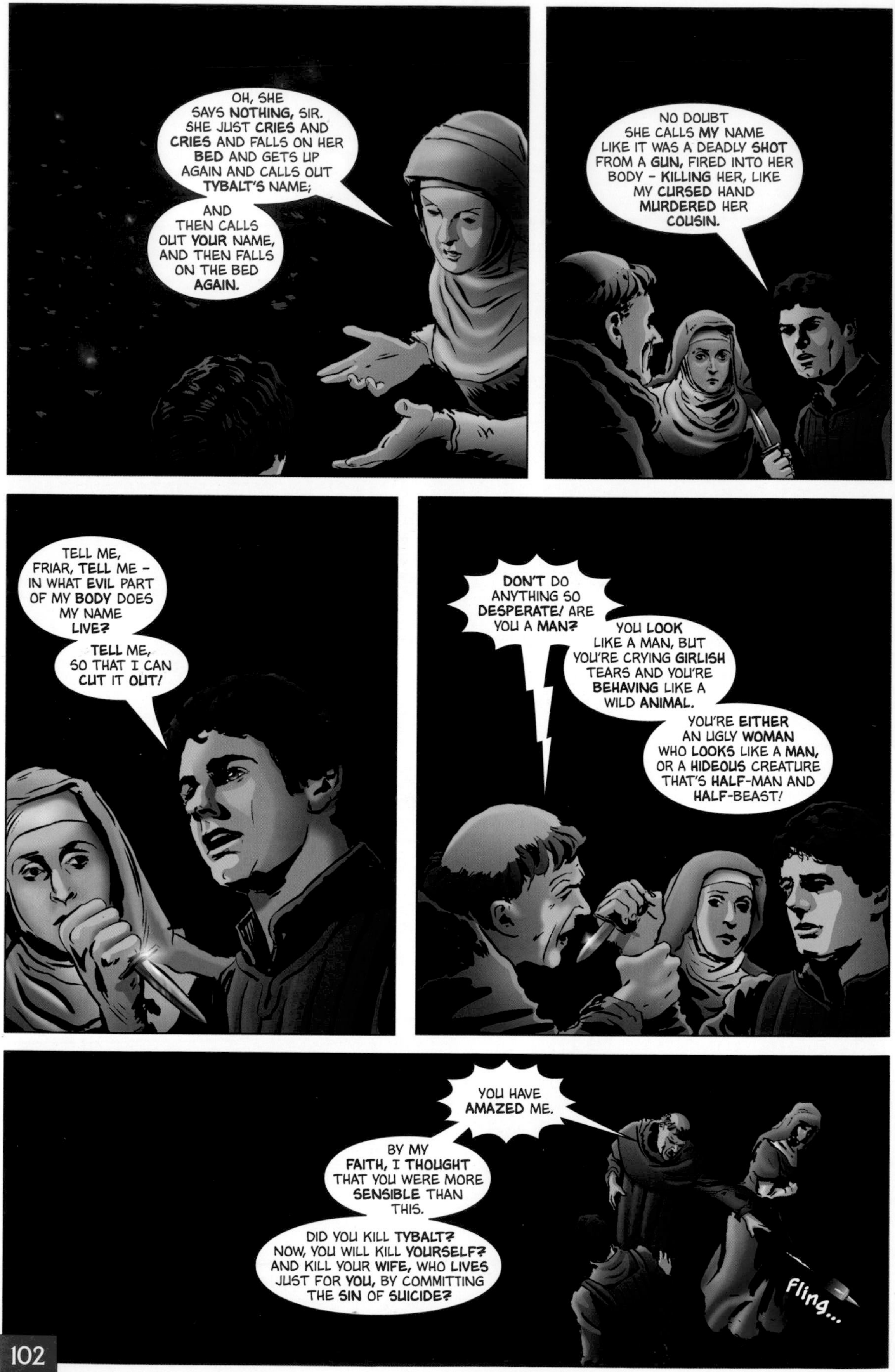
OH, SHE SAYS NOTHING, SIR. SHE JUST CRIES AND CRIES AND FALLS ON HER BED AND GETS UP AGAIN AND CALLS OUT TYBALT'S NAME;
AND THEN CALLS OUT YOUR NAME, AND THEN FALLS ON THE BED AGAIN.
NO DOUBT SHE CALLS MY NAME LIKE IT WAS A DEADLY SHOT FROM A GUN, FIRED INTO HER BODY – KILLING HER, LIKE MY CURSED HAND MURDERED HER COUSIN.
TELL ME, FRIAR, TELL ME – IN WHAT EVIL PART OF MY BODY DOES MY NAME LIVE?
TELL ME, SO THAT I CAN CUT IT OUT!
DON'T DO ANYTHING SO DESPERATE! ARE YOU A MAN?
YOU LOOK LIKE A MAN, BUT YOU'RE CRYING GIRLISH TEARS AND YOU'RE BEHAVING LIKE A WILD ANIMAL.
YOU'RE EITHER AN UGLY WOMAN WHO LOOKS LIKE A MAN, OR A HIDEOUS CREATURE THAT'S HALF-MAN AND HALF-BEAST!
YOU HAVE AMAZED ME.
BY MY FAITH, I THOUGHT THAT YOU WERE MORE SENSIBLE THAN THIS.
DID YOU KILL TYBALT? NOW, YOU WILL KILL YOURSELF? AND KILL YOUR WIFE, WHO LIVES JUST FOR YOU, BY COMMITTING THE SIN OF SUICIDE?
Fling...

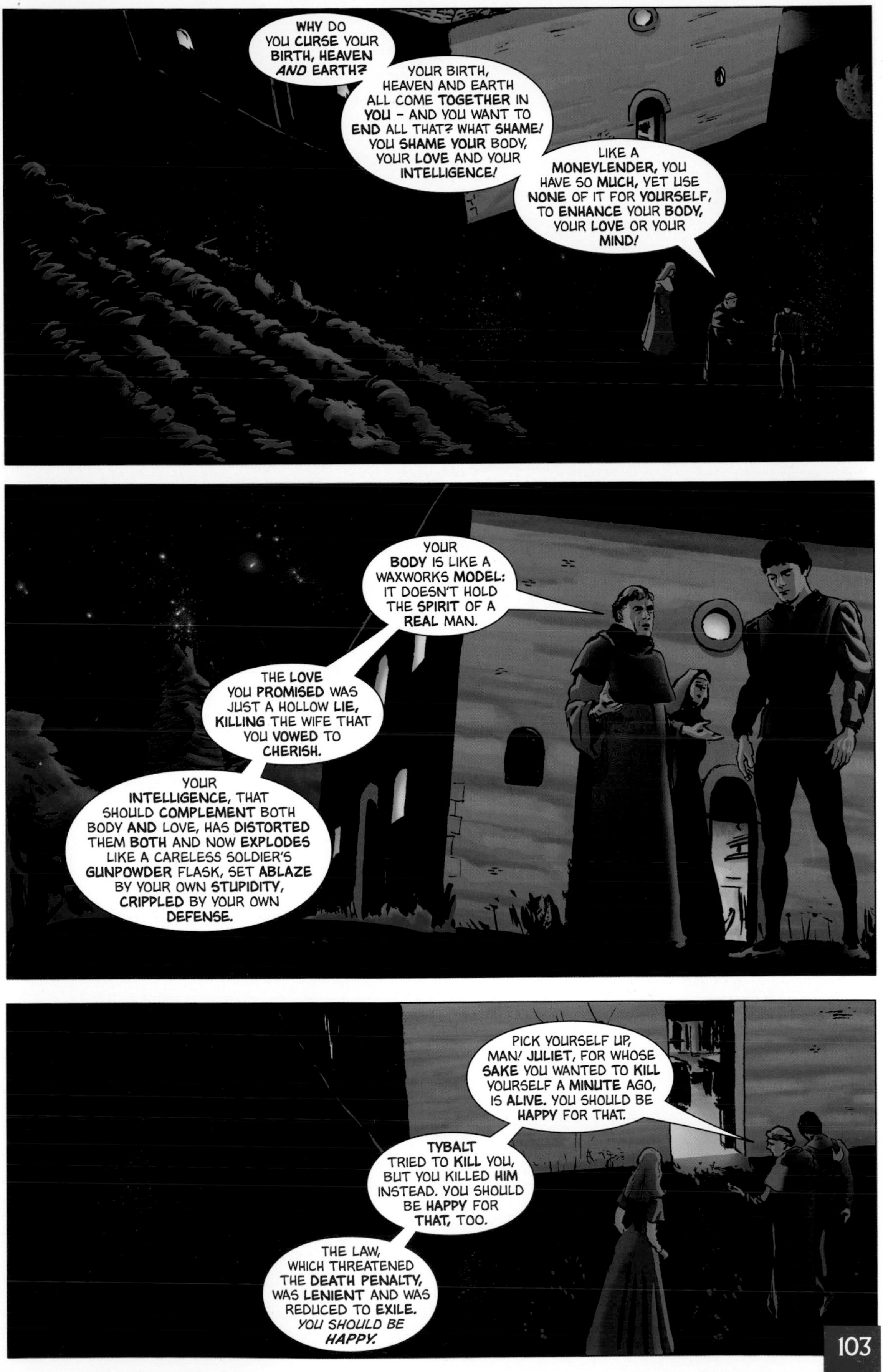
WHY DO YOU CURSE YOUR BIRTH, HEAVEN AND EARTH?
YOUR BIRTH, HEAVEN AND EARTH ALL COME TOGETHER IN YOU - AND YOU WANT TO END ALL THAT? WHAT SHAME! YOU SHAME YOUR BODY, YOUR LOVE AND YOUR INTELLIGENCE!
LIKE A MONEYLENDER, YOU HAVE SO MUCH, YET USE NONE OF IT FOR YOURSELF, TO ENHANCE YOUR BODY, YOUR LOVE OR YOUR MIND!
YOUR BODY IS LIKE A WAXWORKS MODEL: IT DOESN'T HOLD THE SPIRIT OF A REAL MAN.
THE LOVE YOU PROMISED WAS JUST A HOLLOW LIE, KILLING THE WIFE THAT YOU VOWED TO CHERISH.
YOUR INTELLIGENCE, THAT SHOULD COMPLEMENT BOTH BODY AND LOVE, HAS DISTORTED THEM BOTH AND NOW EXPLODES LIKE A CARELESS SOLDIER'S GUNPOWDER FLASK, SET ABLAZE BY YOUR OWN STUPIDITY, CRIPPLED BY YOUR OWN DEFENSE.
PICK YOURSELF UP, MAN! JULIET, FOR WHOSE SAKE YOU WANTED TO KILL YOURSELF A MINUTE AGO, IS ALIVE. YOU SHOULD BE HAPPY FOR THAT.
TYBALT TRIED TO KILL YOU, BUT YOU KILLED HIM INSTEAD. YOU SHOULD BE HAPPY FOR THAT, TOO.
THE LAW, WHICH THREATENED THE DEATH PENALTY, WAS LENIENT AND WAS REDUCED TO EXILE. YOU SHOULD BE HAPPY.

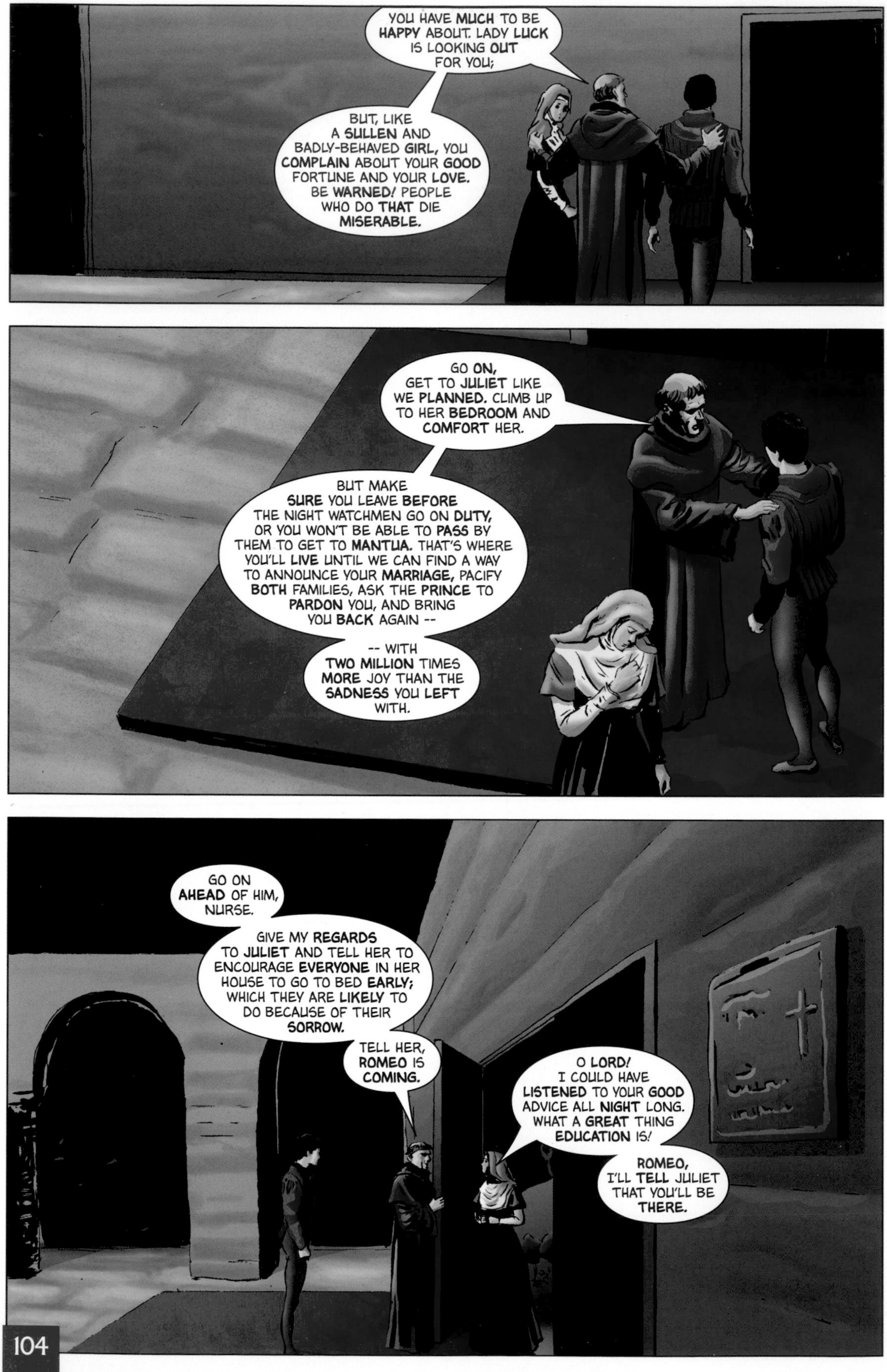
YOU HAVE MUCH TO BE HAPPY ABOUT. LADY LUCK IS LOOKING OUT FOR YOU;
BUT, LIKE A SULLEN AND BADLY-BEHAVED GIRL, YOU COMPLAIN ABOUT YOUR GOOD FORTUNE AND YOUR LOVE. BE WARNED! PEOPLE WHO DO THAT DIE MISERABLE.
GO ON, GET TO JULIET LIKE WE PLANNED. CLIMB UP TO HER BEDROOM AND COMFORT HER.
BUT MAKE SURE YOU LEAVE BEFORE THE NIGHT WATCHMEN GO ON DUTY, OR YOU WON'T BE ABLE TO PASS BY THEM TO GET TO MANTUA. THAT'S WHERE YOU'LL LIVE UNTIL WE CAN FIND A WAY TO ANNOUNCE YOUR MARRIAGE, PACIFY BOTH FAMILIES, ASK THE PRINCE TO PARDON YOU, AND BRING YOU BACK AGAIN --
-- WITH TWO MILLION TIMES MORE JOY THAN THE SADNESS YOU LEFT WITH.
GO ON AHEAD OF HIM, NURSE.
GIVE MY REGARDS TO JULIET AND TELL HER TO ENCOURAGE EVERYONE IN HER HOUSE TO GO TO BED EARLY; WHICH THEY ARE LIKELY TO DO BECAUSE OF THEIR SORROW.
TELL HER, ROMEO IS COMING.
O LORD! I COULD HAVE LISTENED TO YOUR GOOD ADVICE ALL NIGHT LONG. WHAT A GREAT THING EDUCATION IS!
ROMEO, I'LL TELL JULIET THAT YOU'LL BE THERE.

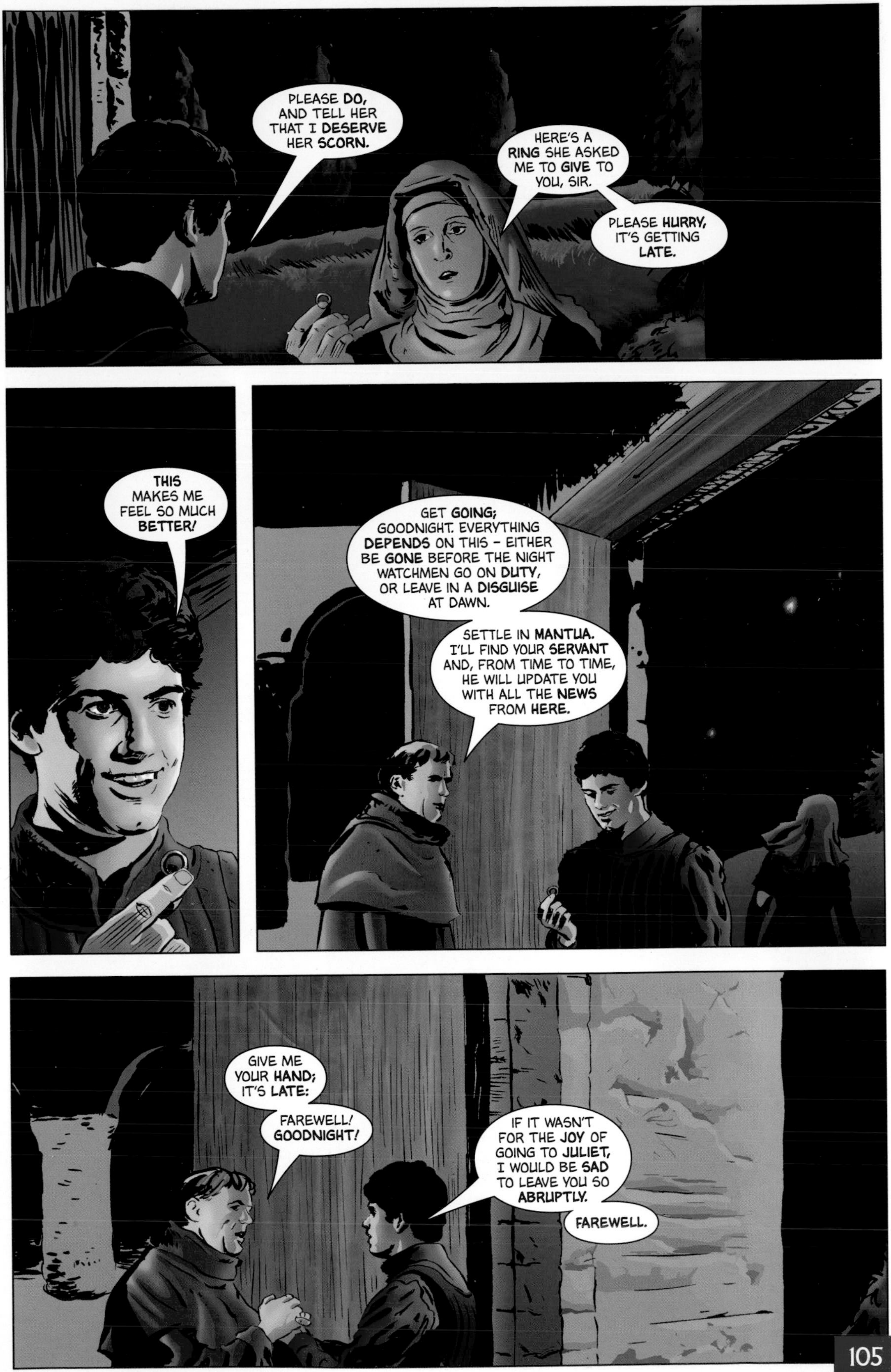
PLEASE DO, AND TELL HER THAT I DESERVE HER SCORN.
HERE'S A RING SHE ASKED ME TO GIVE TO YOU, SIR.
PLEASE HURRY, IT'S GETTING LATE.
THIS MAKES ME FEEL SO MUCH BETTER!
GET GOING; GOODNIGHT. EVERYTHING DEPENDS ON THIS – EITHER BE GONE BEFORE THE NIGHT WATCHMEN GO ON DUTY, OR LEAVE IN A DISGUISE AT DAWN.
SETTLE IN MANTUA. I'LL FIND YOUR SERVANT AND, FROM TIME TO TIME, HE WILL UPDATE YOU WITH ALL THE NEWS FROM HERE.
GIVE ME YOUR HAND; IT'S LATE:
FAREWELL! GOODNIGHT!
IF IT WASN'T FOR THE JOY OF GOING TO JULIET, I WOULD BE SAD TO LEAVE YOU SO ABRUPTLY.
FAREWELL.

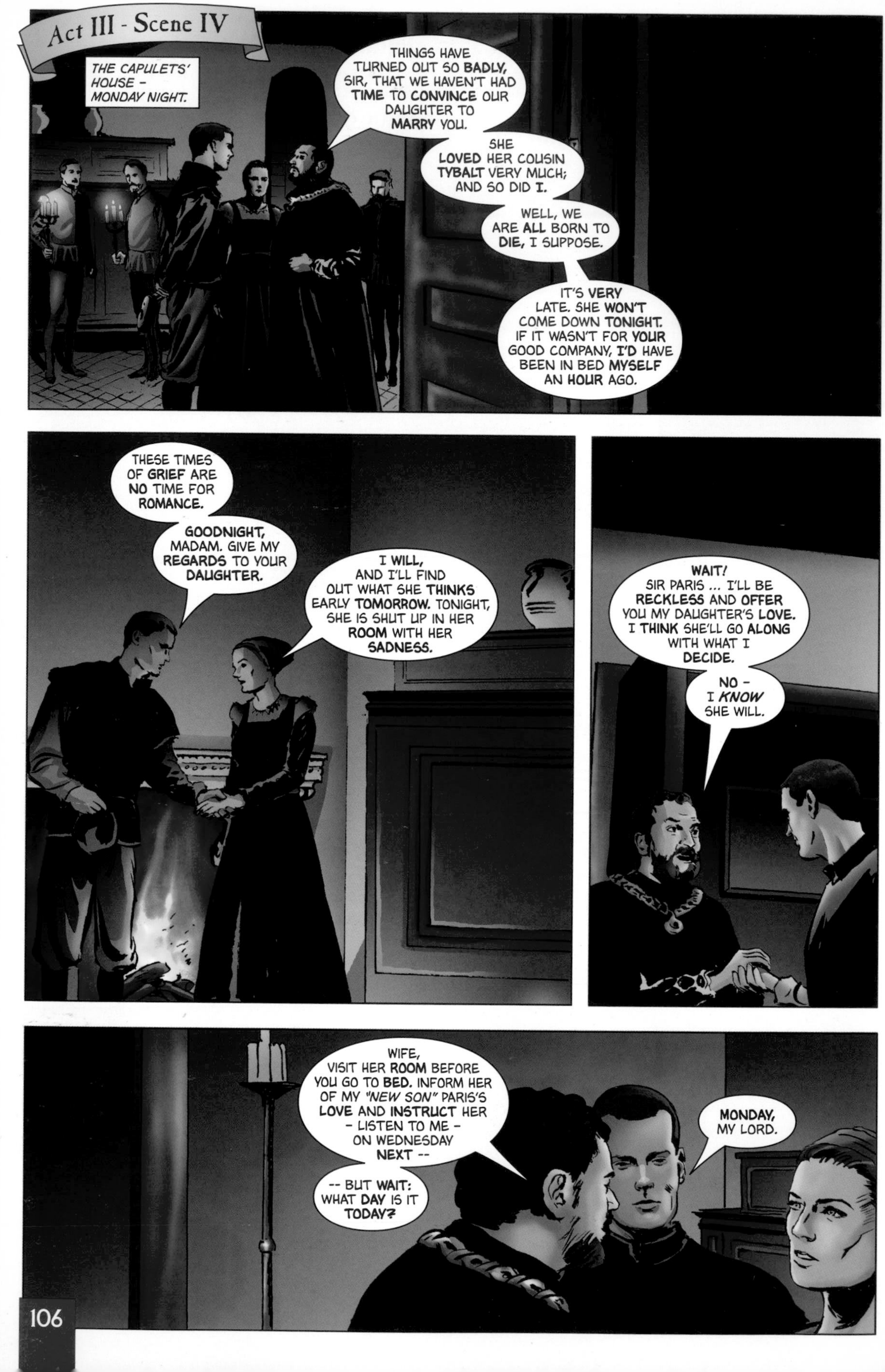
Act III - Scene IV
THE CAPULETS' HOUSE - MONDAY NIGHT.
THINGS HAVE TURNED OUT SO BADLY, SIR, THAT WE HAVEN'T HAD TIME TO CONVINCE OUR DAUGHTER TO MARRY YOU.
SHE LOVED HER COUSIN TYBALT VERY MUCH; AND SO DID I.
WELL, WE ARE ALL BORN TO DIE, I SUPPOSE.
IT'S VERY LATE. SHE WON'T COME DOWN TONIGHT. IF IT WASN'T FOR YOUR GOOD COMPANY, I'D HAVE BEEN IN BED MYSELF AN HOUR AGO.
THESE TIMES OF GRIEF ARE NO TIME FOR ROMANCE.
GOODNIGHT, MADAM. GIVE MY REGARDS TO YOUR DAUGHTER.
I WILL, AND I'LL FIND OUT WHAT SHE THINKS EARLY TOMORROW. TONIGHT, SHE IS SHUT UP IN HER ROOM WITH HER SADNESS.
WAIT! SIR PARIS ... I'LL BE RECKLESS AND OFFER YOU MY DAUGHTER'S LOVE. I THINK SHE'LL GO ALONG WITH WHAT I DECIDE.
NO - I KNOW SHE WILL.
WIFE, VISIT HER ROOM BEFORE YOU GO TO BED. INFORM HER OF MY "NEW SON" PARIS'S LOVE AND INSTRUCT HER - LISTEN TO ME - ON WEDNESDAY NEXT --
-- BUT WAIT: WHAT DAY IS IT TODAY?
MONDAY, MY LORD.

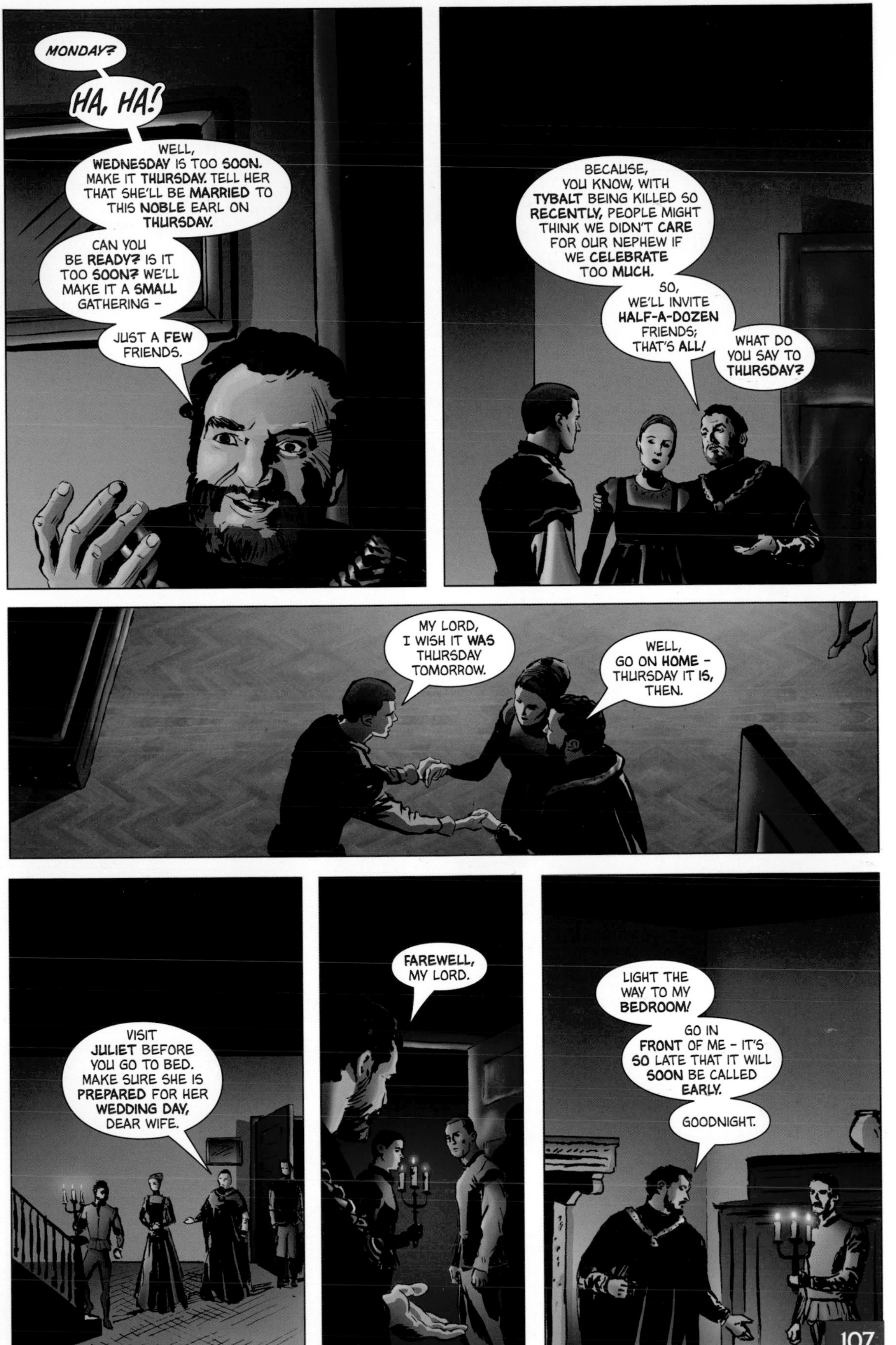
MONDAY?
HA, HA!
WELL, WEDNESDAY IS TOO SOON. MAKE IT THURSDAY. TELL HER THAT SHE'LL BE MARRIED TO THIS NOBLE EARL ON THURSDAY.
CAN YOU BE READY? IS IT TOO SOON? WE'LL MAKE IT A SMALL GATHERING –
JUST A FEW FRIENDS.
BECAUSE, YOU KNOW, WITH TYBALT BEING KILLED SO RECENTLY, PEOPLE MIGHT THINK WE DIDN'T CARE FOR OUR NEPHEW IF WE CELEBRATE TOO MUCH.
SO, WE'LL INVITE HALF-A-DOZEN FRIENDS; THAT'S ALL!
WHAT DO YOU SAY TO THURSDAY?
MY LORD, I WISH IT WAS THURSDAY TOMORROW.
WELL, GO ON HOME – THURSDAY IT IS, THEN.
VISIT JULIET BEFORE YOU GO TO BED. MAKE SURE SHE IS PREPARED FOR HER WEDDING DAY, DEAR WIFE.
FAREWELL, MY LORD.
LIGHT THE WAY TO MY BEDROOM!
GO IN FRONT OF ME – IT'S SO LATE THAT IT WILL SOON BE CALLED EARLY.
GOODNIGHT.

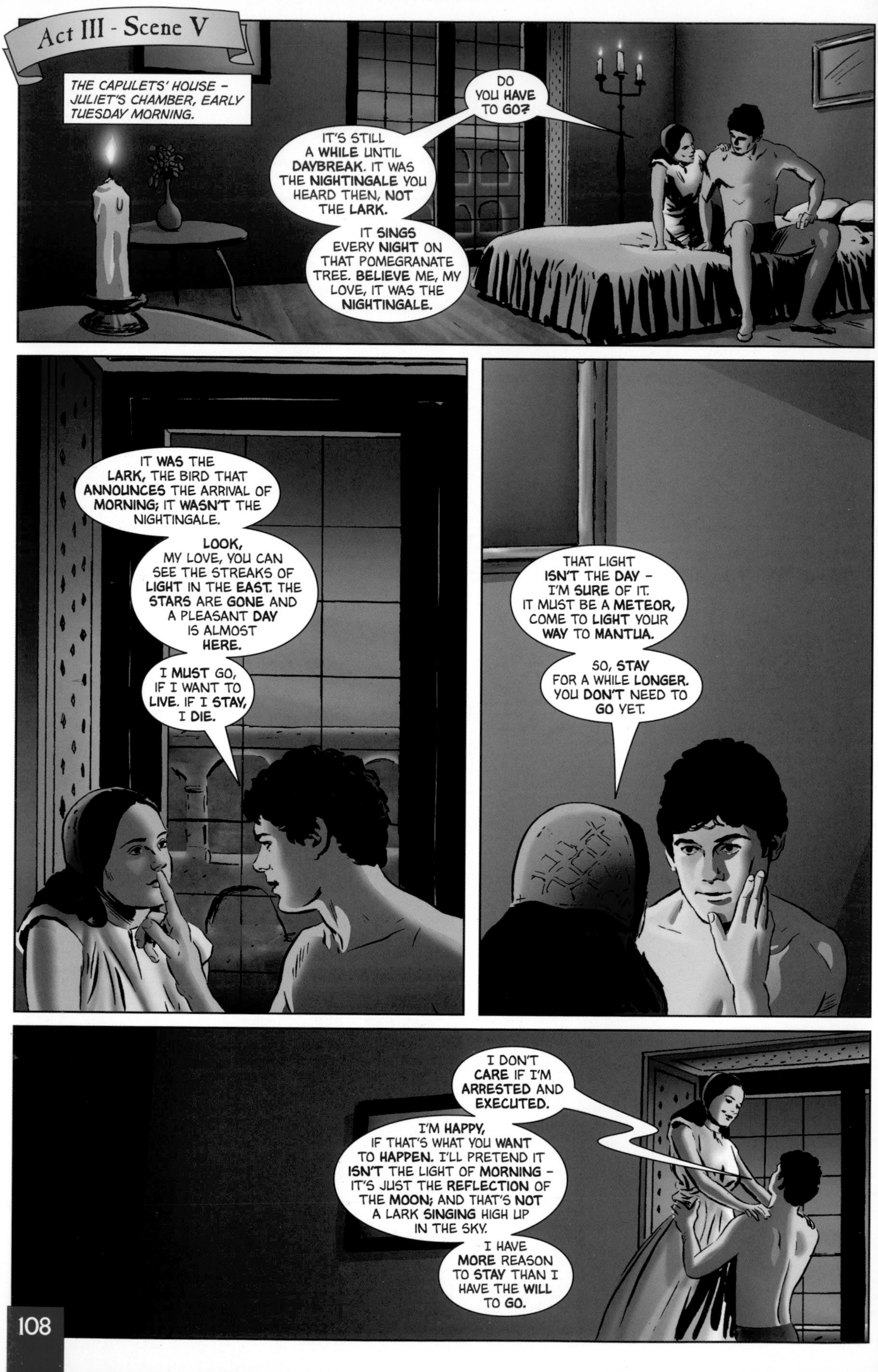
Act III - Scene V
THE CAPULETS' HOUSE – JULIET'S CHAMBER, EARLY TUESDAY MORNING.
DO YOU HAVE TO GO?
IT'S STILL A WHILE UNTIL DAYBREAK. IT WAS THE NIGHTINGALE YOU HEARD THEN, NOT THE LARK.
IT SINGS EVERY NIGHT ON THAT POMEGRANATE TREE. BELIEVE ME, MY LOVE, IT WAS THE NIGHTINGALE.
IT WAS THE LARK, THE BIRD THAT ANNOUNCES THE ARRIVAL OF MORNING; IT WASN'T THE NIGHTINGALE.
LOOK, MY LOVE, YOU CAN SEE THE STREAKS OF LIGHT IN THE EAST. THE STARS ARE GONE AND A PLEASANT DAY IS ALMOST HERE.
I MUST GO, IF I WANT TO LIVE. IF I STAY, I DIE.
THAT LIGHT ISN'T THE DAY – I'M SURE OF IT. IT MUST BE A METEOR, COME TO LIGHT YOUR WAY TO MANTUA.
SO, STAY FOR A WHILE LONGER. YOU DON'T NEED TO GO YET.
I DON'T CARE IF I'M ARRESTED AND EXECUTED.
I'M HAPPY, IF THAT'S WHAT YOU WANT TO HAPPEN. I'LL PRETEND IT ISN'T THE LIGHT OF MORNING – IT'S JUST THE REFLECTION OF THE MOON; AND THAT'S NOT A LARK SINGING HIGH UP IN THE SKY.
I HAVE MORE REASON TO STAY THAN I HAVE THE WILL TO GO.

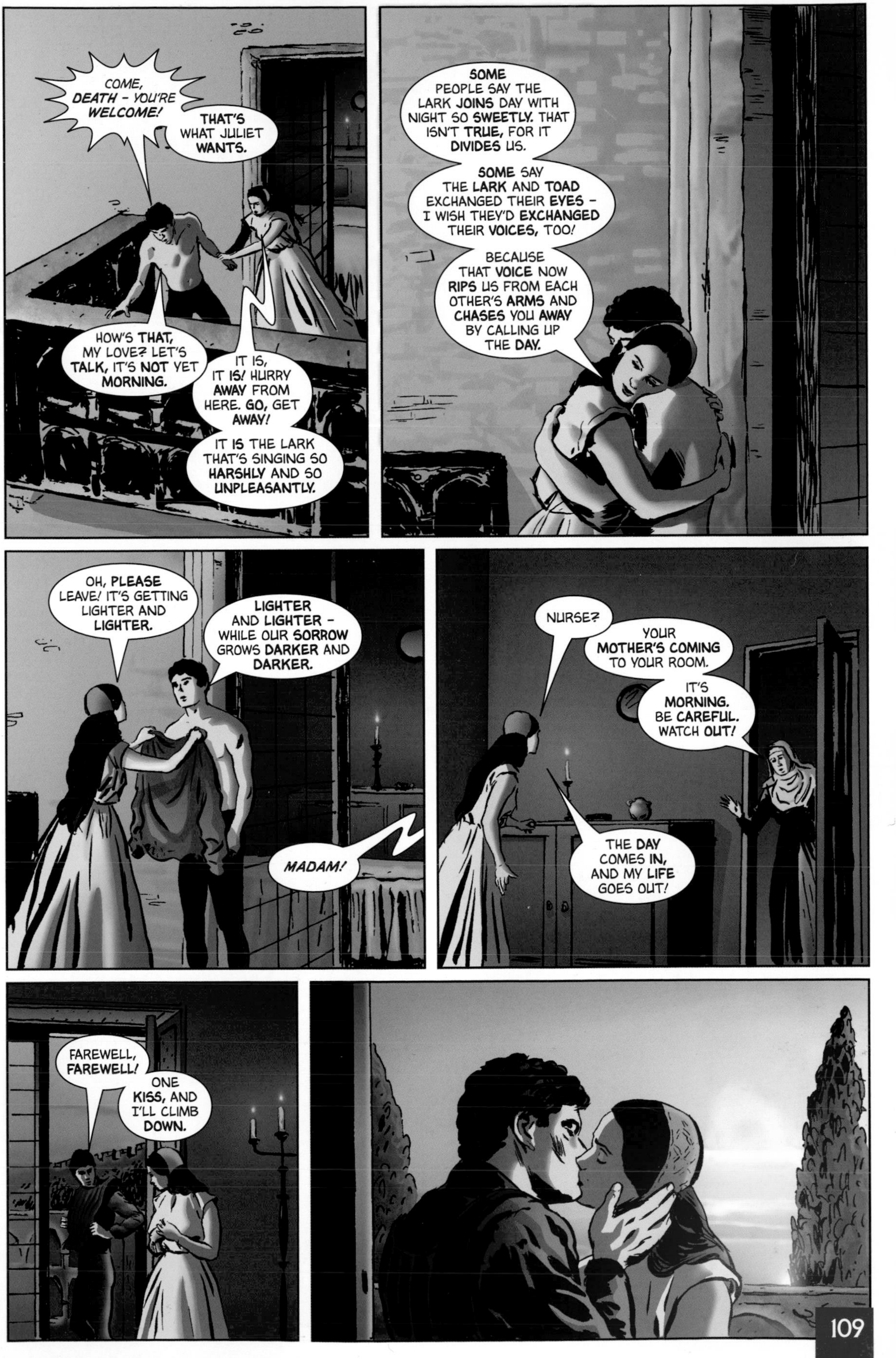
COME, DEATH – YOU'RE WELCOME!
THAT'S WHAT JULIET WANTS.
HOW'S THAT, MY LOVE? LET'S TALK, IT'S NOT YET MORNING.
IT IS, IT IS! HURRY AWAY FROM HERE. GO, GET AWAY!
IT IS THE LARK THAT'S SINGING SO HARSHLY AND SO UNPLEASANTLY.
SOME PEOPLE SAY THE LARK JOINS DAY WITH NIGHT SO SWEETLY. THAT ISN'T TRUE, FOR IT DIVIDES US.
SOME SAY THE LARK AND TOAD EXCHANGED THEIR EYES – I WISH THEY'D EXCHANGED THEIR VOICES, TOO!
BECAUSE THAT VOICE NOW RIPS US FROM EACH OTHER'S ARMS AND CHASES YOU AWAY BY CALLING UP THE DAY.
OH, PLEASE LEAVE! IT'S GETTING LIGHTER AND LIGHTER.
LIGHTER AND LIGHTER – WHILE OUR SORROW GROWS DARKER AND DARKER.
MADAM!
NURSE?
YOUR MOTHER'S COMING TO YOUR ROOM.
IT'S MORNING. BE CAREFUL. WATCH OUT!
THE DAY COMES IN, AND MY LIFE GOES OUT!
FAREWELL, FAREWELL!
ONE KISS, AND I'LL CLIMB DOWN.

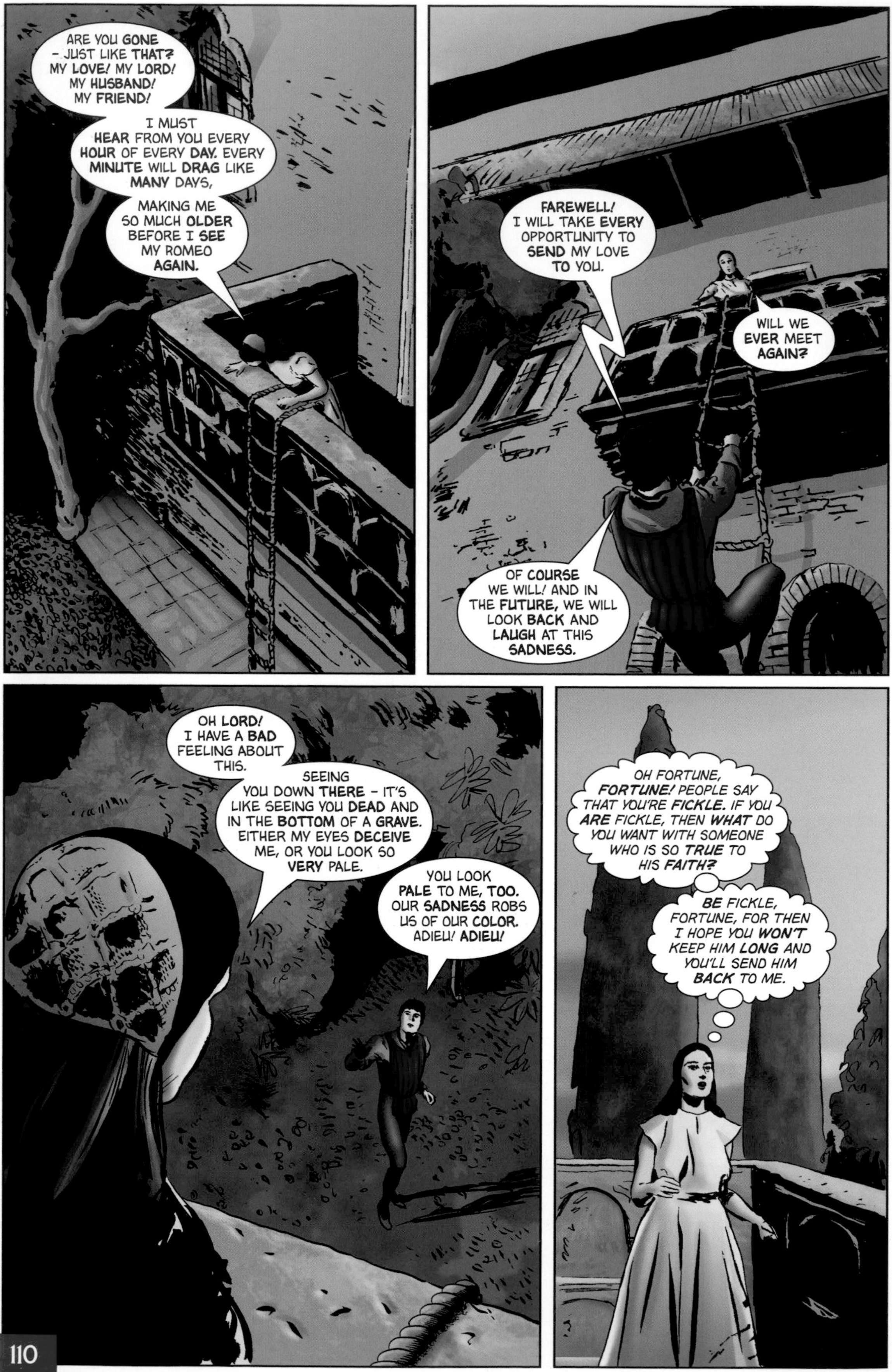
ARE YOU GONE – JUST LIKE THAT? MY LOVE! MY LORD! MY HUSBAND! MY FRIEND!
I MUST HEAR FROM YOU EVERY HOUR OF EVERY DAY. EVERY MINUTE WILL DRAG LIKE MANY DAYS,
MAKING ME SO MUCH OLDER BEFORE I SEE MY ROMEO AGAIN.
FAREWELL! I WILL TAKE EVERY OPPORTUNITY TO SEND MY LOVE TO YOU.
WILL WE EVER MEET AGAIN?
OF COURSE WE WILL! AND IN THE FUTURE, WE WILL LOOK BACK AND LAUGH AT THIS SADNESS.
OH LORD! I HAVE A BAD FEELING ABOUT THIS.
SEEING YOU DOWN THERE – IT'S LIKE SEEING YOU DEAD AND IN THE BOTTOM OF A GRAVE. EITHER MY EYES DECEIVE ME, OR YOU LOOK SO VERY PALE.
YOU LOOK PALE TO ME, TOO. OUR SADNESS ROBS US OF OUR COLOR. ADIEU! ADIEU!
OH FORTUNE, FORTUNE! PEOPLE SAY THAT YOU'RE FICKLE. IF YOU ARE FICKLE, THEN WHAT DO YOU WANT WITH SOMEONE WHO IS SO TRUE TO HIS FAITH?
BE FICKLE, FORTUNE, FOR THEN I HOPE YOU WON'T KEEP HIM LONG AND YOU'LL SEND HIM BACK TO ME.

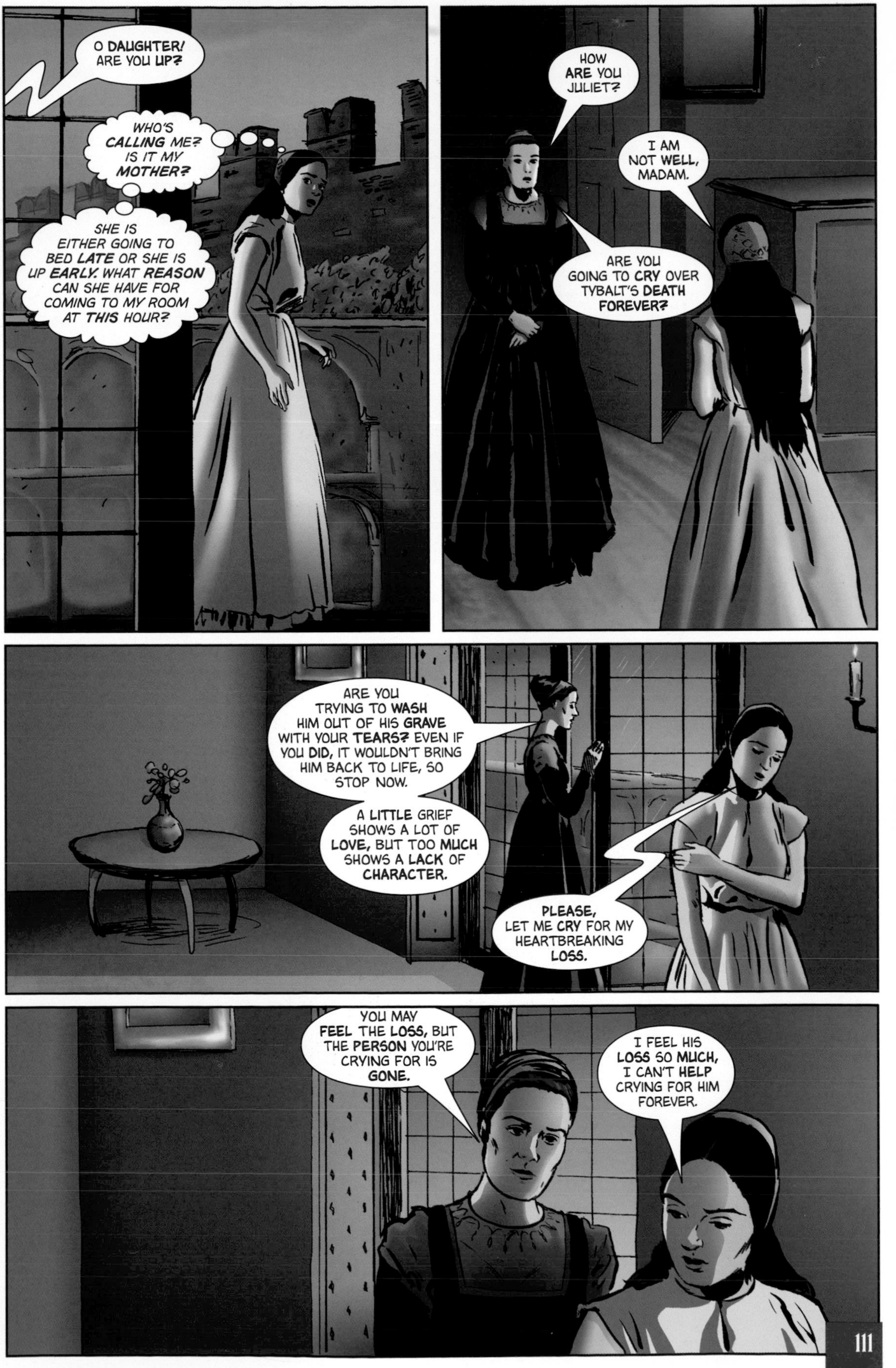
O DAUGHTER! ARE YOU UP?
WHO'S CALLING ME? IS IT MY MOTHER?
SHE IS EITHER GOING TO BED LATE OR SHE IS UP EARLY. WHAT REASON CAN SHE HAVE FOR COMING TO MY ROOM AT THIS HOUR?
HOW ARE YOU JULIET?
I AM NOT WELL, MADAM.
ARE YOU GOING TO CRY OVER TYBALT'S DEATH FOREVER?
ARE YOU TRYING TO WASH HIM OUT OF HIS GRAVE WITH YOUR TEARS? EVEN IF YOU DID, IT WOULDN'T BRING HIM BACK TO LIFE, SO STOP NOW.
A LITTLE GRIEF SHOWS A LOT OF LOVE, BUT TOO MUCH SHOWS A LACK OF CHARACTER.
PLEASE, LET ME CRY FOR MY HEARTBREAKING LOSS.
YOU MAY FEEL THE LOSS, BUT THE PERSON YOU'RE CRYING FOR IS GONE.
I FEEL HIS LOSS SO MUCH, I CAN'T HELP CRYING FOR HIM FOREVER.

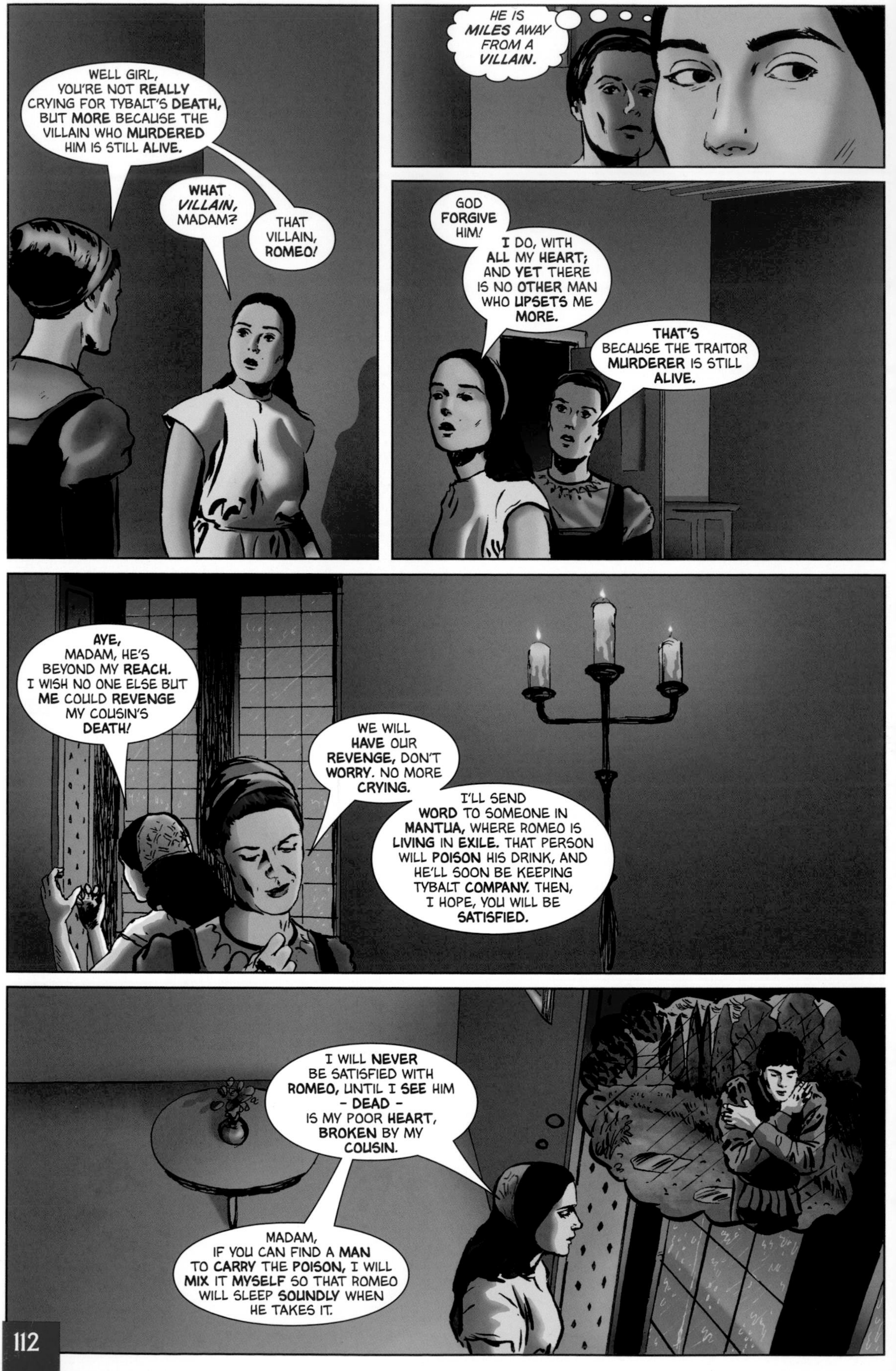

WELL GIRL, YOU'RE NOT REALLY CRYING FOR TYBALT'S DEATH, BUT MORE BECAUSE THE VILLAIN WHO MURDERED HIM IS STILL ALIVE.
WHAT VILLAIN, MADAM?
THAT VILLAIN, ROMEO!
HE IS MILES AWAY FROM A VILLAIN.
GOD FORGIVE HIM!
I DO, WITH ALL MY HEART; AND YET THERE IS NO OTHER MAN WHO UPSETS ME MORE.
THAT'S BECAUSE THE TRAITOR MURDERER IS STILL ALIVE.
AYE, MADAM, HE'S BEYOND MY REACH. I WISH NO ONE ELSE BUT ME COULD REVENGE MY COUSIN'S DEATH!
WE WILL HAVE OUR REVENGE, DON'T WORRY. NO MORE CRYING.
I'LL SEND WORD TO SOMEONE IN MANTUA, WHERE ROMEO IS LIVING IN EXILE. THAT PERSON WILL POISON HIS DRINK, AND HE'LL SOON BE KEEPING TYBALT COMPANY. THEN, I HOPE, YOU WILL BE SATISFIED.
I WILL NEVER BE SATISFIED WITH ROMEO, UNTIL I SEE HIM - DEAD - IS MY POOR HEART, BROKEN BY MY COUSIN.
MADAM, IF YOU CAN FIND A MAN TO CARRY THE POISON, I WILL MIX IT MYSELF SO THAT ROMEO WILL SLEEP SOUNDLY WHEN HE TAKES IT.

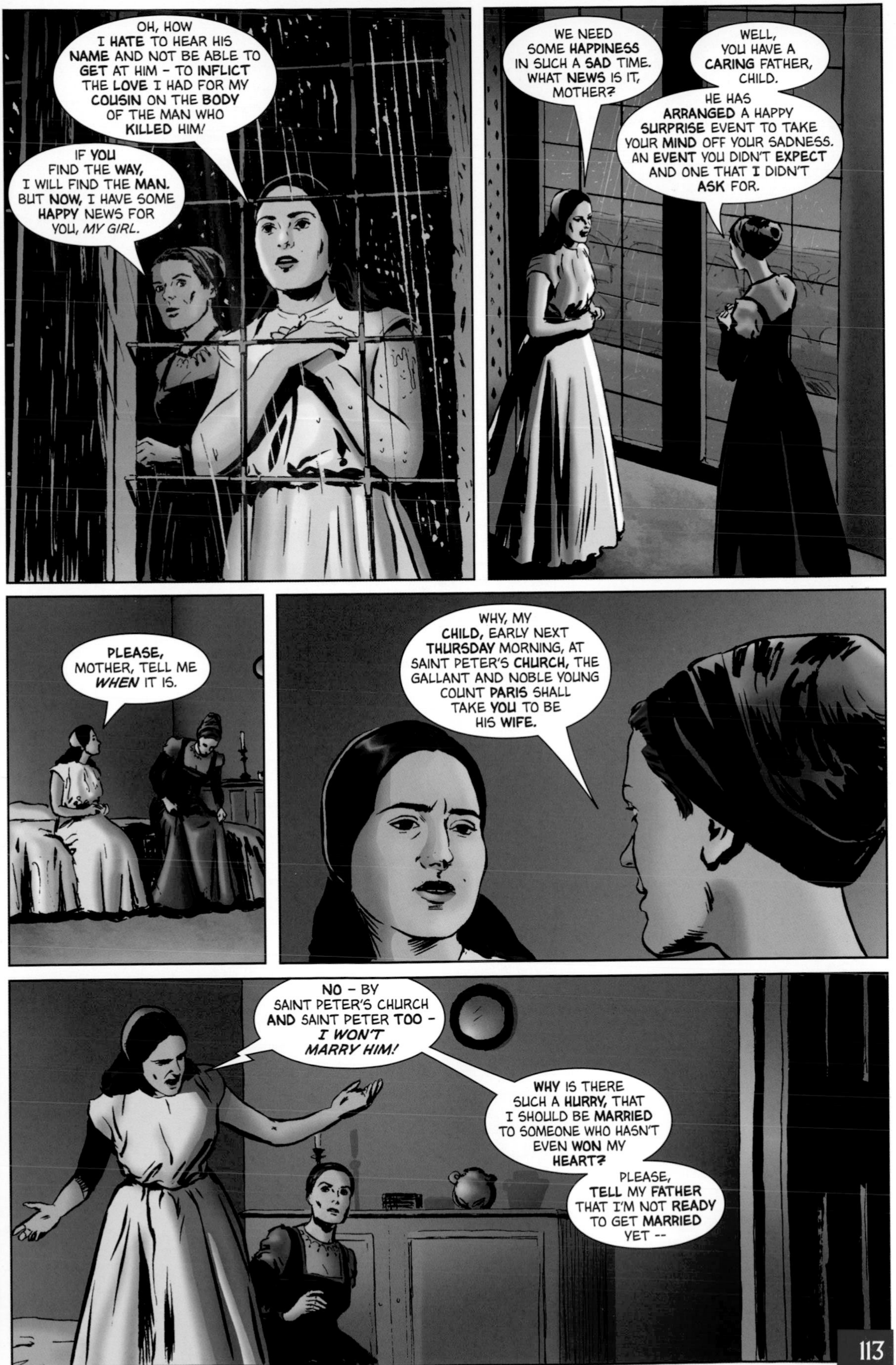
OH, HOW I HATE TO HEAR HIS NAME AND NOT BE ABLE TO GET AT HIM – TO INFLICT THE LOVE I HAD FOR MY COUSIN ON THE BODY OF THE MAN WHO KILLED HIM!
IF YOU FIND THE WAY, I WILL FIND THE MAN. BUT NOW, I HAVE SOME HAPPY NEWS FOR YOU, MY GIRL.
WE NEED SOME HAPPINESS IN SUCH A SAD TIME. WHAT NEWS IS IT, MOTHER?
WELL, YOU HAVE A CARING FATHER, CHILD.
HE HAS ARRANGED A HAPPY SURPRISE EVENT TO TAKE YOUR MIND OFF YOUR SADNESS. AN EVENT YOU DIDN'T EXPECT AND ONE THAT I DIDN'T ASK FOR.
PLEASE, MOTHER, TELL ME WHEN IT IS.
WHY, MY CHILD, EARLY NEXT THURSDAY MORNING, AT SAINT PETER'S CHURCH, THE GALLANT AND NOBLE YOUNG COUNT PARIS SHALL TAKE YOU TO BE HIS WIFE.
NO – BY SAINT PETER'S CHURCH AND SAINT PETER TOO – I WON'T MARRY HIM!
WHY IS THERE SUCH A HURRY, THAT I SHOULD BE MARRIED TO SOMEONE WHO HASN'T EVEN WON MY HEART?
PLEASE, TELL MY FATHER THAT I'M NOT READY TO GET MARRIED YET --

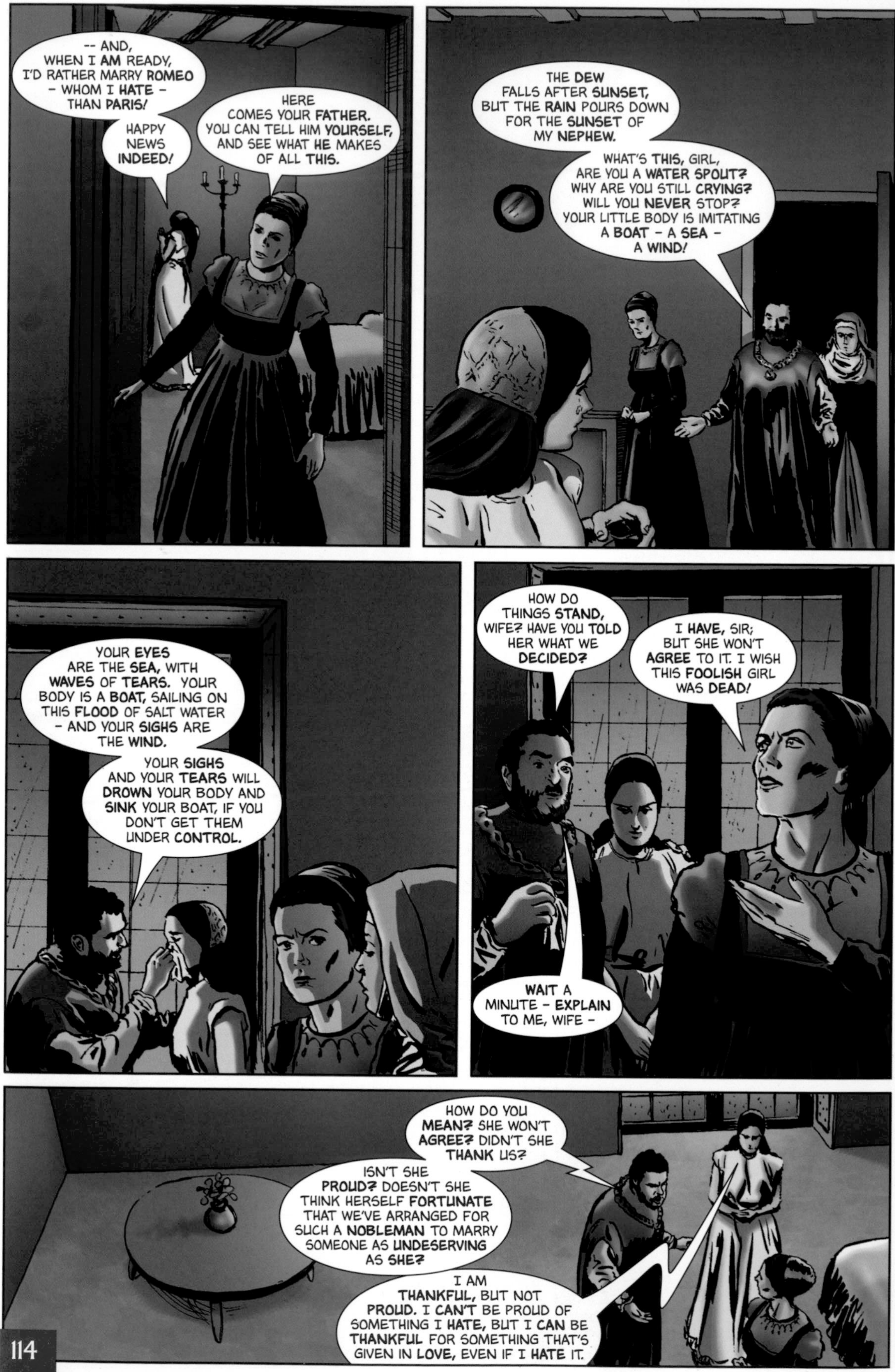
-- AND, WHEN I AM READY, I'D RATHER MARRY ROMEO - WHOM I HATE - THAN PARIS!
HAPPY NEWS INDEED!
HERE COMES YOUR FATHER. YOU CAN TELL HIM YOURSELF, AND SEE WHAT HE MAKES OF ALL THIS.
THE DEW FALLS AFTER SUNSET, BUT THE RAIN POURS DOWN FOR THE SUNSET OF MY NEPHEW.
WHAT'S THIS, GIRL, ARE YOU A WATER SPOUT? WHY ARE YOU STILL CRYING? WILL YOU NEVER STOP? YOUR LITTLE BODY IS IMITATING A BOAT - A SEA - A WIND!
YOUR EYES ARE THE SEA, WITH WAVES OF TEARS. YOUR BODY IS A BOAT, SAILING ON THIS FLOOD OF SALT WATER - AND YOUR SIGHS ARE THE WIND.
YOUR SIGHS AND YOUR TEARS WILL DROWN YOUR BODY AND SINK YOUR BOAT, IF YOU DON'T GET THEM UNDER CONTROL.
HOW DO THINGS STAND, WIFE? HAVE YOU TOLD HER WHAT WE DECIDED?
I HAVE, SIR; BUT SHE WON'T AGREE TO IT. I WISH THIS FOOLISH GIRL WAS DEAD!
WAIT A MINUTE - EXPLAIN TO ME, WIFE -
HOW DO YOU MEAN? SHE WON'T AGREE? DIDN'T SHE THANK US?
ISN'T SHE PROUD? DOESN'T SHE THINK HERSELF FORTUNATE THAT WE'VE ARRANGED FOR SUCH A NOBLEMAN TO MARRY SOMEONE AS UNDESERVING AS SHE?
I AM THANKFUL, BUT NOT PROUD. I CAN'T BE PROUD OF SOMETHING I HATE, BUT I CAN BE THANKFUL FOR SOMETHING THAT'S GIVEN IN LOVE, EVEN IF I HATE IT.

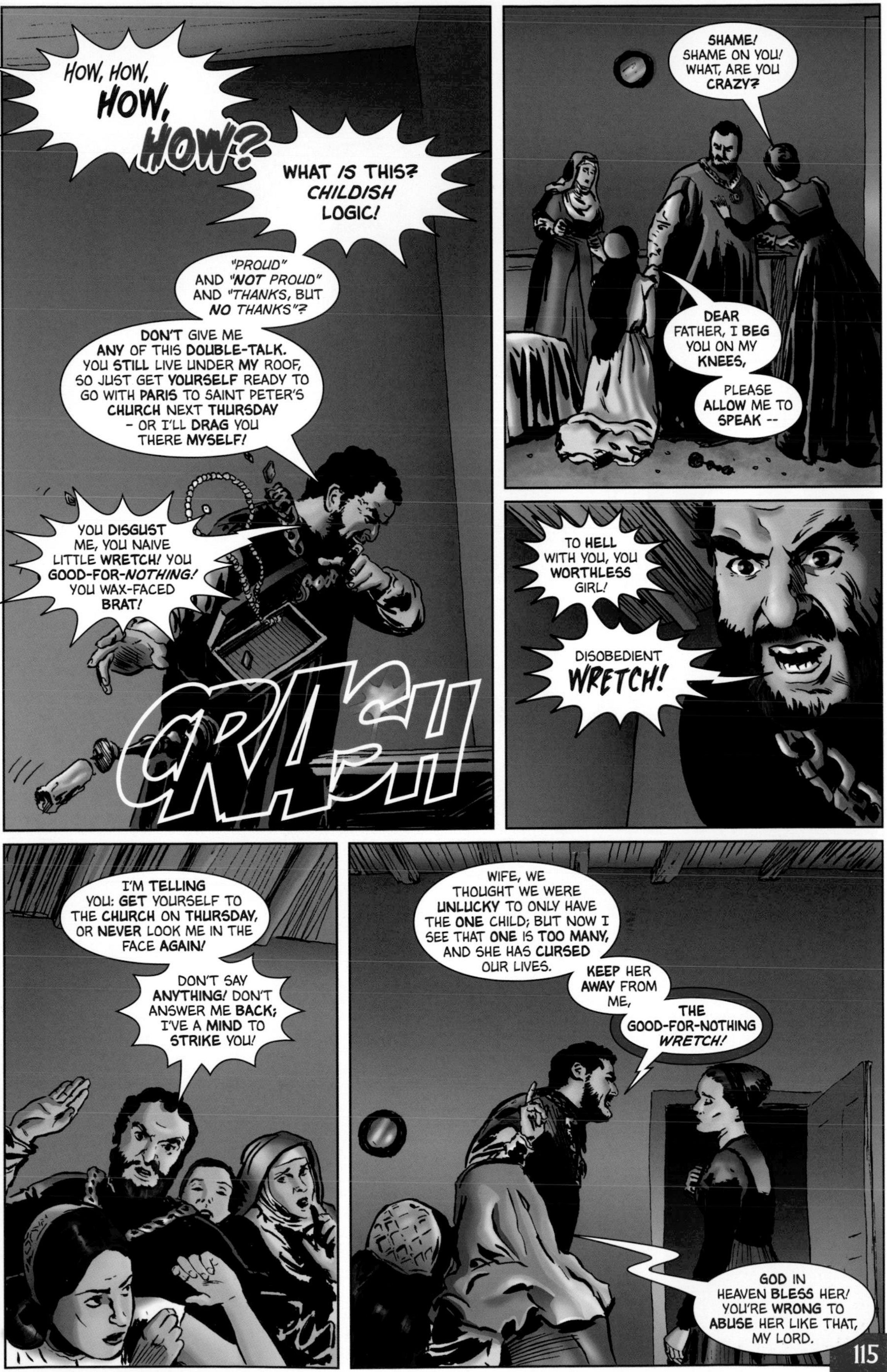
HOW, HOW, HOW, HOW?
WHAT IS THIS? CHILDISH LOGIC!
"PROUD" AND "NOT PROUD" AND "THANKS, BUT NO THANKS"?
DON'T GIVE ME ANY OF THIS DOUBLE-TALK. YOU STILL LIVE UNDER MY ROOF, SO JUST GET YOURSELF READY TO GO WITH PARIS TO SAINT PETER'S CHURCH NEXT THURSDAY - OR I'LL DRAG YOU THERE MYSELF!
YOU DISGUST ME, YOU NAIVE LITTLE WRETCH! YOU GOOD-FOR-NOTHING! YOU WAX-FACED BRAT!
CRASH
SHAME! SHAME ON YOU! WHAT, ARE YOU CRAZY?
DEAR FATHER, I BEG YOU ON MY KNEES,
PLEASE ALLOW ME TO SPEAK --
TO HELL WITH YOU, YOU WORTHLESS GIRL!
DISOBEDIENT WRETCH!
I'M TELLING YOU: GET YOURSELF TO THE CHURCH ON THURSDAY, OR NEVER LOOK ME IN THE FACE AGAIN!
DON'T SAY ANYTHING! DON'T ANSWER ME BACK; I'VE A MIND TO STRIKE YOU!
WIFE, WE THOUGHT WE WERE UNLUCKY TO ONLY HAVE THE ONE CHILD; BUT NOW I SEE THAT ONE IS TOO MANY, AND SHE HAS CURSED OUR LIVES.
KEEP HER AWAY FROM ME,
THE GOOD-FOR-NOTHING WRETCH!
GOD IN HEAVEN BLESS HER! YOU'RE WRONG TO ABUSE HER LIKE THAT, MY LORD.

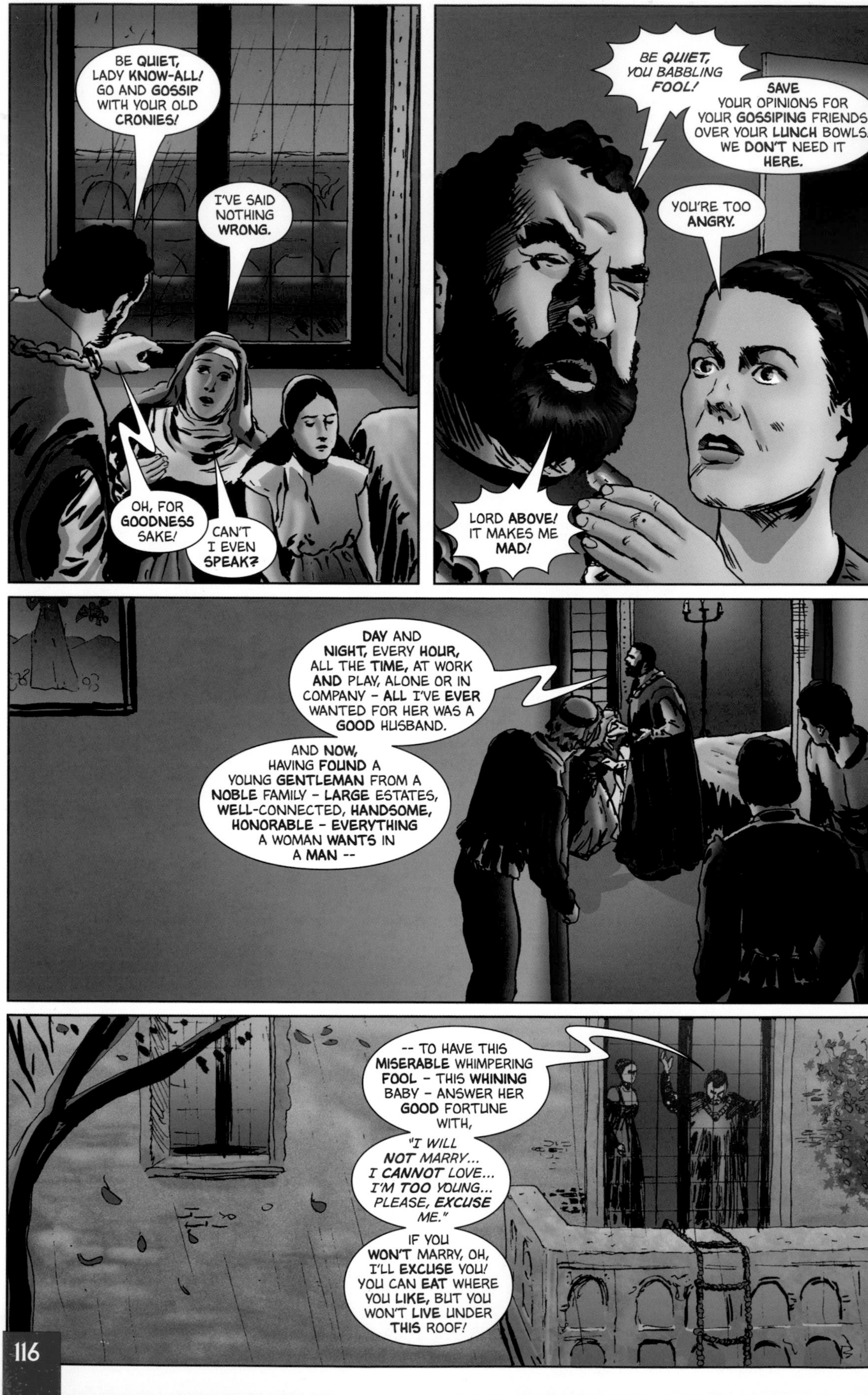
BE QUIET, LADY KNOW-ALL! GO AND GOSSIP WITH YOUR OLD CRONIES!
I'VE SAID NOTHING WRONG.
OH, FOR GOODNESS SAKE!
CAN'T I EVEN SPEAK?
BE QUIET, YOU BABBLING FOOL!
SAVE YOUR OPINIONS FOR YOUR GOSSIPING FRIENDS OVER YOUR LUNCH BOWLS! WE DON'T NEED IT HERE.
YOU'RE TOO ANGRY.
LORD ABOVE! IT MAKES ME MAD!
DAY AND NIGHT, EVERY HOUR, ALL THE TIME, AT WORK AND PLAY, ALONE OR IN COMPANY - ALL I'VE EVER WANTED FOR HER WAS A GOOD HUSBAND.
AND NOW, HAVING FOUND A YOUNG GENTLEMAN FROM A NOBLE FAMILY - LARGE ESTATES, WELL-CONNECTED, HANDSOME, HONORABLE - EVERYTHING A WOMAN WANTS IN A MAN --
-- TO HAVE THIS MISERABLE WHIMPERING FOOL - THIS WHINING BABY - ANSWER HER GOOD FORTUNE WITH,
"I WILL NOT MARRY... I CANNOT LOVE... I'M TOO YOUNG... PLEASE, EXCUSE ME."
IF YOU WON'T MARRY, OH, I'LL EXCUSE YOU! YOU CAN EAT WHERE YOU LIKE, BUT YOU WON'T LIVE UNDER THIS ROOF!

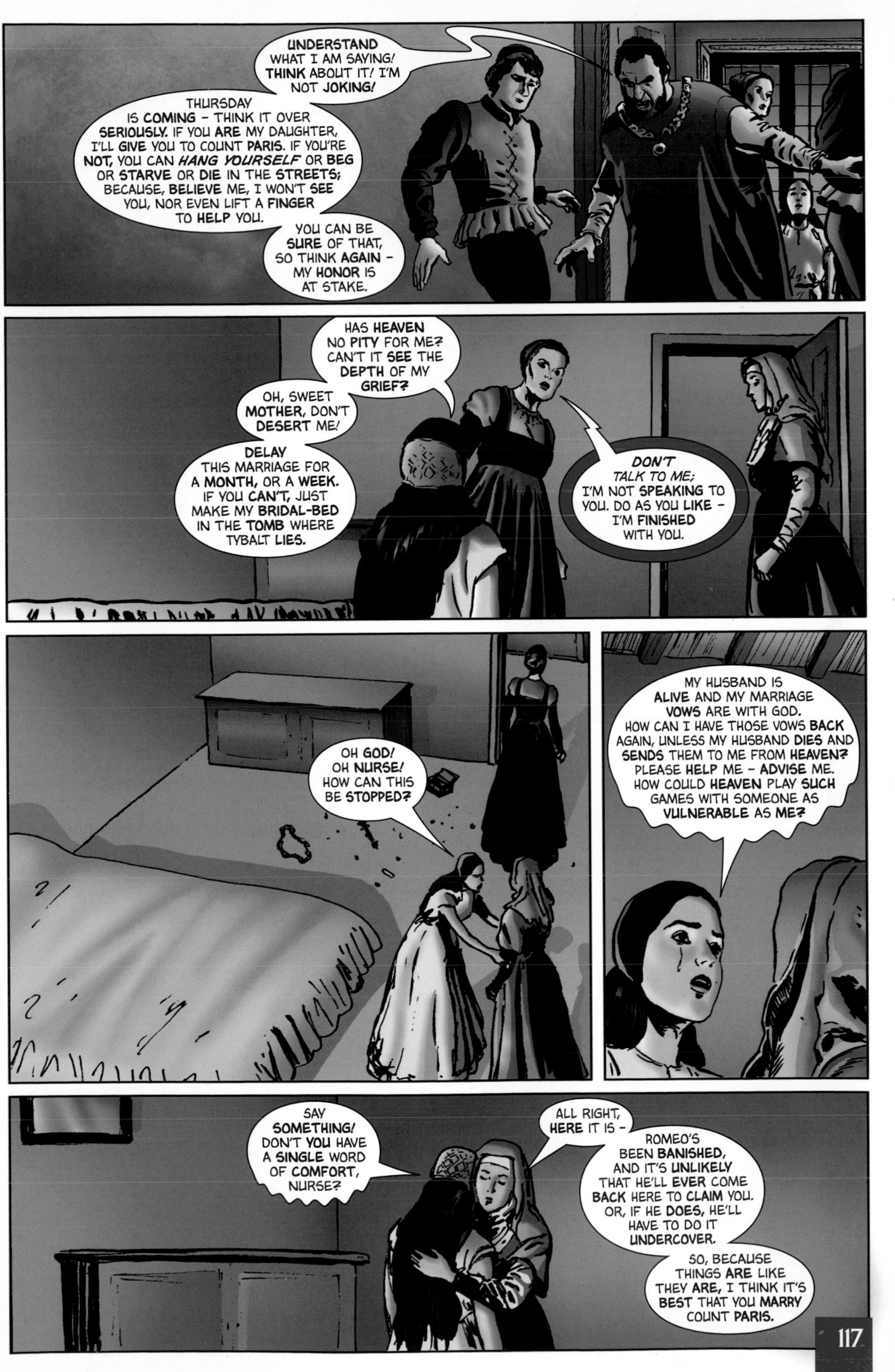
UNDERSTAND WHAT I AM SAYING! THINK ABOUT IT! I'M NOT JOKING!
THURSDAY IS COMING – THINK IT OVER SERIOUSLY. IF YOU ARE MY DAUGHTER, I'LL GIVE YOU TO COUNT PARIS. IF YOU'RE NOT, YOU CAN HANG YOURSELF OR BEG OR STARVE OR DIE IN THE STREETS; BECAUSE, BELIEVE ME, I WON'T SEE YOU, NOR EVEN LIFT A FINGER TO HELP YOU.
YOU CAN BE SURE OF THAT, SO THINK AGAIN – MY HONOR IS AT STAKE.
HAS HEAVEN NO PITY FOR ME? CAN'T IT SEE THE DEPTH OF MY GRIEF?
OH, SWEET MOTHER, DON'T DESERT ME!
DELAY THIS MARRIAGE FOR A MONTH, OR A WEEK. IF YOU CAN'T, JUST MAKE MY BRIDAL-BED IN THE TOMB WHERE TYBALT LIES.
DON'T TALK TO ME; I'M NOT SPEAKING TO YOU. DO AS YOU LIKE – I'M FINISHED WITH YOU.
OH GOD! OH NURSE! HOW CAN THIS BE STOPPED?
MY HUSBAND IS ALIVE AND MY MARRIAGE VOWS ARE WITH GOD. HOW CAN I HAVE THOSE VOWS BACK AGAIN, UNLESS MY HUSBAND DIES AND SENDS THEM TO ME FROM HEAVEN? PLEASE HELP ME – ADVISE ME. HOW COULD HEAVEN PLAY SUCH GAMES WITH SOMEONE AS VULNERABLE AS ME?
SAY SOMETHING! DON'T YOU HAVE A SINGLE WORD OF COMFORT, NURSE?
ALL RIGHT, HERE IT IS –
ROMEO'S BEEN BANISHED, AND IT'S UNLIKELY THAT HE'LL EVER COME BACK HERE TO CLAIM YOU. OR, IF HE DOES, HE'LL HAVE TO DO IT UNDERCOVER.
SO, BECAUSE THINGS ARE LIKE THEY ARE, I THINK IT'S BEST THAT YOU MARRY COUNT PARIS.

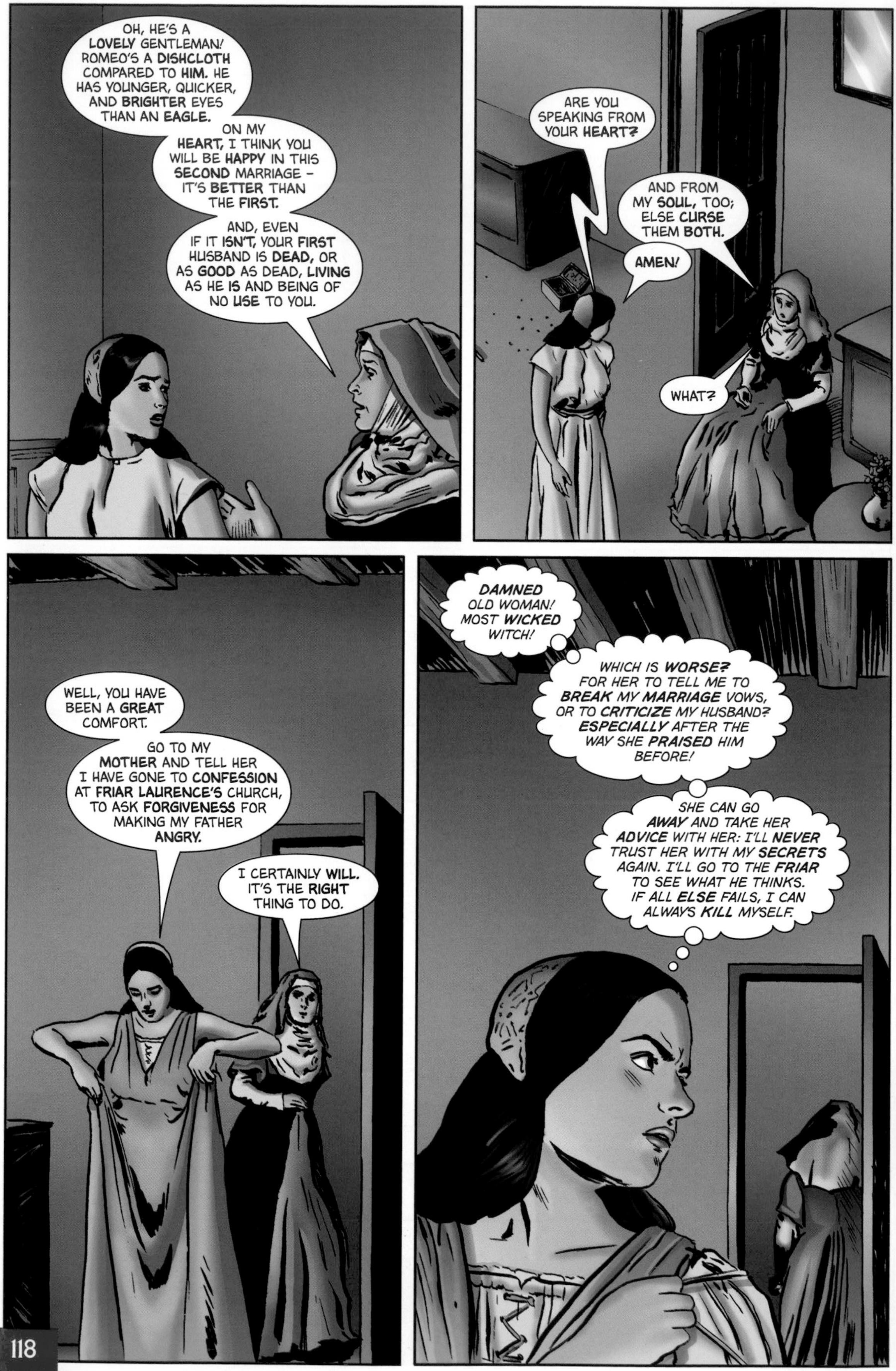
OH, HE'S A LOVELY GENTLEMAN! ROMEO'S A DISHCLOTH COMPARED TO HIM. HE HAS YOUNGER, QUICKER, AND BRIGHTER EYES THAN AN EAGLE.
ON MY HEART, I THINK YOU WILL BE HAPPY IN THIS SECOND MARRIAGE – IT'S BETTER THAN THE FIRST.
AND, EVEN IF IT ISN'T, YOUR FIRST HUSBAND IS DEAD, OR AS GOOD AS DEAD, LIVING AS HE IS AND BEING OF NO USE TO YOU.
ARE YOU SPEAKING FROM YOUR HEART?
AND FROM MY SOUL, TOO; ELSE CURSE THEM BOTH.
AMEN!
WHAT?
WELL, YOU HAVE BEEN A GREAT COMFORT.
GO TO MY MOTHER AND TELL HER I HAVE GONE TO CONFESSION AT FRIAR LAURENCE'S CHURCH, TO ASK FORGIVENESS FOR MAKING MY FATHER ANGRY.
I CERTAINLY WILL. IT'S THE RIGHT THING TO DO.
DAMNED OLD WOMAN! MOST WICKED WITCH!
WHICH IS WORSE? FOR HER TO TELL ME TO BREAK MY MARRIAGE VOWS, OR TO CRITICIZE MY HUSBAND? ESPECIALLY AFTER THE WAY SHE PRAISED HIM BEFORE!
SHE CAN GO AWAY AND TAKE HER ADVICE WITH HER: I'LL NEVER TRUST HER WITH MY SECRETS AGAIN. I'LL GO TO THE FRIAR TO SEE WHAT HE THINKS. IF ALL ELSE FAILS, I CAN ALWAYS KILL MYSELF.

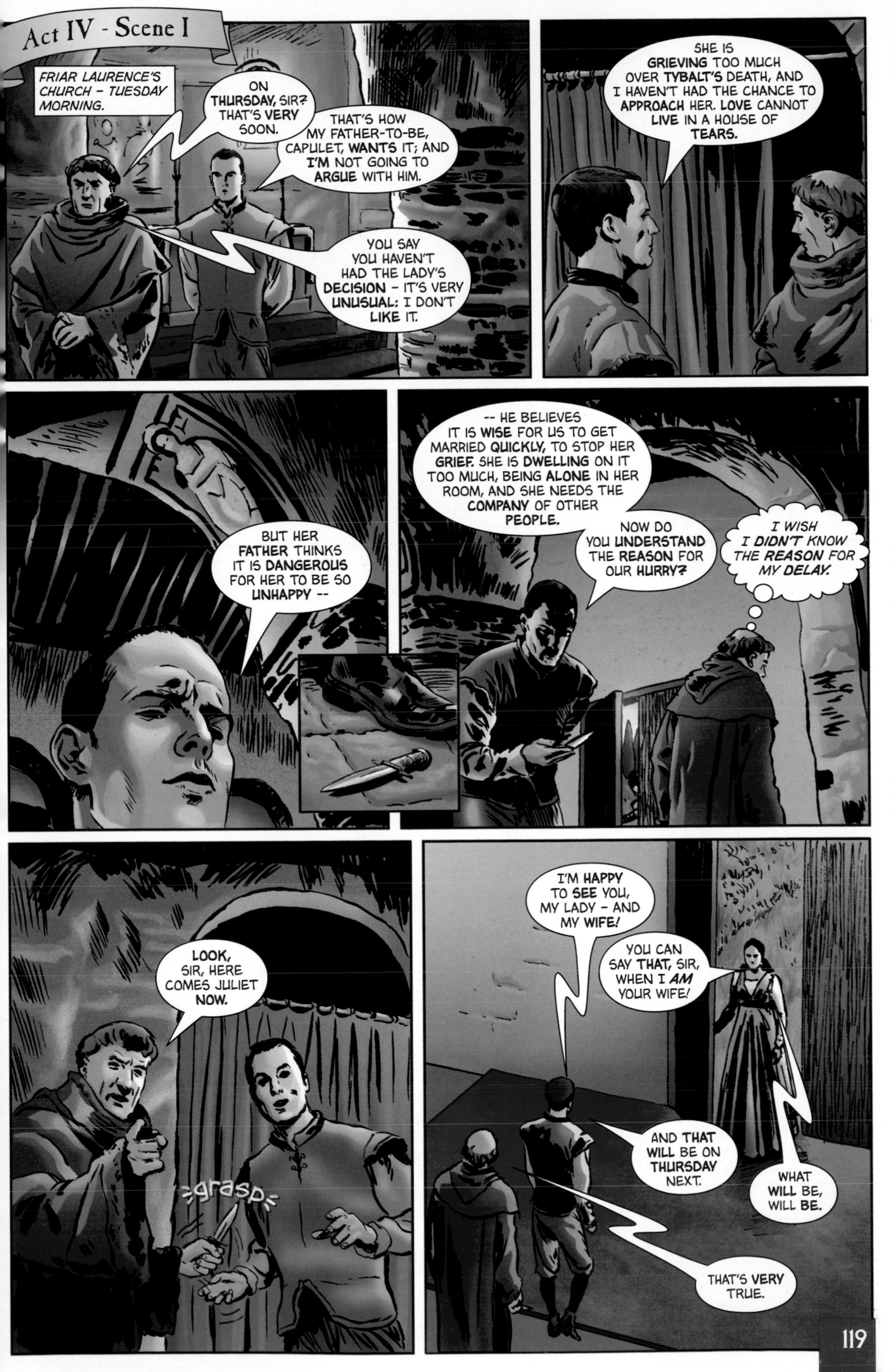
Act IV - Scene I
FRIAR LAURENCE'S CHURCH – TUESDAY MORNING.
ON THURSDAY, SIR? THAT'S VERY SOON.
THAT'S HOW MY FATHER-TO-BE, CAPULET, WANTS IT; AND I'M NOT GOING TO ARGUE WITH HIM.
YOU SAY YOU HAVEN'T HAD THE LADY'S DECISION – IT'S VERY UNUSUAL: I DON'T LIKE IT.
SHE IS GRIEVING TOO MUCH OVER TYBALT'S DEATH, AND I HAVEN'T HAD THE CHANCE TO APPROACH HER. LOVE CANNOT LIVE IN A HOUSE OF TEARS.
BUT HER FATHER THINKS IT IS DANGEROUS FOR HER TO BE SO UNHAPPY --
-- HE BELIEVES IT IS WISE FOR US TO GET MARRIED QUICKLY, TO STOP HER GRIEF. SHE IS DWELLING ON IT TOO MUCH, BEING ALONE IN HER ROOM, AND SHE NEEDS THE COMPANY OF OTHER PEOPLE.
NOW DO YOU UNDERSTAND THE REASON FOR OUR HURRY?
I WISH I DIDN'T KNOW THE REASON FOR MY DELAY.
LOOK, SIR, HERE COMES JULIET NOW.
grasp
I'M HAPPY TO SEE YOU, MY LADY – AND MY WIFE!
YOU CAN SAY THAT, SIR, WHEN I AM YOUR WIFE!
AND THAT WILL BE ON THURSDAY NEXT.
WHAT WILL BE, WILL BE.
THAT'S VERY TRUE.

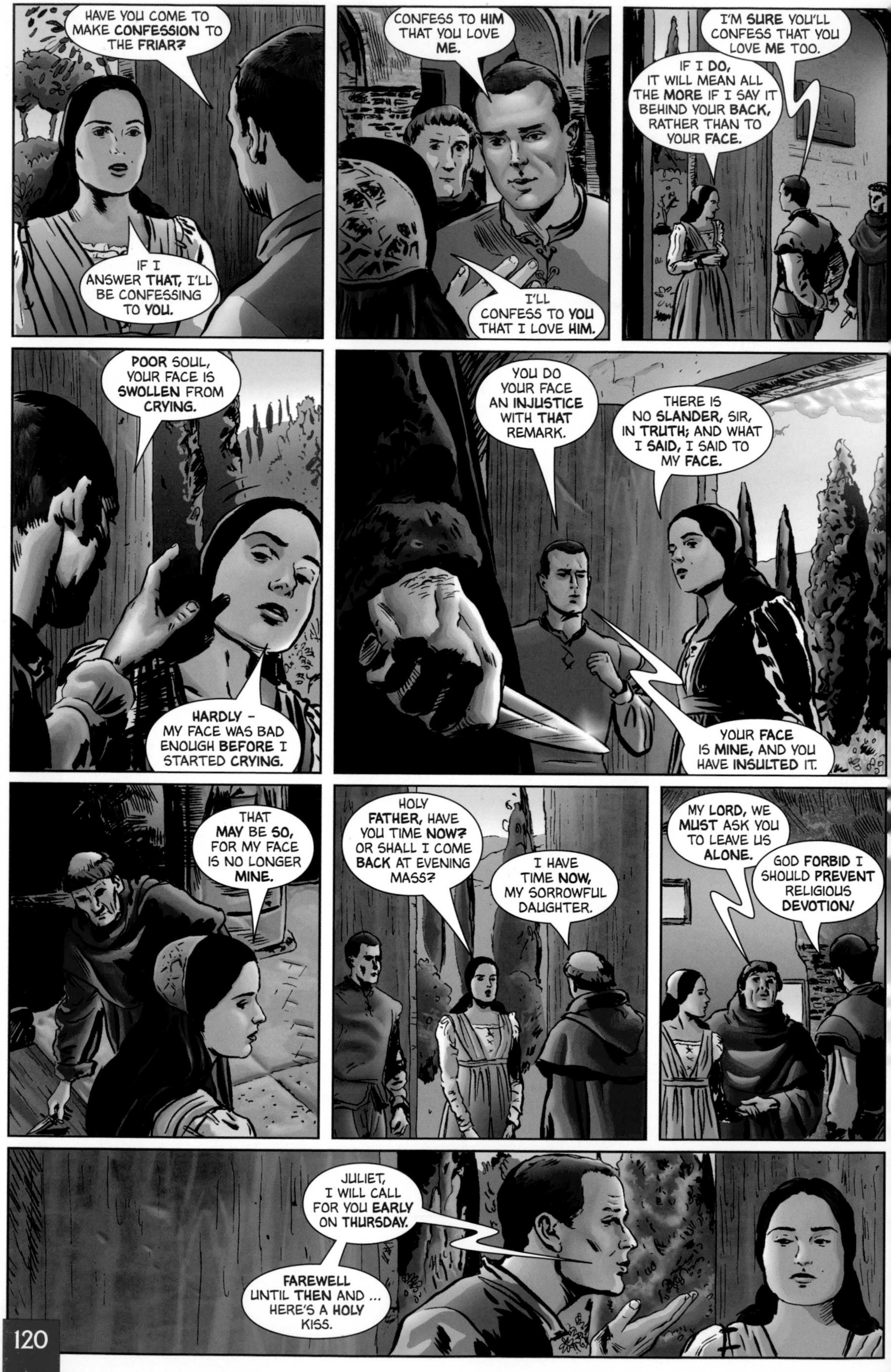
HAVE YOU COME TO MAKE CONFESSION TO THE FRIAR?
IF I ANSWER THAT, I'LL BE CONFESSING TO YOU.
CONFESS TO HIM THAT YOU LOVE ME.
I'LL CONFESS TO YOU THAT I LOVE HIM.
I'M SURE YOU'LL CONFESS THAT YOU LOVE ME TOO.
IF I DO, IT WILL MEAN ALL THE MORE IF I SAY IT BEHIND YOUR BACK, RATHER THAN TO YOUR FACE.
POOR SOUL, YOUR FACE IS SWOLLEN FROM CRYING.
HARDLY – MY FACE WAS BAD ENOUGH BEFORE I STARTED CRYING.
YOU DO YOUR FACE AN INJUSTICE WITH THAT REMARK.
THERE IS NO SLANDER, SIR, IN TRUTH; AND WHAT I SAID, I SAID TO MY FACE.
YOUR FACE IS MINE, AND YOU HAVE INSULTED IT.
THAT MAY BE SO, FOR MY FACE IS NO LONGER MINE.
HOLY FATHER, HAVE YOU TIME NOW? OR SHALL I COME BACK AT EVENING MASS?
I HAVE TIME NOW, MY SORROWFUL DAUGHTER.
MY LORD, WE MUST ASK YOU TO LEAVE US ALONE.
GOD FORBID I SHOULD PREVENT RELIGIOUS DEVOTION!
JULIET, I WILL CALL FOR YOU EARLY ON THURSDAY.
FAREWELL UNTIL THEN AND ... HERE'S A HOLY KISS.

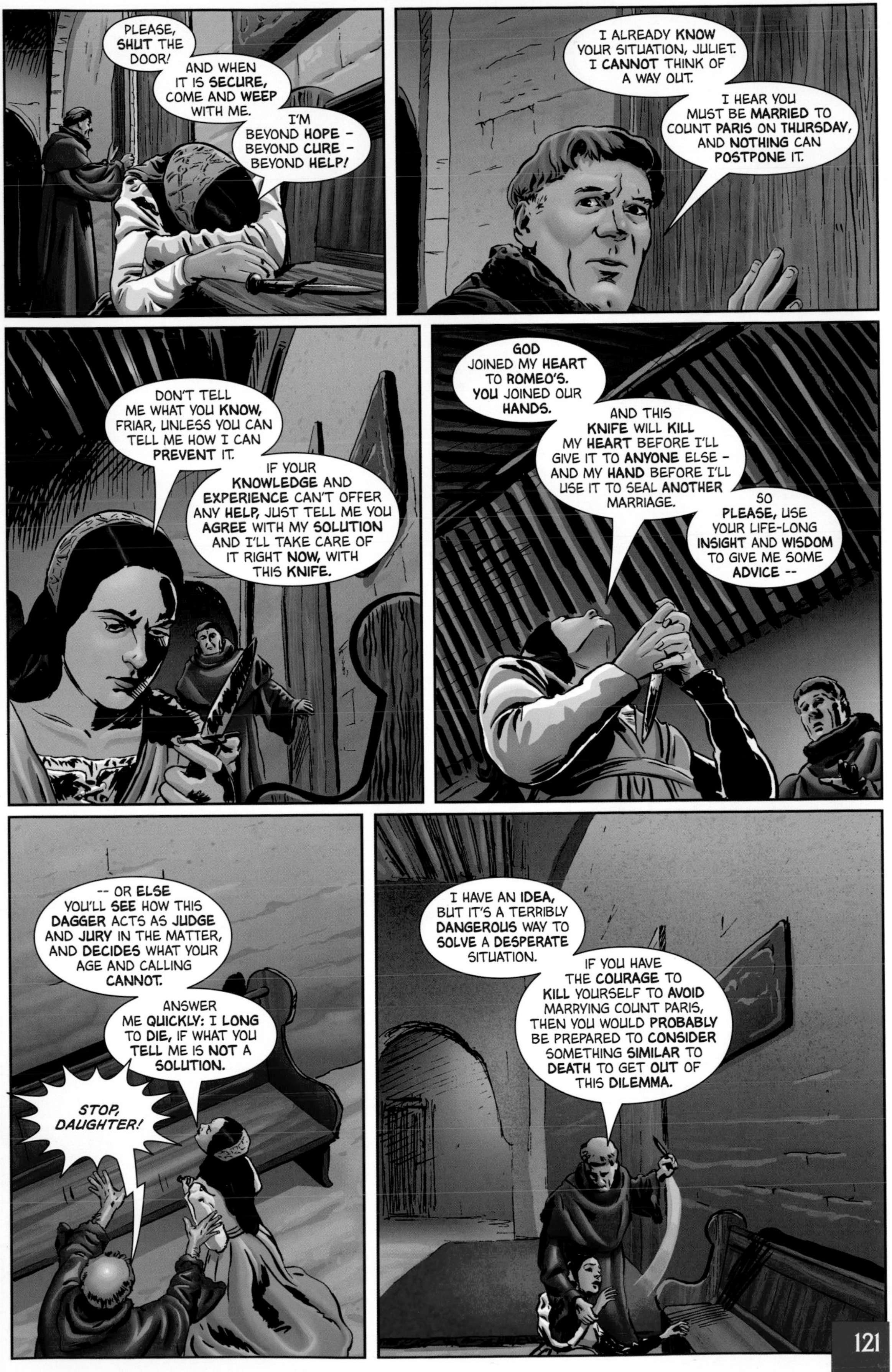
PLEASE, SHUT THE DOOR!
AND WHEN IT IS SECURE, COME AND WEEP WITH ME.
I'M BEYOND HOPE – BEYOND CURE – BEYOND HELP!
I ALREADY KNOW YOUR SITUATION, JULIET. I CANNOT THINK OF A WAY OUT.
I HEAR YOU MUST BE MARRIED TO COUNT PARIS ON THURSDAY, AND NOTHING CAN POSTPONE IT.
DON'T TELL ME WHAT YOU KNOW, FRIAR, UNLESS YOU CAN TELL ME HOW I CAN PREVENT IT.
IF YOUR KNOWLEDGE AND EXPERIENCE CAN'T OFFER ANY HELP, JUST TELL ME YOU AGREE WITH MY SOLUTION AND I'LL TAKE CARE OF IT RIGHT NOW, WITH THIS KNIFE.
GOD JOINED MY HEART TO ROMEO'S. YOU JOINED OUR HANDS.
AND THIS KNIFE WILL KILL MY HEART BEFORE I'LL GIVE IT TO ANYONE ELSE – AND MY HAND BEFORE I'LL USE IT TO SEAL ANOTHER MARRIAGE.
SO PLEASE, USE YOUR LIFE-LONG INSIGHT AND WISDOM TO GIVE ME SOME ADVICE --
-- OR ELSE YOU'LL SEE HOW THIS DAGGER ACTS AS JUDGE AND JURY IN THE MATTER, AND DECIDES WHAT YOUR AGE AND CALLING CANNOT.
ANSWER ME QUICKLY: I LONG TO DIE, IF WHAT YOU TELL ME IS NOT A SOLUTION.
STOP, DAUGHTER!
I HAVE AN IDEA, BUT IT'S A TERRIBLY DANGEROUS WAY TO SOLVE A DESPERATE SITUATION.
IF YOU HAVE THE COURAGE TO KILL YOURSELF TO AVOID MARRYING COUNT PARIS, THEN YOU WOULD PROBABLY BE PREPARED TO CONSIDER SOMETHING SIMILAR TO DEATH TO GET OUT OF THIS DILEMMA.

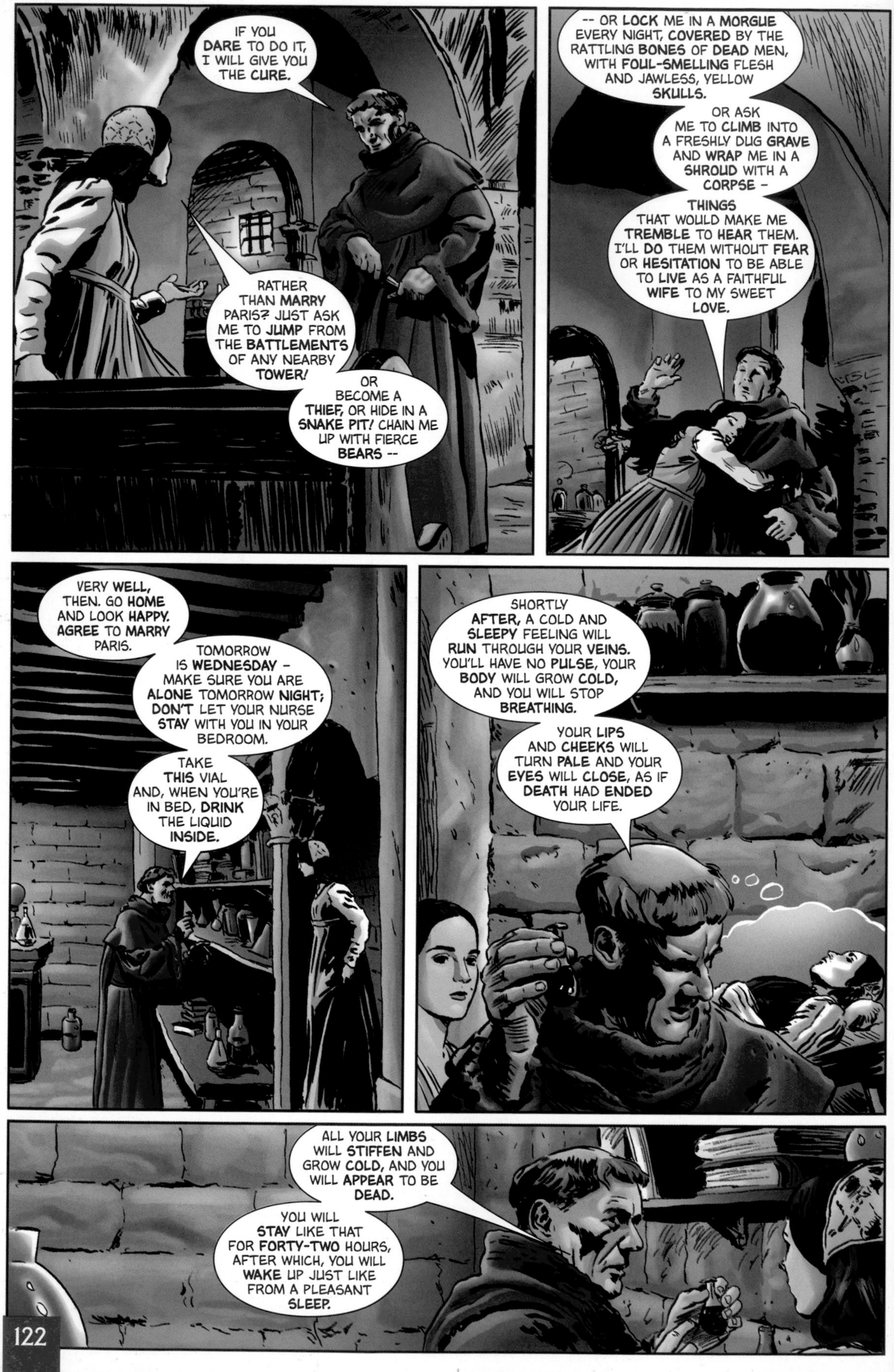
IF YOU DARE TO DO IT, I WILL GIVE YOU THE CURE.
RATHER THAN MARRY PARIS? JUST ASK ME TO JUMP FROM THE BATTLEMENTS OF ANY NEARBY TOWER!
OR BECOME A THIEF, OR HIDE IN A SNAKE PIT! CHAIN ME UP WITH FIERCE BEARS --
-- OR LOCK ME IN A MORGUE EVERY NIGHT, COVERED BY THE RATTLING BONES OF DEAD MEN, WITH FOUL-SMELLING FLESH AND JAWLESS, YELLOW SKULLS.
OR ASK ME TO CLIMB INTO A FRESHLY DUG GRAVE AND WRAP ME IN A SHROUD WITH A CORPSE –
THINGS THAT WOULD MAKE ME TREMBLE TO HEAR THEM. I'LL DO THEM WITHOUT FEAR OR HESITATION TO BE ABLE TO LIVE AS A FAITHFUL WIFE TO MY SWEET LOVE.
VERY WELL, THEN. GO HOME AND LOOK HAPPY. AGREE TO MARRY PARIS.
TOMORROW IS WEDNESDAY – MAKE SURE YOU ARE ALONE TOMORROW NIGHT; DON'T LET YOUR NURSE STAY WITH YOU IN YOUR BEDROOM.
TAKE THIS VIAL AND, WHEN YOU'RE IN BED, DRINK THE LIQUID INSIDE.
SHORTLY AFTER, A COLD AND SLEEPY FEELING WILL RUN THROUGH YOUR VEINS. YOU'LL HAVE NO PULSE, YOUR BODY WILL GROW COLD, AND YOU WILL STOP BREATHING.
YOUR LIPS AND CHEEKS WILL TURN PALE AND YOUR EYES WILL CLOSE, AS IF DEATH HAD ENDED YOUR LIFE.
ALL YOUR LIMBS WILL STIFFEN AND GROW COLD, AND YOU WILL APPEAR TO BE DEAD.
YOU WILL STAY LIKE THAT FOR FORTY-TWO HOURS, AFTER WHICH, YOU WILL WAKE UP JUST LIKE FROM A PLEASANT SLEEP.

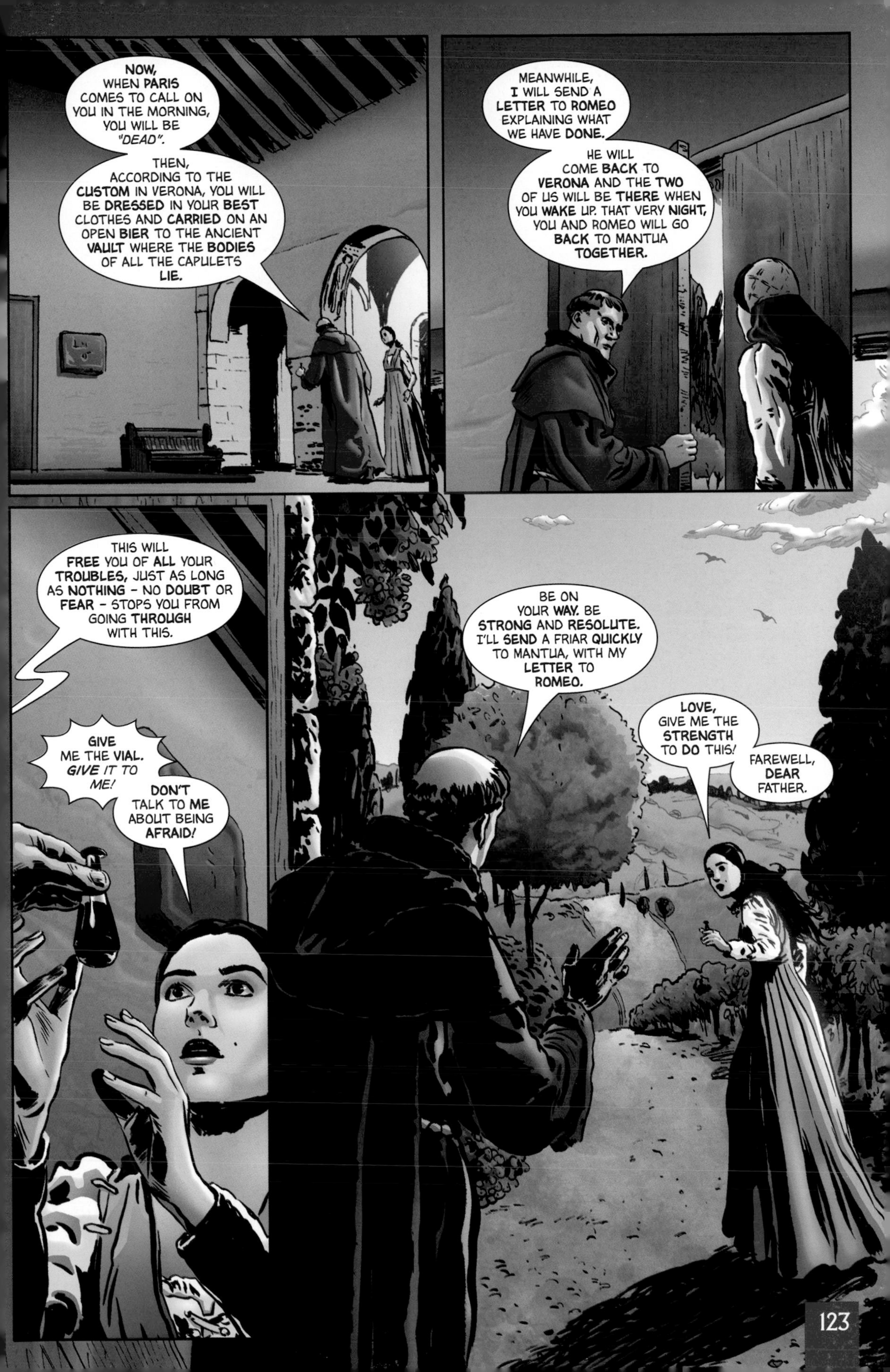
NOW, WHEN PARIS COMES TO CALL ON YOU IN THE MORNING, YOU WILL BE "DEAD".
THEN, ACCORDING TO THE CUSTOM IN VERONA, YOU WILL BE DRESSED IN YOUR BEST CLOTHES AND CARRIED ON AN OPEN BIER TO THE ANCIENT VAULT WHERE THE BODIES OF ALL THE CAPULETS LIE.
MEANWHILE, I WILL SEND A LETTER TO ROMEO EXPLAINING WHAT WE HAVE DONE.
HE WILL COME BACK TO VERONA AND THE TWO OF US WILL BE THERE WHEN YOU WAKE UP. THAT VERY NIGHT, YOU AND ROMEO WILL GO BACK TO MANTUA TOGETHER.
THIS WILL FREE YOU OF ALL YOUR TROUBLES, JUST AS LONG AS NOTHING - NO DOUBT OR FEAR - STOPS YOU FROM GOING THROUGH WITH THIS.
GIVE ME THE VIAL. GIVE IT TO ME!
DON'T TALK TO ME ABOUT BEING AFRAID!
BE ON YOUR WAY. BE STRONG AND RESOLUTE. I'LL SEND A FRIAR QUICKLY TO MANTUA, WITH MY LETTER TO ROMEO.
LOVE, GIVE ME THE STRENGTH TO DO THIS!
FAREWELL, DEAR FATHER.

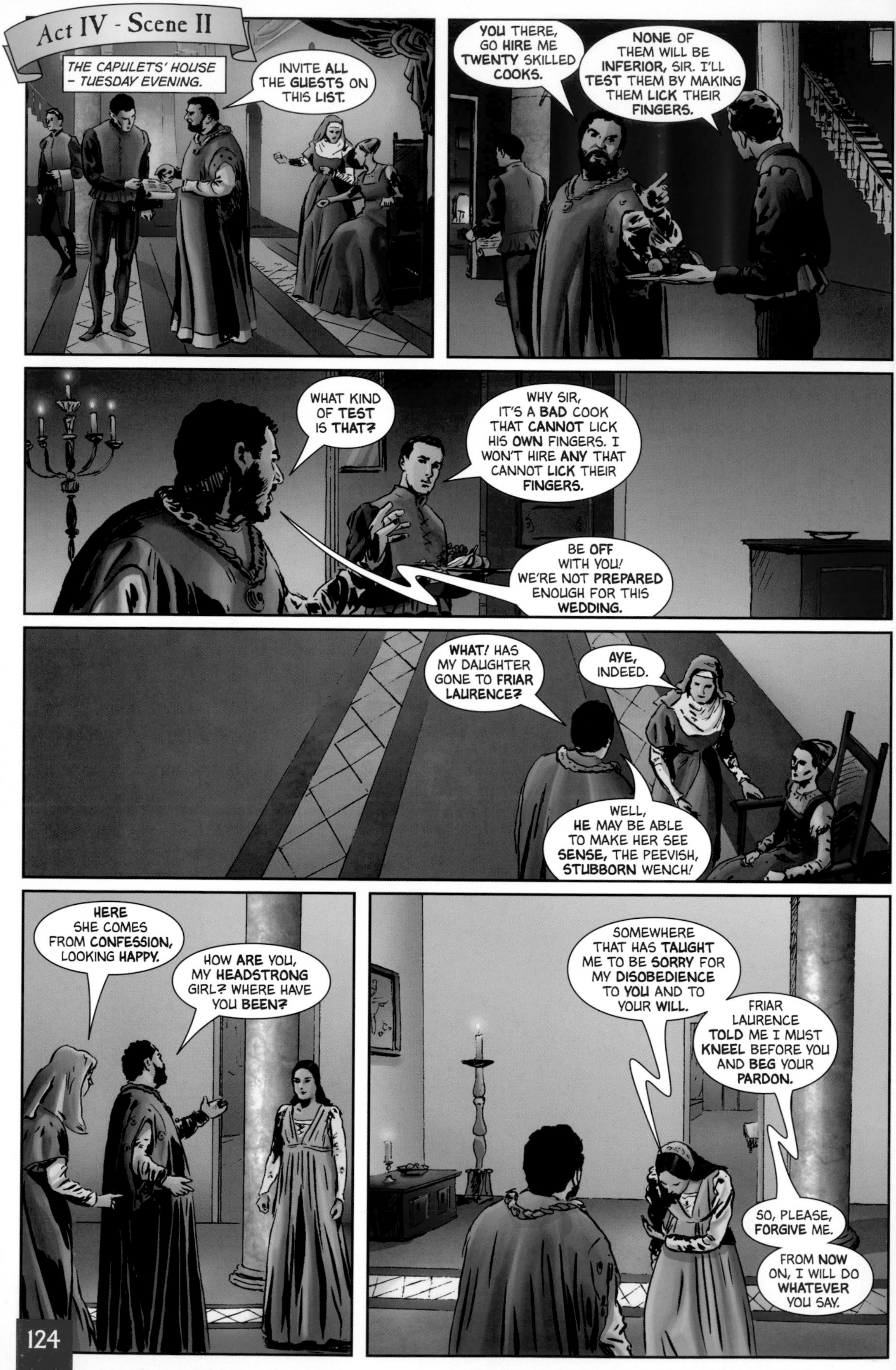
Act IV - Scene II
THE CAPULETS' HOUSE – TUESDAY EVENING.
INVITE ALL THE GUESTS ON THIS LIST.
YOU THERE, GO HIRE ME TWENTY SKILLED COOKS.
NONE OF THEM WILL BE INFERIOR, SIR. I'LL TEST THEM BY MAKING THEM LICK THEIR FINGERS.
WHAT KIND OF TEST IS THAT?
WHY SIR, IT'S A BAD COOK THAT CANNOT LICK HIS OWN FINGERS. I WON'T HIRE ANY THAT CANNOT LICK THEIR FINGERS.
BE OFF WITH YOU! WE'RE NOT PREPARED ENOUGH FOR THIS WEDDING.
WHAT! HAS MY DAUGHTER GONE TO FRIAR LAURENCE?
AYE, INDEED.
WELL, HE MAY BE ABLE TO MAKE HER SEE SENSE, THE PEEVISH, STUBBORN WENCH!
HERE SHE COMES FROM CONFESSION, LOOKING HAPPY.
HOW ARE YOU, MY HEADSTRONG GIRL? WHERE HAVE YOU BEEN?
SOMEWHERE THAT HAS TAUGHT ME TO BE SORRY FOR MY DISOBEDIENCE TO YOU AND TO YOUR WILL.
FRIAR LAURENCE TOLD ME I MUST KNEEL BEFORE YOU AND BEG YOUR PARDON.
SO, PLEASE, FORGIVE ME.
FROM NOW ON, I WILL DO WHATEVER YOU SAY.

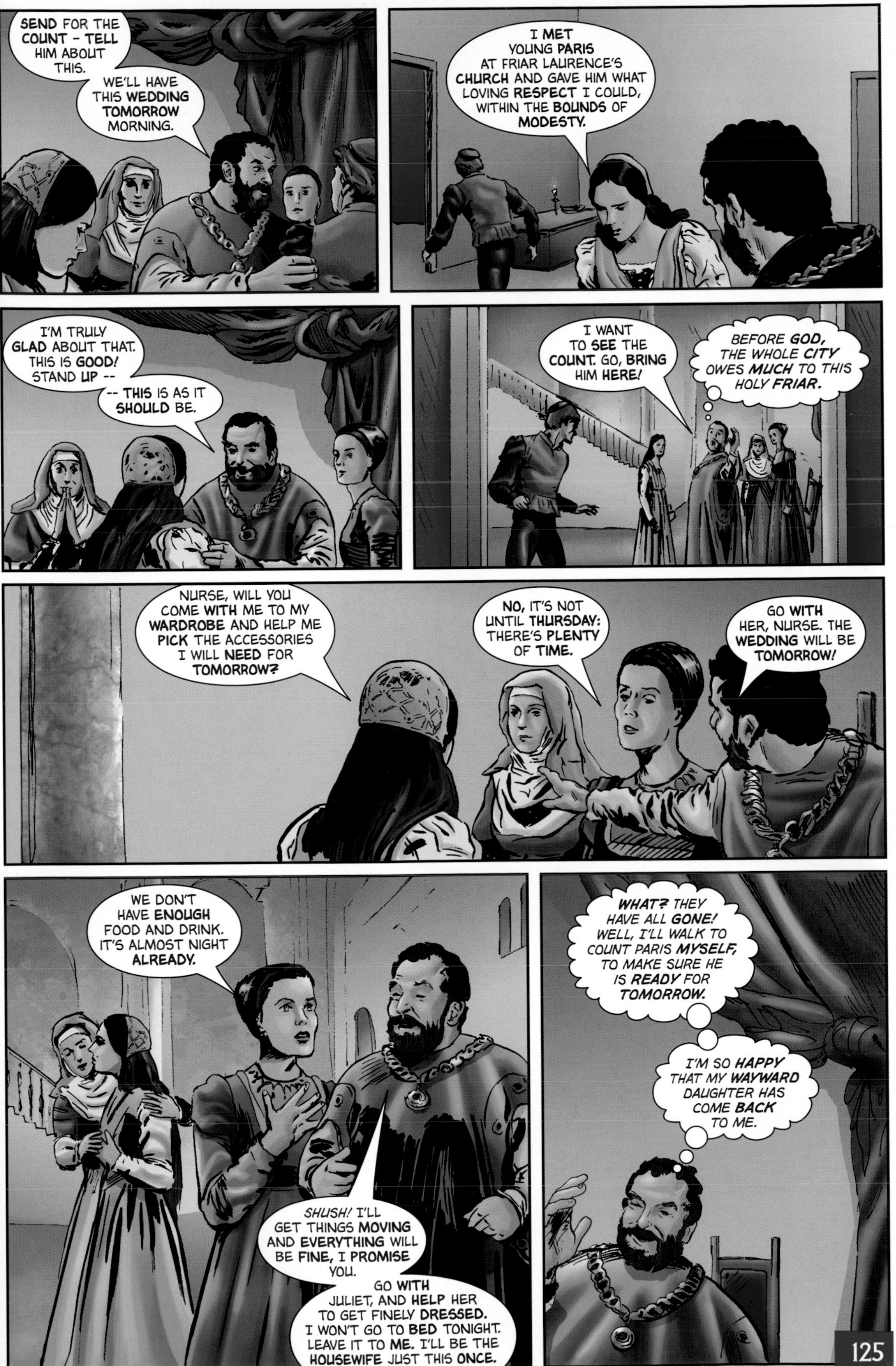

SEND FOR THE COUNT – TELL HIM ABOUT THIS.
WE'LL HAVE THIS WEDDING TOMORROW MORNING.
I MET YOUNG PARIS AT FRIAR LAURENCE'S CHURCH AND GAVE HIM WHAT LOVING RESPECT I COULD, WITHIN THE BOUNDS OF MODESTY.
I'M TRULY GLAD ABOUT THAT. THIS IS GOOD! STAND UP --
-- THIS IS AS IT SHOULD BE.
I WANT TO SEE THE COUNT. GO, BRING HIM HERE!
BEFORE GOD, THE WHOLE CITY OWES MUCH TO THIS HOLY FRIAR.
NURSE, WILL YOU COME WITH ME TO MY WARDROBE AND HELP ME PICK THE ACCESSORIES I WILL NEED FOR TOMORROW?
NO, IT'S NOT UNTIL THURSDAY: THERE'S PLENTY OF TIME.
GO WITH HER, NURSE. THE WEDDING WILL BE TOMORROW!
WE DON'T HAVE ENOUGH FOOD AND DRINK. IT'S ALMOST NIGHT ALREADY.
SHUSH! I'LL GET THINGS MOVING AND EVERYTHING WILL BE FINE, I PROMISE YOU.
GO WITH JULIET, AND HELP HER TO GET FINELY DRESSED. I WON'T GO TO BED TONIGHT. LEAVE IT TO ME. I'LL BE THE HOUSEWIFE JUST THIS ONCE.
WHAT? THEY HAVE ALL GONE! WELL, I'LL WALK TO COUNT PARIS MYSELF, TO MAKE SURE HE IS READY FOR TOMORROW.
I'M SO HAPPY THAT MY WAYWARD DAUGHTER HAS COME BACK TO ME.

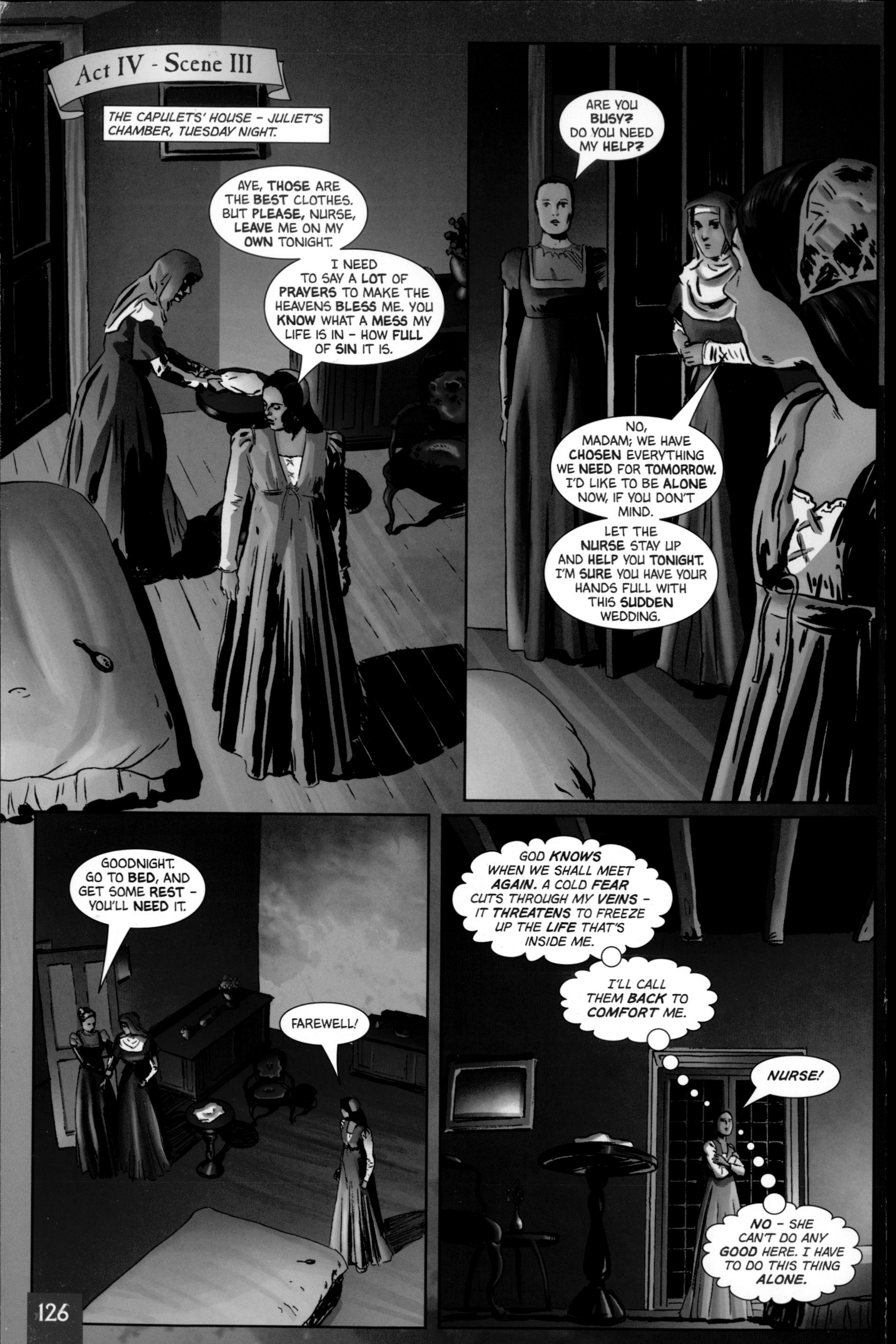
Act IV - Scene III
THE CAPULETS' HOUSE - JULIET'S CHAMBER, TUESDAY NIGHT.
AYE, THOSE ARE THE BEST CLOTHES. BUT PLEASE, NURSE, LEAVE ME ON MY OWN TONIGHT.
I NEED TO SAY A LOT OF PRAYERS TO MAKE THE HEAVENS BLESS ME. YOU KNOW WHAT A MESS MY LIFE IS IN - HOW FULL OF SIN IT IS.
ARE YOU BUSY? DO YOU NEED MY HELP?
NO, MADAM; WE HAVE CHOSEN EVERYTHING WE NEED FOR TOMORROW. I'D LIKE TO BE ALONE NOW, IF YOU DON'T MIND.
LET THE NURSE STAY UP AND HELP YOU TONIGHT. I'M SURE YOU HAVE YOUR HANDS FULL WITH THIS SUDDEN WEDDING.
GOODNIGHT. GO TO BED, AND GET SOME REST - YOU'LL NEED IT.
FAREWELL!
GOD KNOWS WHEN WE SHALL MEET AGAIN. A COLD FEAR CUTS THROUGH MY VEINS - IT THREATENS TO FREEZE UP THE LIFE THAT'S INSIDE ME.
I'LL CALL THEM BACK TO COMFORT ME.
NURSE!
NO - SHE CAN'T DO ANY GOOD HERE. I HAVE TO DO THIS THING ALONE.

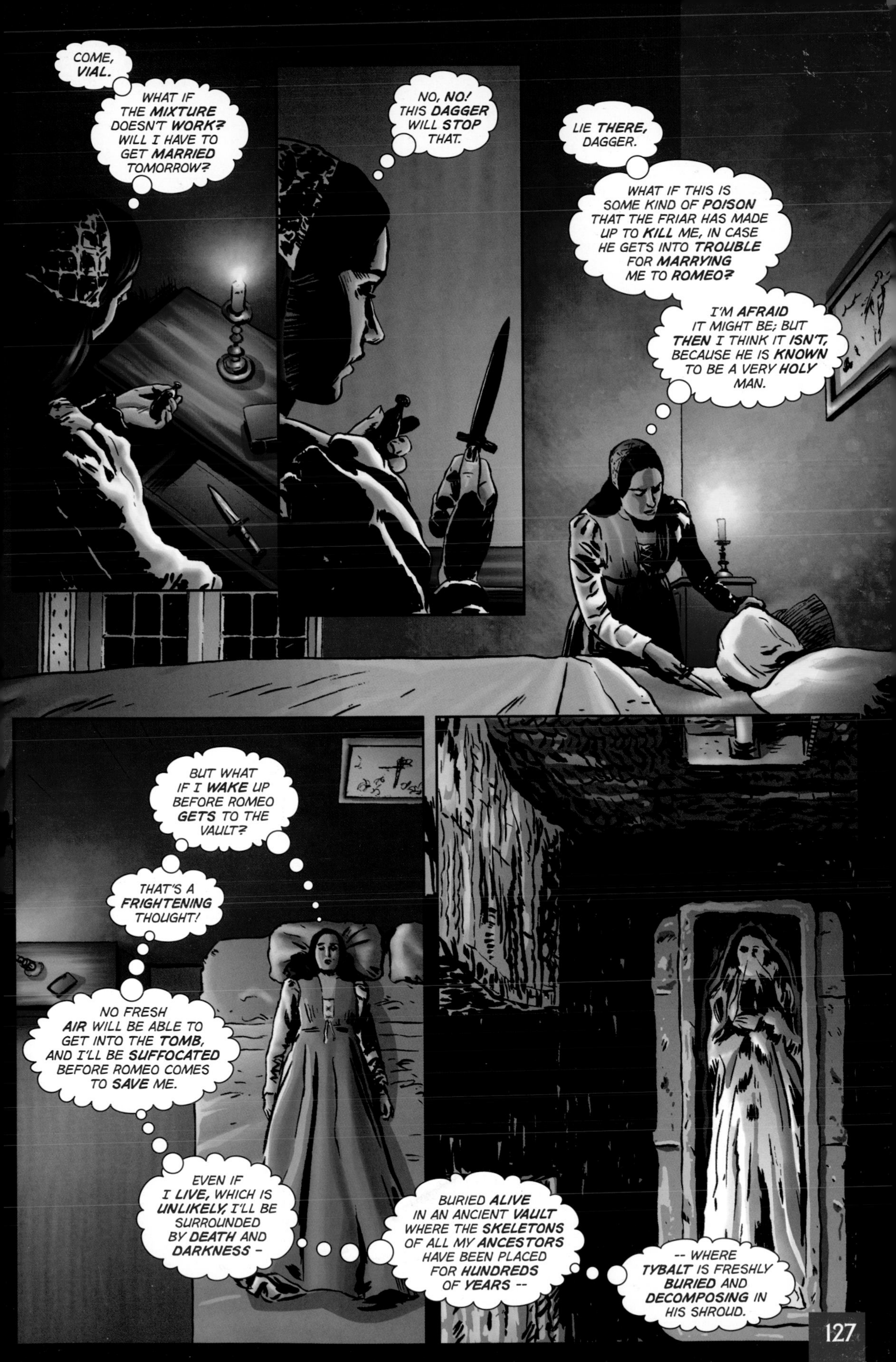
COME, VIAL.
WHAT IF THE MIXTURE DOESN'T WORK? WILL I HAVE TO GET MARRIED TOMORROW?
NO, NO! THIS DAGGER WILL STOP THAT.
LIE THERE, DAGGER.
WHAT IF THIS IS SOME KIND OF POISON THAT THE FRIAR HAS MADE UP TO KILL ME, IN CASE HE GETS INTO TROUBLE FOR MARRYING ME TO ROMEO?
I'M AFRAID IT MIGHT BE; BUT THEN I THINK IT ISN'T, BECAUSE HE IS KNOWN TO BE A VERY HOLY MAN.
BUT WHAT IF I WAKE UP BEFORE ROMEO GETS TO THE VAULT?
THAT'S A FRIGHTENING THOUGHT!
NO FRESH AIR WILL BE ABLE TO GET INTO THE TOMB, AND I'LL BE SUFFOCATED BEFORE ROMEO COMES TO SAVE ME.
EVEN IF I LIVE, WHICH IS UNLIKELY, I'LL BE SURROUNDED BY DEATH AND DARKNESS -
BURIED ALIVE IN AN ANCIENT VAULT WHERE THE SKELETONS OF ALL MY ANCESTORS HAVE BEEN PLACED FOR HUNDREDS OF YEARS --
-- WHERE TYBALT IS FRESHLY BURIED AND DECOMPOSING IN HIS SHROUD.

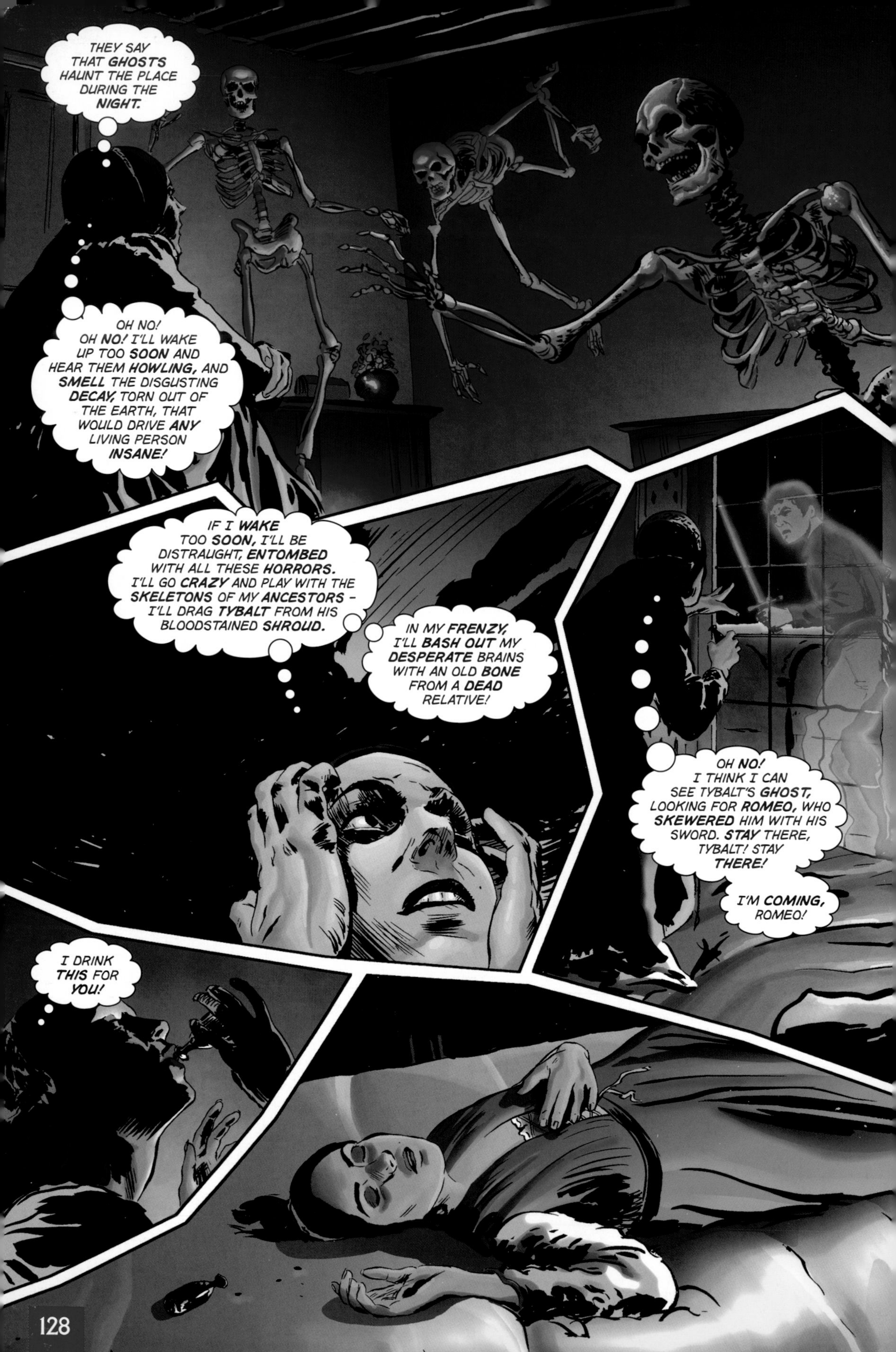
THEY SAY THAT GHOSTS HAUNT THE PLACE DURING THE NIGHT.
OH NO! OH NO! I'LL WAKE UP TOO SOON AND HEAR THEM HOWLING, AND SMELL THE DISGUSTING DECAY, TORN OUT OF THE EARTH, THAT WOULD DRIVE ANY LIVING PERSON INSANE!
IF I WAKE TOO SOON, I'LL BE DISTRAUGHT, ENTOMBED WITH ALL THESE HORRORS. I'LL GO CRAZY AND PLAY WITH THE SKELETONS OF MY ANCESTORS – I'LL DRAG TYBALT FROM HIS BLOODSTAINED SHROUD.
IN MY FRENZY, I'LL BASH OUT MY DESPERATE BRAINS WITH AN OLD BONE FROM A DEAD RELATIVE!
OH NO! I THINK I CAN SEE TYBALT'S GHOST, LOOKING FOR ROMEO, WHO SKEWERED HIM WITH HIS SWORD. STAY THERE, TYBALT! STAY THERE!
I'M COMING, ROMEO!
I DRINK THIS FOR YOU!

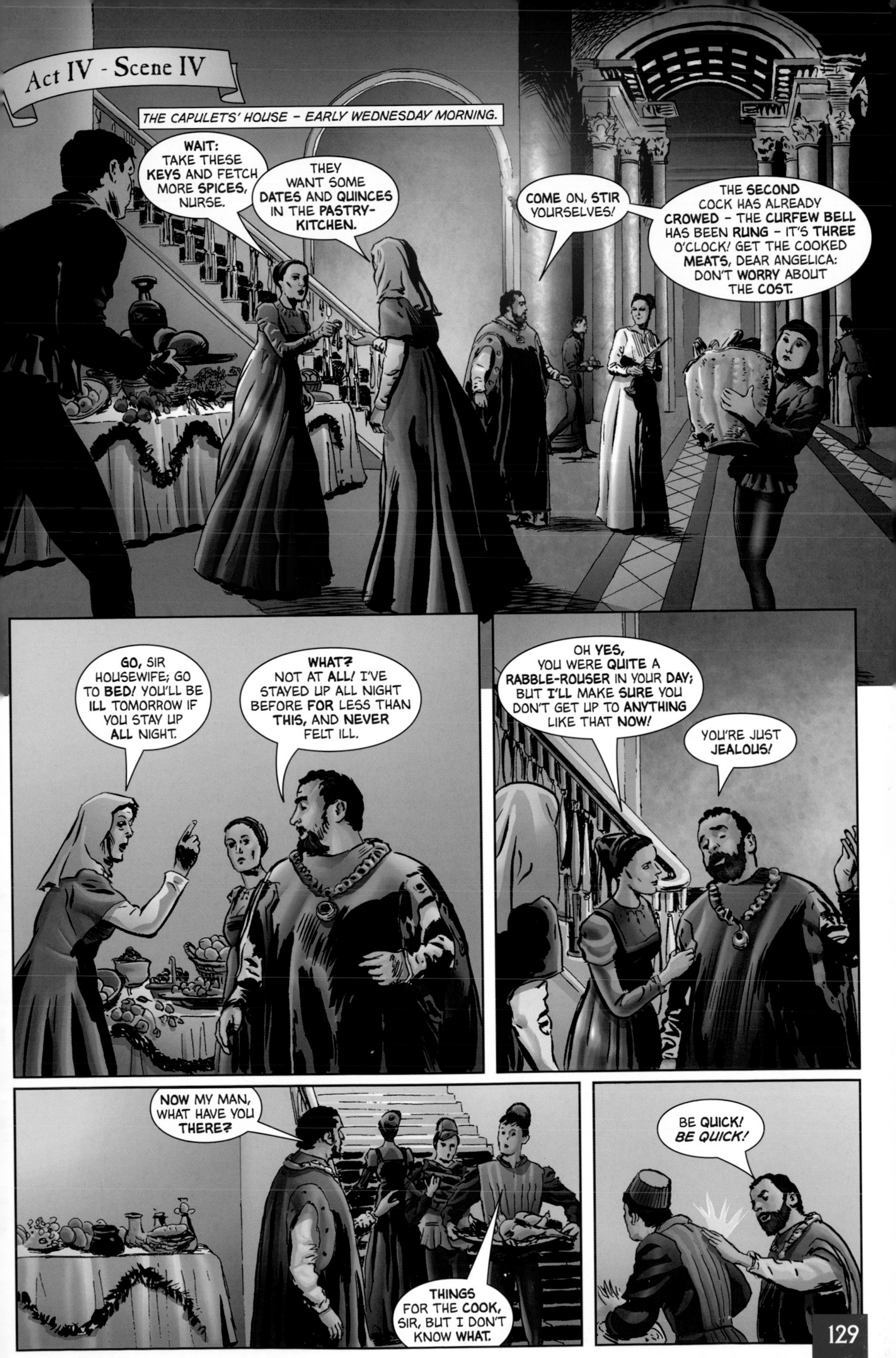
Act IV - Scene IV
THE CAPULETS' HOUSE – EARLY WEDNESDAY MORNING.
WAIT: TAKE THESE KEYS AND FETCH MORE SPICES, NURSE.
THEY WANT SOME DATES AND QUINCES IN THE PASTRY-KITCHEN.
COME ON, STIR YOURSELVES!
THE SECOND COCK HAS ALREADY CROWED – THE CURFEW BELL HAS BEEN RUNG – IT'S THREE O'CLOCK! GET THE COOKED MEATS, DEAR ANGELICA: DON'T WORRY ABOUT THE COST.
GO, SIR HOUSEWIFE; GO TO BED! YOU'LL BE ILL TOMORROW IF YOU STAY UP ALL NIGHT.
WHAT? NOT AT ALL! I'VE STAYED UP ALL NIGHT BEFORE FOR LESS THAN THIS, AND NEVER FELT ILL.
OH YES, YOU WERE QUITE A RABBLE-ROUSER IN YOUR DAY; BUT I'LL MAKE SURE YOU DON'T GET UP TO ANYTHING LIKE THAT NOW!
YOU'RE JUST JEALOUS!
NOW MY MAN, WHAT HAVE YOU THERE?
THINGS FOR THE COOK, SIR, BUT I DON'T KNOW WHAT.
BE QUICK! BE QUICK!

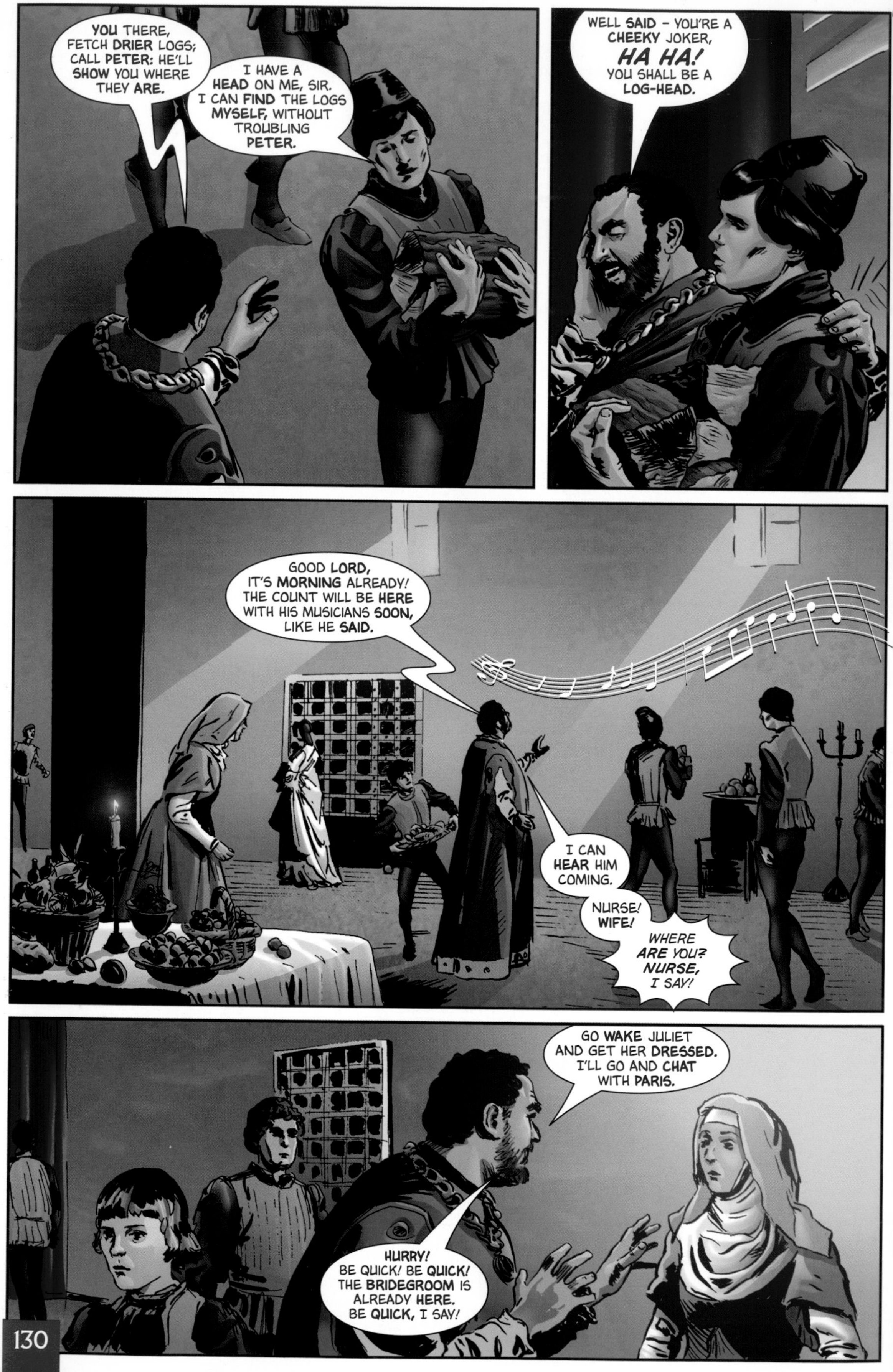
YOU THERE, FETCH DRIER LOGS; CALL PETER: HE'LL SHOW YOU WHERE THEY ARE.
I HAVE A HEAD ON ME, SIR. I CAN FIND THE LOGS MYSELF, WITHOUT TROUBLING PETER.
WELL SAID - YOU'RE A CHEEKY JOKER, HA HA! YOU SHALL BE A LOG-HEAD.
GOOD LORD, IT'S MORNING ALREADY! THE COUNT WILL BE HERE WITH HIS MUSICIANS SOON, LIKE HE SAID.
I CAN HEAR HIM COMING.
NURSE! WIFE!
WHERE ARE YOU? NURSE, I SAY!
GO WAKE JULIET AND GET HER DRESSED. I'LL GO AND CHAT WITH PARIS.
HURRY! BE QUICK! BE QUICK! THE BRIDEGROOM IS ALREADY HERE. BE QUICK, I SAY!

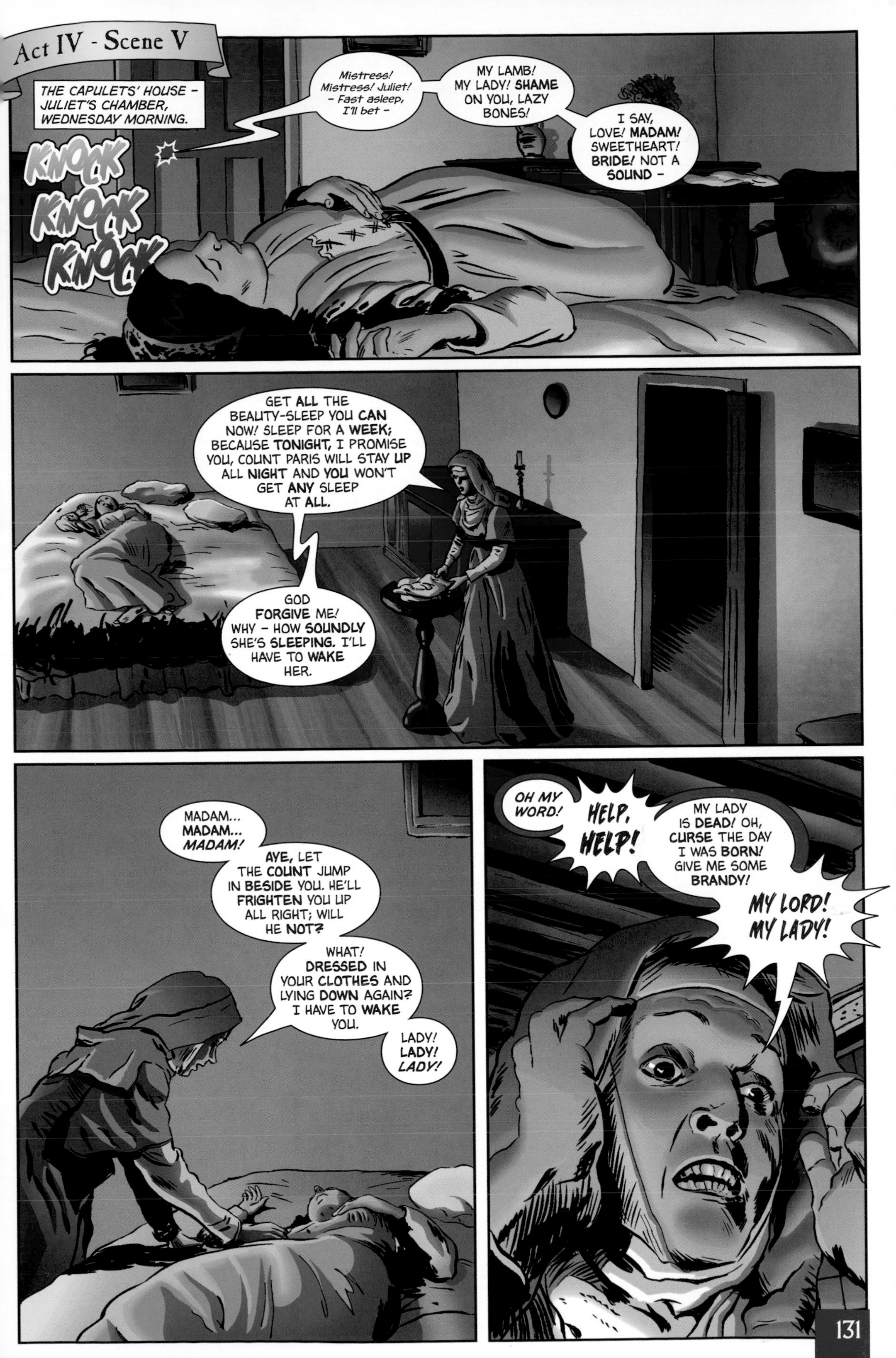
Act IV - Scene V
THE CAPULETS' HOUSE - JULIET'S CHAMBER, WEDNESDAY MORNING.
KNOCK KNOCK KNOCK
Mistress! Mistress! Juliet! - Fast asleep, I'll bet -
MY LAMB! MY LADY! SHAME ON YOU, LAZY BONES!
I SAY, LOVE! MADAM! SWEETHEART! BRIDE! NOT A SOUND -
GET ALL THE BEAUTY-SLEEP YOU CAN NOW! SLEEP FOR A WEEK; BECAUSE TONIGHT, I PROMISE YOU, COUNT PARIS WILL STAY UP ALL NIGHT AND YOU WON'T GET ANY SLEEP AT ALL.
GOD FORGIVE ME! WHY - HOW SOUNDLY SHE'S SLEEPING. I'LL HAVE TO WAKE HER.
MADAM... MADAM... MADAM!
AYE, LET THE COUNT JUMP IN BESIDE YOU. HE'LL FRIGHTEN YOU UP ALL RIGHT; WILL HE NOT?
WHAT! DRESSED IN YOUR CLOTHES AND LYING DOWN AGAIN? I HAVE TO WAKE YOU.
LADY! LADY! LADY!
OH MY WORD!
HELP, HELP!
MY LADY IS DEAD! OH, CURSE THE DAY I WAS BORN! GIVE ME SOME BRANDY!
MY LORD! MY LADY!

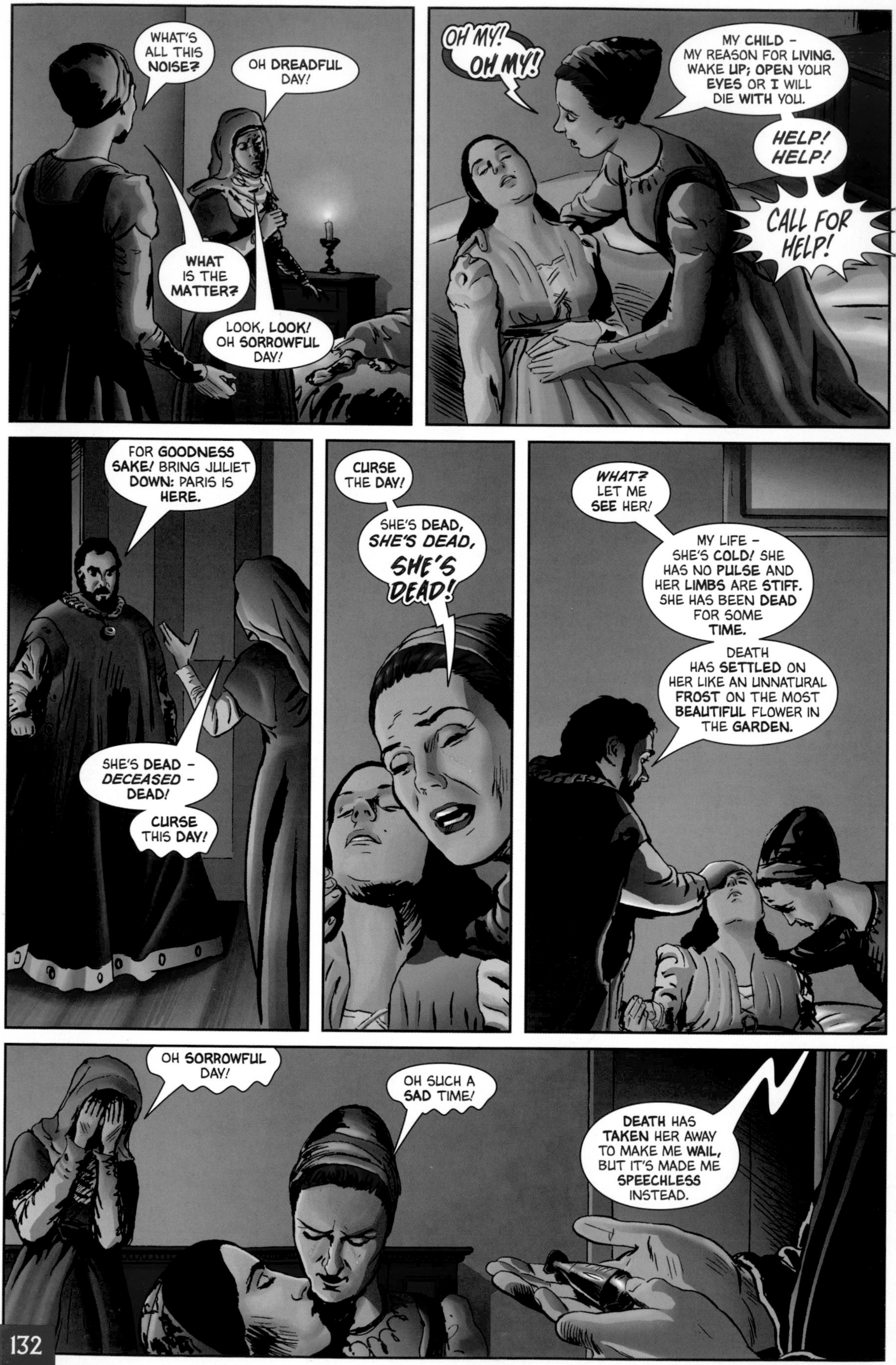
WHAT'S ALL THIS NOISE?
OH DREADFUL DAY!
WHAT IS THE MATTER?
LOOK, LOOK! OH SORROWFUL DAY!
OH MY! OH MY!
MY CHILD – MY REASON FOR LIVING. WAKE UP; OPEN YOUR EYES OR I WILL DIE WITH YOU.
HELP! HELP!
CALL FOR HELP!
FOR GOODNESS SAKE! BRING JULIET DOWN: PARIS IS HERE.
SHE'S DEAD – DECEASED – DEAD!
CURSE THIS DAY!
CURSE THE DAY!
SHE'S DEAD, SHE'S DEAD, SHE'S DEAD!
WHAT? LET ME SEE HER!
MY LIFE – SHE'S COLD! SHE HAS NO PULSE AND HER LIMBS ARE STIFF. SHE HAS BEEN DEAD FOR SOME TIME.
DEATH HAS SETTLED ON HER LIKE AN UNNATURAL FROST ON THE MOST BEAUTIFUL FLOWER IN THE GARDEN.
OH SORROWFUL DAY!
OH SUCH A SAD TIME!
DEATH HAS TAKEN HER AWAY TO MAKE ME WAIL, BUT IT'S MADE ME SPEECHLESS INSTEAD.

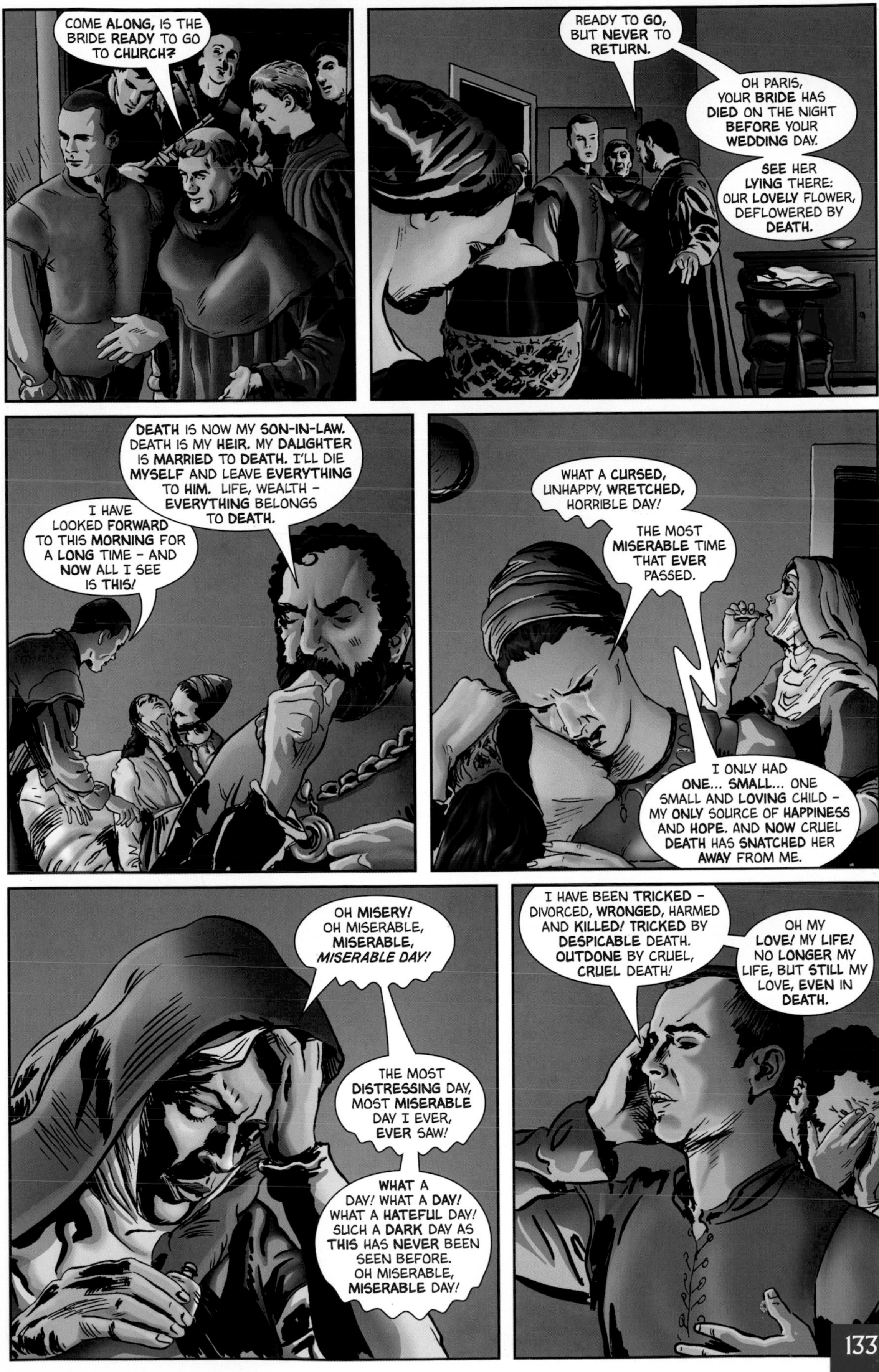

COME ALONG, IS THE BRIDE READY TO GO TO CHURCH?
READY TO GO, BUT NEVER TO RETURN.
OH PARIS, YOUR BRIDE HAS DIED ON THE NIGHT BEFORE YOUR WEDDING DAY.
SEE HER LYING THERE: OUR LOVELY FLOWER, DEFLOWERED BY DEATH.
DEATH IS NOW MY SON-IN-LAW. DEATH IS MY HEIR. MY DAUGHTER IS MARRIED TO DEATH. I'LL DIE MYSELF AND LEAVE EVERYTHING TO HIM. LIFE, WEALTH – EVERYTHING BELONGS TO DEATH.
I HAVE LOOKED FORWARD TO THIS MORNING FOR A LONG TIME – AND NOW ALL I SEE IS THIS!
WHAT A CURSED, UNHAPPY, WRETCHED, HORRIBLE DAY!
THE MOST MISERABLE TIME THAT EVER PASSED.
I ONLY HAD ONE... SMALL... ONE SMALL AND LOVING CHILD – MY ONLY SOURCE OF HAPPINESS AND HOPE. AND NOW CRUEL DEATH HAS SNATCHED HER AWAY FROM ME.
OH MISERY! OH MISERABLE, MISERABLE, *MISERABLE DAY!*
THE MOST DISTRESSING DAY, MOST MISERABLE DAY I EVER, EVER SAW!
WHAT A DAY! WHAT A DAY! WHAT A HATEFUL DAY! SUCH A DARK DAY AS THIS HAS NEVER BEEN SEEN BEFORE. OH MISERABLE, MISERABLE DAY!
I HAVE BEEN TRICKED – DIVORCED, WRONGED, HARMED AND KILLED! TRICKED BY DESPICABLE DEATH. OUTDONE BY CRUEL, CRUEL DEATH!
OH MY LOVE! MY LIFE! NO LONGER MY LIFE, BUT STILL MY LOVE, EVEN IN DEATH.

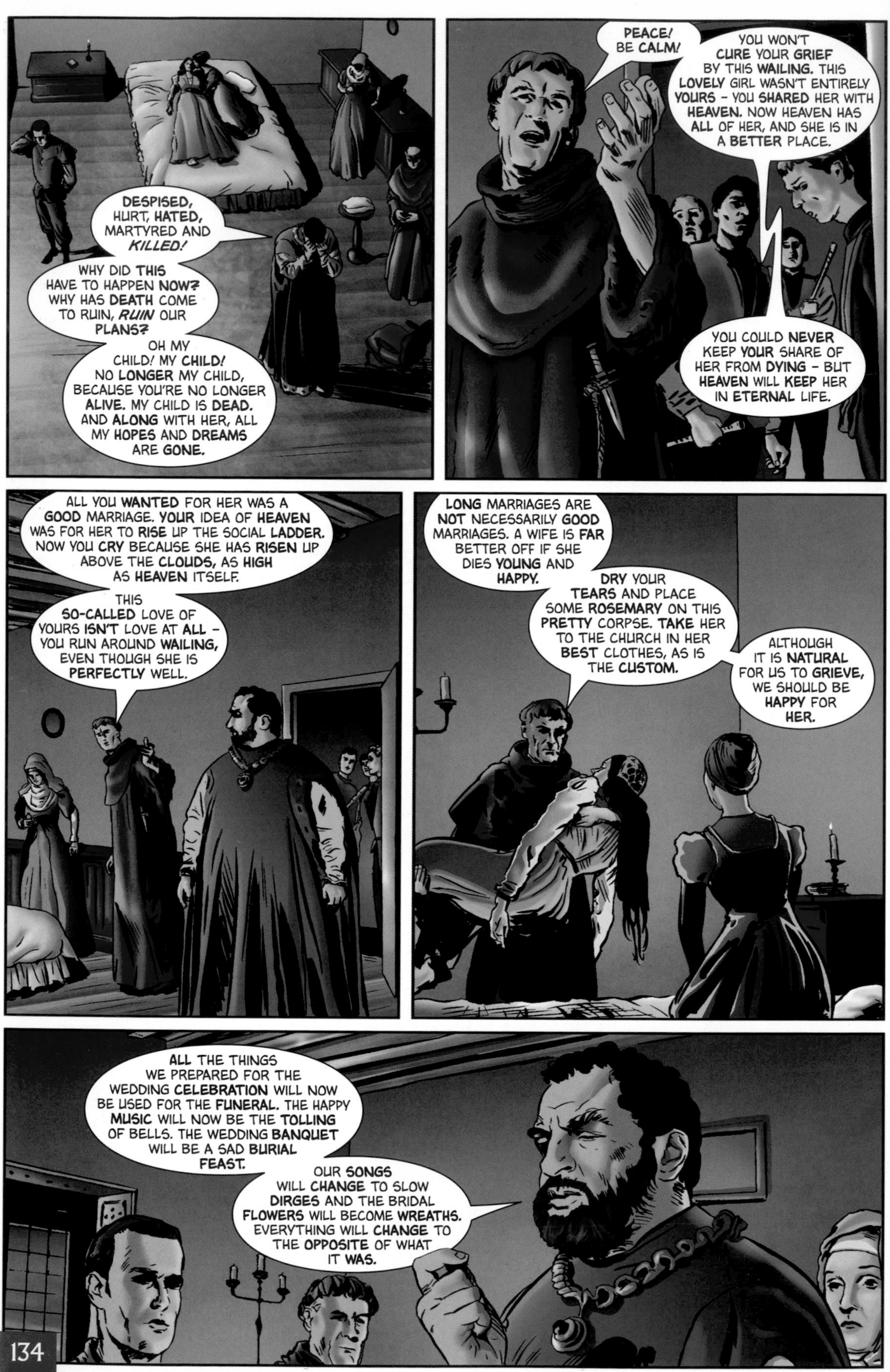
DESPISED, HURT, HATED, MARTYRED AND KILLED!
WHY DID THIS HAVE TO HAPPEN NOW? WHY HAS DEATH COME TO RUIN, RUIN OUR PLANS?
OH MY CHILD! MY CHILD! NO LONGER MY CHILD, BECAUSE YOU'RE NO LONGER ALIVE. MY CHILD IS DEAD. AND ALONG WITH HER, ALL MY HOPES AND DREAMS ARE GONE.
PEACE! BE CALM!
YOU WON'T CURE YOUR GRIEF BY THIS WAILING. THIS LOVELY GIRL WASN'T ENTIRELY YOURS – YOU SHARED HER WITH HEAVEN. NOW HEAVEN HAS ALL OF HER, AND SHE IS IN A BETTER PLACE.
YOU COULD NEVER KEEP YOUR SHARE OF HER FROM DYING – BUT HEAVEN WILL KEEP HER IN ETERNAL LIFE.
ALL YOU WANTED FOR HER WAS A GOOD MARRIAGE. YOUR IDEA OF HEAVEN WAS FOR HER TO RISE UP THE SOCIAL LADDER. NOW YOU CRY BECAUSE SHE HAS RISEN UP ABOVE THE CLOUDS, AS HIGH AS HEAVEN ITSELF.
THIS SO-CALLED LOVE OF YOURS ISN'T LOVE AT ALL – YOU RUN AROUND WAILING, EVEN THOUGH SHE IS PERFECTLY WELL.
LONG MARRIAGES ARE NOT NECESSARILY GOOD MARRIAGES. A WIFE IS FAR BETTER OFF IF SHE DIES YOUNG AND HAPPY.
DRY YOUR TEARS AND PLACE SOME ROSEMARY ON THIS PRETTY CORPSE. TAKE HER TO THE CHURCH IN HER BEST CLOTHES, AS IS THE CUSTOM.
ALTHOUGH IT IS NATURAL FOR US TO GRIEVE, WE SHOULD BE HAPPY FOR HER.
ALL THE THINGS WE PREPARED FOR THE WEDDING CELEBRATION WILL NOW BE USED FOR THE FUNERAL. THE HAPPY MUSIC WILL NOW BE THE TOLLING OF BELLS. THE WEDDING BANQUET WILL BE A SAD BURIAL FEAST.
OUR SONGS WILL CHANGE TO SLOW DIRGES AND THE BRIDAL FLOWERS WILL BECOME WREATHS. EVERYTHING WILL CHANGE TO THE OPPOSITE OF WHAT IT WAS.

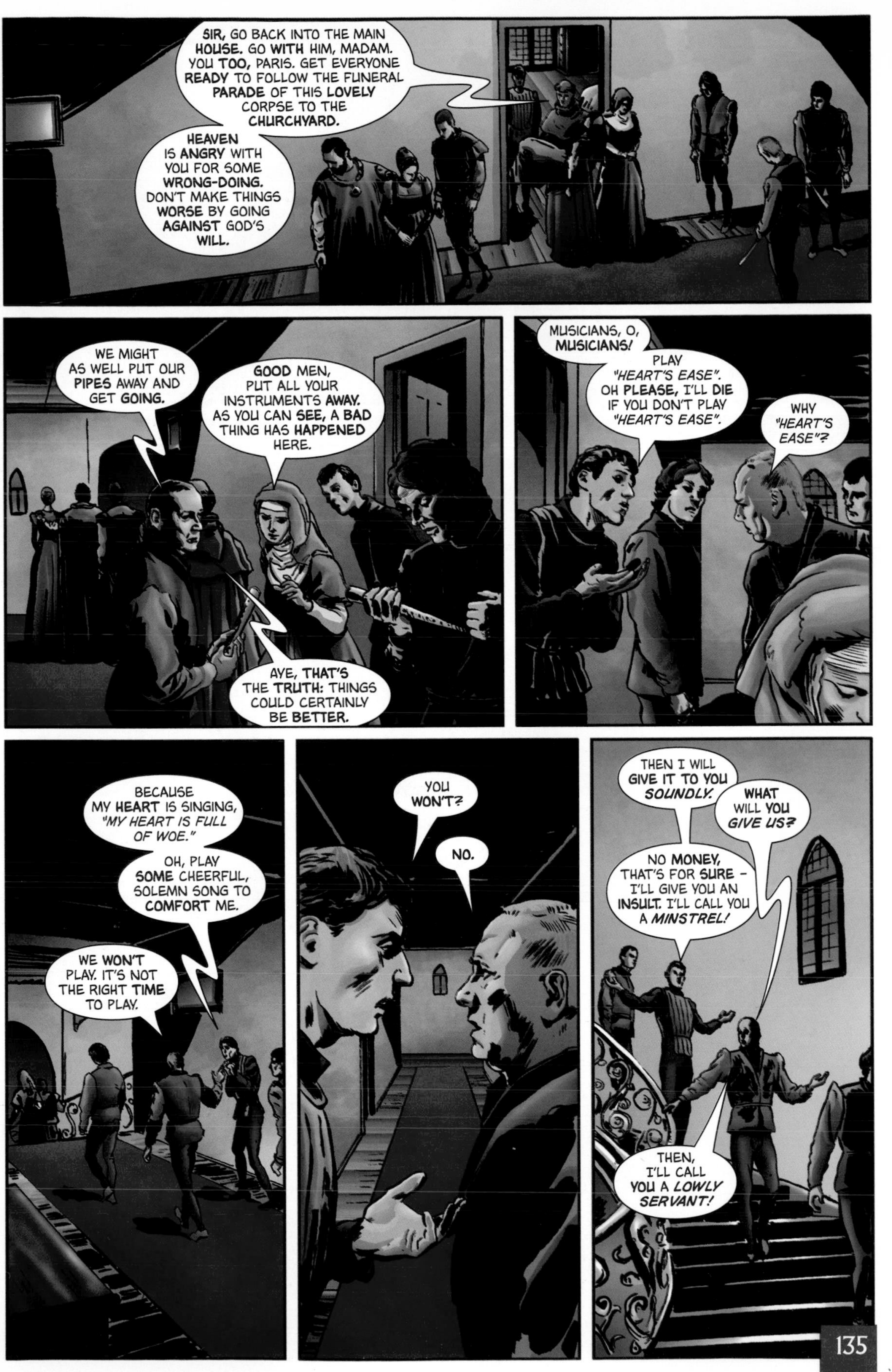
SIR, GO BACK INTO THE MAIN HOUSE. GO WITH HIM, MADAM. YOU TOO, PARIS. GET EVERYONE READY TO FOLLOW THE FUNERAL PARADE OF THIS LOVELY CORPSE TO THE CHURCHYARD.
HEAVEN IS ANGRY WITH YOU FOR SOME WRONG-DOING. DON'T MAKE THINGS WORSE BY GOING AGAINST GOD'S WILL.
WE MIGHT AS WELL PUT OUR PIPES AWAY AND GET GOING.
GOOD MEN, PUT ALL YOUR INSTRUMENTS AWAY. AS YOU CAN SEE, A BAD THING HAS HAPPENED HERE.
AYE, THAT'S THE TRUTH: THINGS COULD CERTAINLY BE BETTER.
MUSICIANS, O, MUSICIANS!
PLAY "HEART'S EASE". OH PLEASE, I'LL DIE IF YOU DON'T PLAY "HEART'S EASE".
WHY "HEART'S EASE"?
BECAUSE MY HEART IS SINGING, "MY HEART IS FULL OF WOE."
OH, PLAY SOME CHEERFUL, SOLEMN SONG TO COMFORT ME.
WE WON'T PLAY. IT'S NOT THE RIGHT TIME TO PLAY.
YOU WON'T?
NO.
THEN I WILL GIVE IT TO YOU SOUNDLY.
WHAT WILL YOU GIVE US?
NO MONEY, THAT'S FOR SURE – I'LL GIVE YOU AN INSULT. I'LL CALL YOU A MINSTREL!
THEN, I'LL CALL YOU A LOWLY SERVANT!

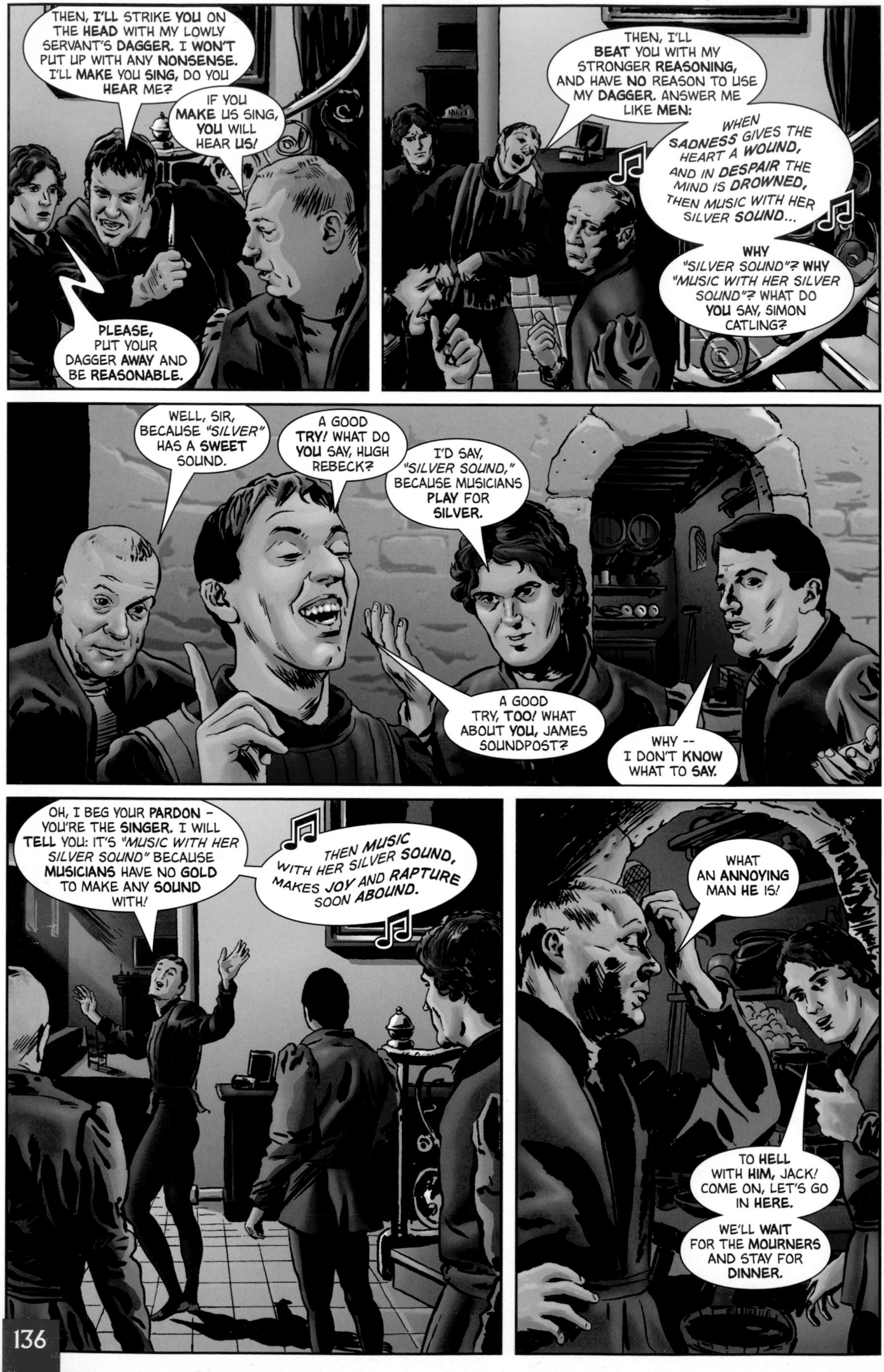
THEN, I'LL STRIKE YOU ON THE HEAD WITH MY LOWLY SERVANT'S DAGGER. I WON'T PUT UP WITH ANY NONSENSE. I'LL MAKE YOU SING, DO YOU HEAR ME?
IF YOU MAKE US SING, YOU WILL HEAR US!
PLEASE, PUT YOUR DAGGER AWAY AND BE REASONABLE.
THEN, I'LL BEAT YOU WITH MY STRONGER REASONING, AND HAVE NO REASON TO USE MY DAGGER. ANSWER ME LIKE MEN:
WHEN SADNESS GIVES THE HEART A WOUND, AND IN DESPAIR THE MIND IS DROWNED, THEN MUSIC WITH HER SILVER SOUND...
WHY "SILVER SOUND"? WHY "MUSIC WITH HER SILVER SOUND"? WHAT DO YOU SAY, SIMON CATLING?
WELL, SIR, BECAUSE "SILVER" HAS A SWEET SOUND.
A GOOD TRY! WHAT DO YOU SAY, HUGH REBECK?
I'D SAY, "SILVER SOUND," BECAUSE MUSICIANS PLAY FOR SILVER.
A GOOD TRY, TOO! WHAT ABOUT YOU, JAMES SOUNDPOST?
WHY -- I DON'T KNOW WHAT TO SAY.
OH, I BEG YOUR PARDON - YOU'RE THE SINGER. I WILL TELL YOU: IT'S "MUSIC WITH HER SILVER SOUND" BECAUSE MUSICIANS HAVE NO GOLD TO MAKE ANY SOUND WITH!
THEN MUSIC WITH HER SILVER SOUND, MAKES JOY AND RAPTURE SOON ABOUND.
WHAT AN ANNOYING MAN HE IS!
TO HELL WITH HIM, JACK! COME ON, LET'S GO IN HERE.
WE'LL WAIT FOR THE MOURNERS AND STAY FOR DINNER.

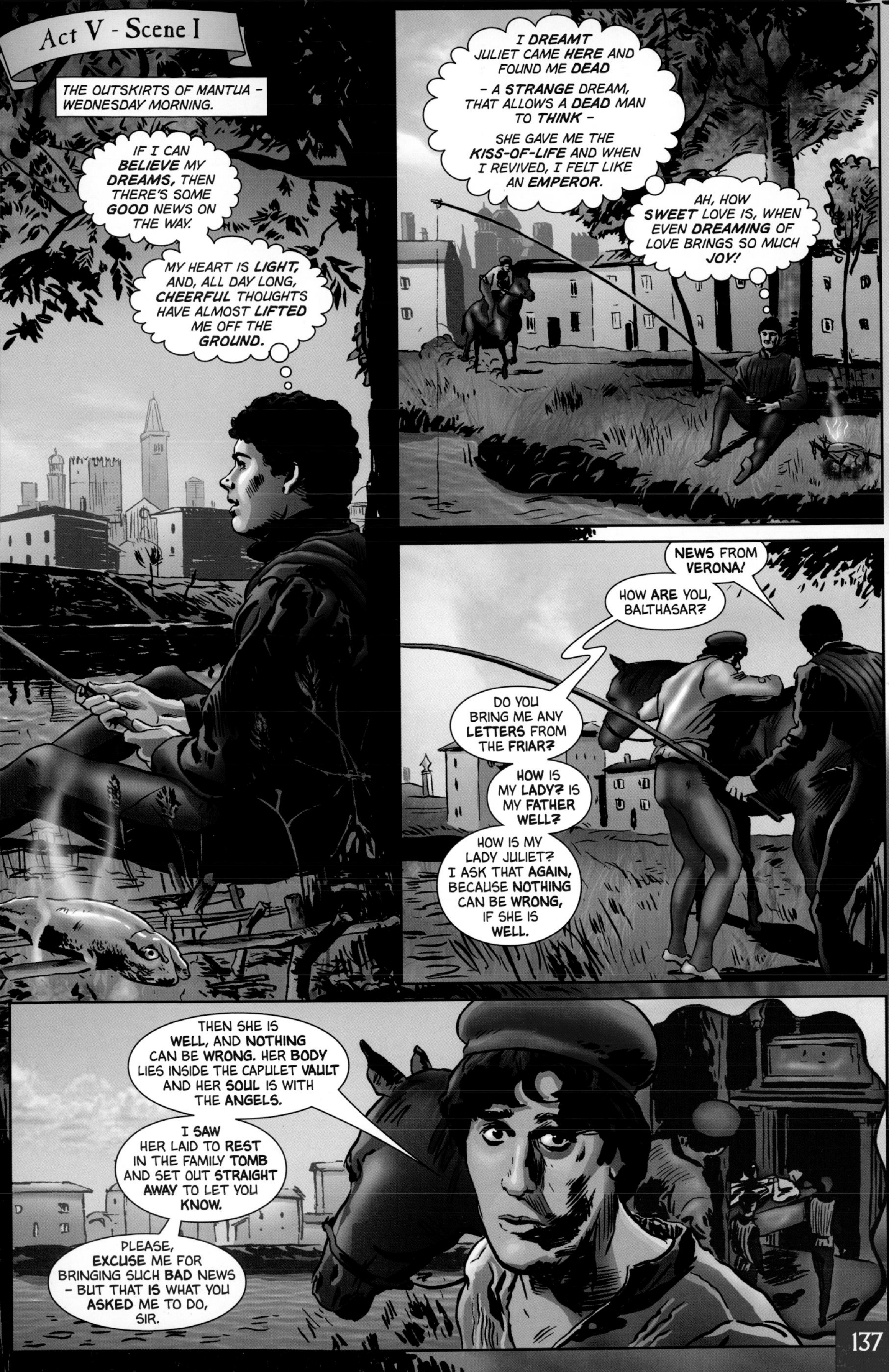
Act V - Scene I
THE OUTSKIRTS OF MANTUA - WEDNESDAY MORNING.
IF I CAN BELIEVE MY DREAMS, THEN THERE'S SOME GOOD NEWS ON THE WAY.
MY HEART IS LIGHT, AND, ALL DAY LONG, CHEERFUL THOUGHTS HAVE ALMOST LIFTED ME OFF THE GROUND.
I DREAMT JULIET CAME HERE AND FOUND ME DEAD
- A STRANGE DREAM, THAT ALLOWS A DEAD MAN TO THINK -
SHE GAVE ME THE KISS-OF-LIFE AND WHEN I REVIVED, I FELT LIKE AN EMPEROR.
AH, HOW SWEET LOVE IS, WHEN EVEN DREAMING OF LOVE BRINGS SO MUCH JOY!
NEWS FROM VERONA!
HOW ARE YOU, BALTHASAR?
DO YOU BRING ME ANY LETTERS FROM THE FRIAR?
HOW IS MY LADY? IS MY FATHER WELL?
HOW IS MY LADY JULIET? I ASK THAT AGAIN, BECAUSE NOTHING CAN BE WRONG, IF SHE IS WELL.
THEN SHE IS WELL, AND NOTHING CAN BE WRONG. HER BODY LIES INSIDE THE CAPULET VAULT AND HER SOUL IS WITH THE ANGELS.
I SAW HER LAID TO REST IN THE FAMILY TOMB AND SET OUT STRAIGHT AWAY TO LET YOU KNOW.
PLEASE, EXCUSE ME FOR BRINGING SUCH BAD NEWS - BUT THAT IS WHAT YOU ASKED ME TO DO, SIR.

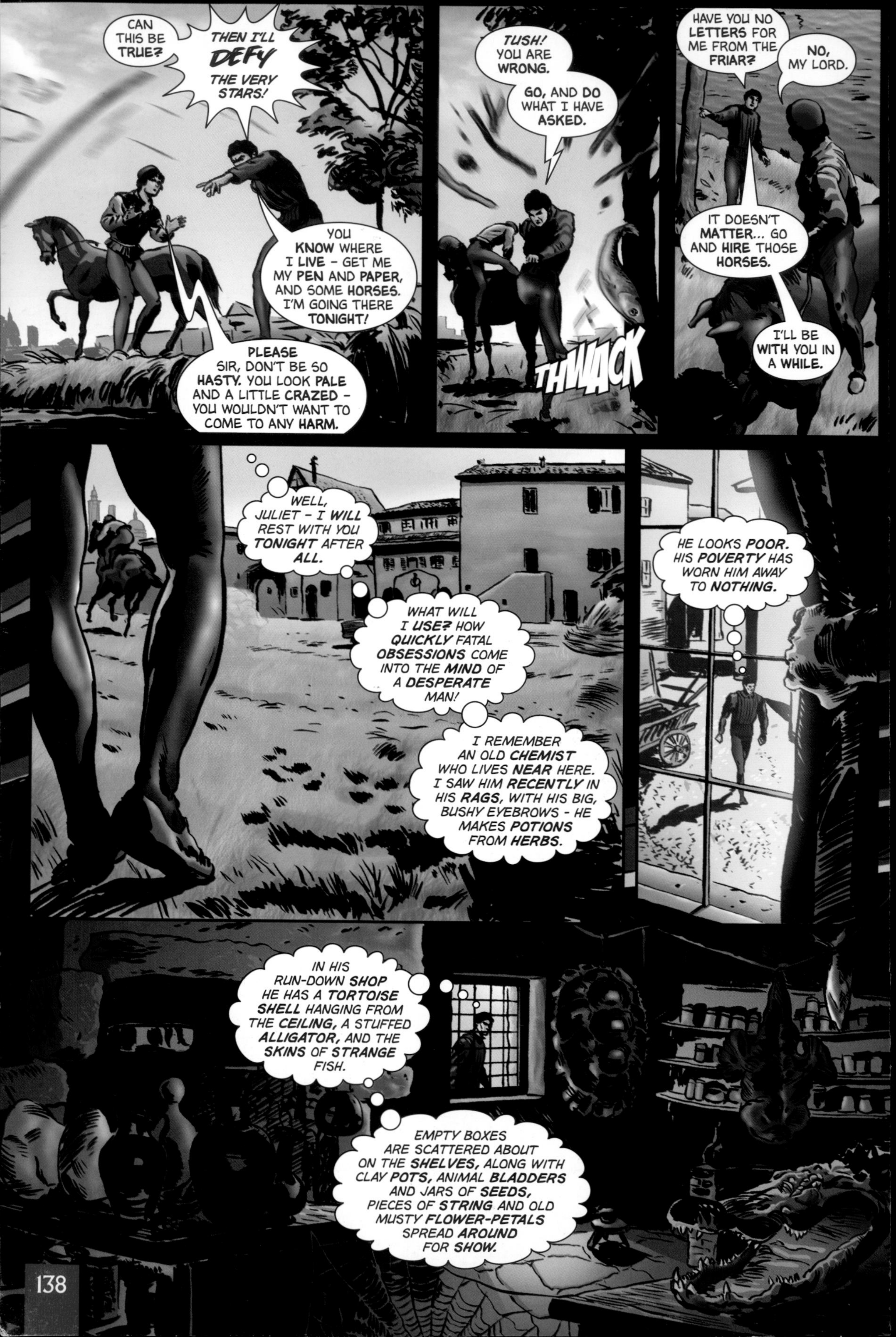
CAN THIS BE TRUE?
THEN I'LL DEFY THE VERY STARS!
YOU KNOW WHERE I LIVE - GET ME MY PEN AND PAPER, AND SOME HORSES. I'M GOING THERE TONIGHT!
PLEASE SIR, DON'T BE SO HASTY. YOU LOOK PALE AND A LITTLE CRAZED - YOU WOULDN'T WANT TO COME TO ANY HARM.
TUSH! YOU ARE WRONG.
GO, AND DO WHAT I HAVE ASKED.
THWACK
HAVE YOU NO LETTERS FOR ME FROM THE FRIAR?
NO, MY LORD.
IT DOESN'T MATTER... GO AND HIRE THOSE HORSES.
I'LL BE WITH YOU IN A WHILE.
WELL, JULIET - I WILL REST WITH YOU TONIGHT AFTER ALL.
WHAT WILL I USE? HOW QUICKLY FATAL OBSESSIONS COME INTO THE MIND OF A DESPERATE MAN!
I REMEMBER AN OLD CHEMIST WHO LIVES NEAR HERE. I SAW HIM RECENTLY IN HIS RAGS, WITH HIS BIG, BUSHY EYEBROWS - HE MAKES POTIONS FROM HERBS.
HE LOOKS POOR. HIS POVERTY HAS WORN HIM AWAY TO NOTHING.
IN HIS RUN-DOWN SHOP HE HAS A TORTOISE SHELL HANGING FROM THE CEILING, A STUFFED ALLIGATOR, AND THE SKINS OF STRANGE FISH.
EMPTY BOXES ARE SCATTERED ABOUT ON THE SHELVES, ALONG WITH CLAY POTS, ANIMAL BLADDERS AND JARS OF SEEDS, PIECES OF STRING AND OLD MUSTY FLOWER-PETALS SPREAD AROUND FOR SHOW.

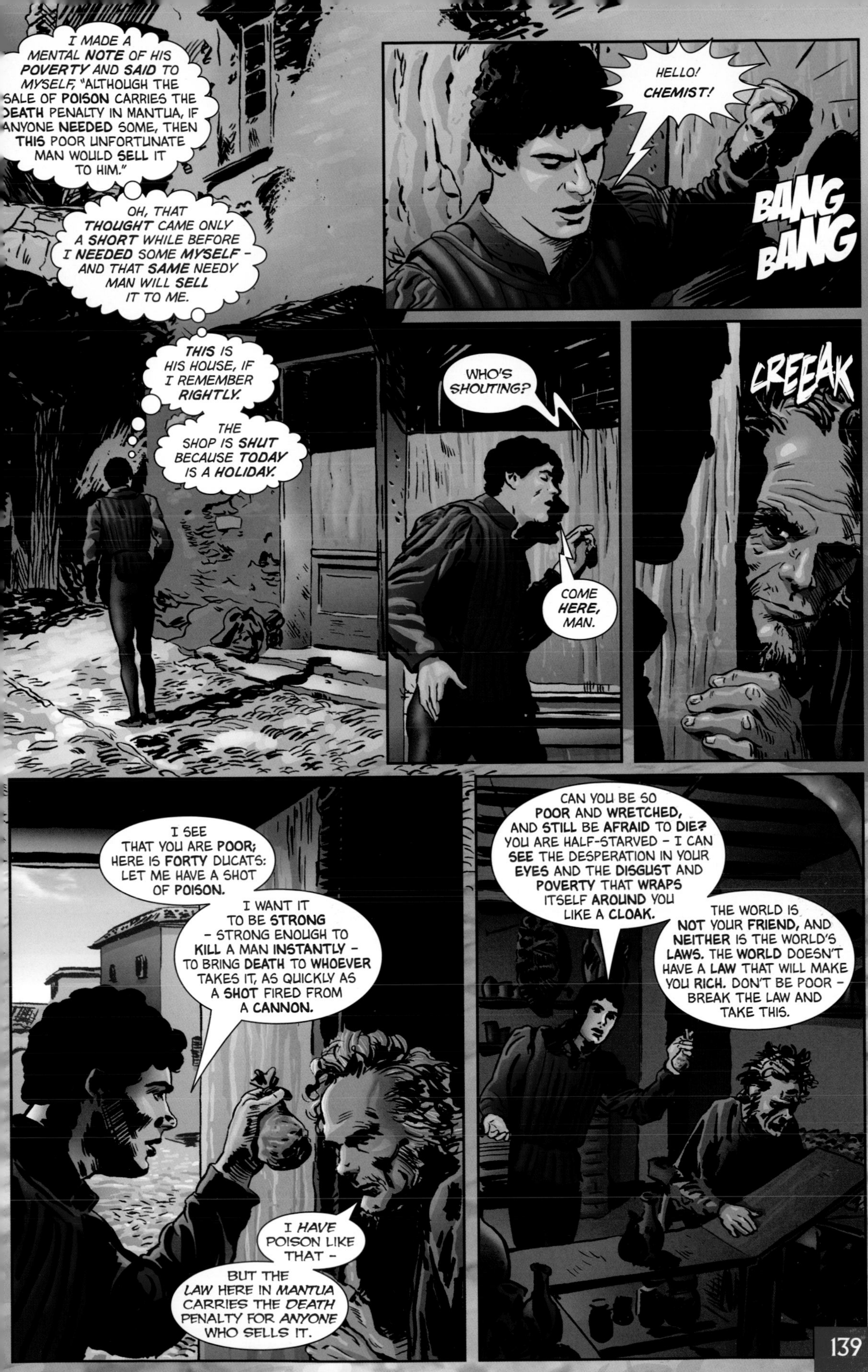

I MADE A MENTAL NOTE OF HIS POVERTY AND SAID TO MYSELF, "ALTHOUGH THE SALE OF POISON CARRIES THE DEATH PENALTY IN MANTUA, IF ANYONE NEEDED SOME, THEN THIS POOR UNFORTUNATE MAN WOULD SELL IT TO HIM."
OH, THAT THOUGHT CAME ONLY A SHORT WHILE BEFORE I NEEDED SOME MYSELF - AND THAT SAME NEEDY MAN WILL SELL IT TO ME.
HELLO! CHEMIST!
BANG BANG
THIS IS HIS HOUSE, IF I REMEMBER RIGHTLY.
THE SHOP IS SHUT BECAUSE TODAY IS A HOLIDAY.
WHO'S SHOUTING?
COME HERE, MAN.
CREEAK
I SEE THAT YOU ARE POOR; HERE IS FORTY DUCATS: LET ME HAVE A SHOT OF POISON.
I WANT IT TO BE STRONG - STRONG ENOUGH TO KILL A MAN INSTANTLY - TO BRING DEATH TO WHOEVER TAKES IT, AS QUICKLY AS A SHOT FIRED FROM A CANNON.
I HAVE POISON LIKE THAT -
BUT THE LAW HERE IN MANTUA CARRIES THE DEATH PENALTY FOR ANYONE WHO SELLS IT.
CAN YOU BE SO POOR AND WRETCHED, AND STILL BE AFRAID TO DIE? YOU ARE HALF-STARVED - I CAN SEE THE DESPERATION IN YOUR EYES AND THE DISGUST AND POVERTY THAT WRAPS ITSELF AROUND YOU LIKE A CLOAK.
THE WORLD IS NOT YOUR FRIEND, AND NEITHER IS THE WORLD'S LAWS. THE WORLD DOESN'T HAVE A LAW THAT WILL MAKE YOU RICH. DON'T BE POOR - BREAK THE LAW AND TAKE THIS.

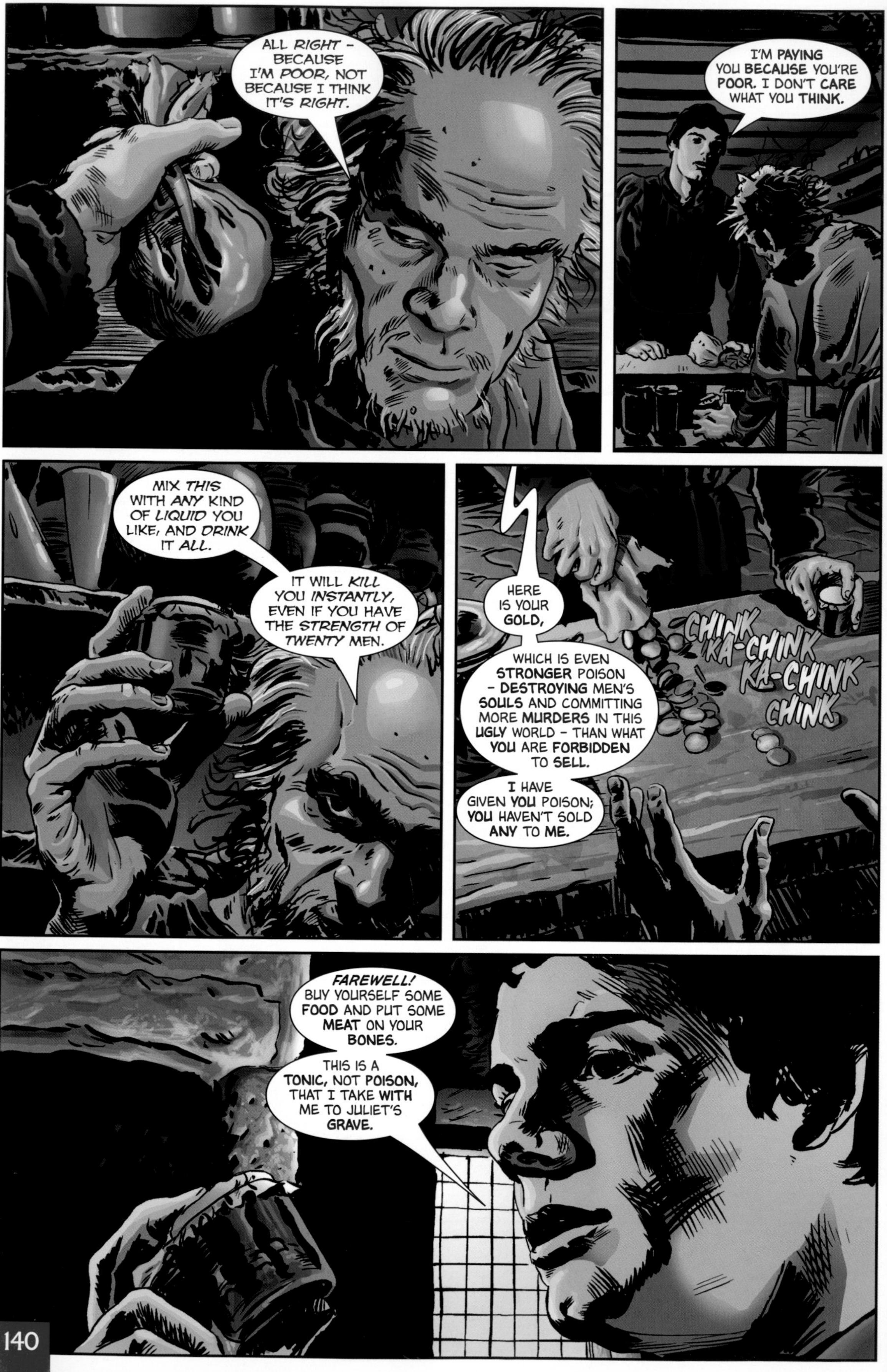
ALL RIGHT – BECAUSE I'M POOR, NOT BECAUSE I THINK IT'S RIGHT.
I'M PAYING YOU BECAUSE YOU'RE POOR. I DON'T CARE WHAT YOU THINK.
MIX THIS WITH ANY KIND OF LIQUID YOU LIKE, AND DRINK IT ALL.
IT WILL KILL YOU INSTANTLY, EVEN IF YOU HAVE THE STRENGTH OF TWENTY MEN.
HERE IS YOUR GOLD,
WHICH IS EVEN STRONGER POISON – DESTROYING MEN'S SOULS AND COMMITTING MORE MURDERS IN THIS UGLY WORLD – THAN WHAT YOU ARE FORBIDDEN TO SELL.
I HAVE GIVEN YOU POISON; YOU HAVEN'T SOLD ANY TO ME.
CHINK KA-CHINK KA-CHINK CHINK
FAREWELL! BUY YOURSELF SOME FOOD AND PUT SOME MEAT ON YOUR BONES.
THIS IS A TONIC, NOT POISON, THAT I TAKE WITH ME TO JULIET'S GRAVE.

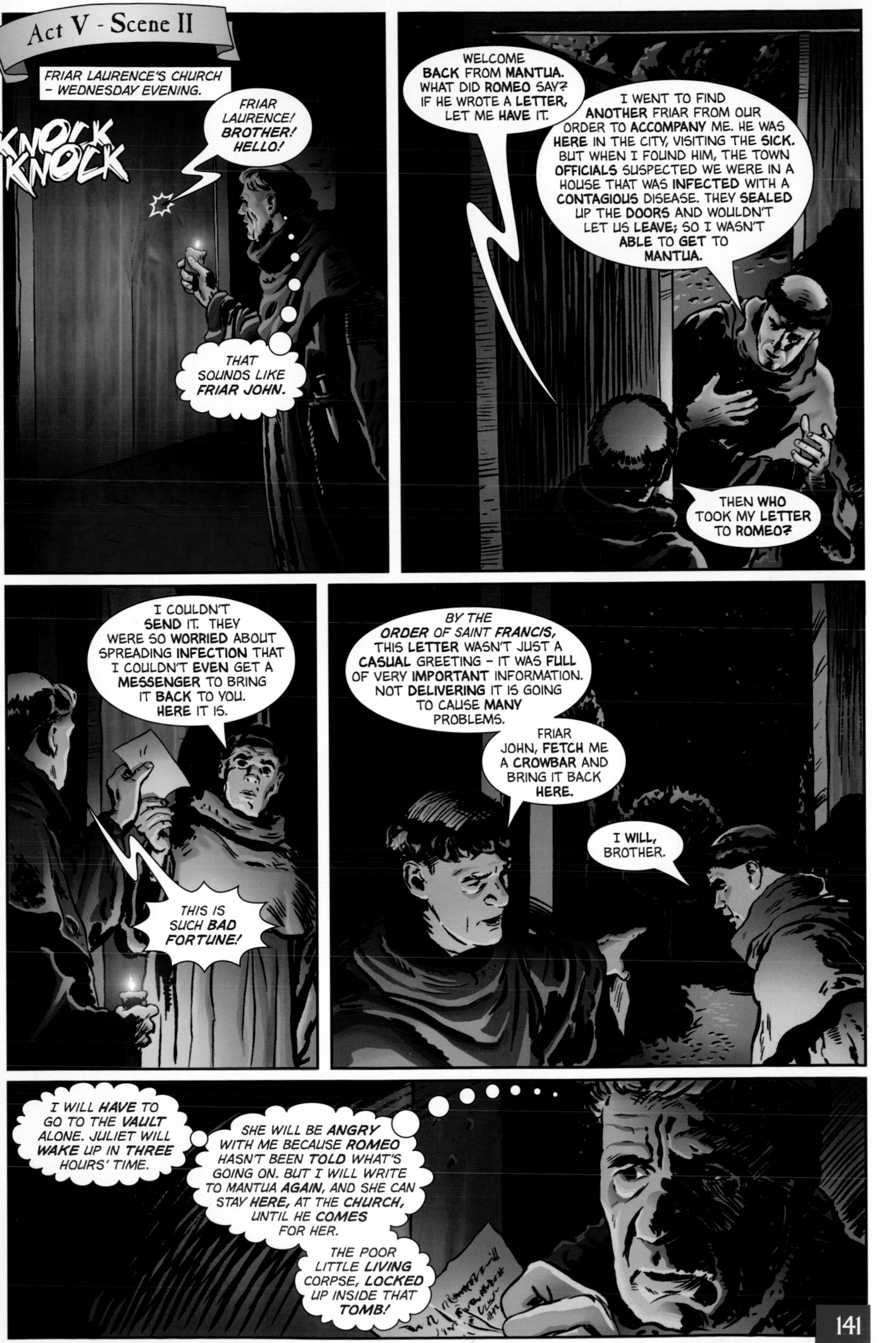
Act V - Scene II
FRIAR LAURENCE'S CHURCH – WEDNESDAY EVENING.
KNOCK KNOCK
FRIAR LAURENCE! BROTHER! HELLO!
THAT SOUNDS LIKE FRIAR JOHN.
WELCOME BACK FROM MANTUA. WHAT DID ROMEO SAY? IF HE WROTE A LETTER, LET ME HAVE IT.
I WENT TO FIND ANOTHER FRIAR FROM OUR ORDER TO ACCOMPANY ME. HE WAS HERE IN THE CITY, VISITING THE SICK. BUT WHEN I FOUND HIM, THE TOWN OFFICIALS SUSPECTED WE WERE IN A HOUSE THAT WAS INFECTED WITH A CONTAGIOUS DISEASE. THEY SEALED UP THE DOORS AND WOULDN'T LET US LEAVE; SO I WASN'T ABLE TO GET TO MANTUA.
THEN WHO TOOK MY LETTER TO ROMEO?
I COULDN'T SEND IT. THEY WERE SO WORRIED ABOUT SPREADING INFECTION THAT I COULDN'T EVEN GET A MESSENGER TO BRING IT BACK TO YOU. HERE IT IS.
THIS IS SUCH BAD FORTUNE!
BY THE ORDER OF SAINT FRANCIS, THIS LETTER WASN'T JUST A CASUAL GREETING – IT WAS FULL OF VERY IMPORTANT INFORMATION. NOT DELIVERING IT IS GOING TO CAUSE MANY PROBLEMS.
FRIAR JOHN, FETCH ME A CROWBAR AND BRING IT BACK HERE.
I WILL, BROTHER.
I WILL HAVE TO GO TO THE VAULT ALONE. JULIET WILL WAKE UP IN THREE HOURS' TIME.
SHE WILL BE ANGRY WITH ME BECAUSE ROMEO HASN'T BEEN TOLD WHAT'S GOING ON. BUT I WILL WRITE TO MANTUA AGAIN, AND SHE CAN STAY HERE, AT THE CHURCH, UNTIL HE COMES FOR HER.
THE POOR LITTLE LIVING CORPSE, LOCKED UP INSIDE THAT TOMB!

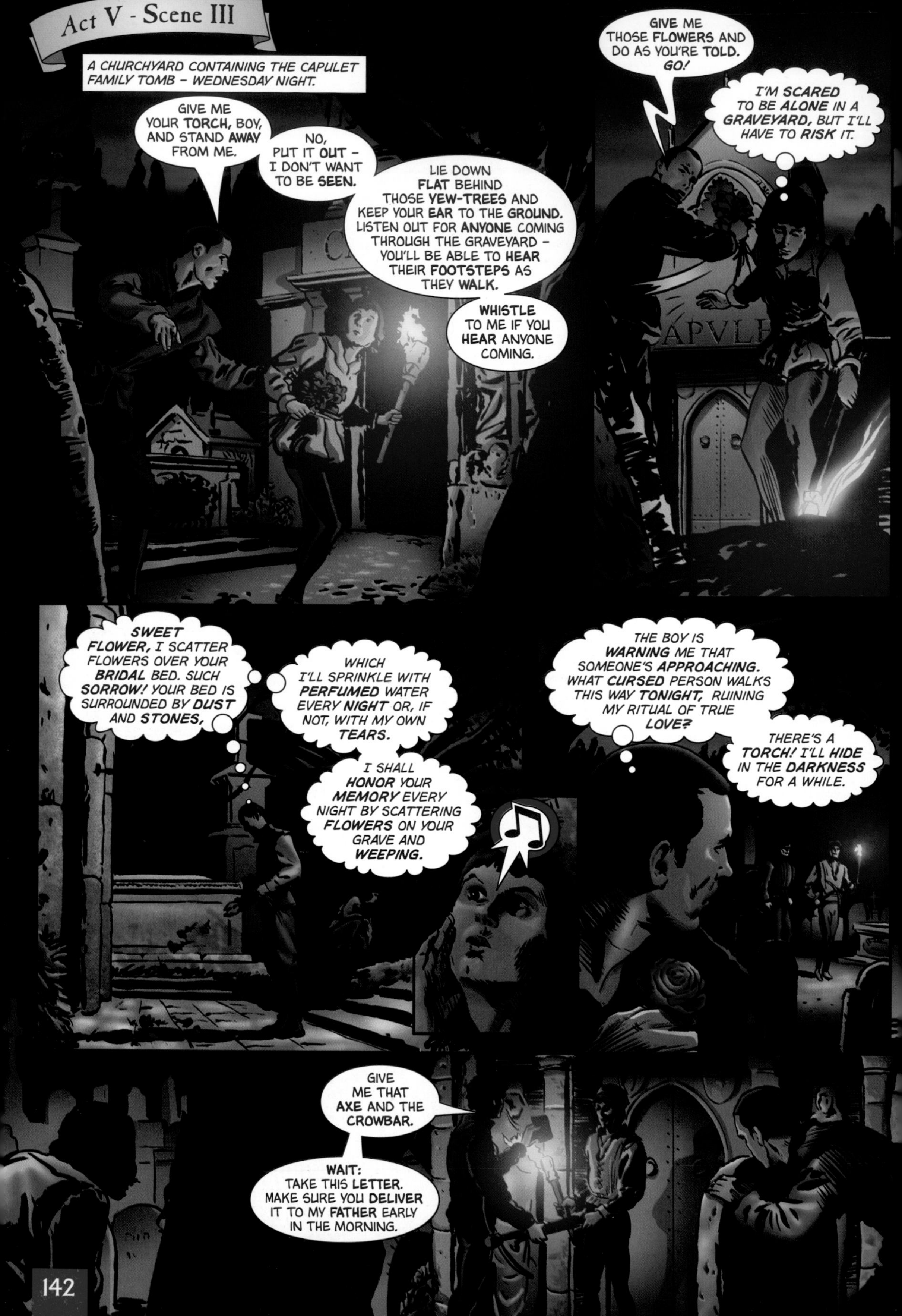
Act V - Scene III
A CHURCHYARD CONTAINING THE CAPULET FAMILY TOMB – WEDNESDAY NIGHT.
GIVE ME YOUR TORCH, BOY, AND STAND AWAY FROM ME.
NO, PUT IT OUT – I DON'T WANT TO BE SEEN.
LIE DOWN FLAT BEHIND THOSE YEW-TREES AND KEEP YOUR EAR TO THE GROUND. LISTEN OUT FOR ANYONE COMING THROUGH THE GRAVEYARD – YOU'LL BE ABLE TO HEAR THEIR FOOTSTEPS AS THEY WALK.
WHISTLE TO ME IF YOU HEAR ANYONE COMING.
GIVE ME THOSE FLOWERS AND DO AS YOU'RE TOLD. GO!
I'M SCARED TO BE ALONE IN A GRAVEYARD, BUT I'LL HAVE TO RISK IT.
SWEET FLOWER, I SCATTER FLOWERS OVER YOUR BRIDAL BED. SUCH SORROW! YOUR BED IS SURROUNDED BY DUST AND STONES,
WHICH I'LL SPRINKLE WITH PERFUMED WATER EVERY NIGHT OR, IF NOT, WITH MY OWN TEARS.
I SHALL HONOR YOUR MEMORY EVERY NIGHT BY SCATTERING FLOWERS ON YOUR GRAVE AND WEEPING.
THE BOY IS WARNING ME THAT SOMEONE'S APPROACHING. WHAT CURSED PERSON WALKS THIS WAY TONIGHT, RUINING MY RITUAL OF TRUE LOVE?
THERE'S A TORCH! I'LL HIDE IN THE DARKNESS FOR A WHILE.
GIVE ME THAT AXE AND THE CROWBAR.
WAIT: TAKE THIS LETTER. MAKE SURE YOU DELIVER IT TO MY FATHER EARLY IN THE MORNING.

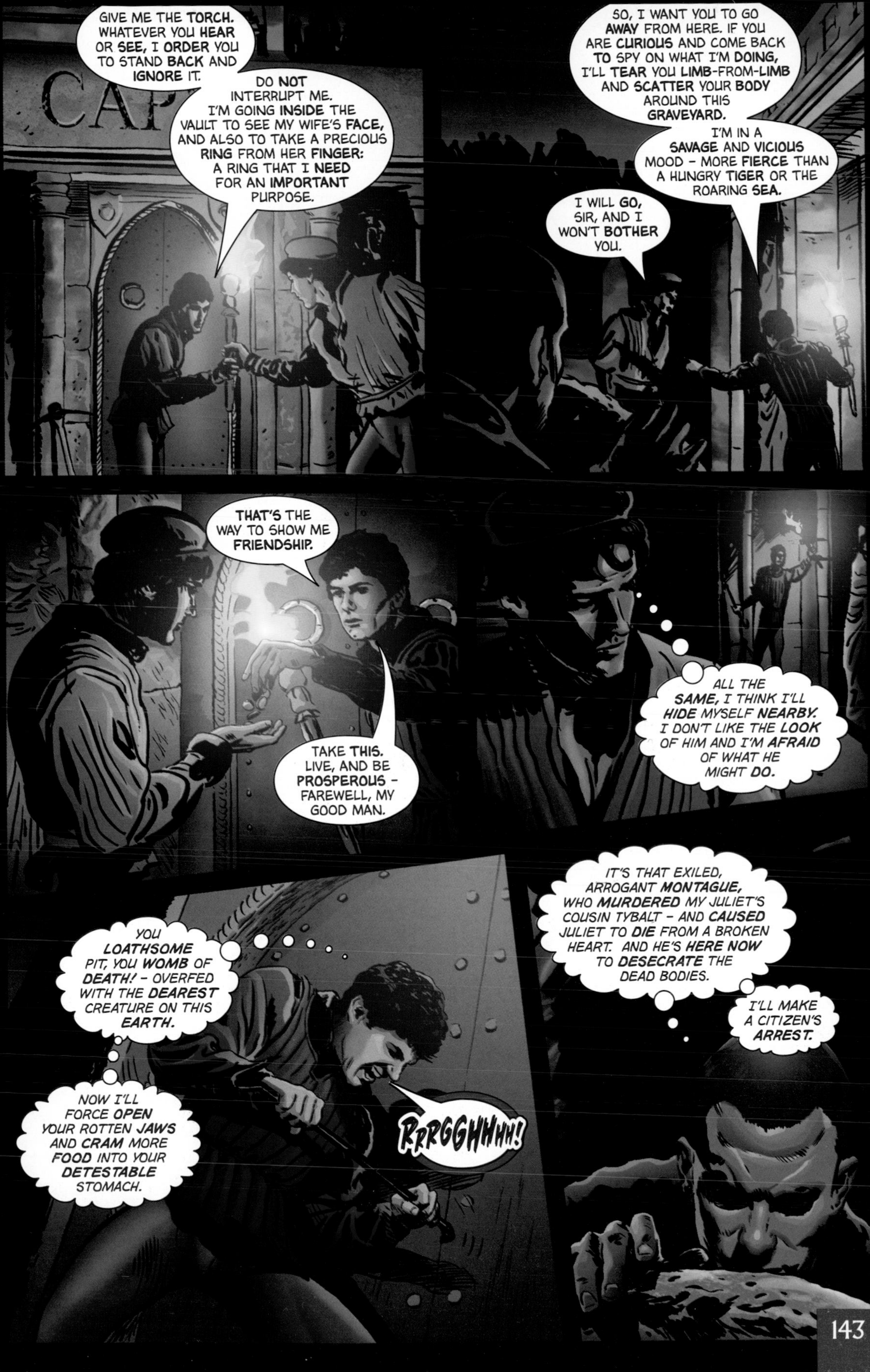
GIVE ME THE TORCH. WHATEVER YOU HEAR OR SEE, I ORDER YOU TO STAND BACK AND IGNORE IT.
DO NOT INTERRUPT ME. I'M GOING INSIDE THE VAULT TO SEE MY WIFE'S FACE, AND ALSO TO TAKE A PRECIOUS RING FROM HER FINGER: A RING THAT I NEED FOR AN IMPORTANT PURPOSE.
SO, I WANT YOU TO GO AWAY FROM HERE. IF YOU ARE CURIOUS AND COME BACK TO SPY ON WHAT I'M DOING, I'LL TEAR YOU LIMB-FROM-LIMB AND SCATTER YOUR BODY AROUND THIS GRAVEYARD.
I'M IN A SAVAGE AND VICIOUS MOOD – MORE FIERCE THAN A HUNGRY TIGER OR THE ROARING SEA.
I WILL GO, SIR, AND I WON'T BOTHER YOU.
THAT'S THE WAY TO SHOW ME FRIENDSHIP.
TAKE THIS. LIVE, AND BE PROSPEROUS – FAREWELL, MY GOOD MAN.
ALL THE SAME, I THINK I'LL HIDE MYSELF NEARBY. I DON'T LIKE THE LOOK OF HIM AND I'M AFRAID OF WHAT HE MIGHT DO.
YOU LOATHSOME PIT, YOU WOMB OF DEATH! – OVERFED WITH THE DEAREST CREATURE ON THIS EARTH.
NOW I'LL FORCE OPEN YOUR ROTTEN JAWS AND CRAM MORE FOOD INTO YOUR DETESTABLE STOMACH.
RRRGGHHHH!
IT'S THAT EXILED, ARROGANT MONTAGUE, WHO MURDERED MY JULIET'S COUSIN TYBALT – AND CAUSED JULIET TO DIE FROM A BROKEN HEART. AND HE'S HERE NOW TO DESECRATE THE DEAD BODIES.
I'LL MAKE A CITIZEN'S ARREST.

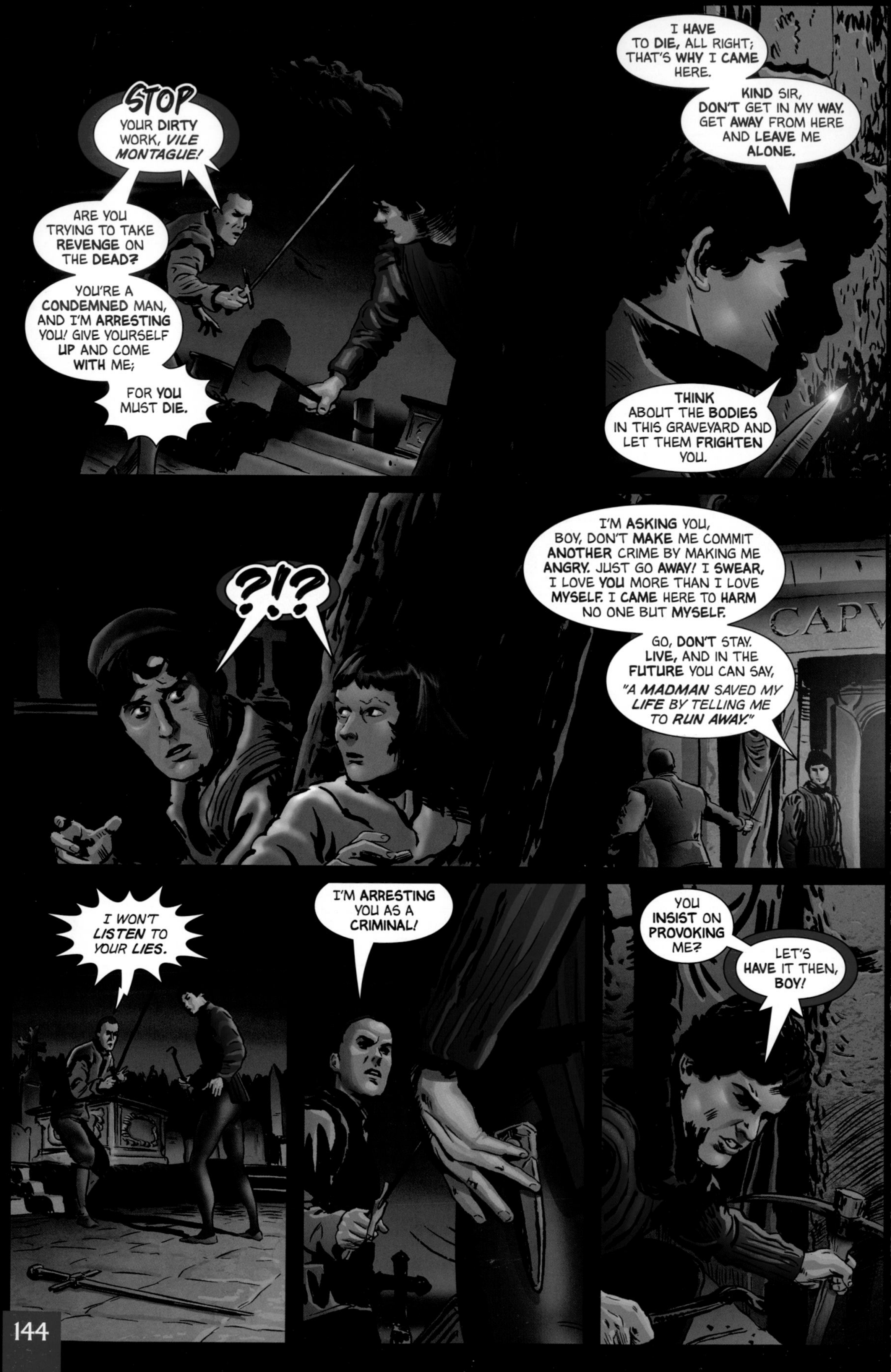
STOP YOUR DIRTY WORK, VILE MONTAGUE!
ARE YOU TRYING TO TAKE REVENGE ON THE DEAD?
YOU'RE A CONDEMNED MAN, AND I'M ARRESTING YOU! GIVE YOURSELF UP AND COME WITH ME;
FOR YOU MUST DIE.
I HAVE TO DIE, ALL RIGHT; THAT'S WHY I CAME HERE.
KIND SIR, DON'T GET IN MY WAY. GET AWAY FROM HERE AND LEAVE ME ALONE.
THINK ABOUT THE BODIES IN THIS GRAVEYARD AND LET THEM FRIGHTEN YOU.
?!?
I'M ASKING YOU, BOY, DON'T MAKE ME COMMIT ANOTHER CRIME BY MAKING ME ANGRY. JUST GO AWAY! I SWEAR, I LOVE YOU MORE THAN I LOVE MYSELF. I CAME HERE TO HARM NO ONE BUT MYSELF.
GO, DON'T STAY. LIVE, AND IN THE FUTURE YOU CAN SAY, "A MADMAN SAVED MY LIFE BY TELLING ME TO RUN AWAY."
CAPV
I WON'T LISTEN TO YOUR LIES.
I'M ARRESTING YOU AS A CRIMINAL!
YOU INSIST ON PROVOKING ME?
LET'S HAVE IT THEN, BOY!

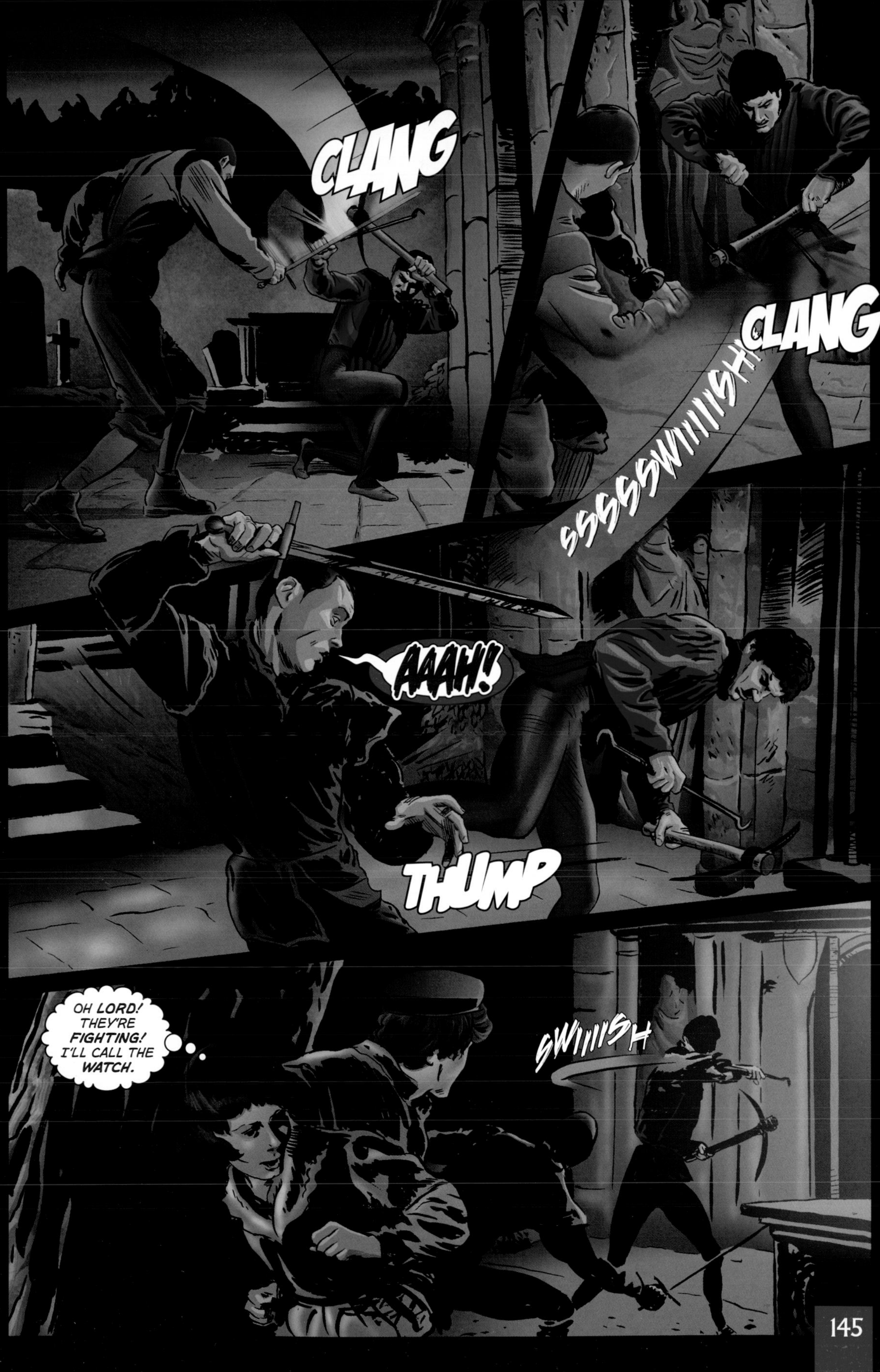

CLANG
CLANG
SSSSSWIIIIISH
AAAH!
THUMP
OH LORD! THEY'RE FIGHTING! I'LL CALL THE WATCH.
SWIIIISH

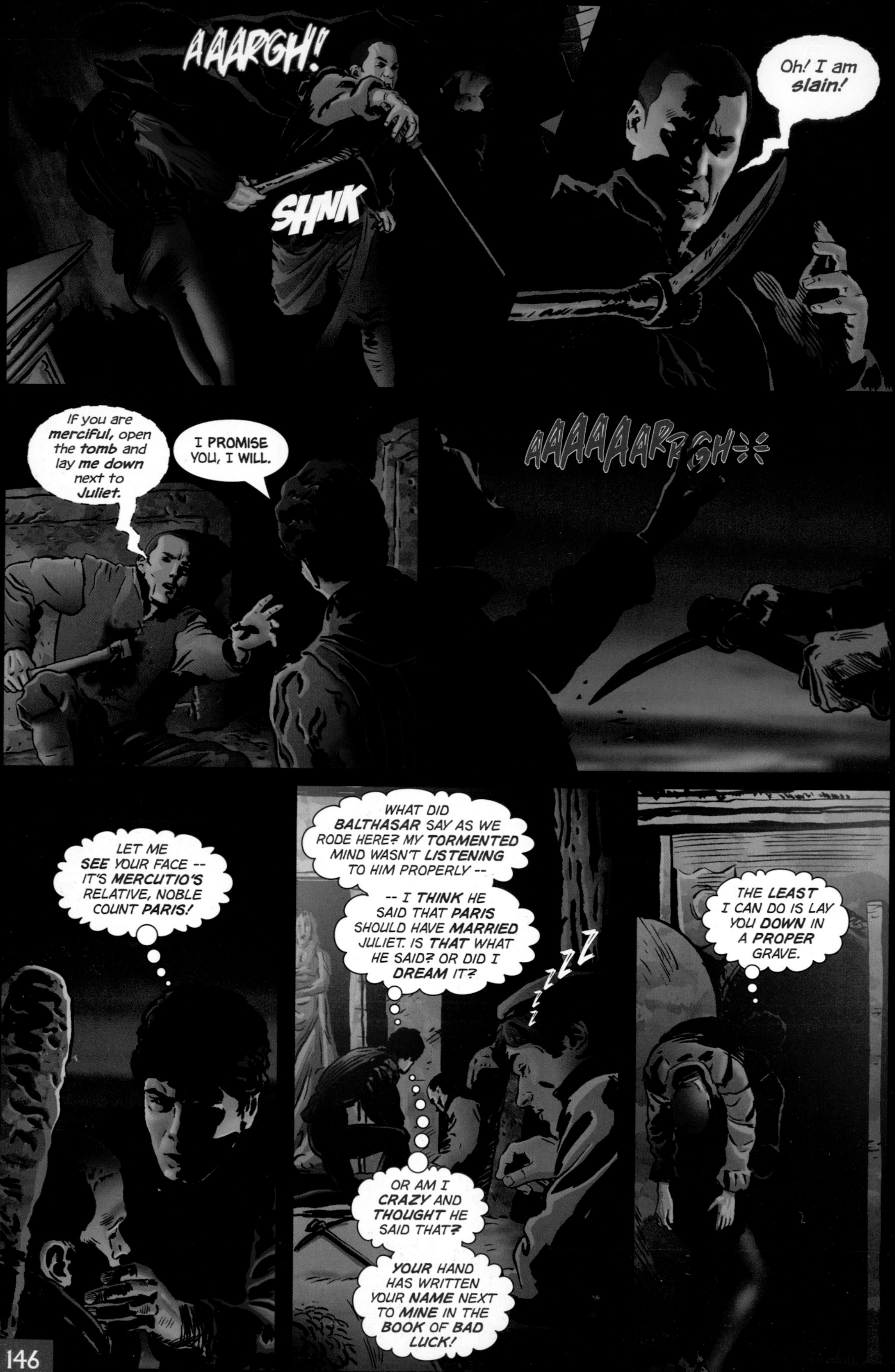
AAARGH!
SHNK
Oh! I am slain!
If you are merciful, open the tomb and lay me down next to Juliet.
I PROMISE YOU, I WILL.
AAAAAARRGH...
LET ME SEE YOUR FACE -- IT'S MERCUTIO'S RELATIVE, NOBLE COUNT PARIS!
WHAT DID BALTHASAR SAY AS WE RODE HERE? MY TORMENTED MIND WASN'T LISTENING TO HIM PROPERLY --
-- I THINK HE SAID THAT PARIS SHOULD HAVE MARRIED JULIET. IS THAT WHAT HE SAID? OR DID I DREAM IT?
ZZZZ
OR AM I CRAZY AND THOUGHT HE SAID THAT?
YOUR HAND HAS WRITTEN YOUR NAME NEXT TO MINE IN THE BOOK OF BAD LUCK!
THE LEAST I CAN DO IS LAY YOU DOWN IN A PROPER GRAVE.

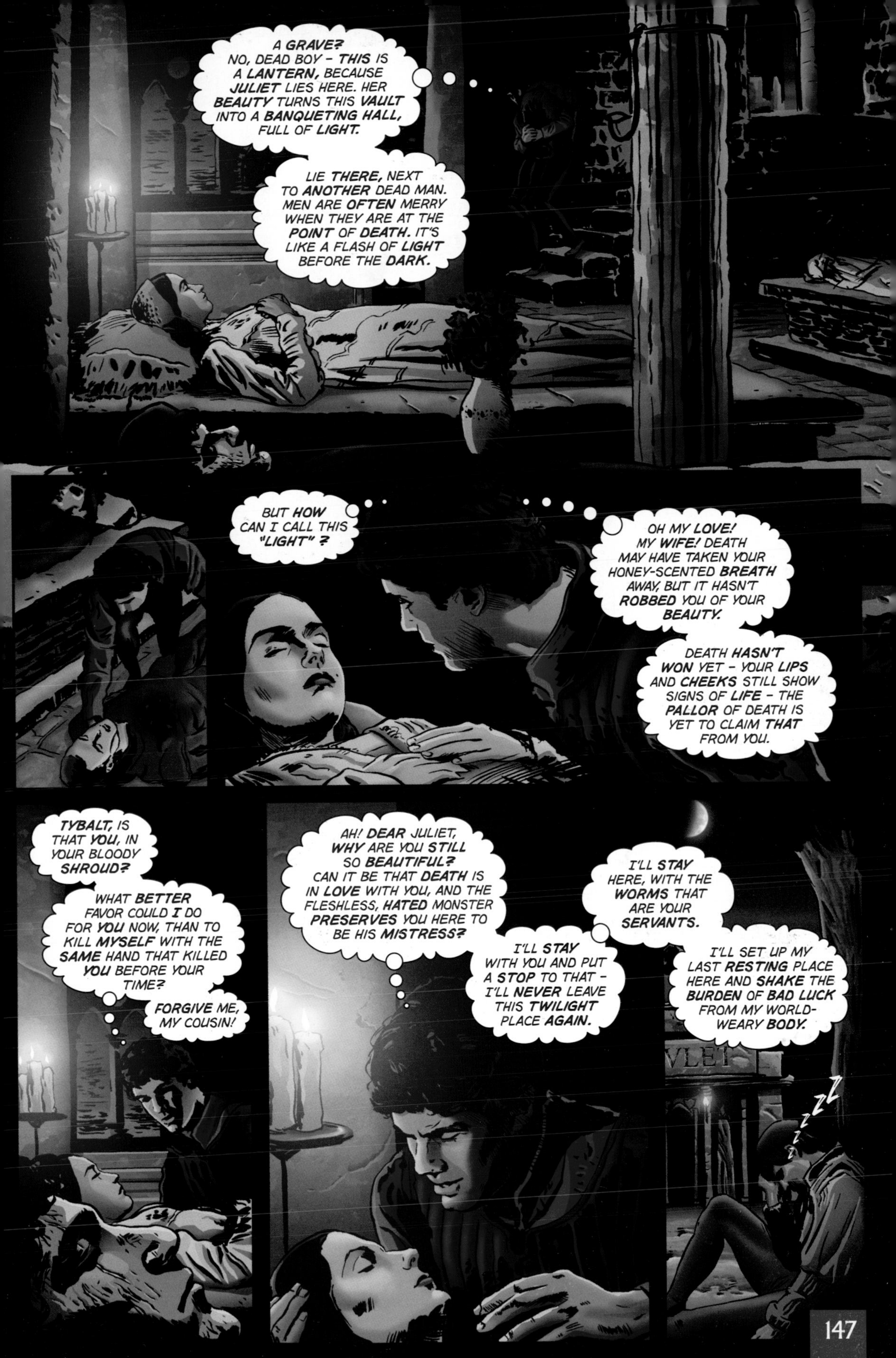
A GRAVE? NO, DEAD BOY - THIS IS A LANTERN, BECAUSE JULIET LIES HERE. HER BEAUTY TURNS THIS VAULT INTO A BANQUETING HALL, FULL OF LIGHT.
LIE THERE, NEXT TO ANOTHER DEAD MAN. MEN ARE OFTEN MERRY WHEN THEY ARE AT THE POINT OF DEATH. IT'S LIKE A FLASH OF LIGHT BEFORE THE DARK.
BUT HOW CAN I CALL THIS "LIGHT"?
OH MY LOVE! MY WIFE! DEATH MAY HAVE TAKEN YOUR HONEY-SCENTED BREATH AWAY, BUT IT HASN'T ROBBED YOU OF YOUR BEAUTY.
DEATH HASN'T WON YET - YOUR LIPS AND CHEEKS STILL SHOW SIGNS OF LIFE - THE PALLOR OF DEATH IS YET TO CLAIM THAT FROM YOU.
TYBALT, IS THAT YOU, IN YOUR BLOODY SHROUD?
WHAT BETTER FAVOR COULD I DO FOR YOU NOW, THAN TO KILL MYSELF WITH THE SAME HAND THAT KILLED YOU BEFORE YOUR TIME?
FORGIVE ME, MY COUSIN!
AH! DEAR JULIET, WHY ARE YOU STILL SO BEAUTIFUL? CAN IT BE THAT DEATH IS IN LOVE WITH YOU, AND THE FLESHLESS, HATED MONSTER PRESERVES YOU HERE TO BE HIS MISTRESS?
I'LL STAY WITH YOU AND PUT A STOP TO THAT - I'LL NEVER LEAVE THIS TWILIGHT PLACE AGAIN.
I'LL STAY HERE, WITH THE WORMS THAT ARE YOUR SERVANTS.
I'LL SET UP MY LAST RESTING PLACE HERE AND SHAKE THE BURDEN OF BAD LUCK FROM MY WORLD-WEARY BODY.
ZZZZZ

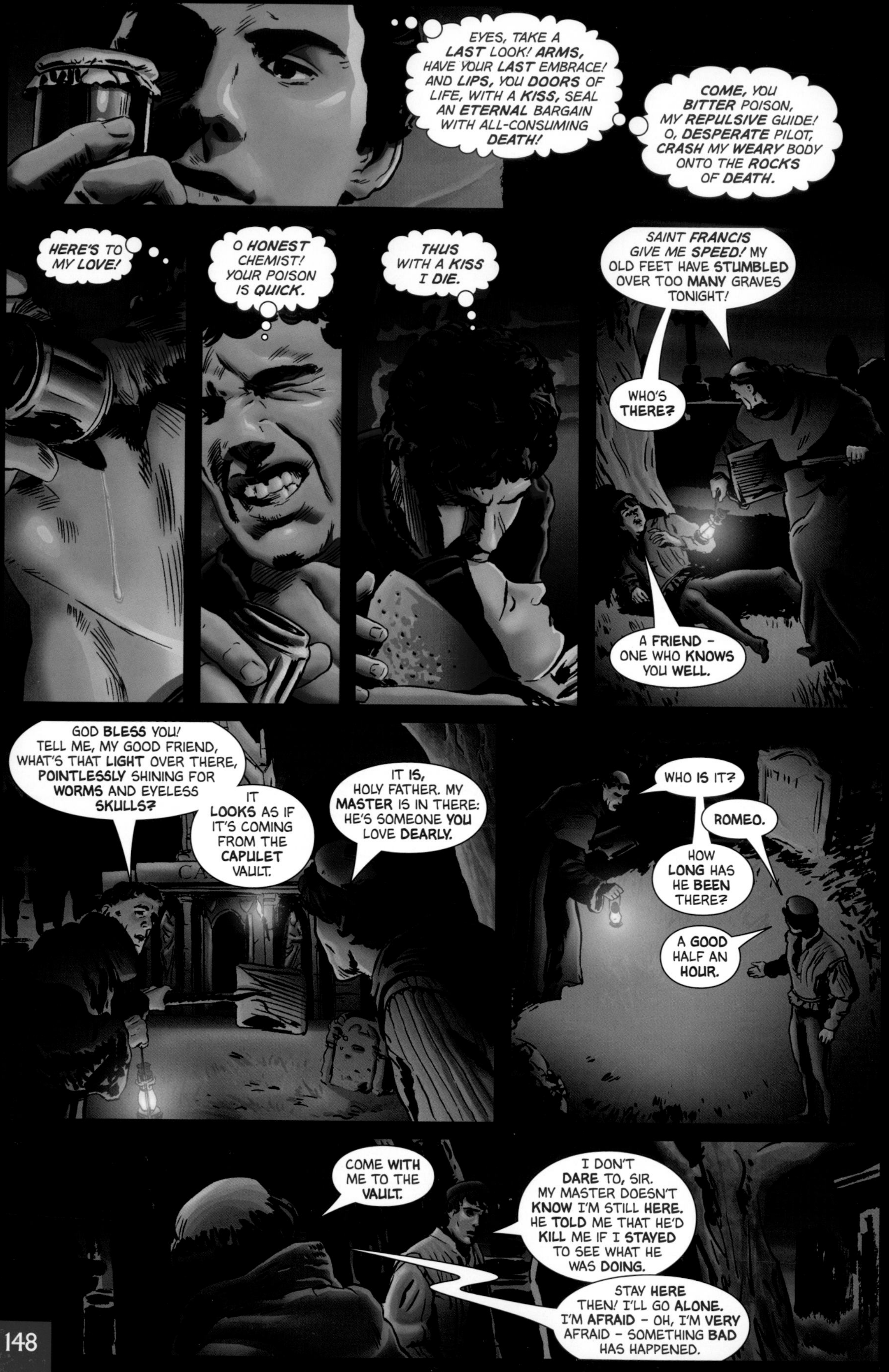
EYES, TAKE A LAST LOOK! ARMS, HAVE YOUR LAST EMBRACE! AND LIPS, YOU DOORS OF LIFE, WITH A KISS, SEAL AN ETERNAL BARGAIN WITH ALL-CONSUMING DEATH!
COME, YOU BITTER POISON, MY REPULSIVE GUIDE! O, DESPERATE PILOT, CRASH MY WEARY BODY ONTO THE ROCKS OF DEATH.
HERE'S TO MY LOVE!
O HONEST CHEMIST! YOUR POISON IS QUICK.
THUS WITH A KISS I DIE.
SAINT FRANCIS GIVE ME SPEED! MY OLD FEET HAVE STUMBLED OVER TOO MANY GRAVES TONIGHT!
WHO'S THERE?
A FRIEND – ONE WHO KNOWS YOU WELL.
GOD BLESS YOU! TELL ME, MY GOOD FRIEND, WHAT'S THAT LIGHT OVER THERE, POINTLESSLY SHINING FOR WORMS AND EYELESS SKULLS?
IT LOOKS AS IF IT'S COMING FROM THE CAPULET VAULT.
IT IS, HOLY FATHER. MY MASTER IS IN THERE: HE'S SOMEONE YOU LOVE DEARLY.
WHO IS IT?
ROMEO.
HOW LONG HAS HE BEEN THERE?
A GOOD HALF AN HOUR.
COME WITH ME TO THE VAULT.
I DON'T DARE TO, SIR. MY MASTER DOESN'T KNOW I'M STILL HERE. HE TOLD ME THAT HE'D KILL ME IF I STAYED TO SEE WHAT HE WAS DOING.
STAY HERE THEN! I'LL GO ALONE. I'M AFRAID – OH, I'M VERY AFRAID – SOMETHING BAD HAS HAPPENED.

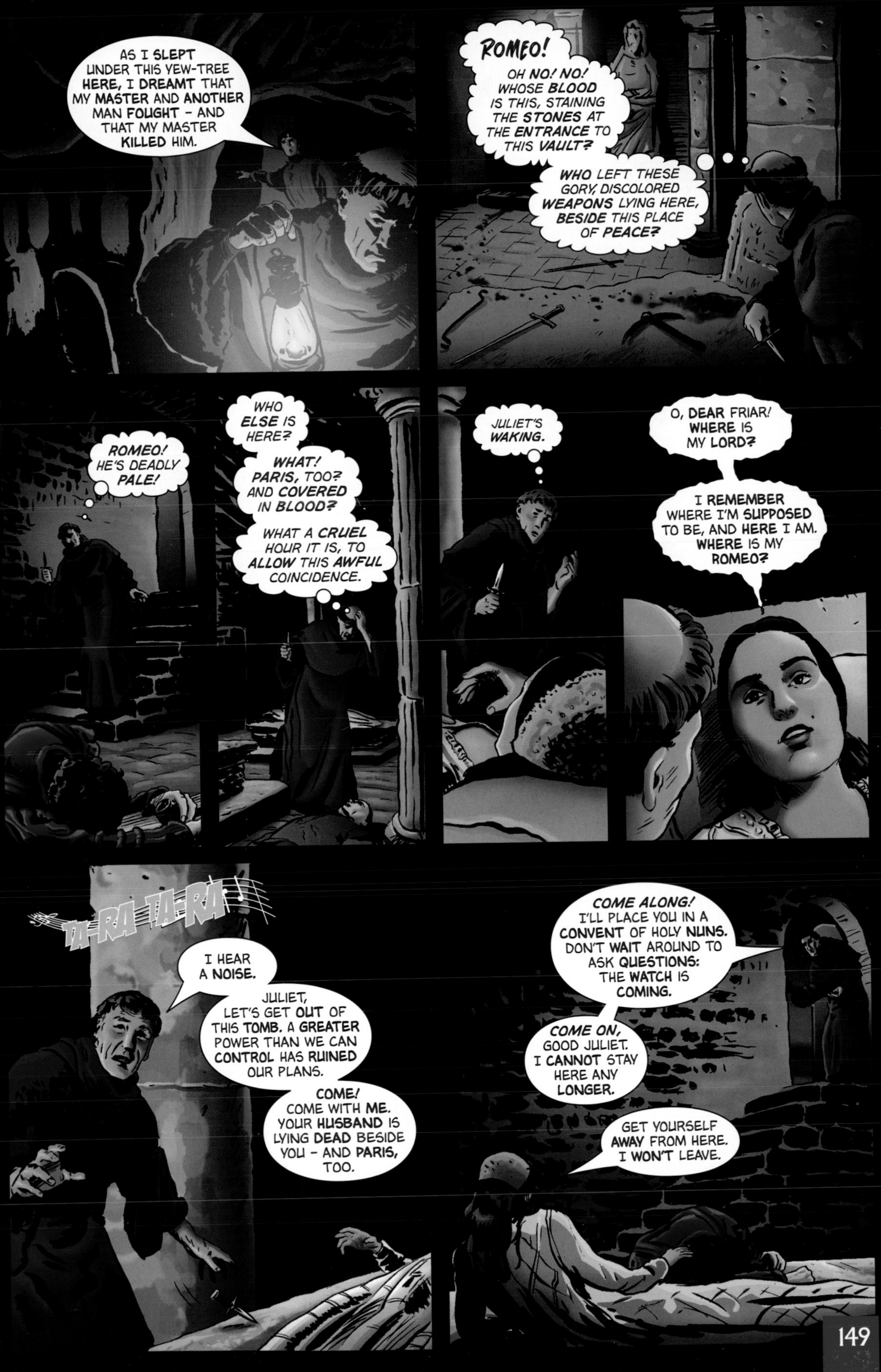
AS I SLEPT UNDER THIS YEW-TREE HERE, I DREAMT THAT MY MASTER AND ANOTHER MAN FOUGHT – AND THAT MY MASTER KILLED HIM.
ROMEO!
OH NO! NO! WHOSE BLOOD IS THIS, STAINING THE STONES AT THE ENTRANCE TO THIS VAULT?
WHO LEFT THESE GORY, DISCOLORED WEAPONS LYING HERE, BESIDE THIS PLACE OF PEACE?
ROMEO! HE'S DEADLY PALE!
WHO ELSE IS HERE?
WHAT! PARIS, TOO? AND COVERED IN BLOOD?
WHAT A CRUEL HOUR IT IS, TO ALLOW THIS AWFUL COINCIDENCE.
JULIET'S WAKING.
O, DEAR FRIAR! WHERE IS MY LORD?
I REMEMBER WHERE I'M SUPPOSED TO BE, AND HERE I AM. WHERE IS MY ROMEO?
TA-RA TA-RA
I HEAR A NOISE.
JULIET, LET'S GET OUT OF THIS TOMB. A GREATER POWER THAN WE CAN CONTROL HAS RUINED OUR PLANS.
COME! COME WITH ME. YOUR HUSBAND IS LYING DEAD BESIDE YOU – AND PARIS, TOO.
COME ALONG! I'LL PLACE YOU IN A CONVENT OF HOLY NUNS. DON'T WAIT AROUND TO ASK QUESTIONS: THE WATCH IS COMING.
COME ON, GOOD JULIET. I CANNOT STAY HERE ANY LONGER.
GET YOURSELF AWAY FROM HERE. I WON'T LEAVE.

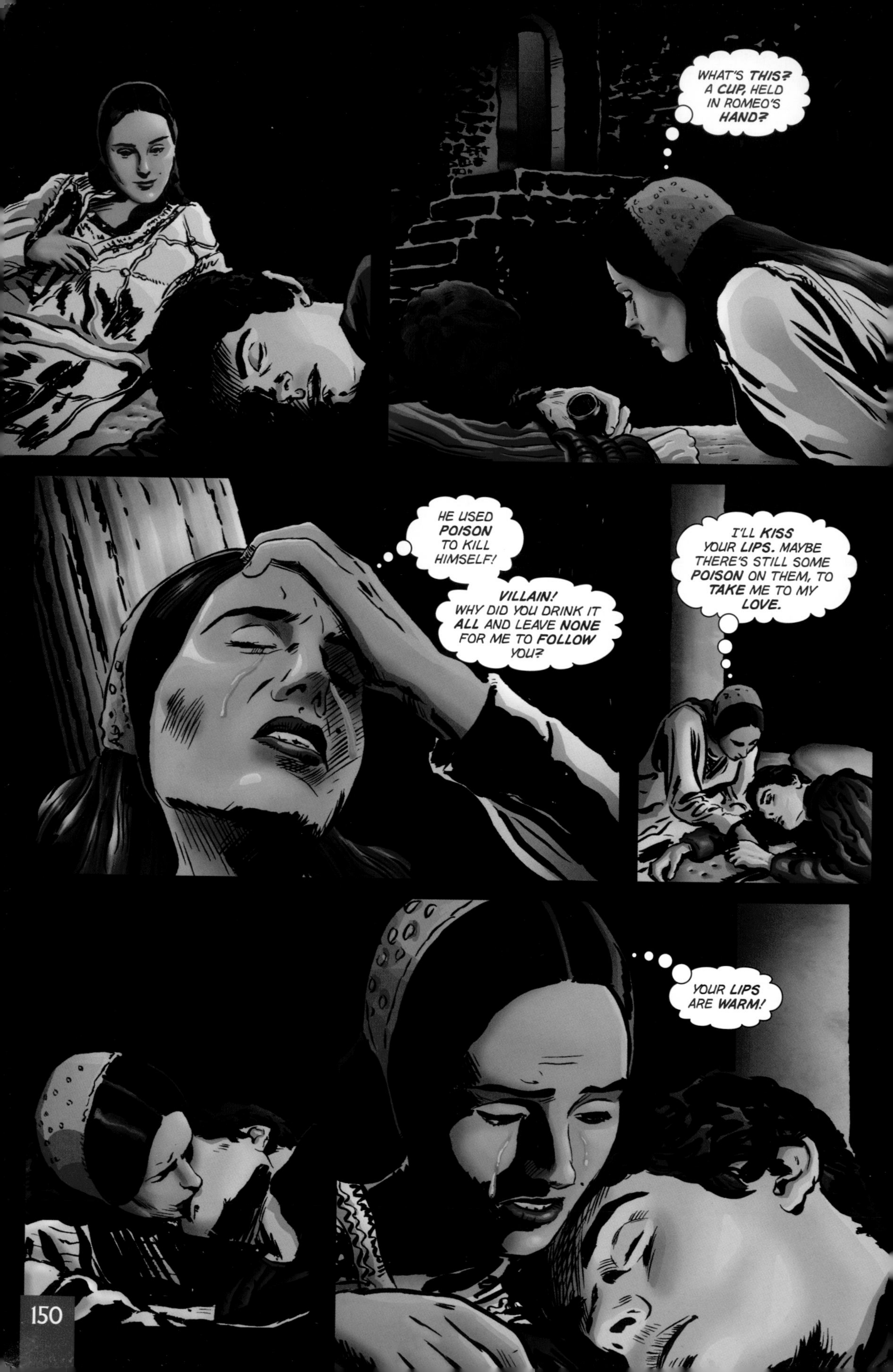
WHAT'S THIS? A CUP, HELD IN ROMEO'S HAND?
HE USED POISON TO KILL HIMSELF!
VILLAIN! WHY DID YOU DRINK IT ALL AND LEAVE NONE FOR ME TO FOLLOW YOU?
I'LL KISS YOUR LIPS. MAYBE THERE'S STILL SOME POISON ON THEM, TO TAKE ME TO MY LOVE.
YOUR LIPS ARE WARM!

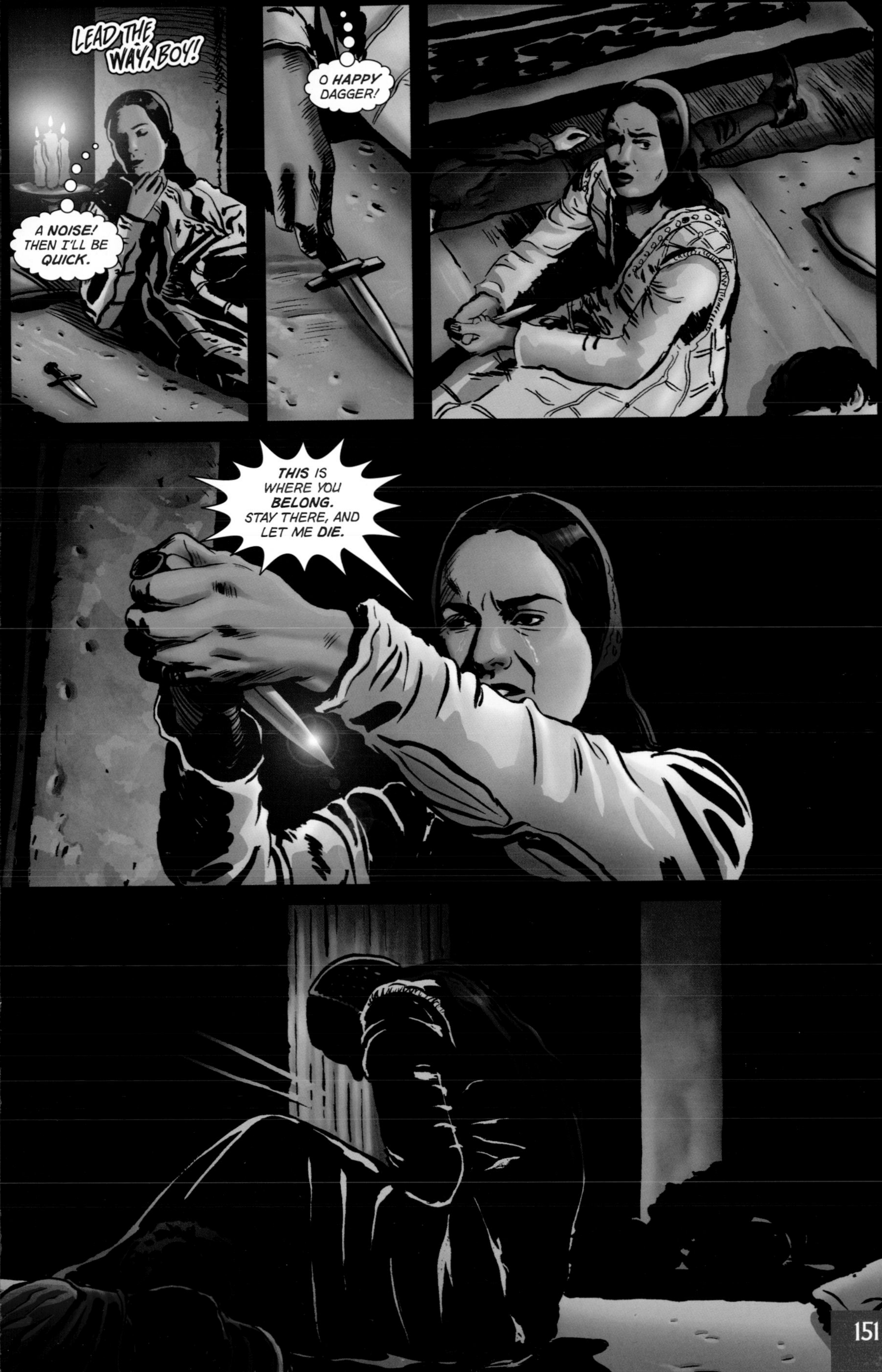
LEAD THE WAY, BOY!
A NOISE! THEN I'LL BE QUICK.
O HAPPY DAGGER!
THIS IS WHERE YOU BELONG. STAY THERE, AND LET ME DIE.

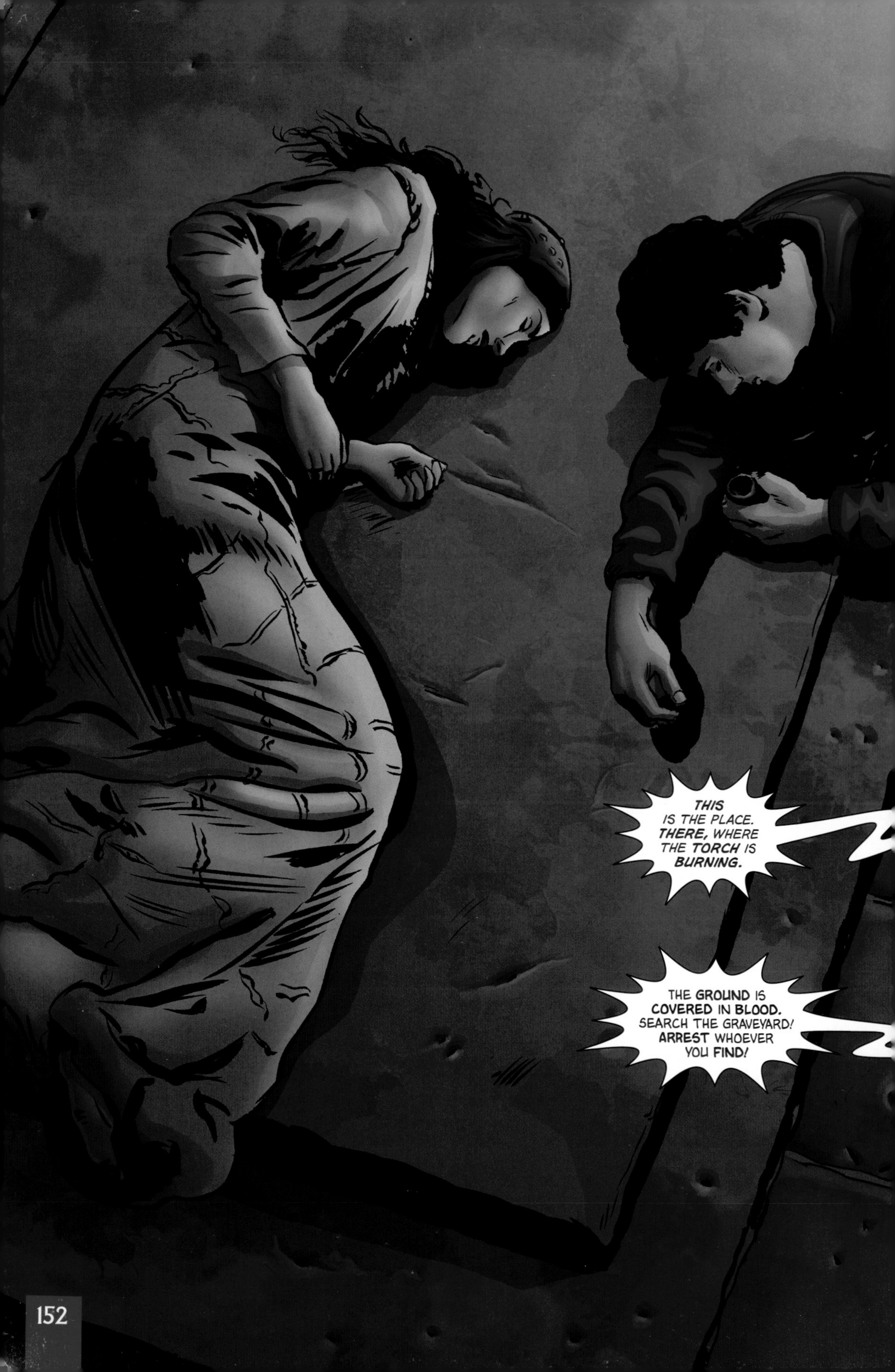
THIS IS THE PLACE. THERE, WHERE THE TORCH IS BURNING.
THE GROUND IS COVERED IN BLOOD. SEARCH THE GRAVEYARD! ARREST WHOEVER YOU FIND!

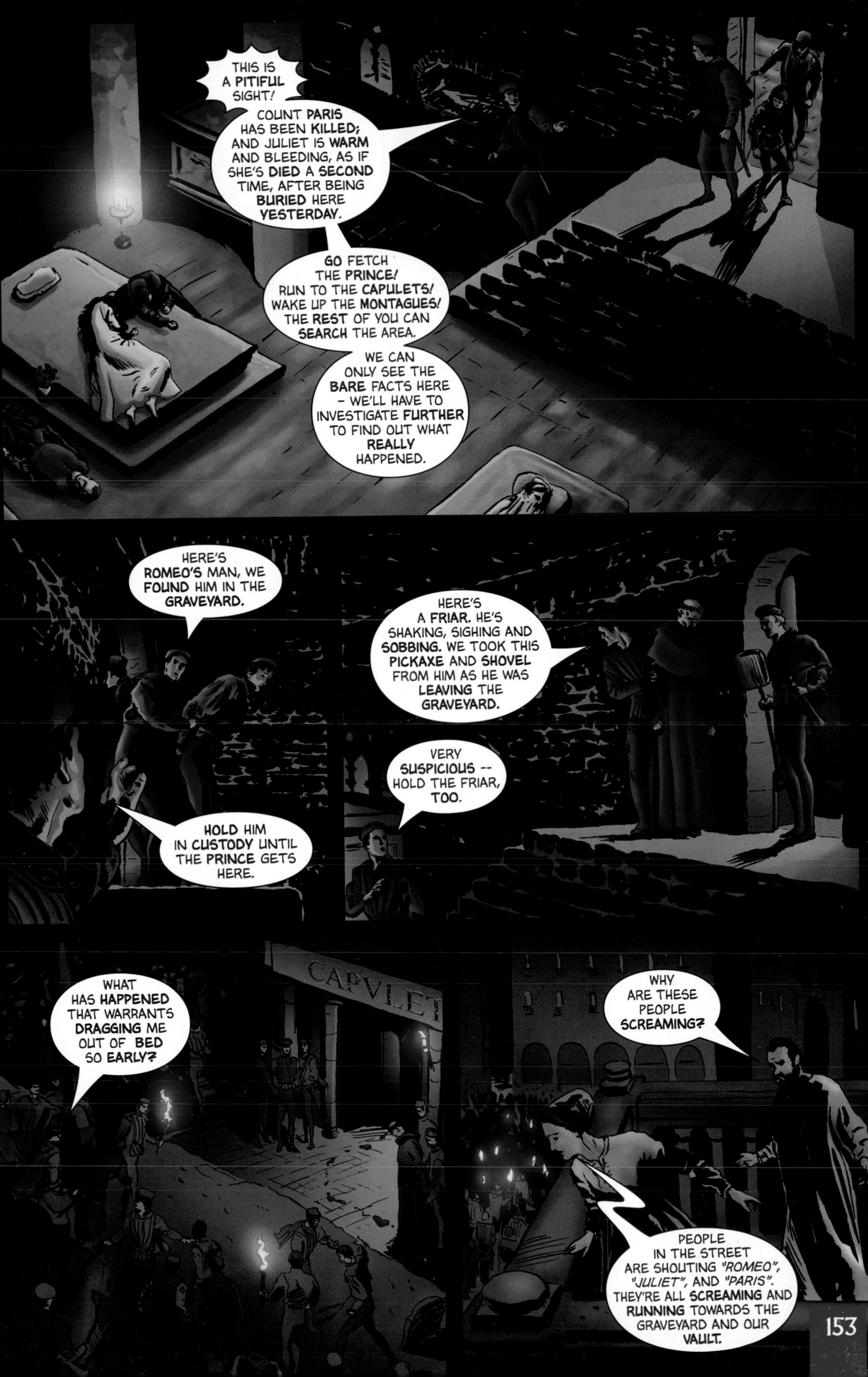
THIS IS A PITIFUL SIGHT!
COUNT PARIS HAS BEEN KILLED; AND JULIET IS WARM AND BLEEDING, AS IF SHE'S DIED A SECOND TIME, AFTER BEING BURIED HERE YESTERDAY.
GO FETCH THE PRINCE! RUN TO THE CAPULETS! WAKE UP THE MONTAGUES! THE REST OF YOU CAN SEARCH THE AREA.
WE CAN ONLY SEE THE BARE FACTS HERE - WE'LL HAVE TO INVESTIGATE FURTHER TO FIND OUT WHAT REALLY HAPPENED.
HERE'S ROMEO'S MAN, WE FOUND HIM IN THE GRAVEYARD.
HOLD HIM IN CUSTODY UNTIL THE PRINCE GETS HERE.
HERE'S A FRIAR. HE'S SHAKING, SIGHING AND SOBBING. WE TOOK THIS PICKAXE AND SHOVEL FROM HIM AS HE WAS LEAVING THE GRAVEYARD.
VERY SUSPICIOUS -- HOLD THE FRIAR, TOO.
CAPVLET
WHAT HAS HAPPENED THAT WARRANTS DRAGGING ME OUT OF BED SO EARLY?
WHY ARE THESE PEOPLE SCREAMING?
PEOPLE IN THE STREET ARE SHOUTING "ROMEO", "JULIET", AND "PARIS". THEY'RE ALL SCREAMING AND RUNNING TOWARDS THE GRAVEYARD AND OUR VAULT.

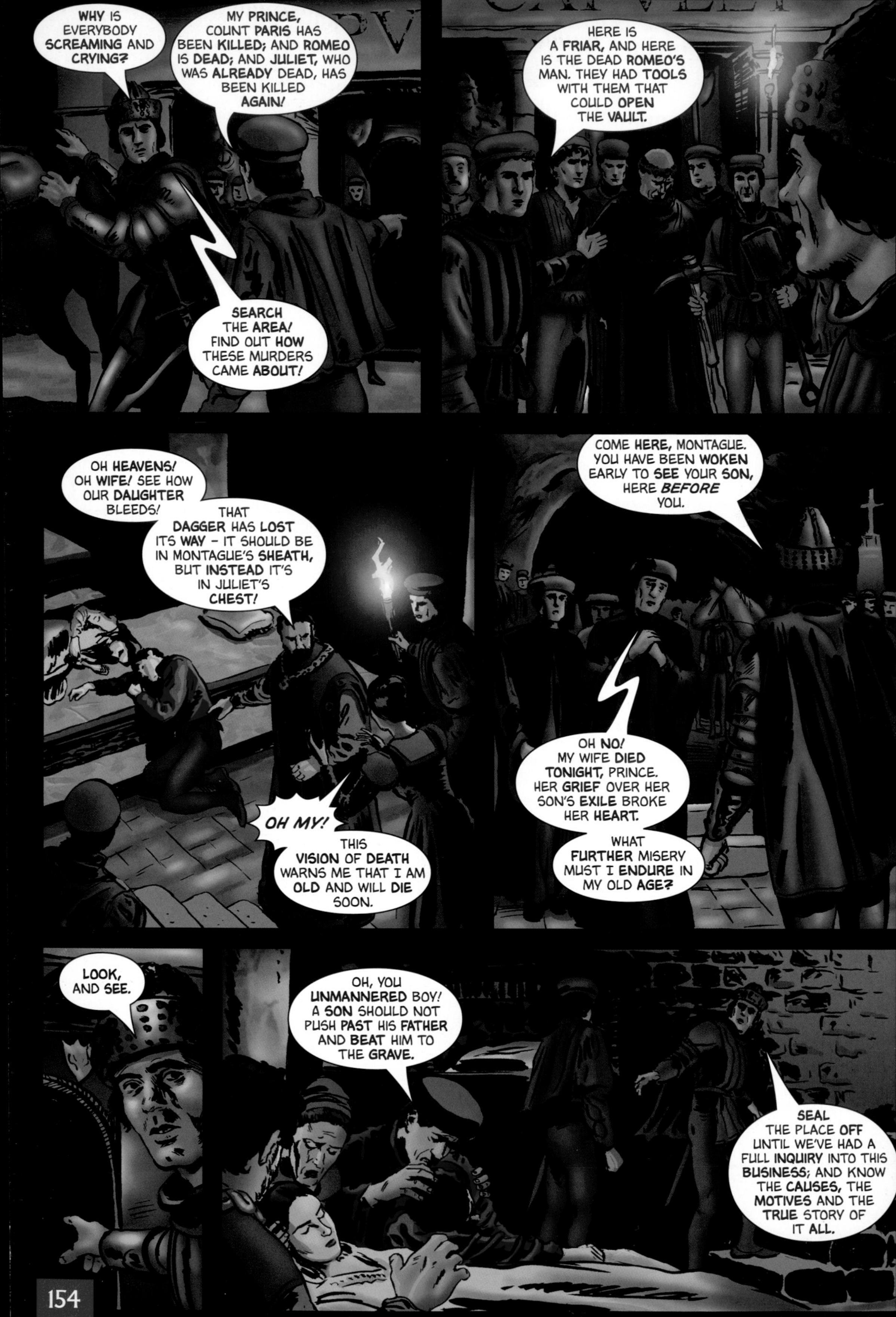

WHY IS EVERYBODY SCREAMING AND CRYING?
MY PRINCE, COUNT PARIS HAS BEEN KILLED; AND ROMEO IS DEAD; AND JULIET, WHO WAS ALREADY DEAD, HAS BEEN KILLED AGAIN!
SEARCH THE AREA! FIND OUT HOW THESE MURDERS CAME ABOUT!
HERE IS A FRIAR, AND HERE IS THE DEAD ROMEO'S MAN. THEY HAD TOOLS WITH THEM THAT COULD OPEN THE VAULT.
OH HEAVENS! OH WIFE! SEE HOW OUR DAUGHTER BLEEDS!
THAT DAGGER HAS LOST ITS WAY – IT SHOULD BE IN MONTAGUE'S SHEATH, BUT INSTEAD IT'S IN JULIET'S CHEST!
OH MY!
THIS VISION OF DEATH WARNS ME THAT I AM OLD AND WILL DIE SOON.
COME HERE, MONTAGUE. YOU HAVE BEEN WOKEN EARLY TO SEE YOUR SON, HERE BEFORE YOU.
OH NO! MY WIFE DIED TONIGHT, PRINCE. HER GRIEF OVER HER SON'S EXILE BROKE HER HEART.
WHAT FURTHER MISERY MUST I ENDURE IN MY OLD AGE?
LOOK, AND SEE.
OH, YOU UNMANNERED BOY! A SON SHOULD NOT PUSH PAST HIS FATHER AND BEAT HIM TO THE GRAVE.
SEAL THE PLACE OFF UNTIL WE'VE HAD A FULL INQUIRY INTO THIS BUSINESS; AND KNOW THE CAUSES, THE MOTIVES AND THE TRUE STORY OF IT ALL.

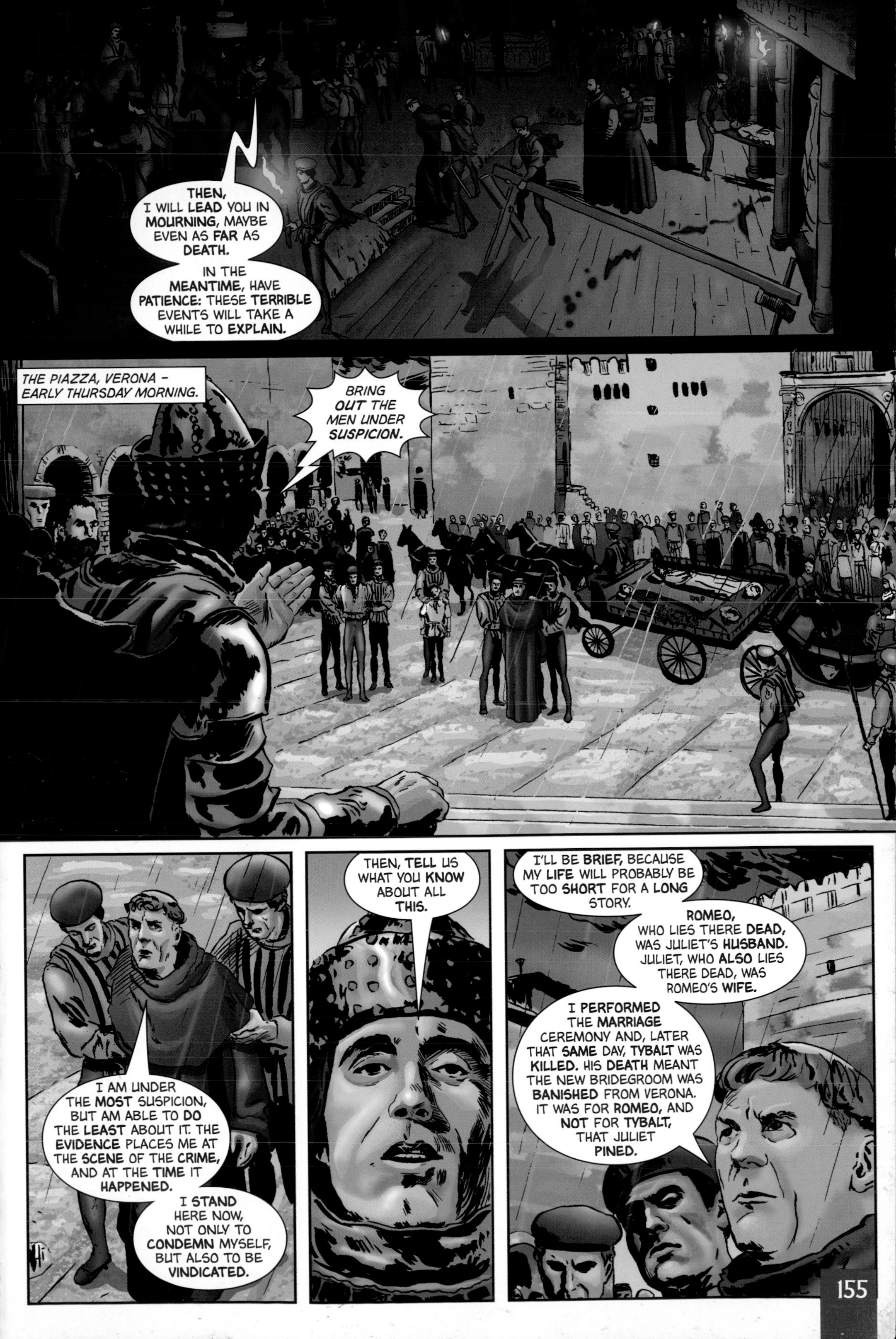

THEN, I WILL LEAD YOU IN MOURNING, MAYBE EVEN AS FAR AS DEATH.
IN THE MEANTIME, HAVE PATIENCE: THESE TERRIBLE EVENTS WILL TAKE A WHILE TO EXPLAIN.
THE PIAZZA, VERONA – EARLY THURSDAY MORNING.
BRING OUT THE MEN UNDER SUSPICION.
I AM UNDER THE MOST SUSPICION, BUT AM ABLE TO DO THE LEAST ABOUT IT. THE EVIDENCE PLACES ME AT THE SCENE OF THE CRIME, AND AT THE TIME IT HAPPENED.
I STAND HERE NOW, NOT ONLY TO CONDEMN MYSELF, BUT ALSO TO BE VINDICATED.
THEN, TELL US WHAT YOU KNOW ABOUT ALL THIS.
I'LL BE BRIEF, BECAUSE MY LIFE WILL PROBABLY BE TOO SHORT FOR A LONG STORY.
ROMEO, WHO LIES THERE DEAD, WAS JULIET'S HUSBAND. JULIET, WHO ALSO LIES THERE DEAD, WAS ROMEO'S WIFE.
I PERFORMED THE MARRIAGE CEREMONY AND, LATER THAT SAME DAY, TYBALT WAS KILLED. HIS DEATH MEANT THE NEW BRIDEGROOM WAS BANISHED FROM VERONA. IT WAS FOR ROMEO, AND NOT FOR TYBALT, THAT JULIET PINED.

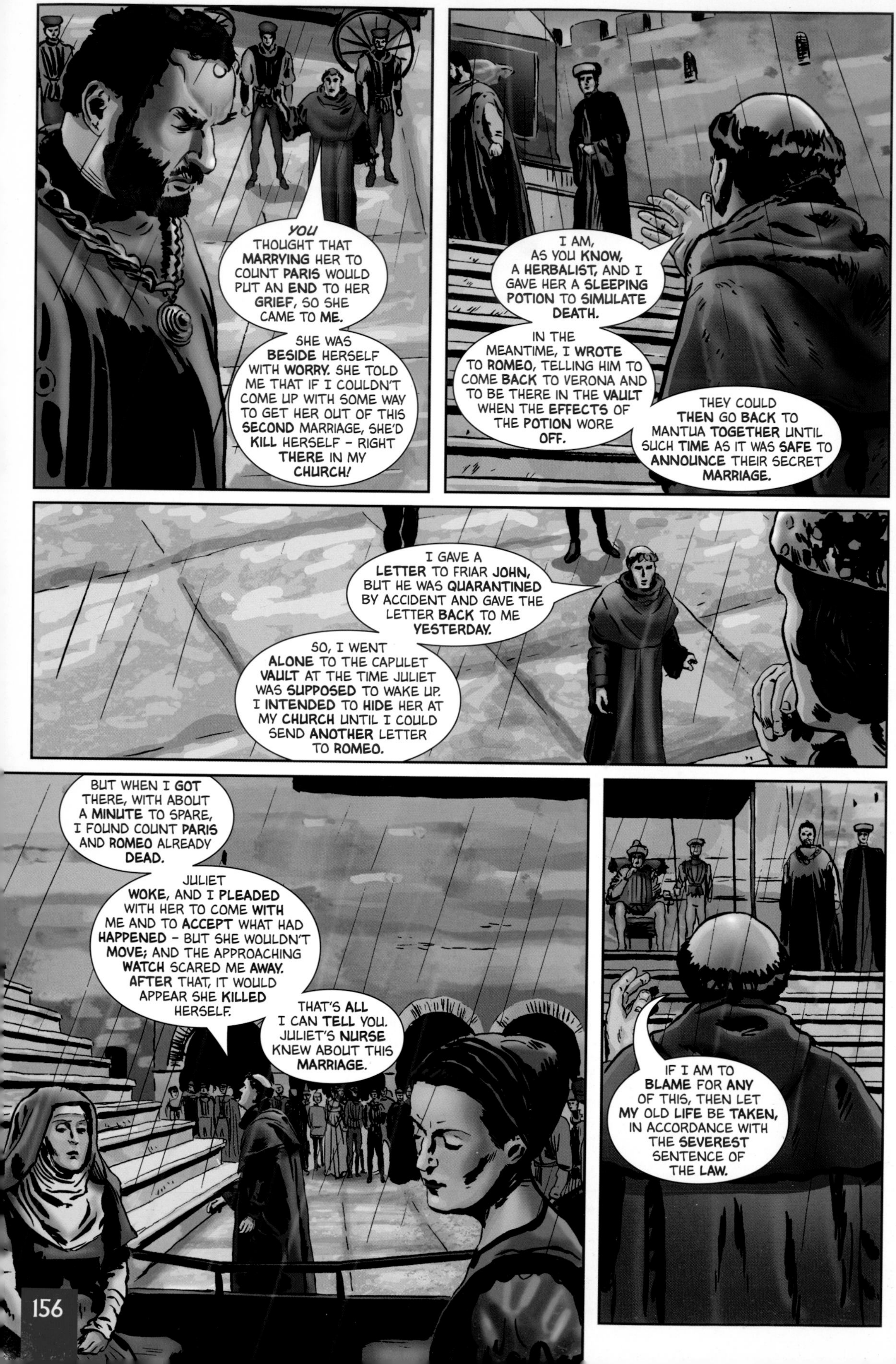
YOU THOUGHT THAT MARRYING HER TO COUNT PARIS WOULD PUT AN END TO HER GRIEF, SO SHE CAME TO ME.
SHE WAS BESIDE HERSELF WITH WORRY. SHE TOLD ME THAT IF I COULDN'T COME UP WITH SOME WAY TO GET HER OUT OF THIS SECOND MARRIAGE, SHE'D KILL HERSELF - RIGHT THERE IN MY CHURCH!
I AM, AS YOU KNOW, A HERBALIST, AND I GAVE HER A SLEEPING POTION TO SIMULATE DEATH.
IN THE MEANTIME, I WROTE TO ROMEO, TELLING HIM TO COME BACK TO VERONA AND TO BE THERE IN THE VAULT WHEN THE EFFECTS OF THE POTION WORE OFF.
THEY COULD THEN GO BACK TO MANTUA TOGETHER UNTIL SUCH TIME AS IT WAS SAFE TO ANNOUNCE THEIR SECRET MARRIAGE.
I GAVE A LETTER TO FRIAR JOHN, BUT HE WAS QUARANTINED BY ACCIDENT AND GAVE THE LETTER BACK TO ME YESTERDAY.
SO, I WENT ALONE TO THE CAPULET VAULT AT THE TIME JULIET WAS SUPPOSED TO WAKE UP. I INTENDED TO HIDE HER AT MY CHURCH UNTIL I COULD SEND ANOTHER LETTER TO ROMEO.
BUT WHEN I GOT THERE, WITH ABOUT A MINUTE TO SPARE, I FOUND COUNT PARIS AND ROMEO ALREADY DEAD.
JULIET WOKE, AND I PLEADED WITH HER TO COME WITH ME AND TO ACCEPT WHAT HAD HAPPENED - BUT SHE WOULDN'T MOVE; AND THE APPROACHING WATCH SCARED ME AWAY. AFTER THAT, IT WOULD APPEAR SHE KILLED HERSELF.
THAT'S ALL I CAN TELL YOU. JULIET'S NURSE KNEW ABOUT THIS MARRIAGE.
IF I AM TO BLAME FOR ANY OF THIS, THEN LET MY OLD LIFE BE TAKEN, IN ACCORDANCE WITH THE SEVEREST SENTENCE OF THE LAW.

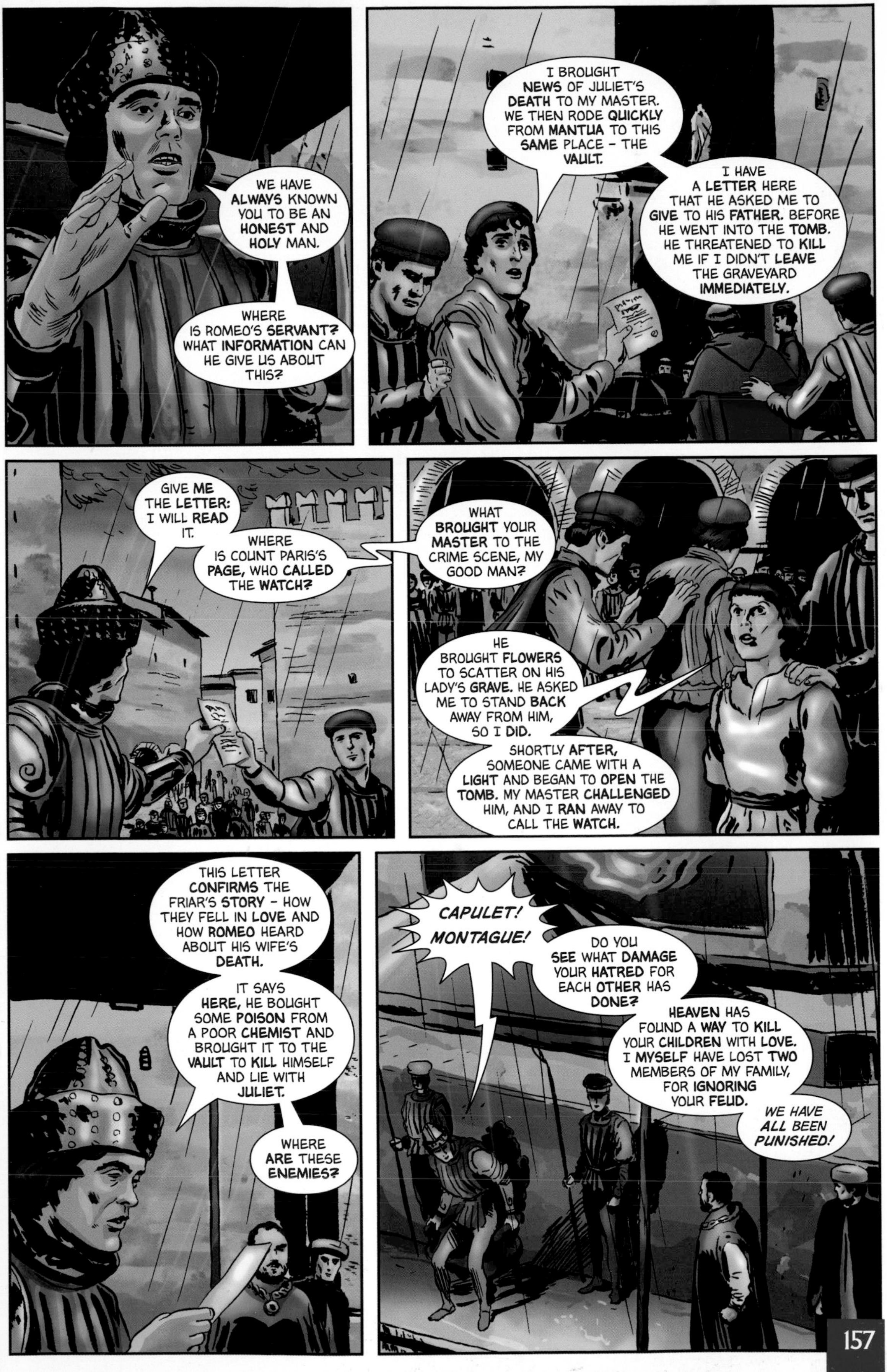
WE HAVE ALWAYS KNOWN YOU TO BE AN HONEST AND HOLY MAN.
WHERE IS ROMEO'S SERVANT? WHAT INFORMATION CAN HE GIVE US ABOUT THIS?
I BROUGHT NEWS OF JULIET'S DEATH TO MY MASTER. WE THEN RODE QUICKLY FROM MANTUA TO THIS SAME PLACE – THE VAULT.
I HAVE A LETTER HERE THAT HE ASKED ME TO GIVE TO HIS FATHER. BEFORE HE WENT INTO THE TOMB. HE THREATENED TO KILL ME IF I DIDN'T LEAVE THE GRAVEYARD IMMEDIATELY.
GIVE ME THE LETTER: I WILL READ IT.
WHERE IS COUNT PARIS'S PAGE, WHO CALLED THE WATCH?
WHAT BROUGHT YOUR MASTER TO THE CRIME SCENE, MY GOOD MAN?
HE BROUGHT FLOWERS TO SCATTER ON HIS LADY'S GRAVE. HE ASKED ME TO STAND BACK AWAY FROM HIM, SO I DID.
SHORTLY AFTER, SOMEONE CAME WITH A LIGHT AND BEGAN TO OPEN THE TOMB. MY MASTER CHALLENGED HIM, AND I RAN AWAY TO CALL THE WATCH.
THIS LETTER CONFIRMS THE FRIAR'S STORY – HOW THEY FELL IN LOVE AND HOW ROMEO HEARD ABOUT HIS WIFE'S DEATH.
IT SAYS HERE, HE BOUGHT SOME POISON FROM A POOR CHEMIST AND BROUGHT IT TO THE VAULT TO KILL HIMSELF AND LIE WITH JULIET.
WHERE ARE THESE ENEMIES?
CAPULET! MONTAGUE!
DO YOU SEE WHAT DAMAGE YOUR HATRED FOR EACH OTHER HAS DONE?
HEAVEN HAS FOUND A WAY TO KILL YOUR CHILDREN WITH LOVE. I MYSELF HAVE LOST TWO MEMBERS OF MY FAMILY, FOR IGNORING YOUR FEUD.
WE HAVE ALL BEEN PUNISHED!

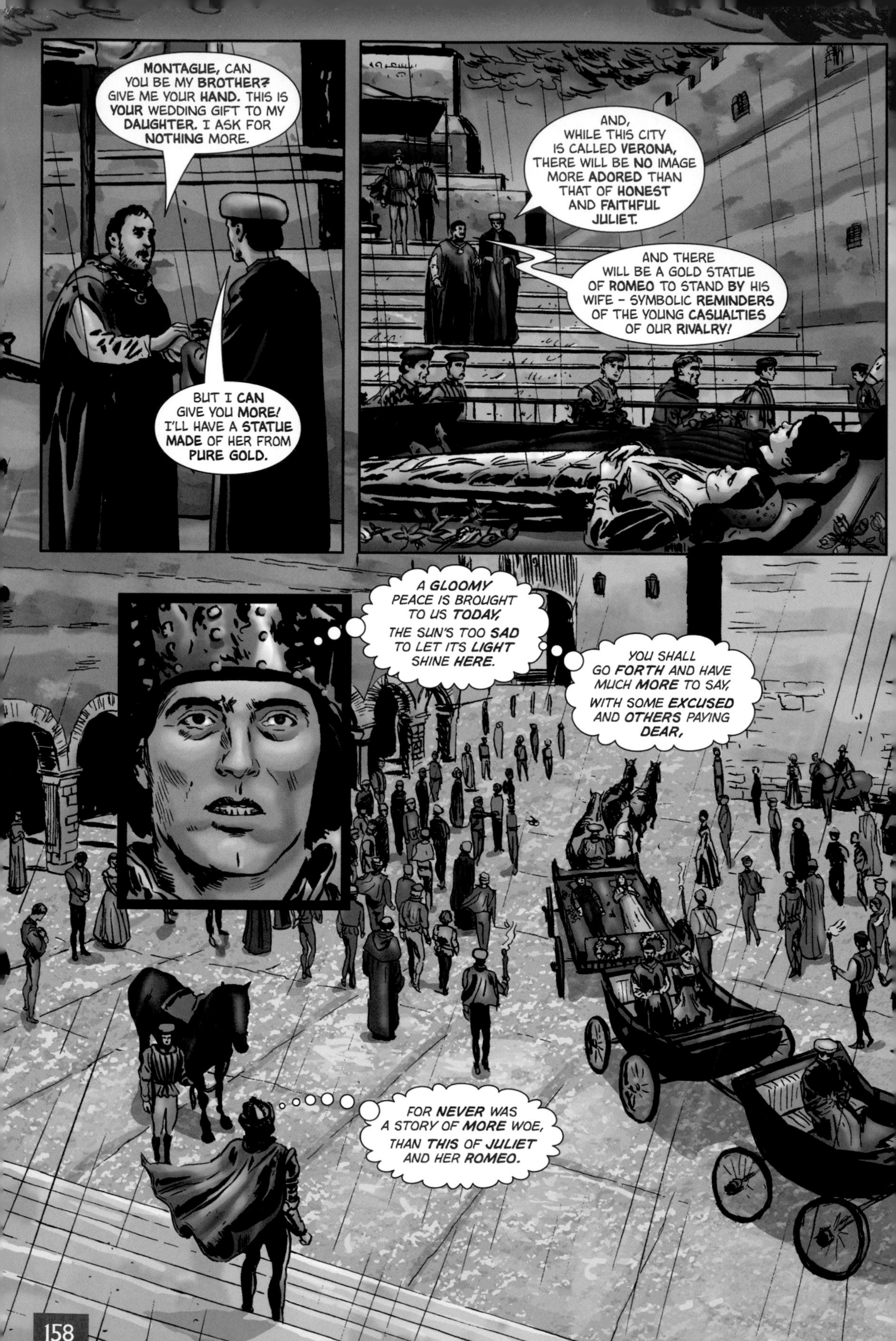
MONTAGUE, CAN YOU BE MY BROTHER? GIVE ME YOUR HAND. THIS IS YOUR WEDDING GIFT TO MY DAUGHTER. I ASK FOR NOTHING MORE.
BUT I CAN GIVE YOU MORE! I'LL HAVE A STATUE MADE OF HER FROM PURE GOLD.
AND, WHILE THIS CITY IS CALLED VERONA, THERE WILL BE NO IMAGE MORE ADORED THAN THAT OF HONEST AND FAITHFUL JULIET.
AND THERE WILL BE A GOLD STATUE OF ROMEO TO STAND BY HIS WIFE – SYMBOLIC REMINDERS OF THE YOUNG CASUALTIES OF OUR RIVALRY!
A GLOOMY PEACE IS BROUGHT TO US TODAY, THE SUN'S TOO SAD TO LET ITS LIGHT SHINE HERE.
YOU SHALL GO FORTH AND HAVE MUCH MORE TO SAY, WITH SOME EXCUSED AND OTHERS PAYING DEAR,
FOR NEVER WAS A STORY OF MORE WOE, THAN THIS OF JULIET AND HER ROMEO.

Romeo & Juliet

≥ The End ≤

William Shakespeare

(c.1564 - 1616 AD)

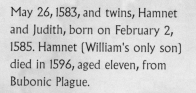

National Portrait Gallery, London

Shakespeare is, without question, the world's most famous playwright. Yet, despite his fame, very few records and artifacts exist for him — we don't even know the exact date of his birth! April 23, 1564 (St George's Day) is taken to be his birthday, as this was three days before his baptism (for which we do have a record). Records also tell us that he died on the same date in 1616, aged fifty-two.

The life of William Shakespeare can be divided into three acts.

Act One – Stratford-upon-Avon

William was the eldest son of tradesman John Shakespeare and Mary Arden, and the third of eight children (he had two older sisters). The Shakespeares were a respectable family. The year after William was born, John (who made gloves and traded leather) became an alderman of Stratford-upon-Avon, and four years later he became High Bailiff (or mayor) of the town.

Little is known of William's childhood. He learned to read and write at the local primary school, and later is believed to have attended the local grammar school, where he studied Latin and English Literature. In 1582, aged eighteen, William married a local farmer's daughter, Anne Hathaway. Anne was eight years his senior and three months pregnant. During their marriage they had three children: Susanna, born on May 26, 1583, and twins, Hamnet and Judith, born on February 2, 1585. Hamnet (William's only son) died in 1596, aged eleven, from Bubonic Plague.

Act Two – London

Five years into his marriage, in 1587, William's wife and children stayed in Stratford, while he moved to London. He appeared as an actor at *The Theatre* (England's first permanent theater) and gave public recitals of his own poems; but it was his playwriting that created the most interest. His fame soon spread far and wide. When Queen Elizabeth I died in 1603, the new King James I (who was already King James VI of Scotland) gave royal consent for Shakespeare's acting company, *The Lord Chamberlain's Men* to be called *The King's Men* in return for entertaining the court. This association was to shape a number of plays, such as *Macbeth*, which was written to please the Scottish King.

William Shakespeare is attributed with writing and collaborating on 38 plays, 154 sonnets and 5 poems, in just twenty-three years between 1590 and 1613. No original manuscript exists for any of his plays, making it hard to accurately date any of them. Printing was still in its infancy, and plays tended to change as they were performed. Shakespeare would write manuscript for the actors and continue to refine them over a number of performances. The plays we know today have survived from written copies taken at various stages of each play and usually written by the actors from memory. This has given rise to variations in texts of what is now known as "quarto" versions of the plays, until we reach the first official printing of each play in the 1623 *"folio" Mr William Shakespeare's Comedies, Histories, & Tragedies*. His last solo-authored work was *The Tempest* in 1611, which was only followed by collaborative work on two plays (*Henry VIII* and *Two Noble Kinsmen*) with John Fletcher. Shakespeare is strongly associated with the famous *Globe Theatre*. Built by his troupe in 1599, it became his "spiritual home", with thousands of people crammed into the small space for each performance. There were 3,000 people in the building in 1613 when a cannon-shot during a performance of *Henry VIII* set fire to the thatched roof and the entire theater was burned to the ground. Although it was rebuilt a year later, it marked an end to Shakespeare's writing and to his time in London.

Act Three - Retirement

Shortly after the 1613 accident at *The Globe*, Shakespeare left the capital and returned to live once more with his family in Stratford-upon-Avon. He died on April 23, 1616 and was buried two days later at the Church of the Holy Trinity (the same church where he had been baptized fifty-two years earlier). The cause of his death remains unknown.

Epilogue

At the time of his death, Shakespeare had substantial properties, which he bestowed on his family and associates from the theater. He had no son to inherit his wealth, and he left the majority of his possessions to his eldest daughter Susanna. Curiously, the only thing that he left to his wife Anne was his second-best bed! (although she continued to live in the family home after his death). William Shakespeare's last direct descendant died in 1670. She was his granddaughter, Elizabeth.

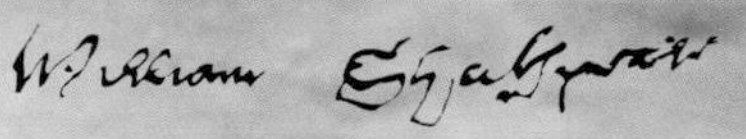

Shakespeare Birthplace Trust

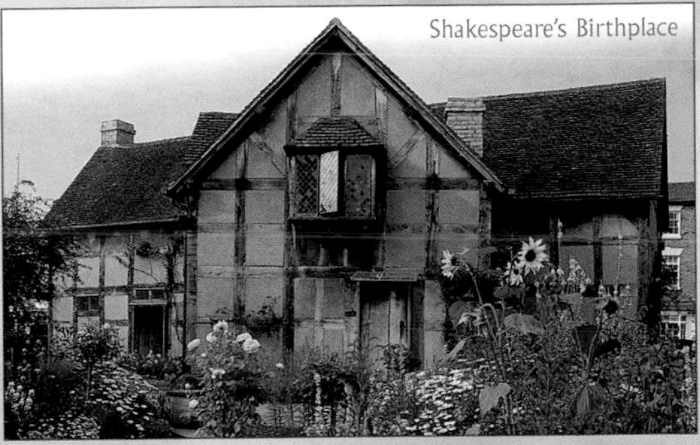

Shakespeare's Birthplace

As so few relics survive from Shakespeare's life, it is amazing that the house where he was born and raised remains intact. It is owned and cared for by the Shakespeare Birthplace Trust, which looks after a number of houses in the area:

- Shakespeare's Birthplace.
- Mary Arden's Farm: The childhood home of Shakespeare's mother.
- Anne Hathaway's Cottage: The childhood home of Shakespeare's wife.
- Hall's Croft: The home of Shakespeare's eldest daughter, Susanna.
- New Place: Only the grounds exist of the house where Shakespeare died in 1616.
- Nash's House: The home of Shakespeare's granddaughter.

www.shakespeare.org.uk

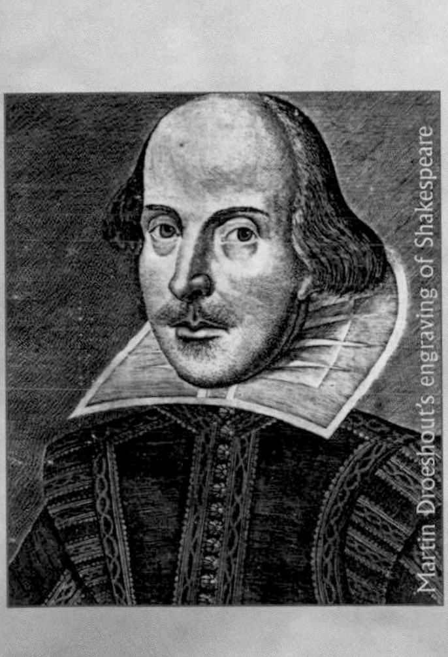

Martin Droeshout's engraving of Shakespeare

Formed in 1847, the Trust also works to promote Shakespeare around the world. In early 2009, it announced that it had found a new Shakespeare portrait, believed to have been painted within his lifetime, with a trail of provenance that links it to Shakespeare himself.

It is accepted that Martin Droeshout's engraving (left) that appears on the First Folio of 1623 is an authentic likeness of Shakespeare because the people involved in its publication would have personally known him. This new portrait (once owned by Henry Wriothesley, 3rd Earl of Southampton, one of Shakespeare's most loyal supporters) is so similar in all facial aspects that it is now suspected to have been the source that Droeshout used for his famous engraving.

www.shakespearefound.org.uk

History of the Play

The tale of ill-fated love between Romeo and Juliet is intrinsically linked with Shakespeare, with the famous "balcony scene" providing some of his most enduring phrases:

"But, soft! What light through yonder window breaks?
It is the east, and Juliet is the sun!"
(p55)

"O Romeo, Romeo! Wherefore art thou Romeo?" (p56)

"What's in a name? That which we call a rose
By any other word would smell as sweet;" (p56)

However, as with the vast majority of his works, Shakespeare's play is an adaptation of a story that already existed (*The Tempest* is his only play without a clear source).

Stories of frustrated love are as old as civilization itself and can be found even in ancient myths. The first recognizable form of *Romeo and Juliet* appeared around 1460 by Masuccio Salernitano. In it, Mariotto Mignanelli and Gianozza Saraceni of Siena fall in love and are married in secret by a friar. Shortly afterwards, Mariotto quarrels, fights with and kills a noble citizen. Mariotto is banished from the town, and Gianozza is forced into marriage by her father (who is unaware of her marriage with Mariotto). The friar creates a potion for Gianozza that makes her appear dead, and she is taken to the family tomb. From there, the friar escorts her to husband, who receives word of her death before she can reach him. Mariotto returns to Siena, where he is seized and executed. Gianozza shuts herself away in a convent and soon dies from grief.

Salernitano's story became the inspiration for Luigi da Porto's *Giulietta e Romeo.* Da Porto set the story in Verona, where he was inspired by the two castles just outside the city, each owned by a different family: the Capuleti and the Montecchi, thus introducing the notion of the feuding families. The ending is more tragic than Shakespeare's, with Romeo killing himself by the side of Giulietta, but seeing her revive in his final moments.

In 1554, an Italian writer by the name of Matteo Bandello published his own version of *Giulietta e Romeo.* This story was much more popular than its predecessors. Not only was it translated into English but, importantly for Shakespeare, it became the basis of a 3,020-line poem by Arthur Brooke called *The Tragicall Historye of Romeus and Juliet* (1562). Brooke's poem has all the main characters, albeit with some spelling differences: Romeus Montagew, Juliet Capilet, Prince Escalus, Tybalt, Paris, Friar Lawrence, Juliet's nurse [sic] and even Peter (although he is cited as one of Romeus's men).

Although Shakespeare embellished the story (and of course added his beautiful language) the events can all be found in Brooke's poem — even Friar John being unable to deliver the message to Romeus because of quarantine. It is possible that Shakespeare worked with other sources, too. He may have read the French translation of Bandello's novel, as well as an English version of the story by William Painter called *Palace of Pleasure.* Yet it is Brooke's poem that most closely matches the Bard's great play, as shown in the excerpt, opposite, in which Juliet discovers the name of her new love as the guests leave the masked ball.

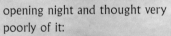

The Tragicall Historye of Romeus and Juliet
by Arthur Brooke (1562)

As carefull was the mayde what way were best deuise
To learne his name, that intertaind her in so gentle wise.
Of whome her hart receiued so deepe, so wyde a wounde,
An auncient dame she calde to her, and in her eare gan rounde.
This olde dame in her youth, had nurst her with her mylke,
With slender nedle taught her sow, and how to spin with silke.
What twayne are those (quoth she) which prease vnto the doore,
Whose pages in theyr hand doe beare, two toorches light before.
And then as eche of them had of his houshold name,
So she him namde yet once agayne the yong and wyly dame.
And tell me who is he with vysor in his hand
That yender doth in masking weede besyde the window stand.
His name is Romeus (sayd she) a Montegewe,
Whose fathers pryde first styrd the strife which both your
                          housholdes rewe.
The woord of Montegew, her ioyes did ouerthrow,
And straight in steade of happy hope, dyspayre began to growe.
What hap haue I quoth she, to loue my fathers foe?
What, am I wery of my wele? what, doe I wishe my woe?
But though her grieuous paynes distraind her tender hart,
Yet with an outward shewe of ioye she cloked inward smart.
And of the courtlyke dames her leaue so courtly tooke,
That none dyd gesse the sodain change by changing of her looke.

Shakespeare contracted the nine months of events within the poem into just five days. While that adds to the tension of the play in performance, it is likely to have been a conscious and practical decision to tailor the story for the stage, as the passing of time is hard to capture in theater.

The play appeared in print for the first time (the *First Quarto*) in 1597. The introduction of that edition tells us that it had already been performed by the time it was published:

An Excellent conceited Tragedie of Romeo and Iuliet, As it hath been often (with great applause) plaid publiquely, by the Honourable the L. of Hunsdon and his Seruants.

It was written before the *Globe Theatre* was built (1599), in the reign of Elizabeth I (which ended in 1603), while Shakespeare was writing for *The Lord Chamberlain's Men.*

The Lord Chamberlain's Men

Until the 1660s, the law prevented women and girls from acting. All parts, even Juliet, were played by males!

Even though Shakespeare's plays were hugely popular, only sparse records exist of actual performances. The earliest official recording of a production of *Romeo and Juliet* doesn't occur until as late as 1662, in a theater in Lincoln's Inn Fields. The famous diarist Samuel Pepys attended the opening night and thought very poorly of it:

"It is a play of itself the worst that I have ever heard in my life, and the worst acted that I ever saw these people do; and am resolved to go no more to see the first time of acting, for they were all of them out more or less."

Despite that early criticism, *Romeo and Juliet* remains one of Shakespeare's best-loved plays, being performed regularly throughout the world, as well as being adapted into other media: classical music (*Berlioz* [1839] and *Tchaikovsky* [1870]), opera (*Gounod* [1867]), ballet (*Prokofiev* [1935]), musical (Leonard Bernstein's *West Side Story* [1957]), movie (many!), and, of course, this graphic novel.

Page Creation

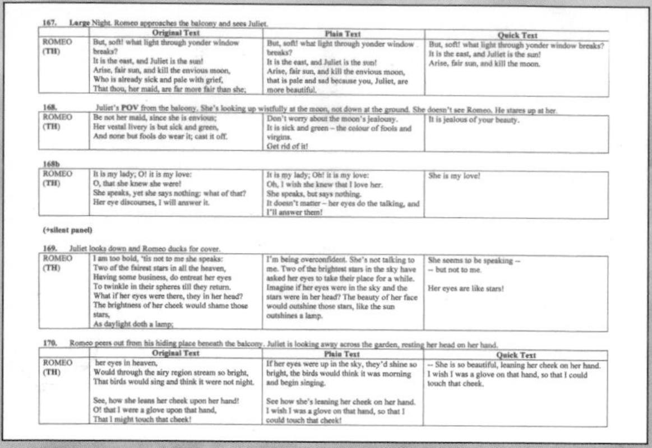

167. Large Night. Romeo approaches the balcony and sees Juliet.

	Original Text	Plain Text	Quick Text
ROMEO (TH)	But, soft! what light through yonder window breaks? It is the east, and Juliet is the sun! Arise, fair sun, and kill the envious moon, Who is already sick and pale with grief, That thou, her maid, are far more fair than she;	But, soft! what light through yonder window breaks? It is the east, and Juliet is the sun! Arise, fair sun, and kill the envious moon, that is pale and sad because you, Juliet, are more beautiful.	But, soft! what light through yonder window breaks? It is the east, and Juliet is the sun! Arise, fair sun, and kill the moon.

168. Juliet's **POV** from the balcony. She's looking up wistfully at the moon, not down at the ground. She doesn't see Romeo. He stares up at her.

ROMEO (TH)	Be not her maid, since she is envious; Her vestal livery is but sick and green, And none but fools do wear it; cast it off.	Don't worry about the moon's jealousy. It is sick and green – the colour of fools and virgins. Get rid of it!	It is jealous of your beauty.

168b

ROMEO (TH)	It is my lady; O! it is my love: O, that she knew she were! She speaks, yet she says nothing: what of that? Her eye discourses, I will answer it.	It is my lady; Oh! it is my love: Oh, I wish she knew that I love her. She speaks, but says nothing. It doesn't matter – her eyes do the talking, and I'll answer them!	She is my love!

(+silent panel)

169. Juliet looks down and Romeo ducks for cover.

ROMEO (TH)	I am too bold, 'tis not to me she speaks: Two of the fairest stars in all the heaven, Having some business, do entreat her eyes To twinkle in their spheres till they return. What if her eyes were there, they in her head? The brightness of her cheek would shame those stars, As daylight doth a lamp;	I'm being overconfident. She's not talking to me. Two of the brightest stars in the sky have asked her eyes to take their place for a while. Imagine if her eyes were in the sky and the stars were in her head? The beauty of her face would outshine those stars, like the sun outshines a lamp.	She seems to be speaking -- -- but not to me. Her eyes are like stars!

170. Romeo peers out from his hiding place beneath the balcony. Juliet is looking away across the garden, resting her head on her hand.

	Original Text	Plain Text	Quick Text
ROMEO (TH)	her eyes in heaven, Would through the airy region stream so bright, That birds would sing and think it were not night. See, how she leans her cheek upon her hand! O! that I were a glove upon that hand, That I might touch that cheek!	If her eyes were up in the sky, they'd shine so bright, the birds would think it was morning and begin singing. See how she's leaning her cheek on her hand. I wish I was a glove on that hand, so that I could touch that cheek!	-- She is so beautiful, leaning her cheek on her hand. I wish I was a glove on that hand, so that I could touch that cheek.

Page 55 from the script of *Romeo & Juliet* showing the three text versions.

1. Script

The first stage in creating a graphic novel adaptation of a Shakespeare play is to split the original script into comic book panels, describing the images to be drawn as well as the dialogue and any captions. To do this, not only does the script writer need to know the play well, but he also needs to visualize each page in his head as he writes the art descriptions for each panel (there are over 600 panels in *Romeo and Juliet*).

Once this is created, the dialogue is adapted into Plain Text and Quick Text to create the three versions of the book, which all use the same artwork.

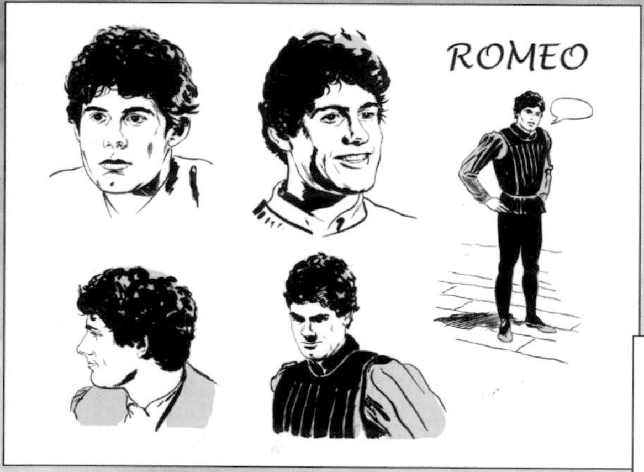
ROMEO

2. Character Sheets

Because *Romeo and Juliet* is such a well-known play, Will Volley needed very little time to familiarize himself with the characters. However, an artist still needs to "climb into the story" while deciding on the right approach for the artwork. Here you can see Will's designs for Romeo and Juliet, which we instantly agreed upon. The whole process moves steadily towards bringing the play to life and, suddenly, the names "Romeo" and "Juliet" are no longer simply names in a script – they have turned into real people!

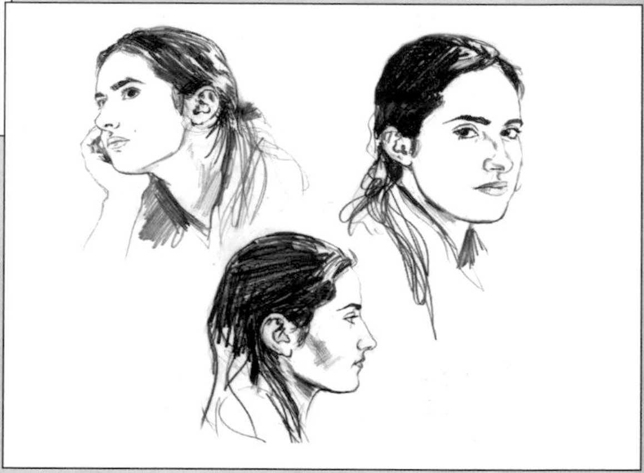

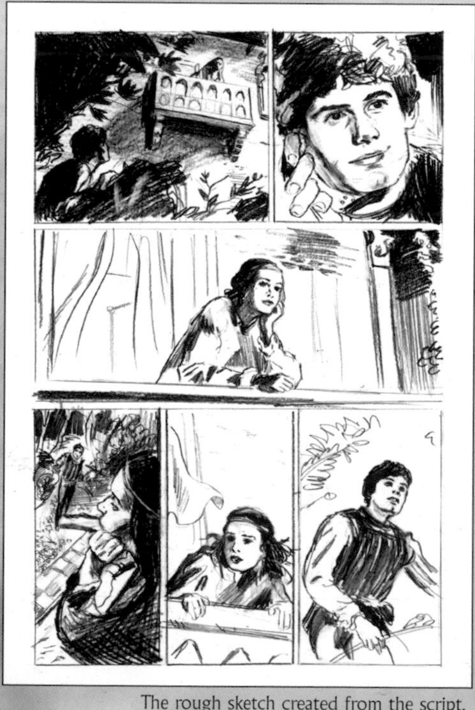

The rough sketch created from the script.

3. Rough Sketch

Armed with the character visualizations, the artist begins work on the 152 pages required for the book. Each page is first sketched out quickly in order to check panel layouts, ensure there is enough space for the lettering, explore continuity elements and to establish the pacing of the action. Will's roughs are very descriptive. As you can see here, he is already considering the lighting of the scenes, how the shadows will fall across surfaces, and so on. These rough layouts are then sent to the editor for approval. If any changes need to be made, it is far easier to make them at this stage from the fast rough layouts than to make changes to finished linework.

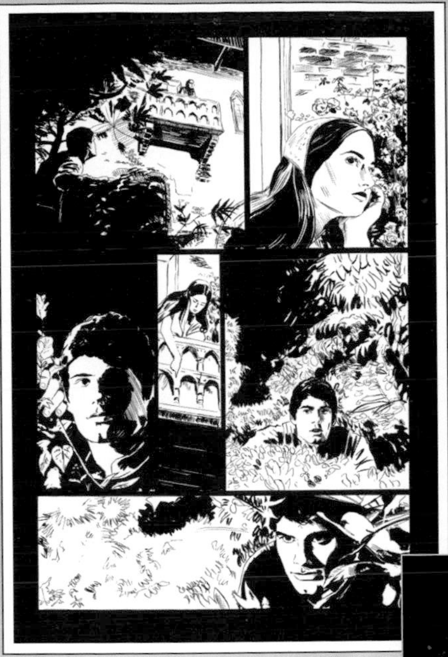

The inked image, ready to be colored.

4. Linework

The process to create the finished artwork begins as soon as the editor agrees to the rough sketch. The artwork is created on A3 art board at approximately 150% of the finished printed size. That magnification allows more freedom when creating the linework and makes for a better final image. As the linework is reduced, it has the effect of "tightening" the art, improving the overall look of the page.

Interestingly, the rough sketch details some artistic elements that won't be tackled until the coloring stage. For example, the sketchy coloring on the sides of faces due to the moonlit scene doesn't appear in the linework because it only deals in stark black and white (and Will doesn't use a technique called "feathering" which is the traditional way to render a curved surface in black and white artwork). Certain textures are added at this stage, such as the folds in the clothing and the rendering of materials, like the stone of the balcony and wall.

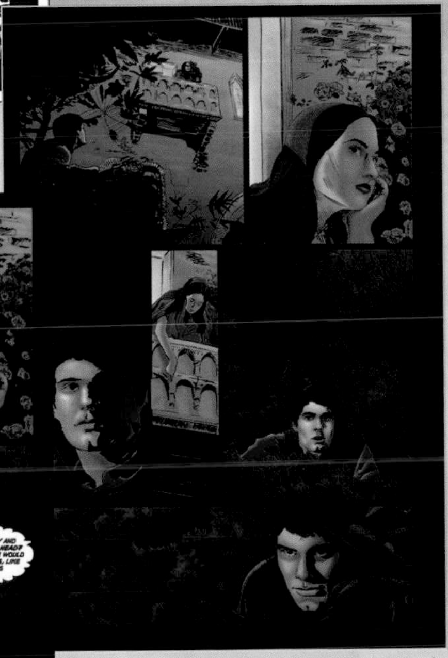

The final colored artwork.

5. Coloring

Adding color really brings the page and its characters to life. There is far more to the coloring stage than simply replacing the white areas with flat color. Some of the linework itself is shaded, while great emphasis is placed upon texture and light sources to get realistic shadows and highlights. Effects are also considered, such as the glow coming from the light in Juliet's bedroom. Finally, the whole page is color-balanced to the other pages of that scene, and to the overall book.

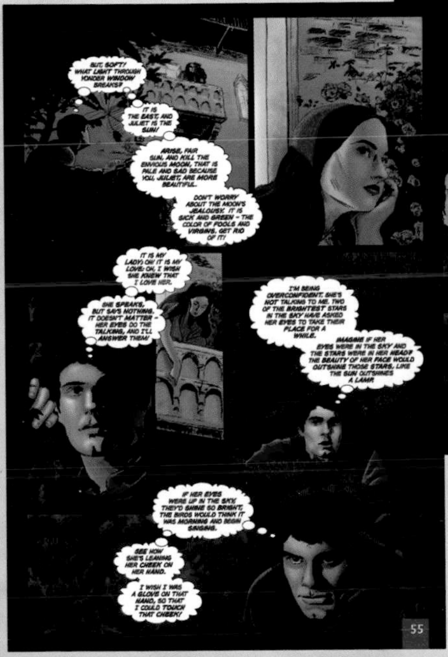
BUT, SOFT! WHAT LIGHT THROUGH YONDER WINDOW BREAKS?
IT IS THE EAST, AND JULIET IS THE SUN!
ARISE, FAIR SUN, AND KILL THE ENVIOUS MOON, THAT IS PALE AND SAD BECAUSE YOU, JULIET, ARE MORE BEAUTIFUL.
DON'T WORRY ABOUT THE MOON'S JEALOUSY. IT IS SICK AND GREEN - THE COLOR OF FOOLS AND VIRGINS. GET RID OF IT!
IT IS MY LADY; OH IT IS MY LOVE: OH, I WISH SHE KNEW THAT I LOVE HER.
SHE SPEAKS, BUT SAYS NOTHING. IT DOESN'T MATTER - HER EYES DO THE TALKING, AND I'LL ANSWER THEM!
I'M BEING OVERCONFIDENT. SHE'S NOT TALKING TO ME. TWO OF THE BRIGHTEST STARS IN THE SKY HAVE ASKED HER EYES TO TAKE THEIR PLACE FOR A WHILE.
IMAGINE IF HER EYES WERE IN THE SKY AND THE STARS WERE IN HER HEAD? THE BEAUTY OF HER FACE WOULD OUTSHINE THOSE STARS, LIKE THE SUN OUTSHINES A LAMP.
IF HER EYES WERE UP IN THE SKY, THEY'D SHINE SO BRIGHT, THE BIRDS WOULD THINK IT WAS MORNING AND BEGIN SINGING.
SEE HOW SHE'S LEANING HER CHEEK ON HER HAND.
I WISH I WAS A GLOVE ON THAT HAND, SO THAT I COULD TOUCH THAT CHEEK!
55

The finished page 55 with Plain Text lettering.

6. Lettering

The final stage is to add the captions, sound effects, and speech bubbles from the script. These are placed on top of the finished, colored pages. Three versions of each page are lettered, one for each of the three versions of the book (Original Text, Plain Text and Quick Text).

Original Text

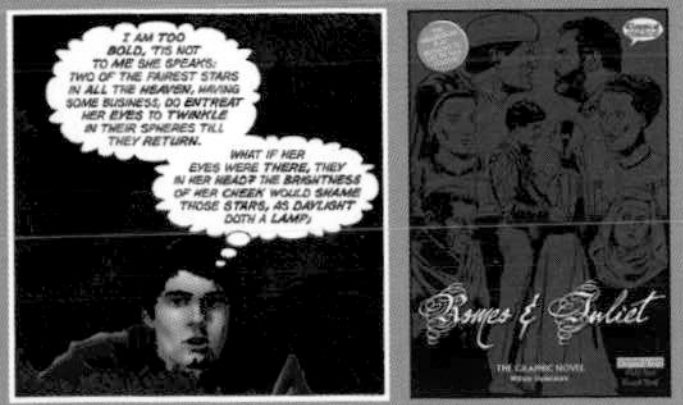
I AM TOO BOLD, 'TIS NOT TO ME SHE SPEAKS: TWO OF THE FAIREST STARS IN ALL THE HEAVEN, HAVING SOME BUSINESS, DO ENTREAT HER EYES TO TWINKLE IN THEIR SPHERES TILL THEY RETURN.
WHAT IF HER EYES WERE THERE, THEY IN HER HEAD? THE BRIGHTNESS OF HER CHEEK WOULD SHAME THOSE STARS, AS DAYLIGHT DOTH A LAMP;

ISBN: 978-1-906332-61-7

Plain Text

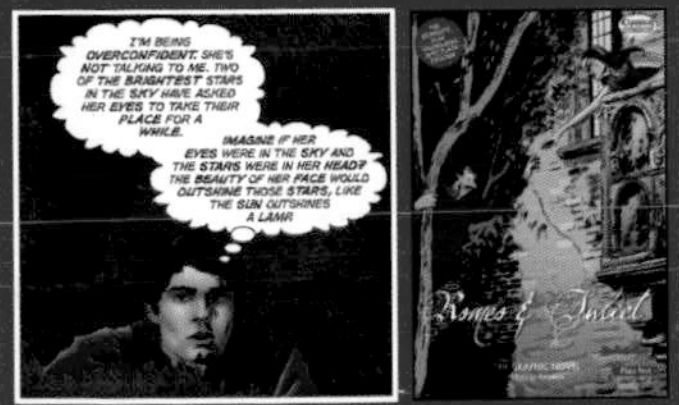
I'M BEING OVERCONFIDENT. SHE'S NOT TALKING TO ME. TWO OF THE BRIGHTEST STARS IN THE SKY HAVE ASKED HER EYES TO TAKE THEIR PLACE FOR A WHILE.
IMAGINE IF HER EYES WERE IN THE SKY AND THE STARS WERE IN HER HEAD? THE BEAUTY OF HER FACE WOULD OUTSHINE THOSE STARS, LIKE THE SUN OUTSHINES A LAMP.

ISBN: 978-1-906332-62-4

Quick Text

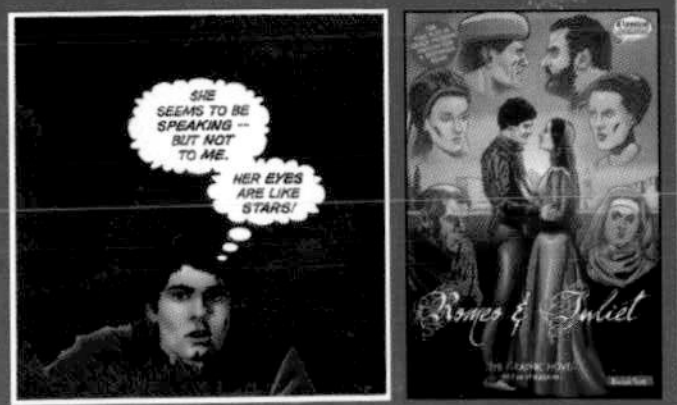
SHE SEEMS TO BE SPEAKING -- BUT NOT TO ME.
HER EYES ARE LIKE STARS!

ISBN: 978-1-906332-63-1

Teaching Resource Packs

HELPING YOU PREPARE MOTIVATING AND STIMULATING LESSONS

CLASSICAL COMICS
TEACHING RESOURCE PACK
Romeo & Juliet
THE GRAPHIC NOVEL
COMIC CARD 1
Includes CD-ROM

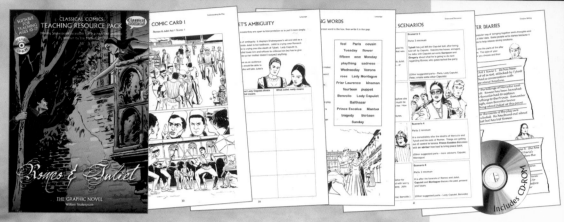

To accompany each title in our series of graphic novels and to help with their application in the classroom, we also publish teaching resource packs. These widely acclaimed 100+ page books are spiral-bound, making the pages easy to photocopy. They also include a CD-ROM with the pages in PDF format, ideal for whole-class teaching on whiteboards, laptops, etc or for direct digital printing. These books are written by teachers, for teachers, helping students to engage in the play or novel. Suitable for teaching ages 10-17, each book provides exercises that cover structure, listening, understanding, motivation and character as well as key words, themes and literary techniques. Although the majority of the tasks focus on the use of language and comprehension, there are also many cross-curriculum topics, covering areas within history, IT, drama, reading, speaking, writing and art. An extensive Educational Links section provides further study opportunities. Devised to encompass a broad range of skill levels, they provide many opportunities for differentiated teaching and the tailoring of lessons to meet individual needs.

"Thank you! These will be fantastic for all our students. It is a brilliant resource and to have the lesson ideas too are great. Thanks again to all your team who have created these."
B.P. KS3

"As to the resource, I can't wait to start using it! Well done on a fantastic service."
Will

"...you've certainly got a corner of East Anglia convinced that this is a fantastic way to teach and progress English literature and language!"
Chris

OUR RANGE OF TEACHING RESOURCE PACKS AVAILABLE

Romeo & Juliet

Romeo & Juliet
978-1-906332-74-7

Macbeth

Macbeth
978-1-906332-54-9

Henry V

Henry V
978-1-906332-53-2

TEMPEST

The Tempest
978-1-906332-77-8

Frankenstein

Frankenstein
978-1-906332-56-3

Jane Eyre

Jane Eyre
978-1-906332-55-6

A Christmas Carol

A Christmas Carol
978-1-906332-57-0

GREAT EXPECTATIONS

Great Expectations
978-1-906332-58-7

- Only $22.95 each
- 100+ spiral-bound, photocopiable pages.
- Electronic version included for whole-class teaching and digital printing.
- Cross-curricular topics and activities.
- Ideal for differentiated teaching.